About the Authors

Terry Pratchett was the acclaimed creator of the global bestselling Discworld series, the first of which, *The Colour of Magic*, was published in 1983. His fortieth Discworld novel, *Raising Steam*, was published in 2013. His books have been widely adapted for stage and screen, and he was the winner of multiple prizes, including the Carnegie Medal, as well as being awarded a knighthood for services to literature. He died in March 2015.

To find out more about the genius of Terry Pratchett, visit www.terrypratchett.co.uk

Stephen Baxter is one of the UK's most acclaimed writers of science fiction and a multi-award winner. His many books include the classic *Xeelee* sequence, the *Time's Odyssey* novels (written with Arthur C. Clarke) and *Time Ships*, a sequel to H. G. Wells's *The Time Machine*, a Doctor Who novel, *The Wheel of Ice*, and most recently the epic, far-future novels *Proxima* and *Ultima*. He lives in Northumberland.

More details of Stephen Baxter's works can be found on www.stephen-baxter.com

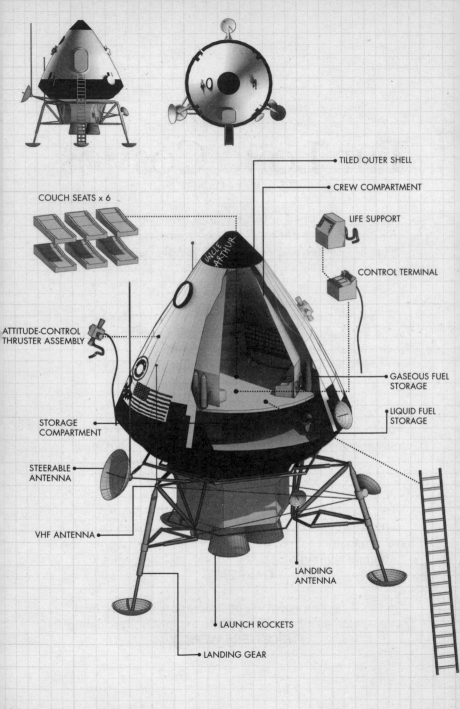

COUCH SEATS x 6

TILED OUTER SHELL

CREW COMPARTMENT

LIFE SUPPORT

CONTROL TERMINAL

ATTITUDE-CONTROL
THRUSTER ASSEMBLY

GASEOUS FUEL
STORAGE

LIQUID FUEL
STORAGE

STORAGE
COMPARTMENT

STEERABLE
ANTENNA

VHF ANTENNA

LANDING
ANTENNA

LAUNCH ROCKETS

LANDING GEAR

UNCLE ARTHUR CAPSULE

THE LONG COSMOS

Terry Pratchett and
Stephen Baxter

CORGI BOOKS

TRANSWORLD PUBLISHERS
61–63 Uxbridge Road, London W5 5SA
www.penguin.co.uk

Transworld is part of the Penguin Random House group of companies
whose addresses can be found at global.penguinrandomhouse.com

 Penguin
Random House
UK

First published in Great Britain in 2016 by Doubleday
an imprint of Transworld Publishers
Corgi edition published 2017

A CIP catalogue record for this book
is available from the British Library.

ISBN
9780552169370 (B format)
9780552173902 (A format)

Typeset in 11.5/14pt Minion by Falcon Oast Graphic Art Ltd.
Printed and bound by Clays Ltd, Bungay, Suffolk.

Penguin Random House is committed to a sustainable
future for our business, our readers and our planet. This book
is made from Forest Stewardship Council® certified paper.

 MIX
Paper from
responsible sources
FSC® C018179

1 3 5 7 9 10 8 6 4 2

For Jacks Thomas and Malcolm Edwards, for their prodigious dinner parties at one of which the Long Earth series was reborn

T.P.

Seconded. And to Sandra, as always

S.B.

Foreword

THE LONG EARTH project was born in the course of a dinner party conversation in early 2010, when Terry Pratchett mentioned to me a science-fiction storyline he'd set aside long ago. Before that party was over, we'd decided to develop the idea as a collaboration. Initially we planned two books, but by December 2011, when we had completed our draft of Volume 1 (*The Long Earth*), that first book had split into two, we couldn't resist exploring a 'Long Mars' in Volume 3, and we were planning how to reach a grand cosmic climax for the whole series . . . So at that point we were able to present our heroically patient publishers with plans for a five-book series.

The books have been published annually, but we worked faster than that; time was not on our side, and Terry had other projects he wanted to pursue. Volumes 1 and 2 of the series were published in 2012 and 2013 respectively. But by August 2013 we had presented our publishers with drafts of the final three volumes of the series, including the present book. We did continue to work on the books subsequently. The last time I saw Terry was in the autumn of 2014, when we worked on, among other things, the 'big trees' passages of *The Long Cosmos* (chapter 39 onwards). It has been my duty to see this book through its editorial and publishing stages.

S.B.

1

JOIN US

ON THE MOVE, 'down' was always the direction of Datum Earth. Down to the bustling worlds. Down to the millions of people. 'Up' was the direction of the silent worlds and the clean air of the High Meggers.

Five steps West of Datum Madison, Wisconsin, in a small cemetery plot outside a children's home, Joshua Valienté stood over his wife's marker stone. Down almost as far as it was possible for him to be down. It was a bitterly cold March day. *Helen Green Valienté Doak.* 'What's it all about, honey?' he asked softly. 'How did we come to this?'

He'd brought no flowers. He didn't need to, so well did the children tend the little plot, presumably under the kindly supervision of Sister John, the old friend of Joshua's who now ran the place. It had been Sister John's idea to set up this marker, in fact, as a consolation for Joshua when he visited; Helen had insisted on being buried in the Datum, at a much less accessible site.

The stone was marked with the date of Helen's death, in 2067. Three years on, Joshua supposed he was still trying to come to terms with the brutal reality.

He was a man who had always sought to be alone, for big chunks of his life at least. Even his experiences on Step Day had come about because of that drive for solitude. It was now more than half a century since an irresponsible genius called Willis Linsay had posted the specifications of a simple home-workshop gadget called a 'Stepper box' online. And when you built it, strapped it on your belt, and turned the switch on the top, you found yourself *stepping*, a transition out of the old world, which everybody now called Datum Earth, and into another: a world silent and choked by forest, if you stepped over from a location like Madison, Wisconsin, as thirteen-year-old Joshua had. Turn the switch the other way and you went back to where you started – or if you were bold enough, as Joshua had been, you could take a step further away, on into one world after another . . . Suddenly the Long Earth was open for business. A chain of parallel worlds, similar but not identical – and all save the original Earth, Datum Earth, empty of humanity.

For a loner kid like Joshua Valienté, a perfect refuge. But wherever you fled to, you had to come back in the end. Now, sixty-seven years old, his wife dead, Sally Linsay long lost – the two women, polar opposites, who had defined his life – with even his only son more or less estranged, Joshua had no choice but to be alone, it seemed.

Joshua had a sudden, sharp headache, like a shock through the temples.

And, standing there, he thought he *heard* something. Perhaps like the subsonic rumble of a deep quake, sound waves so huge and energy-dense they were felt rather than heard.

Joshua tried to focus on the here and now – this plot, his wife's name on the stone, the slab-like buildings of this Low Earth, all timber walls and solar panels. But the distant sound nagged.

Something calling. Echoing in the High Meggers.

JOIN US

And, much further from the Datum, in an empty star-littered sky where an Earth should have been:

'It's impossible,' said Stella Welch, staring at a tablet.

Dev Bilaniuk sighed. 'I know.' Stella was in her sixties, more than thirty years older than Dev. Not only that, Stella was Next: so smart that when she really took off on some line of speculation or analysis, Dev, who with a doctorate from Valhalla U was no dummy himself, could barely see her dust on the horizon. Granted she didn't look all that smart now, from Dev's perspective, dangling upside down in the cavernous volume of this chamber deep within the Brick Moon, with her mass of zero-gravity grey hair stuck out at all angles.

And she did seem to be as baffled by the 'Invitation', the message the radio telescope called Cyclops had picked up, as Dev was.

'For one thing,' she said, 'we haven't even *finished* Cyclops yet.'

'Sure. But the tests of the sub-arrays have proved successful so far. And we were just switching around various sample targets when this – this SETI thing – just showed up in the data feed and downloaded itself and—'

'Also we've had reports that other 'scopes, mostly in the

Low Earths and the Datum, have been picking this up too. That is, on other worlds stepwise. This isn't just some beacon firing off radio messages in this particular sky. This is a *Long Earth wide* phenomenon. How the hell can *that* be?'

Hesitantly Dev said, 'There have been some odd reports on the outernet too. Funny stuff out in the Long Earth. Nothing to do with radio astronomy. Strange stuff in the trolls' long call—'

She seemed to dismiss that. 'And then there's the decryption.' She looked again at the tablet screen, the two blunt words, in plain English: JOIN US.

'There seems to be a lot of information buried under that basic pattern,' Dev said now. 'Maybe we'll need the full Cyclops array to be up and running to extract all of that.'

'But the point is,' she said heavily, 'that what we have received came with its own decryption algorithm encoded into it, like some kind of computer virus. An algorithm capable of translating its own meaning into *English*.'

'And other languages too,' Dev said. 'Human languages, I mean. We tested that. We downloaded the thing into a tablet owned by a native Chinese speaker among the crew here . . .'

Dev had got a corporate reprimand for that. But the tense relations between China and the western nations down on the Datum meant nothing here, two million worlds away.

'*How?*' Stella snapped now. 'How the hell can it *speak* to us? Presumably without any prior knowledge of humanity and our languages? We think this was sent by some

4

civilization far off in the direction of Sagittarius, many light years away, maybe even somewhere close to the centre of the Galaxy. Our radio leakage can't have got that far, even from the Datum.'

Dev, bombarded, lost his patience. 'Professor Welch. You're senior to me in the field by decades. You wrote the texts I studied from. Also you're a Next. Why are you asking me?'

She eyed him, and he saw a glint of humour under her irritated impatience. 'Tell me what you think anyway. Any ideas?'

He shrugged. 'I guess that, unlike *you*, I'm used to sharing a world with beings smarter than I am. These – Sagittarians – are smarter than that again. Smarter than *you*. They wanted to talk to us, and they knew how. The important thing, Professor, is to figure out what to do next.'

She smiled. 'We both know the answer to that.'

He grinned back. 'We're gonna need a bigger telescope.'

JOIN US

And even further from Datum Earth:

One day Joshua Valienté would call this elderly troll Sancho. But he already had a name, of sorts, in this troll band – not a name any human could recognize or pronounce, more like a complex summary of his identity, a motif in the trolls' endless song.

And now, feeding with the others on rich bison meat, as the light of an early spring day slowly faded, Sancho was disturbed. He dropped his chunk of rib, stood up and scanned the horizon. The others grunted, briefly distracted, but they soon returned to their meal. Sancho, though, stood still, listening, watching.

It had been a good day for these trolls, here at the heart of a different North America. For some days they had been tracking a herd of animals that were like bison but not quite, with the trolls' cooperative, communal eye on one particular elderly male who, limping heavily, had been trailing behind the migration. As the trolls had moved steadily towards the setting sun, invisibly paralleling the bison's motion in worlds a few steps away, their scouts had continually flicked across to watch the prey, stepping back to report their observations in dance and gesture and hooting cries.

At last the elderly bison had stumbled.

For the bison himself it was the end of a slow-burning, lifelong story. One hind leg had never properly healed from a splintering break he had suffered as a mere calf; now that leg finally betrayed him.

And the bison, downed, panting in the heat, was immediately surrounded by hunters, big heavy humanoids, their hair black as night, stone blades and sharpened sticks in their massive hands. They closed in, cutting and slashing, aiming for tendons and hamstrings, seeking to sever veins, trying to stab to the heart. Trolls were sublimely intelligent in their way, but not as toolmakers. They did use shaped stones and sharpened sticks, but they had no way of striking at a prey from a distance; they had no bows, not even throwing spears. And so their hunting was direct and close-up and gloriously physical – big muscular bodies thrown at the prey until it was worn down through the sheer application of strength.

The bison was old and proud, and he bellowed as he tried to stand, to fight back. But he fell again under waves of assault from the hunters.

It had been Sancho who had struck the final blow, smashing the bison's skull with a single blow from a massive rock.

The trolls had gathered over the fallen beast and sung their victory song, of joy at the prospect of a meal, of respect for the bison's gift of life. Then they had fallen to the work of butchering the carcass, and the feasting began: the liver first, the kidneys, the heart. Soon the news of this kill would resonate in the trolls' long call, shared by bands across thousands of worlds – and it would lodge for ever in the deep memories of certain older trolls, like Sancho.

But now, as this happy day was ending, Sancho was distracted from the kill, the feasting. He had *heard* something. Or . . . not heard.

What was it? His mind was not like a human's, but it was roomy and full of dusty memory. He knew no human words. But if he had, he might have called what he heard, or sensed, the Invitation.

Sancho looked around at the pack, males and females and cubs feeding contentedly. He had spent years with this band, seen the little ones born, the old fail and die. He knew them as well as he knew himself. They were his whole world. Yet now he saw them for what they were: a handful of animals lost in an empty, echoing landscape. Huddling, vulnerable in the dark.

And, from beyond the horizon, something was coming.

JOIN US

And in a world only a few steps from the Datum, in a new stone-built chapel in the footprint of an ancient English parish called St John on the Water:

Nelson Azikiwe was seventy-eight years old and officially retired. Indeed, he had come back to this place because his old parish on the Datum, although icebound on a world still suffering through a long volcano winter, was the place where, in his long and peripatetic life, he had felt most at home. Where else to retire?

But to a man like Nelson retirement was only a label. He continued to work to the limits of his strength on his various projects, as much as he ever had. It was just that now he was entitled to call it play, not work.

Of course it helped greatly that the growing technological infrastructure of this Low Earth provided the communications he needed to keep in touch with the wider world, and indeed worlds, without his needing to leave the comfort of his lounge. Thus he spent time each day communicating with the Quizmasters, an online group of ageing, grumpy, paranoid obsessives – none of whom, as far as he knew, he had ever met in person – who were now scattered over the Low Earths and beyond, and yet across the decades had managed to remain in regular touch with each other, if necessary through the stepwise swapping of memory chips. It was an odd fact of the Long

Earth that, more than half a century after Step Day, still nobody had figured out how to send a message across the stepwise worlds save by carrying it by hand.

Just now the phenomenon that was becoming known as the Invitation was snagging the Quizmasters' attention. The news of the receipt of an apparent SETI signal by a radio telescope at the Gap had been a nine-day wonder in the news media of the Low Earths, insular and inward-looking and obsessed with local politics and celebrities as they were. There had been a flurry of reports, a firestorm of speculation over mankind's galactic future or its imminent cosmic doom, before it was all forgotten. But not by the Quizmasters.

Some believed it must be what it most obviously looked like, some kind of SETI message from the sky: the fulfilment of the dreams of the decades-long Search for Extraterrestrial Intelligence, a message whispering into radio telescopes on any stepwise world where they had been established. Others believed it couldn't be that precisely *because* that was the most obvious explanation. Maybe this was a covert military experiment, or some kind of corporate viral infiltration, or the first moves in the long-anticipated Chinese invasion of a prostrate post-Yellowstone America.

And it was as Nelson was sifting through another day's communications on this burning topic that he received an invitation of his own.

The screens of all his tablets and other devices suddenly blanked. Nelson sat back in his chair, startled, suspecting a power outage – not uncommon in a world that relied on the careful burning of wood for its electricity supplies.

But then one screen after another lit up with a familiar face: a man's face, calm, head shaven.

Nelson felt a tingle of anticipation. 'Hello, Lobsang. I thought you'd gone away again.'

The face smiled back, and the multiple devices in Nelson's room resounded to a voice like the beating of a gong in a Buddhist temple. 'Good afternoon, Nelson. Yes, I have – gone away. Think of this presence merely as a kind of messaging service . . .'

Nelson wondered *how much* of Lobsang he was talking to. Since Lobsang, when fully functioning, had seemed to run much of Datum Earth, for him vocal speech must have been about as efficient a method of communication as yodelling in Morse. Probably this avatar wasn't much more than a sophisticated speech generator. And yet, Nelson reflected, he had taken the trouble to have this 'messaging service' smile at his old friend.

Lobsang said now, 'I have some news for you.' The tablet before Nelson cleared again, and Lobsang's face was replaced by that of a child, a sun-kissed boy aged maybe ten or eleven. 'This is somebody I only just discovered myself. A remote probe called in, rather belatedly . . .'

'Who is he?'

'Nelson, he's your grandson.'

JOIN US

And much further from the Datum, indeed more than two hundred *million* steps out:

The USS *Charles M. Duke* wasn't Admiral Maggie Kauffman's boat. At sixty-eight she was much too old for operational command, and was in fact formally retired, not that that kept her from troubling her former superiors and nominal successors in the echelons of what remained of the US Navy. Yet this latest mission into the deep Long Earth was her idea, her inspiration – hell, the result of a twenty-five-year-long campaign on her part to resolve an item of unfinished business.

And, she realized, when Captain Jane Sheridan told her about the note that had been received from Datum Hawaii, it was a bit of business that was going to have to be left unfinished a while longer yet.

Maggie did put up a fight, though. 'But we've come so close. Two hundred million worlds plus change!'

'With another fifty thousand to go yet, Admiral, and the most hazardous stretch—'

'Bah. I could pilot this tub through that "hazardous stretch" in my sleep.'

'I'm afraid the recall is quite unambiguous, ma'am. We have to turn back. They don't send out fast-pursuit boats to deliver such a command every day. And after all, the note is for *you*. Admiral Cutler is calling for your return specifically.'

'Why, Ed Cutler couldn't command a leaky bathtub.'

'I couldn't comment on that, ma'am.'

'I'm retired!'

'Of course you are, Admiral.'

'I don't have to take any damn orders from that old desk jockey.'

'But I do, ma'am,' said Sheridan softly.

Maggie sighed, and looked out through the sturdy windows of this observation deck, at the churning volcanic landscape of the latest stepwise Earth, and at the pursuit boat, a sleek craft that hung in the sky alongside the *Duke*. 'But we came so far,' she said plaintively. 'And it's been so long.' Twenty-five years since she'd left a science party on West 247,830,855, a *very* strange Earth, an Earth that was a mere moon of a greater planet. More than twenty years since a relief mission found they'd vanished. 'They're my people, Jane.'

'I know, ma'am.' Sheridan was in her late twenties but, highly capable, had the air of someone significantly older. 'But the way I see it is this. After twenty-five years they're either dead, or they found a way to survive. Either way they'll keep a little longer.'

'Damn it. Not only are you ridiculously young, you're also ridiculously right. And damn Cutler. What's all this about – some kind of invitation?'

'I don't know any more than you right now, Admiral . . .'

Even as they argued, the *Duke* began its long trip home, and the subtle swing-like sense of regular stepping resumed. Beyond the windows whole worlds flapped by, one a second, then two, then four: sun and rain, heat and cold, landscapes and suites of life and climate systems, there and gone in the blink of an eye. But nobody was watching this routine miracle.

JOIN US

And elsewhere:

On this chill March day the shaven-headed novice, sitting cross-legged behind a low desk and labouring over texts that had originated in the eighth century after Christ, was distracted by a distant noise. A faint call.

Not the talk and laughter of the villagers in the clean Himalayan air, the old men with their smoky pipes, the women with their laundry, the little children playing with their home-made wooden toys. Not the clank of cow bells from the passes. It had been like a voice, the boy thought, echoing from the cold, white, ice-draped face of the mountain that loomed over this valley, deep in old Tibet.

A voice that chimed inside his own head.

Words, softly spoken:

. . . *Humanity must progress. This is the logic of our finite cosmos; ultimately we must rise up to meet its challenges if we are not to expire with it . . . Consider. We call ourselves the wise ones, but what would a true* Homo sapiens *be like? What would it do? Surely it would first of all treasure its world, or worlds. It would look to the skies for other sapient life forms. And it would look to the universe as a whole . . .*

The boy called, 'Joshua?'

The master slammed the palm of his hand flat on the desk, making the boy jump. 'Pay attention, Lobsang!'

JOIN US
JOIN US

The words rained down from the sky across the Long Earth, wherever there were ears to hear and eyes to see and minds to understand.

Standing by his wife's grave marker, Joshua Valienté didn't want any invitation. 'Leave me alone, damn it!' He stepped away angrily.

13

The air he displaced created a soft breeze that touched the petals of the flowers on the grave.

Yet the voice from the sky did not cease.

JOIN US

JOIN US

JOIN US

2

WHEN BILL CHAMBERS arrived at the office, the final April morning before Joshua left for his latest sabbatical, he had trouble opening the door – and it was the door of his own office, Bill being the current mayor of Hell-Knows-Where, Joshua realized with chagrin.

Joshua was in the small private bathroom. When he heard muffled cusses he came out bare to the waist, towel around his neck, half his face covered with shaving foam. Though the morning was well advanced, the blinds were still down, and the room was gloomy. Bill was trying to get across the office without stepping on some crucial piece of travelling gear, and it was a challenge. Not only did Joshua have Bill's fold-out cot still piled with bedding, but the rest of his kit was strewn out in rows and heaps across the floor, even on the desk.

'Mother of mercy, Josh, what is it ye're packing here?' Bill's faux Irish got stronger every time they met. 'Hell-Knows-Where is a sophisticated place now, you know. I've got to sort out the quarterly cross-taxes by the end of the week.'

'Bill, I thought you had a computer to handle that sort of stuff.'

Bill looked pained. That is to say, more pained than previously. 'Ye can't leave it to the computer, man! True accountancy is the last refuge of the creative mind.'

'I did once sit in that chair myself, remember? I'll be out of your hair—'

'What hair?' Bill tried to push a bit further into the room, taking long strides, tottering on awkwardly placed feet. 'And by God it smells like a troll's jockstrap in here.' He pulled up a blind and yanked a cord to open the wooden sash window.

Cool air flowed in, laden with a scent of dust, hay and spring flowers: air from a world that was chilly compared to others in this stretch of the Long Earth, cool enough to deliver a frost as late as June, sometimes. Kind of refreshing, Joshua had always found it.

And this was the air of home for Joshua now, as much as anywhere – the place he kept his most significant stash of stuff, anyhow. Hell-Knows-Where wasn't a place Joshua had founded, or helped to found, but a place he'd made his home for decades, with his wife Helen and his son Rod. When he'd come here, in fact, the nascent town's only fixed point had been the smithy. As iron couldn't be stepped between worlds, the smithy was a kind of thumbtack that had pinned the community to this particular Earth, and back then it had served as a meeting point and a gossip focus. Later, it was no coincidence that Joshua and Bill and the others had used the location to build this, Hell-Knows-Where's first town hall. And on its inauguration they had hung an iron horseshoe over the door. An oddity when you thought about it, making horseshoes on a world without horses yet, but people wanted the good luck that came with it.

But Joshua's marriage had broken down. Helen had moved out of here to go back to her Corn Belt home town of Reboot. And then she had died. Now Joshua hardly ever saw his son Rod; he was supposed to show up today, but . . . Well, that was the plan.

Stepping back from the window into the gloom, Bill ran straight into a row of Joshua's lightweight shirts and pants, hanging on a line. 'Feck! Funnily enough I don't remember a clothesline in here. So where have ye fixed it? Ah, I see, to the bust of the town's founder on top of the bookcase here. Knotted around her *neck*. It's what she would have wanted.'

'Sorry, man. I had to improvise. You want a coffee? I have a pot running in the kitchen space back here.'

'You mean, would I like some of my best coffee before it walks out of here in your bladder? Ah, what the hey, give me a shot.'

Joshua, mopping foam from his face, poured the brew into the least disreputable mug he could find in the small cupboard over the sink. 'Here you go. No milk, no sugar.'

'Never.' Bill cleared a corner of his desk and sat.

'Cheers.' They touched their mugs.

'You know, Bill, there was a time when you'd have asked for – how did you use to put it? – a drop of something a bit fortifying in there. Even at this hour of the morning.'

'I did have a mature man's tastes—'

'Started when you were fourteen years old, as I recall,

Billy Chambers, whenever you could swing it, and don't deny it.'

'Ah, well, I've changed since those days. Those *decades*. And I've got Morningtide to thank for that.'

'You're lucky to have her, and your kids.'

'My liver generally agrees with that sentiment. Just as you were lucky to have Helen.'

'So I was.'

There was an awkward silence.

'Absent friends,' Bill said at last, and they touched their mugs again. Bill gingerly moved a broad-brimmed hat from the seat behind his desk. 'All these piles of shite, man. Is it all strictly necessary?'

'You bet.'

'And all laid out in order.' He glanced around the room. 'Cold-weather gear, I see, so you're planning to be out for a few months. Universal maps . . .' These were maps of features that generally persisted as you travelled across the Long Earth: nothing human like towns and roads, but the underlying mountains, rivers, coastlines, landmarks. 'Silver-foil emergency blankets – check. Where's your roll-up mattress?'

'You're out of touch. Look at this.' In his left hand Joshua hefted a pack the size of a baseball. 'Aerogel – a whole mattress that you can hold in your fist.'

'Or in your case your Terminator cyber-claw.'

'Yeah, yeah.'

'Boots. Camp sandals. Socks! You can never have enough socks. Water tablets. Food, jerky and stuff – emergency rations, I take it?'

'I'll be living off the land. Hunting and trapping.'

'You always were a bit rubbish at that, but you could afford to lose a little weight.'

'Thanks.'

'A med pack, check: anti-diarrhoea pills, antihistamines, painkillers, laxatives, antifungal treatments, disinfectant, bug killers, vitamin tablets . . . What else? Arrowheads. Line for making bows. Snares. Nets. Lightweight bronze axe. More knives than a butcher's back drawer. The usual electronic gadgets: a radio transceiver, a tablet, a location finder.' This would exploit GPS on worlds developed enough to host such systems, but would otherwise deliver a best-guess location based on the position of the sun and moon, the constellations, the length of the day, any fortuitous events like solar or lunar eclipses. All this was technology that encoded the hard-won wisdom of decades of travelling in the Long Earth. 'A flint firestarter. And matches, good move. A solar oven.' A little inverted open-out umbrella, its inner surface reflective, that could be set up on a stand to catch the sunlight and focus it to boil water. 'Colostomy bags. Denture glue.'

'Yeah, yeah.'

'I'm only barely jokin', Methuselah. Coffee. Spices. Pepper! Trade goods, of course. Ah, and weapons. A couple of bronze revolvers – electromagnetic impulse?'

'Yeah.' Joshua hefted one of the small handguns. 'The latest thing. Charges up on solar power, or you can just pump it up by squeezing the grip.' He pointed it downward, fired the thing, and drilled a fine hole through the corner of Bill's desk.

'Hey, show some respect! This desk's an antique.'

'No, it's not. We built it.'

'Well, it never *will* be an antique now. And all this will fit into a single backpack, I take it? Ye've got some lovely widgets, Josh, I'll give you that.'

'And they say that innovation stalled after Step Day.'

Bill said simply, 'Shame it is they haven't yet developed an unbreakable heart.'

Joshua looked away.

'Sorry, man,' Bill said. 'That was cheesier than a mouse's wet dream. I never would have said such things once, would I? We were lads together, you and me. Feelings were for those fecking nuns to have, not us. Well, I changed. And you changed too. But you've changed – well, *back*.'

Joshua was a little shaken by that. To cover, he selected a shirt from the line and pulled it on. Suddenly Bill, sixty-eight years old, sitting on his own junk-cluttered desk, sipping his coffee in the gloom of the office, *looked* like a mayor to Joshua. Mature. As if mad old Bill the fake Irishman had somehow grown up when Joshua wasn't looking. Had, in fact, overtaken Joshua himself. 'What do you mean, changed back?'

Bill spread his hands. 'Well, for instance, when it was all kicking off with those rebel types in Valhalla, and all the trolls in the Long Earth went AWOL, remember? And you and me were handed a twain by that fecker Lobsang and told to go off and find Sally Linsay.'

'Jeez, Bill, that must be thirty years ago.'

'Sure. And as far as I remember we just slept on it, and up and left, and pissed off to the ends of the Long Earth. I don't remember you doing all this *packing*. Counting your fecking socks.'

Joshua looked around the room, at all his gear in its

neat rows and piles. 'You have to do it right, Bill. You've got to make sure you have everything, that it's all in working order. Then you have to *pack* it right—'

'There you go. That's not Joshua the mayor of Hell-Knows-Where talking, Joshua the father, Joshua Valienté the hero of half the fecking Long Earth. That's Josh the boy I used to know at the Home, when we were eleven or twelve or thirteen. When you used to make your crystal radio sets and model kits, just the way you're doing your packing now. You'd lay everything out first, and fix any bits that were damaged—'

'Paint before assemble.'

'What?'

'That's what Agnes used to say to me. "You're the sort of boy who always, but always, paints before assembling."'

'Well, she was right.'

'She usually was. In fact she usually still is . . . And *she's* supposed to come by to see me today, no doubt to be right one more time. Well, Bill, so what?'

'There's always a balance, man. You've got to hit the right proportion. And, just to raise another point, Mister Chairman, aren't you getting too fecking *old* to run off playing Daniel Boone?'

'None of your business,' Joshua snarled.

Bill held up his hands. 'Fair enough. No offence.'

There was a knock at the door.

Bill stood. 'Maybe that's Sister Mary Stigmata now, right on cue. I'll leave you to it. I mean, I won't get any work done in here until you're out of it anyhow.'

'Bill, I appreciate it—'

'Just remember one thing. Put a bloody marker

somewhere high up where a twain can see it, an emergency blanket on top of a rock, so they can find you when you do yourself in.'

'Roger.'

The rap on the door was harder this time.

'All right, all right.'

The opened door revealed, not Agnes, but Joshua's son. Bill Chambers cleared off fast.

3

DANIEL RODNEY VALIENTÉ was thirty-eight years old. Framed in the doorway, taller than his father, he was as pale of complexion as his mother had been, but his hair was as dark as Joshua's. He wore a practical-looking hooded coverall, and carried a small leather bag on a strap slung over one shoulder. Joshua suspected that this would be all the possessions he had with him – all the permanent possessions he owned at all, maybe.

Now he stalked into the mayor's office, looked around with faint disgust at the heaps of gear, vacated Bill's chair of junk, and sat down. All this without a word.

Joshua suppressed a sigh. He felt moved to button up his shirt, however, in his son's stern presence. Then he collected Bill's half-empty mug from the desk and moved to the kitchen area. 'So,' he said.

'So.'

'You want a coffee? There's some in the pot.'

Rod, as he now insisted on being called, shook his head. 'I managed to lose my caffeine addiction years ago. One less craving you have to fulfil out in the High Meggers.'

'Water, then? The town supply's been clean again since—'

'I'm fine.'

Joshua nodded, dumped the mugs, and sat on a stool from which he had to clear a set of climbing grips. 'I'm glad you came.'

'Why?'

Joshua sighed. 'Obviously, because since your mother died we're all we've got, you and I.'

Rod was stone-faced. 'You haven't "got" me, Dad. Nor have I "got" you.'

'Rod—'

'And why, once again, are you disappearing into the wilds of the Long Earth? Just as you did throughout my childhood, periodically. Just as you did when your marriage to my mother broke down. An outernet note to say, "Hi, I'm off again" doesn't really cut it, Dad. Besides, aren't you too damn old for these stunts now?'

'You know, Rod – *Daniel* – I feel like I've had a lifetime of your judgements. Maybe everybody blames their parents—'

Rod cut him off. 'I only came here to talk about your will.'

'OK. Look, it's all duly witnessed and notarized, both here in Hell-Knows-Where and in an Aegis office back in Madison West 5.'

'Dad, I don't care about the legal stuff. And I don't want anything from you. I just want to be sure I understand it before you disappear and break your damn neck in the wilderness, and I never see you again.'

'Fine. Well, you know the basic provision. Aside from a

few gifts, such as to the Home in Madison, I left it all to your aunt Katie back in Reboot, or her surviving descendants. Simple as that . . .'

Katie was Helen's older sister. Along with their parents, just a decade or so after Step Day, the Green sisters had trekked on foot off into the Long Earth, and had taken part in the founding of a new community, Reboot, on the edge of the band of fecund worlds that had become known as the Corn Belt. Helen had left Reboot when she met Joshua, but Katie had stayed, married, raised a couple of healthy daughters – and, eventually, granddaughters.

But there was a dark underside to the story. The Green girls had had a brother, Rodney, who was a phobic, as the jargon had emerged: constitutionally incapable of stepping. As the family trekked away, Rodney was left behind with an aunt. And in the end Rodney had taken part in the destruction of Madison, Wisconsin, with a backpack nuke, and had spent the rest of his life in jail. When he had learned the full family story, Joshua's son Daniel Rodney had abandoned his childhood name, 'Dan', and adopted the name of his broken uncle. It was just one element of the tension between father and son.

Now Joshua said, 'It's not as if there's anybody I *could* give it to on your side, is there?'

Rod sighed. 'It's called an extended marriage, Dad. I'm one of fifteen husbands now. There are eighteen wives and twenty-four kids at the last count. It's kind of vague – we're spread over many worlds, and we keep moving. Look, I'm in a steady relationship with Sofia, for now. Sofia Piper – you never met her, and never will. And kind of foster-uncle to her nephews. Step-uncle, whatever, the old labels don't really apply. It's flexible but stable, and it suits Long Earth migrants like me just fine. It's already two decades since the first pairing that began it all.'

'It's trippy comber bullshit is what it is. And it's not recognized in Aegis law. When it comes to inheritance of property—'

'We don't have any property to speak of, Dad. That's kind of the point.'

'You seem to have made a conscious choice not to have had a kid of your own.'

'And take part in that disgusting old stepper mass-breeding experiment?'

'It needn't be like that—'

'*You yourself* were the product of a planned match, Dad. And look how well *that* turned out. Your mother dead at childbirth, your father a sexual predator and a bum. A centuries-old conspiracy to selectively breed natural steppers! Things like that don't just fade away. And look at what it unleashed on mankind – all the destabilization of Step Day.'

'We wouldn't be sitting here if not for that, Rod. Look – *I* was never approached. So the Fund didn't seem to be functioning in my generation, did it? And certainly your mother and her family had nothing to do with any of that. Your own uncle was a full-on phobic.'

'Bullshit. You can be the carrier of a gene without it necessarily expressing in you. Oh, whatever. For better or worse, this line of the Valienté family, at least, ends with me, along with our tainted genome.'

'Fine,' Joshua snapped. He looked at his son in the mayor's chair, stiff, not remotely at his ease, as if he was about to light out of there at any moment. 'You damn youngsters think you invented it all.'

Rod stood up. 'I think we're done here, don't you? Oh, here, I brought you a gift. Sofia's idea.'

He handed over a slim case. Inside were lightweight sunglasses. Joshua glanced through them and squinted. 'These are prescription.'

'Yeah. *Your* prescription. Found it in Mom's files.'

'Don't need no spectacles—'

'Sure you do. Oh, use them or not. So long, Dad.'

And he walked out. Joshua just stood there, holding the glasses, surrounded by his orderly rows of travel goods, for an unmapped time.

Then there was another knock at the door.

Sister Agnes.

4

AGNES, PRACTICAL AS ever, got to work packing Joshua's bag. 'I remember helping you with this kind of thing when you were a boy. Well, it was a case of you showing me how it was done. Spare trousers at the bottom, soft stuff against your back, knives and guns and other life-saving gear at the top.' She accepted a mug of tea, though she pulled a face at the cleanliness, or otherwise, of the mugs. 'Billy Chambers always was a scruffy boy.'

'You didn't come all this way out just to see me, did you?'

She snorted. 'Don't flatter yourself. I've been visiting some of my old friends from New Springfield. Do you remember Nikos Irwin, who found the silver beetles? Got kids of his own now.'

Her skirt, blouse and cardigan were clean and crisply ironed – no habit for Sister Agnes, not since her return from New Springfield, where she'd built a home with an avatar of Lobsang. Her face was authentically Sister Agnes's face, Joshua thought. Even if it was, eerily, so much *younger* than the last time he'd seen the real Agnes, on her deathbed, all of thirty-five years ago.

'You know, Agnes, I'm sixty-seven now, going on sixty-eight. Suddenly you're younger than *me*.'

'Hmmph. You're not so old that I can't tell you that you're making a foolish mistake by going off alone into the wilderness at your age. Don't come crying to *me*.'

'You're the third person this morning to tell me so.'

'Does that include your conscience?'

'Ha ha.'

She left off folding socks and touched his hand – the flesh-and-blood right hand, as opposed to the prosthetic left. Her skin was nearly as liver-spotted as his, he saw. 'You always have a place with us, you know. At the Home. I pop in myself from time to time, just to make sure young Sister John isn't going too far off the rails.'

Young Sister John was close to Joshua's own age, and had been running the Home for decades. 'I'm sure she appreciates that,' he said dryly.

'And she's told me all about that young boy they're having so much trouble with, Jan – what's his name?'

'Jan Roderick, I think. I met him.'

'Yes. How he's hoovering up all those old books and movies you gave the Home, like a Chicago gangster snorting crack cocaine.'

'Agnes!'

'Oh, hush. Now there's another complicated little boy, just as you were. And I'm sure it would be good for him to see more of you. One thing the Home doesn't excel at, for obvious reasons, is providing good male role models.'

'Well, I'm not sure I've ever been one of those . . . Look, Agnes, I've been drifting these last three years, since Helen died. I need to make some kind of break. I won't be away that long. The Home will still be there when I return—'

'I might not be.'

She said this so bluntly that he was shocked. 'Agnes, your body's artificial, your mind has been downloaded into Black Corporation gel – you could live until the sun goes out—'

'Who would want to hang around to see that?' She touched the papery skin of her cheek. 'There has to be a finish, Joshua. I learned that lesson from Shi-mi, who decided that in the end all she wanted to be was a cat. I wanted to be a mother to Ben, and – well, that was *all* I wanted, and then I would be ready to lay down my burden. My adopted son is nineteen already.'

'Really?'

'Believe it. Time just pours away, doesn't it? And I'm not sure how much longer I can fake all this ageing convincingly. Also there's a question of good manners. I've been through old age myself, but who am I to live in some kind of mannequin, mimicking all that pain and suffering, for the sake of my own vanity? When I know I could switch it off at any time. When I could even be young again, if I chose. No, I think my time should come sooner rather than later. It's right that way.'

'Hmm. And Ben?'

'He knows. He's understood what we are since he was nine years old, myself and "George". He accepts it.'

'Does he have a choice?'

'What choice do any of us have, Joshua?'

Suddenly this was too much for him. He pulled away, stood, and started gathering up more stuff to pack.

'It's hard on you,' she said now. 'I know.'

He grunted. 'Hard on Lobsang too.'

She sighed. 'Well, I think I discharged my obligation to that man long ago, Joshua. Depending which Lobsang you mean. The one I married, "George", was lost when the Next closed off New Springfield's world. The older copy that you brought back from that remote Long Earth became the master edition, so to speak. I know that identity with Lobsang is an odd concept. There's never just one of him; his identity can be split up, joined, one copy poured into the other . . .'

Lobsang had come to awareness as an artificial intelligence running on a substrate of Black Corporation gel. From the beginning he had claimed to be human, in a sense – a reincarnation of a Tibetan motorcycle repairman. To date, nobody had been able to prove him a liar. And since his awakening, his existence had been complicated.

Agnes went on, 'The various copies were synched before "George" was trapped in New Springfield. The new version *remembers* me, our life together. But he was never *my* Lobsang. And anyway he's gone missing.'

It had been years since Joshua had been in touch with any iteration of Lobsang. 'What, again?'

'Selena Jones at transEarth says he's retreated into some kind of virtual environment, where he feels "safe". I've no desire to know where, just now. Of course while his identity – I hesitate to use the word "soul" – has been removed, his outer functions are working just fine. Which is just as well for the fabric of the human world.'

'This is a pattern, isn't it, Agnes?'

'It seems to be. He's fine for a while, then there's some

kind of build-up of stress, and he retreats into a shell – just like when he played at being a farmer in New Springfield. And then the cycle starts all over again. Well.'

'Is this goodbye, Agnes?'

'It doesn't have to be. Oh, it's all so silly, Joshua! You're not Daniel Boone, and you never were. You were just a boy who needed some space—'

'There's something out there calling me back, Agnes,' he blurted. 'I don't have a choice.'

She studied him. 'I remember the words you used as a child. *The Silence.* That's back, is it? You know, I wondered if that might be going on, when I read all those silly news reports about the SETI signal they picked up. If all the oddness might be connected somehow. After all, it usually is.' She sighed. 'I often wish Monica Jansson was still around. Now there was a woman who could speak to that side of you better than I ever could. And she would have told you that whatever you've lost, you won't find it up there.' She stood. 'I've said my piece, and I'll take my leave.'

Suddenly he couldn't look at her.

She said softly, 'Oh, bright eyes.'

And he turned, and she folded him in her arms.

5

Joshua Valienté, and indeed Sister Agnes, were never far from the thoughts of Sister John, superior of the Home on Madison West 5, or her companions.

Take the case of Jan Roderick, who both Agnes and Joshua had met. Ten years old, Jan was a conundrum to the Sisters and staff, even a source of frustration at times, so complicated was the knotted-up personality contained within that small body. Sister John could do nothing but advise patience: what use were nuns and counsellors and teachers if they couldn't show patience at least?

Sister John herself had never found it terribly hard to stay calm around Jan. She didn't pride herself on any special qualities of character, however. It was just that Jan, a slim, dark boy, reminded her in so many ways of Joshua.

The thing with Joshua was that he had always seemed so mundane. His hobbies as a boy in the Home, before Step Day, had been solitary trekking, and exploring the reconstructed prairie in Madison's Arboretum, and back at the Home making ham radio gear and assembling models – in fact, *repairing* incomplete or broken models, and that gave you a clue as to the kind of personality Joshua had harboured under that dark mop of hair.

Then, after Step Day, Joshua had become something of a local celebrity for his calm competence that first bewildering night, when the doors of the stepwise worlds had suddenly swung open, and everybody else had freaked, including most adults.

Sister John had never forgotten what Joshua had done for her that night. She had had utterly no idea what had happened to her: *I never stepped into no wardrobe* . . . Sarah Ann Coates, as she was known then, had already survived nightmares, which was why she had ended up in the Home on Allied Drive in the first place. And there, blundering around in a darkened stepwise forest, she had felt as if all those nightmares had come back for her once more. Hands reaching for her in the night . . . She'd lost it.

Joshua had brought her home. He had saved her.

Step Day had changed his life, but it hadn't changed the essence of Joshua, it seemed to Sister John. He had gone on more solo treks. It was just that now he had jaunted off stepwise, to the High Meggers. He was still methodical and patient to a fault, but now he made and repaired Stepper boxes rather than assembly kits and jigsaw puzzles. There was a spooky side to Joshua – he had been the very first widely known natural stepper, after all, as if Joshua belonged more to the Long Earth than the good old Datum. But he was a man who was in essence *simple*, Sister John thought: not meaning dumb, but simple of construction within, with a short cut between his own deep moral core and the way he behaved.

She'd tried to make it clear to Joshua that there would

always be an open door for him here, whenever he needed it. It had been her idea to set up a memorial stone for Helen Valienté in the rebuilt Home's little cemetery plot. It seemed the very least she could do.

So if Sister Agnes and the rest had been able to help Joshua Valienté, if *he* had eventually grown up so straight and true, surely Sister John in turn could help Jan Roderick.

But Jan was such a puzzle.

One morning Sister Coleen, not far into her twenties herself, came to Sister John in a fluster.

'That boy will do the oddest things.'

'Such as?'

'He *listens*.'

'What's so odd about that? Listens to what?'

'Not what. *Who*. To whoever comes in the door. Officials. Visitors.'

'I thought he didn't get visitors,' Sister John said.

'He doesn't. I mean visitors for the other kids, or even the Sisters. If he gets the chance, he just sits there and listens. And he asks if they've heard any good stories.'

'Stories?'

'Travellers' tales. Urban myths. That kind of thing.'

'Tabloid gossip? Virals?' Sister John asked, feeling it was appropriate to try to sound stern.

'Well, maybe. But he seems to like best the stuff he hears direct from people. And he writes it down on that battered old tablet of his. He even adds times and dates and places. It creeps people out if they notice.'

'Well—'

'And then there's the questions. He will ask the *oddest* things. He's been watching one of Joshua's old movies again.'

'Ah.' Jan's dogged interest in antique pre-Step Day science fiction had prompted the Sisters to curate the Home's collection, left behind mainly by Joshua, with a lot more care. Putting battered paperback books in order was one thing, but it had taken a lot of technical expertise before various hundred-year-old movies had been successfully converted from tape or disc or creaky old file formats to be playable on modern tablets and screens. And after all that effort, the boy returned again and again to a mere handful of favourites. 'Let me guess which one he's watching. *The First Men in the Moon.*'

'No.'

'*Avatar . . . The Mouse on the Moon . . . Galaxy Quest!*'

'That one.'

'Ha! I knew it.'

'He started asking questions, like he'd never seen the movie before, and you know he's seen it twenty times. "What's that place called?" "Well, it's a planet." "But what's its name? Is it real?" "It's just in the movie." "Could you go there for real? What's really out there in space? Are there people like us there?" And so on. Over and over. And you don't dare guess at an answer, not even about a detail of some dumb old movie, or you *know* he'll check it out and come after you.'

'It's not so strange for a ten-year-old boy to be interested in space.'

'I know,' Sister Coleen sighed. 'It's just he's so – you know – *Jan.*'

'I'll speak to him.'

So Sister John quietly arranged to spend an evening with Jan. She promised him they'd sit together on an elderly sofa watching one of his old movies, or reading one of his books, whatever he liked.

They settled down before a big wall-mounted screen that was showing *Contact*, a movie she had seen with him so many times she recognized each frame. Jan was making notes on a handheld tablet. And he had a couple of old novels on the couch beside him: one was *Contact*, the book of the movie – or maybe it was the other way around – and the other was called *Ringworld*. The two of them sat there viewing philosophically, and crunching on popcorn.

Right now the screen showed radio astronomer Ellie Arroway as a kid, with her father. Jan remarked, 'You know, this movie is eighty years old. Something like that. But they talk just the way people talk now.'

What kind of perception was that for a ten-year-old boy? It was the kind of thing Jan came out with that perpetually surprised people. 'I guess so. Why do you think that is?'

He shrugged. 'Because we all watch the same old movies. Nobody makes new stuff any more.'

She supposed that was true. 'I did read that the TV industry suffered after Step Day, because you couldn't transmit stuff between the stepwise worlds. Then Yellowstone kind of killed it off for good. You know, the big volcano back in '40.'

'So we all watch the same stuff, over and over,' Jan said. 'It's like it froze.'

She smiled. 'I guess. Nobody's sure who the Pope is any more, but we all know Captain Kirk.'

'I never heard of *him*.'

'You will, Jan. You will. So why do you like this movie particularly?'

'*Contact*? I like the way she looks for patterns, you know? In the signal from the sky. All those numbers. That's why I wanted to watch this movie, because they really did pick up a signal in the sky, didn't they? At the Gap. Did they find numbers in that signal?'

'I don't know,' Sister John said honestly. She hadn't been much interested in the signal when it was briefly news; most of the reporting she'd seen had been lurid speculation.

Jan munched popcorn complacently. 'I found some books in the library. About finding patterns in numbers and stuff. Patterns in nature, like you get the same kind of spiral in a sunflower and a galaxy.'

'Really?' Sister John had never been a scholar. She was reminded sharply of Sister Georgina, long dead now, who had been the most academic of the nuns. The books Jan had consulted might even have been Georgina's once. Georgina had never ceased to remind everybody that she had studied at Cambridge. Sister John murmured, 'Not-the-one-in-Massachusetts-Cambridge-University-the-real-one-you-know-in-England . . .'

Jan looked at her quizzically. 'Huh?'

'Nothing. Just remembering . . .' And she made an intuitive leap. 'Patterns. Is that why you like listening to the stories people tell? Are there patterns in those too?'

He shrugged, chewing his popcorn.

Maybe he didn't recognize himself what he was doing, Sister John thought. *Pattern-seeking*: looking for logic in a chaotic life. *Contact*: looking for a way to reach the absent other. The movie had made the same connection, actually; there was a slightly cheesy scene where the young Ellie tried to contact her dead father through CB radio.

It made sense, given Jan's background. He'd never even met his father, and his mother had been little more than a kid herself, with significant learning and cognitive difficulties. He'd spent his first four years more or less alone with the mother, in a post-Yellowstone Low Earth refugee camp that had become a sink of poverty and dependence. One downside of the great opening up of the Long Earth was that it offered a lot more room for such cases to go unnoticed. The mother had done her limited best, but she hadn't even taught Jan to speak properly; they had communicated with a kind of home-developed baby talk.

Then the mother too had disappeared. Neighbours had rescued a bewildered and terrified child from starvation. Suddenly, at age four, Jan Roderick had lost his only human contact and his sole means of communication. Bombarded by a blizzard of strangeness, he hadn't uttered a word for a whole year.

Sister John always tried to keep stuff like that in the back of her mind. A kid was a kid, after all, not a bundle of conditions. Yet such knowledge informed.

'So what are you making notes about now?'

'I'm proving Ellie Arroway is from Madison, Wisconsin.'

She did a double take. 'Really?'

39

'It doesn't say so out loud in the movie. But in the book, in the first chapter, Ellie's mom takes her for a walk down State Street.' He squinted. 'There was a State Street in Datum Madison too, wasn't there, Sister?'

'Yes, there was.'

'And it says she lives by a lake in Wisconsin.' He flicked through his tablet, small fingers moving rapidly. 'She goes to see her mother in a care home in Janesville. And look, in the movie . . .' Expertly he scrolled back to a scene where a wall map showed young Ellie's pattern of CB radio contacts: lines of tape connecting thumbtacks. 'See the tack where her home is?'

'Dead-on for Madison,' Sister John said, wondering.

'Later her father says how far away Pensacola is—'

'I believe you. Wow. Who'd have thought it? Cheeseheads make first contact. Whoo hoo!'

They exchanged a high-five slap, and Sister John dared to hug him, tickling him a little to make him laugh; he wasn't generally a physical kind of kid.

Then they subsided and watched more of the ancient movie.

She said carefully, 'Sister Coleen says you've been asking questions about why people haven't gone to other worlds for real.'

'I'm sorry,' he said reflexively.

For all her caution she'd got the tone wrong; too many of the kids in the Home were over-sensitized to criticism, and the punishment that had usually followed before they came here. 'No. Don't be sorry. It's OK. We're just talking. Look, you know Americans did go to the moon and back.'

'Sure. Like a hundred years ago. Not since then.'

'I guess it's because of the Long Earth. Why go to the moon when you've got all those worlds you can just walk into?'

'But they're all *boring*. They're all just Madison, without the people and stuff.'

'I know what you mean. But there's a *lot* of worlds in the Long Earth, and you don't need a spacesuit, you can breathe the air . . .' Sister John remembered that Joshua, as a younger man, had said the same kind of thing: 'Out in the High Meggers I am in fact a planetbound astronaut, which hasn't got the glamour of the old-time spacemen but does have the advantage in that you can stop occasionally for a crap . . .' She suppressed a smile.

'Is the Long Earth bigger than the Ringworld?'

She had to glance at the book cover to get a rough idea of what a "Ringworld" was: some kind of huge structure in space. 'Well, how big is the Ringworld?'

'As big as three million Earths,' he said promptly.

'Oh, the Long Earth is much bigger than *that*.'

'Really?' His eyes widened in wonder. '*Cool*.'

Later, when the spooky stuff began, she would think back to conversations like this. It was a strange thing that Jan Roderick's background had almost pre-adapted him for what followed.

Made him ready to respond to the Invitation.

The thing was, Jan Roderick had been right. Obsessed with SETI and mathematical puzzles and pattern-finding, he was slowly becoming aware of something new in the world – new and *real*. A pattern not of numbers, or

41

contained in radio signals whispered from the sky: a pattern in the stories people were telling each other. Stories spreading across local nets in the Low Earths, and webs of telegraph and telephone cables and micro comsats in the more developed pioneer worlds, and further out through the outernet – the low-tech, self-organized communications system that spanned a million worlds of the Long Earth – even, when push came to shove, spreading by word of mouth, around campfires scattered across otherwise empty planets where travellers met and talked.

And – coincidentally, given Joshua's departing conversation with Agnes, which was the first time he had thought of his old friend Monica Jansson for some time – one such story concerned a strange encounter for Jansson herself, many years earlier . . .

6

WHATEVER THE ULTIMATE destiny of mankind in the unending landscapes of the Long Earth – and in the year 2029, just fourteen years after Step Day, that had been only dimly glimpsed – back on Datum Earth, in Madison, Wisconsin, and its footprints, the agenda of MPD Lieutenant Monica Jansson, then forty-three years old, had been increasingly occupied by the tension between steppers and non-steppers.

The tension, and its victims.

Stuart Mann was a theoretical physicist, not a doctor or a psychologist. Monica Jansson had met him at one of the many academic conferences that she'd attended as she tried to get her head around the whole Long Earth phenomenon. Mann had struck her as one of the more human attendees, humorous, mostly comprehensible in his conversation, and with little of the spiky arrogance that so many academics seemed to display. Now, as he spoke gently to the Damaged Woman, here in the holiday cabin her family had built in this footprint of Maple Bluff – they were in Earth West 31, a fairly remote world but still a community tied to Datum Madison – Jansson thought Mann had a better bedside manner than most doctors she'd come across. Which was why Jansson had suggested he consult.

Mann sat on the sofa beside the patient and smiled, though it was evident the woman couldn't see him. He was around fifty, grey, portly, wearing a tweed jacket and a bright-scarlet bow tie, his one affectation. The patient was in a dressing gown. 'Tell me what you can see,' he said simply.

The Damaged Woman turned her head in his direction. Her eyes weren't like the eyes of a blind person, in Jansson's experience. They flickered, moved, focused. She was seeing *something*. Just not Stu Mann. She plucked at the loops of copper wire around her wrist. She was called Bettany Diamond.

'Trees,' she said. 'I see trees. It's sunny. I mean, I can't feel the sun's heat, but ... The kids are playing. Harry coming down from the tree house we built. Amelia running at me ...' She flinched, sitting on her sofa, and Jansson imagined a little girl running through Bettany's visual field. One side of Bettany's face was a mass of bruises, a relic of the beating she'd taken in hospital, and her speech was distorted as a result. 'Harry's getting his Stepper. He has his sick bag. We always make the kids carry sick bags when they step.'

Mann said gently, 'He's going to step back here?'

'Oh, yes. They're not allowed to go more than one world stepwise without us present.'

'Can you tell me where he is? Where he's going to step back to?'

She pointed, to a spot in the middle of the living room

carpet. 'We laid out tape in the stepwise worlds. The outline of the house. It doesn't harm them if they try to step into a wall. You just get pushed away, you know, but it distresses them.'

And with a puff of displaced air Harry appeared, a grubby, sweating six-year-old, stepping straight from the forest on to the carpet. Exactly where Bettany was pointing.

Where she, stuck in Earth West 31, had seen him standing, in Earth West 32.

Harry's little face crumpled, and he held his sick bag to his mouth, but he didn't throw up. His mother reached for him, unseeing. 'Good boy. Brave boy. Come here now . . .'

Mann and Jansson withdrew to the kitchen.

Bettany's husband made them a pot of coffee. He was in white shirt and tie, crisp slacks, black leather shoes; he'd come home from work when Bettany was released from the hospital so he could get the kids back from her sister where they'd been staying, and the family could be together again here in this holiday home, this refuge from the current anti-stepper madness back on the Datum. When he'd poured the coffee, the husband left them alone.

Mann sipped from his mug. 'I can see why the doctors called you in, Lieutenant Jansson. Knowing of your, umm, vocation. The work you've done on stepping-related crime and social issues.'

'But the doctors don't understand. She's actually a near-phobic, isn't she? Bettany Diamond. She has significant

45

difficulties stepping, even though she's set up this holiday home thirty-one steps out. And though she's wearing a stepper bracelet. She *believes* in stepping and its benefits, even though she can't do it so well herself . . .'

This was a time when evidence was first spreading widely that some people were able to step naturally, that is without the aid of a Linsay Stepper box, despite the official cover-ups. And the tension between non-steppers and natural steppers was mounting. Humanity had found the latest in a long line of sub-groups to pick on, and a kit bag of discriminatory horrors inherited from the past was being rummaged through. In some Central Asian countries, according to human rights activists, they laced the bodies of steppers with iron, so that if you stepped away you'd bleed out of some pierced artery. Some states in the US were considering something horribly similar, where steel-based pacemakers would be installed into the bodies of high-category cons: step away, and your heart stopped.

At minimum, in most states, as in many countries around the world, natural steppers were being forced to wear markers of some kind, such as electronic wristband tags. The argument was that the tags were needed to keep track of potential criminals. *Yellow stars*, the critics called the markers. Jansson imagined this foolishness would pass soon enough. In the meantime it had become a fashion among the young to wear dummy stepper tokens as a badge of defiance. It had even generated a kind of street art, as designers extended the wristband concept into loops of copper or even platinum, supposed representations of the chain of worlds that was the Long Earth.

None of which had anything much to do with Bettany Diamond, lawyer, wife, mother. In the Datum Madison hospital another patient had actually assaulted her just because she was admitted for her sight problems, a condition apparently *related* to stepping. It didn't help that she defiantly wore a pro-stepper bracelet, but that was hardly an invitation to attack.

Jansson asked, 'So what do you make of her condition?'

Mann sipped his coffee. 'It's very early to say. Perhaps we need more cases like hers to make sense of the phenomenon. In the past, after all, we learned a lot about how the brain functions from instances of damage. You broke a bit on the inside, and saw what stopped working on the outside.

'I do firmly believe, however, that stepping is an attribute of human consciousness – or at least humanoid. Animals with significantly different kinds of consciousness do not step, as far as we know. Now, the best theories we have of how the Long Earth works, and they are only tentative, are based on quantum physics: the possibility that many realities exist in a kind of cloud around the actual. And in some quantum theories consciousness has a fundamental role to play.'

'Like the Copenhagen Interpretation.'

He smiled. 'You've done your homework.'

'It's a long way from police academy, so go easy on me . . .'

'Maybe consciousness, observing some quantum phenomenon – the cat in the box, neither dead nor alive until you look at it – chooses one possibility to become the actual. Thus, conscious seeing creates reality, in a way. Or maybe it takes you there. Some believe that what happens, when you step, is that similarly you can suddenly *see* Earth West 32, or whatever, and taste and smell and touch it, and that's what *transports* you there. Almost as if you are collapsing some enormous set of quantum wave functions. Sorry – that's a bit technical.

'It's all very preliminary, because we understand so little of the basics. Even the mechanism of sight itself is a mystery. Think about it.' He picked up his red coffee mug. 'You can recognize this mug from above or below, in bright light or in the shade, against any background. How do you *do* that? What kind of pattern is being matched in your cortex?

'But even beyond the neurology, you have the mystery of consciousness. How does all this information processing relate to *me* – to my internal experience of redness, for instance, or roundness, or mug-ness? And then there's the further mystery of the interaction of consciousness with the quantum world.

'The whole field of Long Earth studies is still nascent, and it's a cross-disciplinary quagmire of neurology, philosophy, quantum physics. What we do know is that even sight comes with a group of barely understood exotic disorders that we call agnosias, usually caused by some kind of brain damage. There's an agnosia for faces, where you can't recognize even your family; there's an agnosia for scenes, for colour . . .'

'So maybe Bettany has some kind of stepwise agnosia?'

'Perhaps, though that's doing little more than attaching

a label to something we don't understand. Look – what *I* believe is that something's gone wrong for Bettany, in that tangle of processing. She does the *seeing* without the *stepping*. For several hours a day, the world she sees is no longer necessarily the one she's living in. So she blunders into furniture while seeing her kids playing in the world next door, but she can't hear them or touch them, and they, of course, can't see her. And meanwhile the doctors can't treat what they don't understand. They do say the time she spends seeing wrongly is increasing. Give her another year and her sight will be stuck permanently stepwise.'

'She won't be able to see her kids, even when they're right beside her.'

'But she can hold them,' Mann said. 'Touch them. Hear them.'

Jansson said, 'She told me today she heard birdsong, of a kind she'd never heard before.'

'Birdsong?'

'Why shouldn't this affect her other senses? Is it possible her whole mind will come adrift, ultimately? And she'll fully experience one world while her body lies comatose in the other?'

'I don't know, Lieutenant. We'll just have to make sure she is protected, whatever happens.'

From elsewhere in the house they heard Bettany calling for her children. Jansson wished Joshua Valienté was around, to help her figure this out.

Just as, later, after her death, Joshua would often miss Jansson's advice.

*   *   *

And Jan Roderick, making his notes on his tablets in his childish vocabulary, would try to figure out what the story of the Damaged Woman meant in terms of seeing, and stepping, and living in an infinite ensemble of potential worlds.

And beyond.

7

THE INVITATION CAME to all the worlds of the Long Earth from space. And it was on a world on the edge of space that the work of responding to the Invitation began.

Dev Bilaniuk and Lee Malone, in identical blue jumpsuits, stood nervously outside the entrance of the GapSpace facility. It was a cool April day. Around them stretched the local version of northern England, a sandy, grass-strewn coastal plain studded with scratchy farms and workers' villages, giving way to rounded hills further inland. The songs of trolls, contentedly labouring in the fields and building yards, lifted on the fresh breeze off the sea. It was a mundane panorama, Dev thought, and it was hard to believe they were some two million steps from the Datum.

But before them stood the tall fence that contained the heavily policed interior of the GapSpace facility, with all its expensive and high-energy engineering. To support the facility was the sole purpose of the scattered community in this landscape.

And beyond *that*, in a sense, lay infinity.

Forty years earlier Joshua Valienté had discovered an alternate Earth that was no Earth at all. Big spaceborne rocks hit the planet all the time, and in that particular universe the all-time champion world smasher had happened to hit dead centre. The result was the Gap, and it had turned out to be damned useful for those elements of humanity who still harboured dreams of spaceflight. Because from here, to reach space, you didn't need Cape Canaveral and rocket stacks the size of cathedrals. You only needed to step sideways, into a Gap where an Earth used to be, into vacuum. People had been venturing into space from this place ever since.

And now the Next were coming here. Dev felt Lee's hand slip into his own.

They had come out a little early; waiting for their Next visitors to arrive, they'd been too nervous to sit around. Lee, tall, slim, dark, wearing her hair shaven close to her scalp, was a few years younger than Dev, in her mid-twenties, and he was her nominal superior in the GapSpace management hierarchy, such as it was. She was ferociously bright, however, and he had a feeling that their working relationship wouldn't stay the same for long – even if their tentative personal relationship lasted. For now, though, she needed his support.

He squeezed her hand. 'Take it easy. I mean, you know Prof Welch from Valhalla U. The Next might browbeat you, but they don't actually bite.'

'It's not that. Well, maybe a little. It's like being back at college, and being brought in before some ferocious supervisor who's going to pick your work apart.'

'And they have been bringing money into GapSpace,

52

remember. Why, the Cyclops radio telescope project was their initiative in the first place.'

'But they weren't interested in *us* before, were they? They saw the Gap as just a handy place to hang a big space antenna. But now there's the Invitation, and here they come, taking over.'

Dev shrugged. 'Well, they're not taking over—'

'And *we'll* get railroaded.'

The Next were a new kind of people – genetically and morphologically distinct – who had emerged in the strange crucible that was the Long Earth. And they were, without a doubt, categorically smarter than regular-issue folk.

'Humans are kind of disposable when the Next are around. That's what they say.'

'We can deal with it . . .'

A sleek airship appeared above their heads with a soft pop of displaced air. As soon as it arrived it began to descend, and a passenger ramp like a long tongue unrolled and reached for the ground not far from the facility's security gate. Shadowy figures moved in the ship's interior.

'I hope you're right,' Lee said nervously.

Even the Next had to follow the proper security procedure when entering the compound.

Not that there was much malevolence directed at GapSpace nowadays, but this was still a fragile, high-technology, high-energy facility, and while security in the Long Earth had always been a challenge, there were ways to achieve it. The only orderly way into GapSpace was the way Stella Welch and Roberta Golding were coming in now: stepping through from the lower worlds to arrive outside the security perimeter and be processed through the gate.

And it was the job of Dev and Lee to welcome them.

Dev led Lee towards the twain. 'To tell the truth I'm more nervous about what they're going to be wearing. There are these rumours about how the Next live, in the wild . . .'

'Nude except for pockets. That's what I heard. But Professor Welch is like a hundred and eight.'

'Not that old—'

'Without her clothes she'll look like she's *melted*.'

He laughed. 'I'll tell her you said so.'

Two women were walking down the ramp from the twain, followed by a crewman pushing a trolley heaped with luggage. To Dev's relief neither of the Next was semi-nude; they wore what looked like serviceable travelling clothes – jackets and slacks in sombre shades. A few more crew followed the party down, and began fixing anchor ropes to the ground.

Dev recognized Stella Welch, of course, who had visited GapSpace several times before. He'd never met Roberta Golding, but she was rumoured to be senior in whatever organization the Next had set up for themselves in the Grange, their secretive base. Slim, dark, bespectacled, with a rather pinched face, she looked younger than he'd expected – mid-forties, maybe.

'See,' Dev said. 'They look normal enough.'

'Hm. For a given value of "normal" . . .'

The introductions, with cursory handshakes, were brief.

Dev said, 'We're honoured you've come out to see us, Ms Golding.'

She looked faintly puzzled, as if he'd said something inappropriate. 'That's polite of you. But this is business, of course. The project we propose—'

Stella Welch interposed, 'Oh, but this goes beyond business, Roberta. At least as far as these two former students of mine are concerned. We're going to ask them to put aside their own personal programmes to help us facilitate the Clarke Project. They are among the most able here.'

Dev felt his own polite expression become strained at this faint praise. And he glanced at Lee. *The Clarke Project? I never heard that name before.*

Roberta said now, 'You have our transport waiting?'

Dev said, 'The stepper shuttle to the Gap? Whenever you're ready. But if you'd like to look around the facility first—'

'We'd rather get on with it,' Stella said. She headed towards the gate – after all, she knew the way. 'We went through the necessary bio-screening on board the twain; the formal permissions are being downloaded now.'

Dev and Lee fell in behind the two of them. 'You seem in a hurry.'

Roberta barely glanced back. 'We are.'

'So,' Lee murmured to Dev, 'we're among the most able here, are we? Maybe we could go swing on a tyre. They might throw us a couple of bananas.'

'Hush,' he whispered, suppressing a grin.

8

THE HANGAR CONTAINING the stepper shuttles was at the heart of the complex, a concrete box surrounded by fuel-store facilities. The shuttles stood in a neat row. Each conical craft looked like an old Apollo command module, but standing on three legs with a stubby engine block and spherical fuel tanks beneath.

Using the Gap, this was all you needed to reach space. You didn't even need to take your shuttle out of this hangar.

The processing was swift. The bulk of the visitors' luggage was taken away to residential facilities elsewhere on the site, leaving them with small items of hand luggage. Supervised by attendants in hooded white coveralls, the four of them were put through a final medical screen, culminating in antiseptic showers. Then they were fitted with fresh coveralls in a rich NASA-type blue, each equipped with temperature-control elements, an emergency oxygen supply, and clumsy sewn-in diapers in case of other kinds of emergency.

The Next visitors put up with all this with a kind of bored patience. Dev, watching them, supposed this must be a posture that Next working among humans got used to adopting. Bored patience.

They all climbed easily into their shuttle, and strapped themselves into couches, selecting them at random from banks fixed on a couple of decks in the interior of the little craft. Automated, the shuttle needed no pilot.

Dev found himself slipping into tour-guide mode. 'This is all very routine,' he said. 'We make hops over in shuttles like this every day—'

'We can do without such trivial observations,' said Roberta mildly. 'We are not – tourists.'

'The safety record they've achieved is a non-trivial matter,' Stella said to her. 'Although it has got better yet since *we* showed up and ran a few reviews.'

Roberta considered Dev. 'And the cultural development here is non-trivial, of course. *Dev Bilaniuk* – I'm guessing your names have different origins? They sound Indian and Slavic—'

'Mother from Delhi, father from Minsk. Both drawn here to the Gap. I'm a second-generation Gapper.'

'You could surely have moved away, had you chosen to. Evidently you inherited their dream of space.'

Lee leaned forward against her straps. 'That's not so unusual. Especially when you see what else is on offer in the Long Earth. Slaving in factories at the feet of space elevators in the Low Earths, or else wandering around in hand-me-down clothes, picking fruit and chasing after funny-looking deer. I'm a second-generation Gapper too. At least here we're pursuing an authentic human aspiration, one that predates stepping itself. And one you people stay out of, unless you need something.'

Dev said, 'Lee—'

Stella held up a hand. 'It's OK.'

And, under the control of the shuttle's AI, they stepped.

One step further West, they fell into a hole where an Earth should be. Beyond the windows, where there had been washed-out English sunlight, there was only darkness. And as always, without gravity it felt to Dev like they were suddenly falling.

Then the shuttle swivelled sharply and fired its thrusters, producing a fierce deceleration.

Every object on the surface of the spinning Earth, at GapSpace's latitude, was moving through space at hundreds of miles per hour, and in the Gap that velocity had to be shed. And that was what the rocket fire was for.

Dev was glad the transition had put a stop to the conversation. And spitefully glad too to observe discomfort on the faces of the two Next – even Stella, who had made this journey a number of times before. Superhuman intellects they might be, but right now he suspected they were discovering that their inner ears and stomachs were just as human and just as maladapted to shifting gravity as his own.

The hard rocket thrust lasted only seconds, and died quickly. They were briefly weightless again. Then the shuttle turned once more, with pops of attitude thrusters that sounded as if somebody was beating the outer hull with a stick, and with a blip of the main engine began to edge towards its docking station.

Now, through the small window before him, Dev glimpsed structures in space.

Directly ahead of the shuttle was a mass of clustered concrete spheres, huge, marked with sunlight-faded black letters, A to K, with an oddly organic look – like a clump of frogspawn, perhaps. This was the Brick Moon, GapSpace's first reception station here in the Gap, tracking the orbits of the Earths to either stepwise side. Further out, brilliant in the unfiltered sunlight, Dev could see the *O'Neill*, a new and much larger facility, like a glass bottle filled with glowing green light and surrounded by big, fragile constructions, paddles and bowls and net-like antennas. The whole affair rotated languidly on the bottle's long axis. It was only the smaller craft swarming around the docking ports at the structure's circular ends that gave a sense of its scale: that 'bottle' was twenty miles long, four miles wide.

And behind all this, dwarfing even the *O'Neill*, hovered a lump of ice and rock. From here Dev could see work going on across its surface: the gleam of mass drivers, the spark of craft landing and taking off. Called only the Lump, this was an immense asteroid that had been nudged, over decades, into a position close to the Brick Moon, and steadily mined for its resources to build such structures as the *O'Neill* and the Cyclops telescope.

'So that's the Brick Moon,' Roberta murmured. 'Concrete mixed by trolls. Ha! What a start to humanity's conquest of space.'

Lee just glared.

Dev began to unbuckle. 'We need not stay long here; this is just a transit point. We've a ferry waiting to transfer us to the *Gerard K. O'Neill*. It's a much more comfortable environment. With gravity, for one thing, provided by the spin. We'd be pleased to show you the projects we're developing out here—'

'Irrelevant,' Roberta said simply. 'Does this Brick Moon, this concrete box, have viewing facilities sufficient to view the progress on Cyclops? Also computational support, some kind of AI?'

'Of course.'

'I have no desire to extend this visit beyond what is necessary. After all, we have to regard the situation as urgent; we have no idea how long we have before the Invitation ceases to transmit, and we must ensure we extract all the information it contains. The Clarke proposal is the one and only reason I am here.' She laughed softly. 'Not to sightsee your new toys.'

Lee was fuming, and Dev tried to suppress his own irritation. He said, 'Well, let's hope you people are just as happy with *your* new toy, when *we've* built it for you.'

Roberta and Stella exchanged a raised-eyebrow glance. The man-ape was being defiant.

No more was said until the shuttle closed in on the Brick Moon, and docking latches rattled shut.

9

THERE WAS NO gravity in the Brick Moon. You moved by pulling yourself along ropes slung around the walls, and poles that criss-crossed the spherical chambers.

The big spheres were connected by circular orifices, and as they moved deeper into the interior it was as if they were swimming into the centre of some vast honeycomb – or maybe, as one visitor from the Datum Earth had remarked, it was like a huge old Roman-era drainage system, all concrete vaults and cylindrical passages. And after decades of occupation the Brick Moon smelled that way too, despite periodic flushings of the entire volatile content, the water and all the air: a sour stink of people, of stale food and sweat and blood and piss, seemed to seep out of the very walls.

It wasn't a quiet place; there was an endless clatter of pumps and fans. And the walls, where they weren't hidden by cabling and ducts and pipes, were crusted with decades' worth of junk, from antiquated tablets and comms stations, to the relics of abandoned science experiments, to tokens left by those who had lived and worked here: faded photographs, children's paintings, scribbled notes, graffiti on the concrete. Even the residential area, at the centre of the cluster, with bunk beds and galleys and a medical centre and grimy zero-gravity toilets, couldn't have looked less inviting.

Most long-lived space stations got shabby; they weren't places where you could ever open the windows for a good spring-clean. And after all, this rough, decades-old construction had been humanity's first colony in this Earth-less universe; embarrassment wasn't an appropriate reaction. But Dev couldn't help it.

And he kept an eye on his guests. They had little trouble moving around, though their postures were a bit stiff, and Roberta in particular seemed to be recoiling from touching the grimy walls. Here and there boxes and pots held plants and flowers that grew in splashes of sunlight from the windows. The visitors' eyes were drawn to the green – another primitive reaction, and one Dev found grimly satisfying to observe.

They crossed paths with only a couple of people, both in GapSpace coveralls like Dev and his guests, who stared curiously back at the Next. The Brick Moon was never very crowded. There was a small station staff, rotated frequently, whose main job was to maintain the antique fabric and clean up the air and water. Otherwise there were only ever a few passengers in transit from one shuttle to another.

At last they reached the sphere known informally as the observatory. Here much of the original troll-concrete shell had been replaced by a ribbing of steel and aluminium, and plates of toughened glass. There were bars for hands and feet to help visitors keep from drifting around the bubble. It was dark, the artificial light subdued.

Beyond the windows no sun was visible, and the sky was pitch-black. The four of them spread out in the darkness.

To Dev, whose father had been an Orthodox Catholic, this place always felt oddly like a chapel, and he spoke softly. 'It's best to wait a while to allow our eyes to adjust to the dark. The Brick Moon has some limited manoeuvrability, to maintain its station and its orientation. And it's turned, very slowly, to ensure no one section is over-exposed to the sun. But this chamber is kept facing away from the light permanently—'

'I see a planet,' Roberta said. She pointed at a light, emerging from the dark. She thought for a moment, and Dev imagined calculations processing through her high intelligence: an exercise in celestial mechanics, a determination of what she was seeing. 'Mars,' she announced.

'Yes,' Dev said. 'A Mars, at any rate, the Mars of this stepwise universe. But its position is subtly different from that of our own Mars because of—'

'The lack of an Earth here. Of course.'

Again she'd cut him off. He suppressed his irritation. These Next did seem to require an awful lot of forgiveness of the dim-bulbs they dealt with.

He caught Lee grinning at him, her teeth bright in the subdued light.

Roberta ran her finger around the equator of the sky. 'And there are asteroids.'

Dev could just see them now, emerging as a band of sparkles against a wider scatter of stars.

Stella nodded. 'It is the wreckage of the local Earth, of course. Dead Earth, as they call it. Much of the mass of the planet seems to have been lost in the impact – thrown out of the solar system altogether, probably – but what remains is a new asteroid belt, rich in silicate rock, iron.'

Dev said, 'This local belt has been essential in building up our facilities here. The big *O'Neill*, for example, was constructed of iron and aluminium and stocked with volatiles, all gathered from Dead Earth asteroids. The fact that these rocks are so close to us, compared to the classic asteroid belt, has made life a lot easier.'

Roberta looked out with some interest. '"Dead Earth." I understand there are some groups who oppose your exploiting this resource. It's likened to grave-robbing.'

Lee said, 'But some say it's as if we're honouring the planet, by making use of its wreckage.' She faced Roberta defiantly. 'I suppose *you* think either position is illogical.'

'Not at all. One would have to have a very stunted emotional imagination not to have some response to this, the ruin of a world, of, presumably, a planetary biosphere every bit as mature and rich as that of Datum Earth itself. But what you're doing here is neither right nor wrong. It simply is.' She glanced around the sky. 'Where is Cyclops?'

Stella swam over next to her and pointed. 'Up there, at four o'clock.'

Looking that way, Dev could see only a disc of blackness, occluding the stars. He said, 'Actually what you see is just the baffle, shielding the radio telescope from leakage from the habitats, the shuttles.' He tapped a console, and a big display tablet brought up an image of a vast, lacy dish: the antenna of the spaceborne radio telescope itself.

Roberta glanced up at the baffle, itself an immense structure. 'A shame I can't see it with the naked eye, but I sense the scale.'

Stella said, 'You know, astronomy, and particularly radio astronomy, was one of the first great science programmes for the Next, once we had organized our society sufficiently. An area where huge advances in knowledge were available based on a simple expansion of technological scale. We began with a trio of super-Arecibos. On the Datum this was a major radio telescope with its dish built into a volcanic caldera in Puerto Rico. We constructed much larger dishes in calderas on one particular Earth, near Olduvai Gorge, at Pinatubo, one at Yellowstone in North America – a long-dead copy of the parent volcano on the Datum. If you visualize these positions, spread around the globe of the world, you will see we had coverage of the equatorial sky for twenty-four hours of the day.

'But these efforts will be surpassed as we move into space. Our first design was Cyclops, out there. A single parabolic dish antenna five kilometres wide. We named it after a pre-Step Day proposal, from a century ago, to build such a telescope from a conglomeration of a thousand smaller antennas, constructed on the ground. It might be unfinished, but it's good enough to have acquired the clearest version yet of the Invitation.' She fished her own tablet out of her bag, and tapped it to bring up data on the signal. 'In some ways it's a classic SETI discovery. An extremely strong signal. Polarized, as if it has been broadcast by a radio telescope of the kind we can build ourselves. The frequency is around the minimum of the background noise of the Galaxy. We're aware of a lot of detail below the signal's top-level structure, but much of it is lost in the noise. And what we have is complex. Not decipherable, so far anyhow.'

'Which is,' Roberta said calmly, 'why we're all here.'

Dev said, 'We still don't know where it's coming from. The source is stationary against the background of the stars. The source appears to be in Sagittarius—'

'It's logical that it should be.' Roberta glanced over her shoulder, and Dev just *knew* she was looking straight towards the position of the Sagittarius constellation in the sky. 'The overwhelmingly most likely location of high intelligence is towards the centre of the Galaxy. The spiral arms, where we live, are waves of star birth washing around the galactic disc. But at the core, where the stars are crowded close, where the energy fluxes are enormous – a dangerous place, but where the first worlds rich in rock and metal formed billions of years before Earth – *that* is where the peak of galactic civilization must reside. And all of that lies in the direction of Sagittarius.'

Lee said, 'And you think it's imperative that we pick up this Invitation and figure it out.'

Roberta looked back at her. 'Of course. What could be more important than that? For one thing, has it occurred to you to wonder why it should be *now* that they attempt to contact us? Somehow they must know that we, or something like us, are here: a technological civilization, I mean.

This despite the fact that our own radio signals cannot have travelled more than one per cent or so of the distance to the galactic core.'

Stella said, 'Of course we must extract all the information we can from the Invitation – all of it, if we're to make an informed decision on how to react.'

Lee said, 'You mean how to respond.'

Roberta said calmly, 'Not necessarily. We have received an invitation; we don't have to accept it. Not until we're sure it's in our best interest.'

Lee snorted. 'The best interest of the Next?'

'In the interest of all of us, all the inhabitants of the Long Earth.'

Dev smiled. 'It's an old debate – goes back to Carl Sagan and Stephen Hawking. Contact optimists versus the pessimists.'

Roberta nodded gravely. 'It is an authentic dilemma. We too debate these issues. First things first: we must learn what we are dealing with.'

Stella said, 'Well, certainly listening can't do any harm. As for the telescopes, we have a new design that will soon surpass the capabilities of the Cyclops.' She swiped her tablet over the bubble's consoles, and the big display screens on the walls filled with new images.

Dev saw a graphic of a sphere suspended in space, from which towers extended in all directions, like spines, dwarfing the central mass. It looked oddly like a sea urchin.

Lee asked, 'What is this?'

Roberta said, 'Tell me what you see.'

Lee shrugged. 'It looks like an asteroid with towers sticking out of it.'

'It is an asteroid,' Roberta said evenly, 'with towers sticking out of it.'

'This is your Clarke Project?'

'Named after a writer of the last century who proposed—'

Dev swallowed. 'Those spines must be hundreds of miles long.'

'Thousands, actually.'

'And where are you going to get your asteroid?'

Roberta glanced out of the window. 'We will use the object you have already harvested. Your "Lump".'

'That's intended for other purposes. More *O'Neills*—'

'We can pay,' Roberta said dismissively.

Lee said, 'I guess I can see the purpose. With a thing that scale you'd be able to pick up very long wavelength radiation – well beyond the usual radio lengths, tens of kilometres, even. Gravity waves too?'

'That's the idea. We've no reason to think the Invitation is restricted to the wavelengths at which we've detected it so far. We want it *all*.'

Dev's engineering chops began to tingle. 'It's one hell of a construction project. The *O'Neill* took us a decade to build. How long do you estimate it will take you to build that behemoth?'

Roberta said blandly, 'Two months.'

Now it was Dev's turn to laugh. Lee just looked blank. Even Stella seemed surprised.

Dev asked, 'How can you possibly do it so quickly? Given the manufacturing capacity we have at GapSpace – even if you suddenly expanded it one hundred per cent—'

Stella said, '*Replicators*. You're talking about using silver-beetle technology to build the Clarke, aren't you? That's the only way you could get it done so quickly.'

Roberta said, 'It's under consideration.'

Dev glanced at Lee, who winked back. It was nice to see these Next disagreeing with each other, even if Dev had no idea what they were talking about. He asked pleasantly, 'And what is "silver-beetle technology"?'

Stella looked at him. 'I guess you'll find out soon enough. Highly efficient replicator and reassembly technology. *Alien* technology. It already destroyed one stepwise Earth, as far as we know.'

Dev just stared. 'It *destroyed an Earth*?'

'Long story,' Stella said.

Roberta said, 'No technology is dangerous if handled correctly. And it would allow an extremely rapid construction, just as you say. The Clarke telescope would be very large, but mostly structurally simple. An ideal application of replicator techniques. Of course, preliminary results would begin to come in much earlier than full construction – and then we will have decisions to make on how to react. I think I've seen enough here. We must talk in more detail. I need to meet your senior people, while avoiding having them take us for tours of the *O'Neill* – Stella, what *do* they do on that object?'

Stella grinned. 'They walk on grass, and chase zero-gravity chickens along the spin axis.'

Lee flared. 'You dismiss us, don't you? Everything we've built here. Spaceflight is an ancient dream, cherished for longer than people like you have even been in existence, and we're achieving it at last.'

'Perhaps. But, child,' Roberta said sadly, 'can you not see that all of this has already been swept away? Because the Galaxy is now reaching down to you. Well. There is much to do. Shall we return to our shuttle?'

10

JOSHUA SPENT HIS first night alone on Earth West
1,520,875 up a tree.

Not that he tried too hard to keep count; this was a
sabbatical after all, and counting kind of wasn't the point.
And since the deletion of a whole world, of Earth West
1,217,756, doomed by an infestation of alien creatures,
and with the Long Earth sealed up to either side of that
wound, such numbers were probably meaningless
anyhow.

Just now, in fact, the choice of tree had been more
significant than the choice of world.

He had found this tree, standing on this rocky bluff,
had selected a stout branch, and lodged himself in the
angle of branch and trunk. He made sure his pack was
hanging where he could reach it, pulled his outer coat up
over his legs, and then tied himself in place with a few
loops of rope. This had been his habit when striking out
alone since he was a boy, when he had first sought safety
high in trees.

He laughed at himself. 'I learned all I know about
surviving in the wilderness from Robinson Crusoe,' he
told the empty world. Because climbing a tree was exactly

what Crusoe had done, on the first night on his island. As it happened Joshua had a copy of the book itself in his pack – one of just two books he'd brought with him. The Crusoe was an ancient paperback, the very copy he had read himself as a boy in the Home – it was heavily annotated in his own rounded child's handwriting, an act of graffiti that had earned him punishment detail from Sister Georgina. Potato peeling, as he recalled. Well, he fully intended to return this copy to the bookshelf that Sister John, only half joking, called the Joshua Valienté Library. 'I won't be out here for ever,' he told himself.

He was dog tired. He'd tried napping, without success. Then again, the sun had yet to set.

Chewing on jerky, sipping water, he inspected his new home. This was a distant relative of Montana, more than one and a half million steps from the Datum. He was somewhere near the loosely defined border between the band of rich green worlds in which the footprints of North America were dominated by a vast, shallow inland ocean – the so-called Valhallan Belt – and the much more arid, less-travelled worlds further out, worlds so unwelcoming they had only a scientist's label, the Para-Venusian Belt. For sure this looked like a transitional world, with the eroded aridity of a Para-Venus broken up by water courses and clumps of trees of species unknown to him but looking vaguely deciduous, seasonal, water-loving.

He was alone, just like Crusoe. Nobody knew he was here. In fact he'd gone to some trouble to ensure that.

After he'd told Agnes and the Sisters and Bill Chambers and Rod and a few other selected contacts that he was off on a sabbatical, he'd taken one of the few big commercial twains that still sailed the Long Mississippi run from the Low Earths to the city of Valhalla, one point four million steps West. In the few days on board he had fattened himself up with the richest food he could find, and soaked his ageing body repeatedly in clean soapy water, and he'd got his teeth fixed by the onboard dentist. He'd even had his prosthetic left hand serviced by a Black Corporation technician attached to the crew.

Once at Valhalla he'd hitched a ride at random on a smaller twain, a mineral prospector's private vehicle, and sailed off for another hundred thousand worlds or so, letting himself be carried crosswise geographically to the footprints of Montana. And *then* he'd stepped further, on foot, travelling deeper through this band of transitional worlds, heading steadily into the wilderness.

So here he was, in this world, on this bluff, high in this tree.

Plenty of people must have travelled through this world before him, heading on out West. He'd gone further out himself, many times. Maybe a few people had even settled here, although only the hardiest pioneers would be this far out. So what? Even most of the Low Earths, the alternates right next to the Datum, had never really been explored, not beyond the most easily habitable places. Why would you bother to go somewhere difficult? More than five decades after Step Day, go just a little way off the beaten track and you found yourself in exotic, untouched wilderness. Which was the way Joshua liked it.

He'd chosen his geographical location with care too. He wasn't far from a river. This particular tree he sat in, something like a small-leaved sycamore, was one of a clump that had sprouted on top of a sandstone bluff. Further down the bluff, on the south-west face and still a few yards above the sandy ground, he'd found a hollow – not quite a cave, but with some effort he could probably dig his way into the soft rock and deepen it. That would give decent shelter, and he'd get plenty of light and a good view of the landscape.

As for security, a look with an experienced eye had informed him it wouldn't be too much labour to construct a stockade to block off the ground approach to the hollow, the smoke from his fires ought to keep any critters off the bluff itself, and he could lay a few traps for any sneak attacks from humans or humanoids coming from above. And the forest clump above the bluff would serve as a reserve of firewood, if he did manage to get himself besieged in here. He could get it all constructed and stocked up for the winter – he'd arrived at midsummer – and anyhow Joshua hoped the cold wouldn't be too severe on this world.

He would have to learn the local landscape, the essentials like forest clumps and water sources, and landmarks for when he got turned around in a storm, or was fleeing a grizzly bear or some such and had to make snap decisions about which way to run. In time he would extend that mental map into a third dimension, to include similar landmarks in the nearby stepwise worlds. Once he'd invested all the labour in his stockade he was going to be tied to this world, at least until he chose to end the sabbatical altogether. But the stepwise worlds were always there as refuges – only sapients could step – and as alternate sources of food, of escape from bad weather, even hides to use when hunting. He'd never had any trouble with this kind of mental mapping. Lobsang had come to the conclusion that this sort of visualization of the world, or worlds, was at the core of his enhanced ability to step in the first place.

And it paid to be prepared, because there were always threats out there. At least you knew that what animals wanted of you was primal: either to eat you, or to avoid being eaten *by* you. Sapient threats were worse, both from malevolent humans and from some variants of humanoids. Some thought of the Long Earth humanoids as mere animals. Nobody would ever convince Joshua that there was no malice in the heart of some of the killer elves he'd encountered over the years.

'Well, Crusoe had his cannibals,' he told the world now. 'And I got bandits and elves. But he intended to live to tell the tale, and so do I.'

No reply.

This was a quiet world, he thought. No birdsong.

And he hadn't even heard the trolls' long call, not an echo of it. Which was kind of unusual; trolls were to be found most everywhere. But one reason he'd stopped here was precisely because of that absence. He liked trolls, but right now he didn't much want to be around any of them, because if a troll saw you he or she told the pack, who added the news to their long call – the endless improvised opera that united all trolls everywhere in a kind of bath of information. If your name was Joshua Valienté, the news tended to get out, and next thing you knew the whole Long Earth knew what colour your boxers were . . .

Now there *was* a sound in this quiet world. A deep

rumble, from far away to the north, like a lion's roar maybe but deeper, almost like something geological. A big beast advertising its presence. Just as he needed to know his landscape, Joshua was going to have to learn about the creatures he shared his world with, although with any luck he'd never need to get close up and personal with most of them.

It was a classic High Meggers landscape. And, as the sun dipped towards the horizon, Joshua Valienté was king of all he surveyed.

'In Madison, when I was a kid, I was nothing,' he announced. 'Didn't want to be nothing. Soon as I went stepwise, with everybody else stumbling and crying, and I just strode away, I was something. Me. Joshua Valienté! Right here! . . .'

Fine. So why the hell couldn't he sleep?

He took his second book out of his backpack. It was a fat paperback, sheets of coarse Low Earth paper crudely bound together. And it wasn't ageing well. This was Helen's journal, which she had started to keep at age eleven, before she went trekking with her family into the Long Earth. It was pretty much all of his marriage that he'd kept: this book, and his wedding ring. He flicked at random through the pages.

I miss being online. I miss my phone!!! I miss school. Or some of the people in it, anyway. Not some others. I MISS ROD. Even though he could be a weirdo. I miss being a cheerleader. Dad says I should say some of what I like too. Otherwise this journal won't be a fun read for his grandchildren. Grandchildren!? He should be so lucky . . .

76

If he cried himself to sleep, it was nobody the hell's business.

In the dark of night, under a subtly different moon, he was disturbed.

There were the usual cries in the dark, as a population of feeders and hunters came out of the shadows and the burrows and the tree stumps to live out their nocturnal lives: a subtle symphony of hunger and pain, as one little life after another was sacrificed to serve as a few hours' worth of food for something with sharper teeth. No, that didn't bother Joshua Valienté; he was used to it.

It was the Silence. That was what had woken him.

The Silence: the great breathing of the world, of all the worlds, that he'd always sensed in the gaps between the petty noises of life, the rattling of the weather. At times he'd encountered embodiments of it – or so he'd thought. Like the giant compound entity that had called itself First Person Singular, which he'd found on a world far beyond the Gap with Lobsang and Sally Linsay, oh, forty years ago now. But the Silence was more, even more than that. Always had been, always would be. It was the voice of the Long Earth itself, calling to some deep root part of his consciousness.

But here, now, the Silence was different. There was a kind of urgency to it. Almost as if some tremendous beast sat beneath his tree trying to lure him down, to teeth and slashing claws . . . An ambiguous invitation.

Alone in this tree, in this empty world, sleepless, he felt small.

Despite all his banter with Agnes and Bill, having

passed his sixty-eighth birthday since leaving Hell-Knows-Where he was well aware of his increasing frailty, the gradual failure of his senses – yes, he needed those damn glasses of Rod's – the diminishing of his strength. Aware too of the imminent end of his own spark of existence. The world – all the worlds, the great panorama of the Long Earth that he himself had done so much to open up – seemed overwhelming, crushing, vast. It would all go on whether he was alive or dead. What was the meaning of it all – of what he had done with his own life?

And why did the Silence, even now, not leave him alone? Such questions had plagued him all his adult life, when he'd let them, and he seemed to be no closer to any answers.

He said aloud, 'So, Agnes, Lobsang, Sally, are there going to be answers at the back of the book?'

But still there was no reply. He tied his ropes tighter, and, alone in the dark, determinedly closed his eyes.

11

IN THE MORNING Joshua's priority was water.

He left the bulk of his pack in the safety of his tree, and climbed down. Weapons to hand, he made his way towards the bank of the sluggish river that he'd spied out maybe half a mile to the east of his position. He carried plastic fold-out sacks for today's collection of food and water. He'd spotted that some of the trees bore massive nuts, something like coconuts, and he had a medium-term plan to empty out some of those to use as gourds, as he built up a water store in his stockade. All in good time; right now he just needed to find breakfast

As he walked, he kept his eyes open for threats of all kinds – not just the exotic like a dwarf T-Rex bounding out of cover, but more mundane deadliness like snakes and scorpions or their local relatives, even ground traps left by elves or other travellers. His eyes were gritty and sore; he hadn't slept enough, and he felt irritable, impatient. All the labour he was going to have to put in to create a safe encampment, which had been so much fun in the planning, didn't seem so appealing now it was morning and he faced the prospect of actually having to do some of it.

Maybe he was distracted. He didn't even spot the group of bison until he was within fifty yards of them.

He stood stock still.

They were a mass of dusty black bodies, clustered close together, working at a patch of greenish ground. They *looked* like bison, they were clearly cattle-like mammals. But they were eerily silent, and very closely grouped, and they had elaborate, tough-looking horns. He could see young pushing between the parents' legs.

Now they noticed him standing there, watching them.

A big male raised his head and gave off a rumbling bellow of warning. In a heartbeat they pushed even closer together, the young were head-butted into the middle of the pack, and the adults faced outward, a rough circle bristling with horns, as if they were a single armoured beast, a tremendous, ferociously spined hedgehog, perhaps.

It looked a pretty drastic reaction to the presence of a single skinny human. The local dangers must be drastic too. Not a reassuring thought.

Cautiously, Joshua backed away and gave the herd a wide berth.

He went on to the river, passing south of a low scarp, a dusty, eroded feature. When he reached the river bank he eyed the water cautiously; he'd long ago learned that you could expect to find crocs or alligators or some relative in just about any inland body of water, anywhere in the Long Earth. But the river was broad, flowing slowly, laden with mud and green murk, and he could see it stayed shallow a good way out from the bank. He stepped forward, opening out his carrier sacks.

And as he reached the murky water, and his view to the north opened up past the rocky scarp, he saw more big beasts.

Ducking, he moved back to the cover of the scarp and got down on his haunches. Once again he'd got within a few dozen yards of a herd of massive animals without even being aware they were there. But they were upwind – they couldn't smell him, and showed no signs of reacting to him. He murmured, 'Just like you always said, Lobsang. You want to see the wildlife, you go where the water is . . .'

Peering around the scarp he tried to make sense of what he saw. These, at least, were nothing like cattle, though the adults were more massive quadrupeds with muscular bodies. The detail that drew his eye was a mask of armour on each beast's face that flared back from the cheeks and swept around the eyes, and on up to form a gleaming white crest over the brow. At first glance they looked like armoured dinosaurs, like triceratops, like ankylosaurus. He'd devoured reconstructions of such things as a kid, in books and online reference sources, and out in the reaches of the Long Earth he'd seen for himself what might have appeared to be close relations of such beasts, the products of different evolutions. But these creatures had fur coating their hefty bodies, or wool, thick brown layers of it: not the scaly reptilian hide or the feathers he'd come to associate with dinosaur types. Now he made out infants, standing cautiously under the legs of the adults. In them the armour mask wasn't so obvious, not so developed, and the basic form was much more apparent.

And as they bent to drink from the river, he saw trunks uncurling and dipping into the water.

These were elephants, or mammoths. In these creatures the tusks, features always subject to the whims of natural selection, had evidently evolved into that heavy plated mask sweeping back over the face. As to why a beast the size of an elephant should need armour, and should have to creep almost silently in a huddle of its fellows as it dared to sip at the river water—

The thing that burst from the deeper water was like an alligator, but running upright, on two fat hind legs.

Joshua cowered in the shadows of the bluff.

The predator ran like a machine – relentless, purposeful, almost silent – and on each of its stubby forepaws it had one huge claw, long and curved, like Death's sickle. Those blades must be ideal for disembowelling, even when turned on a beast the size of an elephant. Joshua had seen beasts like this before. He'd *run* from such beasts before.

To his huge relief the gator ignored him, evidently intent on the elephants.

For their size, the elephants responded with remarkable speed. With warning trumpets – they didn't need to be quiet any more – they got into a kind of formation, just as rapidly as the bison had, with the adults locking their armoured faces together, while the young scrambled back behind the barrier. They were like, Joshua thought, a cohort of Roman soldiers making a shield wall to face the barbarians.

Then the gator beast leapt. It flew over the shield wall and landed *on top of* the row of elephants. The gator slashed and tore with its blade-claws, while the elephants bellowed and tried to drive the points of their face-armour into the gator's belly. Dust filled the air, and there was a stink of blood and dung, and elephants shrilled in pain and fear.

Joshua, unnoticed, scuttled to the water, filled his sacks hurriedly, and moved away, leaving the crowded battle-field behind.

He didn't feel secure until he was back up his tree, and strapped in.

So maybe this was the pattern here. The big herbivores looked like they came from mammalian stock, but the predators that preyed on them were reptilian.

This kind of mash-up of ecologies, dinosaurs versus mammals, wasn't so uncommon in this stretch of the Long Earth, he'd learned long ago. Each world of the chain of the Long Earth differed from its neighbours, a little or a lot, depending, it seemed, on the chance outcome of some set of past events – and every so often a tipping point would be reached and there would be a more dramatic discontinuity. The further out you went across the Long Earth, the more those differences accumulated, and the deeper back in time came those branching points. It was all a fundamentally random melting pot.

And *this* was a world so remote from his own, it seemed, that the huge event that had eliminated the dinosaur lineages on Datum Earth was no more than a rumour, a near miss, a bad dream of the deep past.

Anyhow he was going to have to be more watchful, that was clear enough. He needed to keep his attention focused on his surroundings, and not the inside of his own sixty-eight-year-old head.

And, he thought with a kind of grim relish, that was a

good thing. Even as a mixed-up thirteen-year-old pioneer stepper, he'd soon learned that no matter how far you travelled, you couldn't leave behind the fears and regrets and grievances that cluttered up the cargo hold of your mind. But at least, alone, focusing on the essentials of life – of survival itself – you could push all that garbage back into the deeper darkness where it belonged. Which was one reason he needed his sabbaticals.

He filled a flask with water from his sacks, dropped in a purification pill, and sipped. He found himself spitting out river-bottom grit; he'd need a filter. He grunted, disappointed with himself. He'd been here the best part of twenty-four hours and he hadn't even secured any drinkable water yet.

Sister Agnes had told him he was too old. Maybe he should have gone camping in some tamed park of a Low Earth world, in the preserved prairie around Madison West 5, maybe. And if he were a mite less stubborn he might at least move to some world where elephants didn't need to wear armour. He grinned. Hell, no.

As soon as his heart had stopped pounding, he climbed down from the tree and began to pace out his stockade.

12

I T WAS THE fifth day.

After a breakfast of small, rather sour local berries, a sliver of hare flesh – or at least it had come from a beast that had looked like a hare – and a strip of what was left of his jerky, Joshua made his rounds. He walked around his traps, checking out the snares he'd set, mostly at the fringes of the forest clumps. He was ever watchful in this deceptively quiet world, and kept his weapons to hand, but he was getting used to the routine now. He was also, unfortunately, getting used to going hungry, and it looked like that streak of bad luck might be continuing. His traps were empty, empty, empty, just like before.

Maybe he'd have to think about going deeper into the forest clumps. He knew there was game in there, at least up in the canopy. He had managed to snare an unlucky hare at a forest edge. Well, it *was* unlucky because it looked like it had already been injured when it fell into his trap. The animal was very hare-like, but it had loose flaps of skin trailing between its wings, like a flying squirrel, perhaps adapted to life in the tree tops. And maybe it had suffered an attack by some other aerial creature, for its left 'wing' was gashed, and most of one cheek torn away, exposing small teeth in a bloody mouth. It was still alive when he'd found it, and he'd apologized more profoundly than usual as he ended its small life with as much kindness as he could.

He'd left the hare a while to cool and for the fleas to clear, then he'd taken it home, skinned it, and flame-roasted it with local berries and some wild garlic. The meat had been tender and delicious, but there just wasn't much of it.

That had been his sole catch so far, which was why he remembered it in such detail. There seemed to be nothing like regular rabbits or hares running around on the ground of this world, nothing for his snares to trap. Maybe the ground-level predators were just too ferocious here – that, and maybe the grass was too sparse.

As he came to his fifth empty snare, a shadow passed over him.

He ducked instinctively into the shade of the trees. Nothing good was going to be moving soundlessly through the sky above.

Peering up warily, he saw a vast form sailing above the forest canopy. At first he thought it was some kind of human-made glider – that wingspan had to be fifty feet – but he soon realized it was too organic a structure for that, the curves of the wings too graceful, the bones clearly visible through flesh stretched so tight it was all but translucent. He saw feet on skinny legs armed with vicious-looking claws, and a beak that must have been as long as he was tall, filled with glinting teeth. No feathers on the wings, but there were splashes of colour on that spindly central body. Some kind of pterosaur, perhaps, the biggest of its kind he'd ever seen, and a tough-looking carnivore even if those wings looked fragile. No wonder there were no birds here – they'd have been easily out-competed by such creatures, the honed products of millions of years of evolution of their own.

And maybe that was another reason why there were so few, if any, small rabbit-like ground-dwelling mammals. Too easy a target for the killers in the sky. He remembered Bill Chambers urging him to spread something bright like his spacesuit-silver emergency blanket on the top of his bluff, in case some disaster befell him and the twains came searching. Now he was glad he'd instinctively rejected that advice and wasn't drawing the attention of the monsters in the sky.

The pterosaur sailed away, off to the west, and Joshua warily watched it go. Whatever was on its menu today didn't include him, at least.

And when he looked down to the ground once more, he saw the troll.

The humanoid was a big older male, a mass of black fur, but with a speckling of grey around his face and on his back: the kind some people called, inaccurately, a silver-back. He was squatting, staring at a bare patch of ground before him. The troll was alone. His troop was nowhere to be seen, but Joshua knew they would be around somewhere.

Joshua sighed, and strode forward, emerging from the shadows of the forest clump. There were plenty of times he'd been glad to see a troll, but this wasn't one of them. 'Well, there goes the neighbourhood—'

The troll glowered at him. He lifted a hand like a steam hammer, and touched one finger to his lips. *Shut up.* The gesture was unmistakeable, and one of the elements of an informal sign language that had evolved across the Long Earth, leaking out from labs and farms and factories and other places where trolls lived and worked alongside people – sometimes, even by choice.

Joshua stood still and shut his mouth. He had learned not to argue with trolls. The troll went back to his earnest inspection of the ground.

An unmeasured time passed. The troll stayed utterly still, apparently relaxed. That was harder for Joshua to manage, as the sun climbed higher in the sky, and he grew thirsty, and his stomach rumbled.

He still saw no sign of this troll's troop, nor heard their calls. It wasn't unknown for trolls to be encountered alone. This one could be a scout, sent out from the pack stepwise to seek out food or water, or spot potential threats. But Joshua didn't think so; scouts were usually a lot younger, their senses still sharp, fleet of foot. Maybe this older male, approaching the end of his life, just wanted some time to himself: he was on a troll sabbatical, just like Joshua's. Even after all these years, and for all the intensive study of their collective behaviour pioneered by the likes of Lobsang, people knew hardly anything about trolls, and certainly not in the wild. If he'd thought to bring a troll-call, Joshua supposed, he could have asked.

Joshua was getting bored, and a little dizzy. Enough of this. He opened his mouth to speak—

Slam.

The troll brought his two great fists down on the ground

with a smash, and Joshua was amazed to see the ground crumble under the impact, a thin crust cracking to reveal some kind of earth-walled chamber down there, a couple of feet deep, with rough tunnels leading off into the dark . . .

And animals. They swarmed over each other, things like furless rabbits or rats, pale beasts with claws and teeth shaped for digging, tiny pink eyes clamped shut against the light. Immediately, the creatures began to escape from the central nest, wriggling, scrambling back down the tunnels. Their movements were liquid; they seemed to flow away from the intrusion of daylight.

With a roar the troll jumped down into the hole, his big feet crushing a couple of the animals, and he started grabbing the creatures one at a time in each big fist, shaking them until they went limp, throwing them aside, bending down for more. He glanced up at Joshua, and the invitation on his crumpled, gorilla-like face was unmistakeable.

Joshua dropped his bits of gear and jumped down into the hole, opposite the troll. He tried to emulate the troll's industry, but *he* needed two hands to get hold of a single rabbit, and when he managed to catch one creature it turned out to be bigger and stronger than it looked, and dug needle-like teeth into the webbing of his thumb until he dropped it.

'Damn it!'

He bent down and tried again, this time favouring his prosthetic hand. 'Bite on *this*.' This time he got a rabbit from the hind end, so he kept those teeth away. With a muttered apology, trying to avoid the spiteful claws on its kicking back feet, he slammed its head against the ground, feeling its neck crack. 'Ha!' Then he tossed the quivering corpse aside, and looked around for more.

But all the surviving rabbits had gone, squirming away into their tunnels. Joshua had that one miserable catch at his side. The troll had two heaps of, count them, ten, fifteen, maybe twenty each. The big old troll looked at Joshua's single specimen, and his own piled-up catch, and back again. 'Hoo!'

Joshua had heard a troll laugh before. It was a sound you never got used to. Soon he was joining in, laughing until his gut ached.

Then the troll threw over one more rabbit carcass to Joshua, gathered up his haul in his huge arms with effortless ease, laughed once more – 'Hoo!' – and stepped away.

That evening, before the sun went down, Joshua gutted and cleaned both rabbit-moles and cooked them on spits over his fire. He could barely wait until he could get his teeth into the smooth, lush meat. But after five days hungry he knew not to overeat; he determined to put the produce of the second rabbit aside for salting and curing in the sun.

Of course these little mammals with their big rodent-like incisors and digging claws weren't rabbits, or rats, or moles, all of which they resembled to some degree. Maybe they were like the mole rats he'd heard of in Africa, living underground in big warrens, clambering over each other in the dark . . . Mole rats lived in societies like hives, like social insects, with just a few breeding pairs supported by a mass of sterile siblings, nephews and nieces. Maybe it was that way here.

'And maybe that's where all the local rabbits and hares went,' he said to the air. 'Underground, where you're safe from the death-gators and super-pterosaurs and whatever else the elephants here are armoured against. Not safe from a clever enough troll, though. Or from Joshua, the mighty hunter. Ha!'

And as he said this, he became aware of the troll watching him.

The big silverback male was back. He was sitting just beyond the glow cast by Joshua's fire. Even by the uncertain light of the evening Joshua could see blood smeared around the big humanoid's mouth. Surely he had been drawn here by the scent of the cooking. Trolls loved cooked meat, and would use fires when they came across one such as after a lightning strike, but had never mastered the art of making fire.

'There never was a King Louie of the trolls, buddy.'

'Hoo?'

'Never mind.'

With a pang of regret, Joshua picked up the rabbit he'd half eaten, and the other, cooked but still whole, and carried them both out to the troll. He sat in the dirt before the troll, and laid the intact carcass before him, like a respectful waiter. 'Your rat, sir, well done just as you ordered . . .'

'Hoo!'

The troll tore into the meat.

Joshua sat down and ate with the troll, if more slowly, and considered his distant relative.

From Step Day, the archaeologists, including a young Nelson Azikiwe, had tried to understand the absence of mankind in the new worlds. They had found flint tools in the dusty footprints of Olduvai. They had found fossil hearths in the depths of caves in stepwise Europes. But a certain spark had never been lit behind heavy brows on any world save Datum Earth. Perhaps, the comedians said, on every other world the black monolith just mislaid the man-apes' address . . .

But what you did get out in those human-free worlds were other kinds of humanoids, evolved from the same basic root stock as mankind, presumably – they were all thought to be descendants of *Homo habilis*, Handy Man, two million years extinct – but with wildly different natures, some more pleasant to encounter than others. And some had evolved to take full advantage of the extended landscape of the Long Earth.

Of which cousins of mankind, the trolls were the epitome.

Joshua said now, 'Look at us, buddy. Two old bookends in the wilderness. Here was me thinking I was Crusoe, and all of a sudden you show up. I can't call you Friday. Sancho – how about that?'

'Ha?'

'Help me, Sister Georgina. We did get through that book together in the original Spanish, just once . . . *La mejor salsa del mundo es el hambre.*'

'Ha!'

'Eat well, my friend.'

The wind picked up, and sparks from the fire rose up into the tall dark of the empty sky.

13

I T WAS ON the ninth day that Joshua tried hunting for rabbit-moles alone.

Sancho the troll couldn't explain how he tracked down his prey, of course. Joshua could only observe, guess, imitate, learn.

But he slowly began to recognize the outward signs of a rabbit nest. There would be a broad, circular discoloration in the earth, maybe twenty paces across – the piss of thousands upon thousands of rabbits in their dense underground warren seeping into the ground, perhaps. And over the central chamber there could be a slight uplift of the ground, a very shallow dome, only barely visible to Joshua if he lay down and spied it with one eye shut. Even then you had to get to the very middle of the mound, where the central chambers with their comparatively thin roofs were to be found, and once there you had to wait a long time, still as a statue, while the rabbits, alarmed by the fall of your footsteps, returned from the deeper tunnels where they would have fled, and got back to whatever business they conducted in the shallower chambers. *Then* all you had to do was smash open the thin roof – Joshua augmented his small human fists with a rock for that – and dive in among the wriggling packets of meat before they could all run away again.

So, after three successful hunts with Sancho, here was Joshua alone, scouting a suspicious-looking area not far from a forest clump. The faintest of circles on the ground – check. The shallowest of domes, barely visible in the dry drifting dust – check. Joshua spent a tough half-hour standing there in the sun, motionless, still as a statue, holding a rock the size of his head.

It was just as he raised his rock that the baby elephant came bursting from the forest clump.

Joshua could barely believe his eyes. He hadn't even known the elephants used the forests, though there was no reason why the hell they shouldn't. It took a heartbeat for him to take in the fact that the calf, fleeing whatever had alarmed it, was heading straight for his precious rabbit warren. Worse, its mother was coming out of the forest after her calf, trumpeting shrilly.

And Joshua himself, the thoughts in his old brain flowing as slowly as jelly sucked through a straw, was standing right in the way of the parade. The baby elephant was fast, faster than he'd expected.

Suddenly it was on him.

He dropped the rock and, at the very last moment, rolled out of the way. The calf's tusk-armour was immature but still hard as steel and bristling with sharp points; it missed him by inches. Now here came the mother, intent on catching her calf, barely giving Joshua a second glance.

It was sheer bad luck that, as he crawled through the

dirt, desperately scrambling to get away, she brought her heavy back foot down on Joshua's leg.

He felt the bone break. He *heard* it, like a twig snapping. And as he rolled away, he felt the raw faces of bone scraping across each other.

'Stupid!' he yelled. How could he have been so slow? Plus he was Joshua Valienté, the world's most famous stepper. Why had he not just stepped away to safety? Because he'd been distracted by wanting to hold on to his prize rabbit-mole warren?

Because you're too old, he heard Sister Agnes whisper in his ear.

And then the pain hit him, and he roared, and blacked out.

When he came to, the pain in his leg seemed to have subsided to a kind of dull throb.

He lay in the dirt where he had fallen. He hadn't moved, hadn't so much as rolled over. On the ground, vivid before his face, he could see the scuff marks where the elephants' huge flat feet had passed, and a little trail of dry shit, a panic evacuation by the calf, probably, as it had run from whatever had spooked it in the forest. Strange, he thought, that elephant dung didn't smell so bad. A benefit of a vegetarian diet, he supposed.

And strange, or just dumb luck, that he was still alive, given he was lying here, inert, unprotected, a sack of meat bleeding into the High Meggers ground.

He ran through his options. He'd thought through scenarios like this many times. He could step away in an emergency, if some set of teeth backed by an empty stomach came for him. Otherwise he would be horribly vulnerable to attack.

But if he could manage it, it was best for him to stay in this world. This was where his gear was, in his barely begun stockade – his food stash, his water, his medical kit. If he could get back to his hollow in the rock, it wasn't so far, maybe even get up into the refuge of his tree, he could try to weather it out until the injury had healed enough for it to be safe for him to move. As long as the winter didn't close in on him first. How bad would winters get in this world? . . .

That was a long way off, he told himself. First he had to get to the damn stockade, or he wouldn't survive a night, let alone a season. He saw nothing he could use as a crutch, to take the weight off the broken leg. If he could drag himself to the forest clump close by, get hold of a fallen branch that he could lean on, hobble back . . .

Good plan, his sceptical side said as he lay there.

Focus, damn it.

The first thing he had to do was turn over, on to his back. He swung his arm and rolled.

And as his busted right leg shifted, the pain returned – worse than anything he'd experienced since those two beagles had, almost kindly, detached his hand at the wrist with their teeth, all those years ago. He was flattened by the pain, dulled, almost knocked back to unconsciousness again.

He forced his head up. At least the leg looked straight, and he could see no jutting bone. His trousers were ruined, though, the leg trampled and bloody. He slumped back.

The break could have been worse, but evidently it was

bad enough. He wasn't going to be able to crawl out of here, let alone stand. What he needed was a medevac, a modern hospital, a surgeon and a team of nurses. Oh, and an anaesthetist. As it was, he didn't even know where his water was, let alone whether he could reach it.

Told you, Sister Agnes said in his ear. *You've gotten too old. Taken one too many chances. You shouldn't have gone out there again, alone.*

Bill Chambers chimed in, *Ye didn't even put the fecking spacesuit-silver blanket on the fecking rock like I fecking told ye, ye great fecking eejit.*

You're going to pay for your pride, Dad, Rod said. *With your life . . .*

'Not yet,' Joshua growled. 'Now here's my plan . . . Sancho? Sancho! Sancho!'

He called until he blacked out again. His last conscious thought was a vague prayer that the troll would in fact be the first beast that responded to his cries.

Sancho tried to be gentle. In his way. He was, for his kind, as Joshua would learn, exceptionally intelligent. But he was a humanoid, the size and strength of a large orangutan, and he had performed no action in his life more delicate than the chipping of a blade from a chunk of rock.

He picked Joshua up and threw him over his shoulder like a sack of coal.

Joshua screamed. But he was unconscious even before the troll had stepped away from the bloodstained ground where he'd been lying.

14

AT PRECISELY 11.30 a.m. the *Reverend William Buckland* lifted into midsummer air, smoothly and silently. Below its prow, the luxurious facilities of the Twenty-Twenty tourist resort diminished: a cluster of glass-walled buildings surrounded by a sprawl of twain landing pads, and further out the brilliant-green absurdity of golf courses cut into the pine forests that dominated this footprint of southern England, here in Earth West 20,000.

Nelson Azikiwe and Sister Agnes sat side by side in front of a big observation window, watching this panorama unfold. A discreet waitress had served tea on a small table before them, with a china service, a pot and cups, a platter of biscuits, small paper napkins. Agnes was dressed in a long black skirt, sensible shoes, and a pale-pink cardigan over a white blouse. Her grey hair was cut short and neat. Nelson had never seen her wear a habit, and yet she seemed always to be in the shadow of the wimple, even now. Unconsciously Nelson touched his own throat, the open neck of his shirt.

Agnes, being Agnes, noticed this and laughed. 'Don't

worry, Nelson. You still look like a vicar – you probably did even before you became one – but I don't think anybody here notices, or cares, do you?'

Nelson glanced around at the other passengers. Many of them were the modern idle rich – mostly elderly couples sitting in silence together, dressed in the out-of-date and impractical pre-Yellowstone Datum Earth styles that had recently become a badge of disposable wealth – but it was their money that mostly kept this twain service in the air. In a corner sat a party of early-teens students with harassed teachers, probably on some kind of expensive ecology field trip out of a Low Earth college. A few more earnest types, young adults, busily made notes and took images on tablets, even as the twain sailed over the golf courses and lakeside saunas. And Nelson and Agnes, the most enigmatic of all if anybody knew their personal stories, were receiving no attention at all.

'You're right, of course. Nobody sees anybody else.'

She twinkled. 'And nobody in all the Low Earths knows you have a secret grandson, Nelson. Nobody but me and Lobsang.'

His heart thumped, even now, months after he'd had that mysterious automated phone call with its extra-ordinary news.

The shadow of the twain crossed a clump of forest and startled a small herd of what looked like deer. Surprising to see them so close to the resort, Nelson thought; maybe they were learning to scavenge garbage. Another subtle modification of animal behaviour by humanity.

And here he was thinking about anything except his unexpected new family. *A grandson . . .*

99

Then the twain began to step.

The deer were whisked out of existence, the splash of concrete and glass that was the resort obliterated, to be replaced by lakes and virgin forest. And then it changed again. And again and again, a rippling of worlds that were soon passing at a rate of one a second or so, about the pace of a human heartbeat. The basic shape of the landscape endured: the river beside which the resort had been established, the contours of the hills of this remote footprint of southern England. But everything else was evanescent, even the trees, the clumping of the pines, the distribution of the grassy plains between them. After a dozen steps they passed out of sunshine into a world where a storm briefly battered the windows – and then out again, blink and it was gone, like a dip of lights powered by a faulty post-Yellowstone power grid.

Agnes sighed, and pressed a finger to her temple.

'Are you all right, Agnes? I'm no stepper myself, but there are medications, at least for an old-fashioned meat human like me. For you—'

'Oh, I'm fine. I'm no Joshua, but I could always step well enough with a box, when I needed to. And when Lobsang, ah, *restored* me, like some bit of old furniture he'd found in a dumpster, I found I'd become some kind of super-stepping steely-eyed android. But I never *enjoyed* stepping very much.' She glanced at him. 'After all, what was the point? Everything I cared about, the people, it was all right where I was – at home. Although of course stepping can be good for the conscience, can't it? Which, I believe, is the idea behind this travel service you've helped set up.'

'The *Buckland*? Yes, I suppose it was my idea, once I learned of the existence of the Twenty-Twenty centre, although I'm a small player in the commercial operation that came out of it . . . Have you noticed how worlds with neat round numbers always attract the big-money facilities? Especially golf courses. I wish I'd thought of that on Step Day and bought up some property! And it did appeal to the founders of Twenty-Twenty to run nature tours out of their resort.

'Everybody talks about Joshua and his adventures, and the romance of the High Meggers, the very remote worlds. I'm no great stepper either, Agnes. And besides, I've always been drawn more to the nearby worlds: what they call the Ice Belt, worlds that are more or less like the Datum, more than thirty thousand of them to both East and West – I'm drawn to them precisely *because* they are like the Datum, our world.'

'But the Datum without human beings.'

'Indeed. Why, even here in Britain in East and West 1 you'll find the wolf and the brown bear and the lynx roaming, beasts who shared these isles with us as recently as the Bronze Age. A landscape without its big predators is unbalanced – a pathology.' He smiled. 'You'll notice I did manage to smuggle in a reference to a hero of mine.'

'The ship's name, you mean? William Buckland? Never heard of him.'

'A churchman and a naturalist, early nineteenth century. And a diluvian. Even as the first fossils were being dug up, and as the geologists were starting to get a handle on how the world really works, Buckland continued to argue for the reality of Noah's flood. But the thing with

Buckland was that he stuck to the evidence. A perfect example of the tension between religion and science.'

'Rather like Lobsang,' Agnes said. 'That Tibetan-Buddhist core within a high-technology body.'

'Buckland himself found the very first dinosaur bone of all, you know, Agnes – of a megalosaurus, here in Britain, in Oxfordshire. Well, a party from the Natural History Museum went out – they had to go beyond the Gap, I think – and found something very like an extant megalosaurus, brought home a clutch of eggs, and now they run wild in a reserve in London West 3. The chicks are almost cute! But all that's for others to explore.'

Agnes peered down, distracted again by the scenery. Nelson saw that the flickering landscapes below were becoming more sparse now, those here-and-gone pine-tree clumps few and far between. The twain slowed, subtly, lingering in the air of one particular world for a few seconds. Huge forms, hairy, a deep mud-brown colour, moved across the landscape like the shadows of clouds. Once the passengers had been given time for a good look and a few photos, the stepping resumed, and the animal herd was whisked away.

Agnes sat back. 'Were they mammoths?'

'I think so. Agnes, the Ice Belt worlds aren't identical; some are more frozen than others. Here, as at the Twenty-Twenty resort, the climate is like southern Scandinavia – that is, Datum Scandinavia before Yellowstone messed up the climate. But around West 17,000 we'll hit a sheaf of more heavily glaciated worlds. Tundra, where the only trees are willows clinging to the ground, and the big animals are mammoths and musk ox and woolly rhinos.'

'Not much to see, I imagine.'

'You can be lucky, but it's a sparse terrain. The inter-glacial worlds – where the ice has retreated for a time – are more spectacular. Lions and hippos and elephants.'

'I guess England is a more interesting place than I ever imagined.'

Nelson smiled. 'Well, not *that* interesting. It was good of you to come all this way to see me. I would have come out to you—'

'Oh, I didn't mind adding another date to what I'm thinking of as a farewell tour. And I did have an ulterior motive, as you know. It was good of *you* to show me the material you found on Joshua's family history – his father's side. It does help me understand that poor boy, and his family, after all this time.'

That 'boy', Nelson reflected wistfully, was now sixty-eight years old.

Agnes said, 'I did try to find the father, you know, when Joshua was growing up. I know he was wary of us Sisters. Well, now he's died, taking his story with him. From what Joshua told me, I think Freddie managed to be proud of his son, in the end. So he did leave a legacy, of sorts, despite the awful circumstances of Joshua's birth.' She eyed him. 'Just as you will, it seems, Nelson, you rogue.'

Nelson felt as if his face was glowing hot. 'Now, Agnes, this isn't the kind of thing to tease me about.'

'No. I'm sorry. I'm sure that answering-machine message from Lobsang was a heck of a shock.'

'So it was.'

'And when you contacted me, asking if I knew anything about this mysterious grandson of yours, I got a shock of my own. Lobsang never just *vanishes*, you see. That's not his style. He leaves me little gifts around the place, in the systems in my home, even in my tablet. Files that pop open given a particular trigger – such as an association of your name with the word "grandson". I'll have a few seconds or minutes with some avatar of the man, sometimes long enough for a conversation. Joshua calls them "Easter eggs" for some reason.'

'An old computer-game term.'

She frowned disapprovingly. 'Well, it's no game to me to get such news.'

Nelson leaned forward, intent. 'All I know is that I have a grandson. And, while my life has hardly been blameless, I can only think of one occasion where I might have . . . Did Lobsang mention Earth West 700,000, or thereabouts?'

Now she smiled. 'Actually, he did. Then you know where to find them.'

'Them?'

'Your grandson, and your son.'

That took him aback. 'Shallow fool that I am, I focused on the grandson. I didn't think of a daughter or a son.'

She leaned over and rested her hand on his; her ambulant unit's artificial flesh was comfortingly warm. 'There are no rules with this kind of thing, Nelson. You just have to find your way through.'

'For all I eschew long stepwise jaunts, I must go to them.'

'Of course you must. And you must come back and tell me all about it, if I'm still here. Oh – sorry.' She squeezed his hand again. 'Didn't mean to be as blunt as that.'

He sat back. 'I did hear about your plans, from mutual friends. Your plans to die.'

'From Joshua?'

'Sister John at the Home, actually. We keep in touch.' He wondered what to say. In his years as a clergyman he had of course had many conversations on this topic – but never with an entity like Sister Agnes. 'This is something you need to do?'

'What's the alternative?' She smiled at him, quite brightly. 'Don't be sad, Nelson. It's already over a hundred years since I was born. I've had a far richer life, or lives, than I could ever have imagined. Or deserved, probably.'

He snorted. 'I won't accept *that.*'

'Now I just want it all to have a tidy ending.' She thought that over and nodded. 'Yes, that's it. Tidy. And you could help me with that, dear Nelson.'

'Of course. How?'

'Help *them.* Anybody who misses me, anybody who cares.'

'Such as Joshua.'

She smiled. 'I can't think of anybody better to ask.'

'It's this invisible dog collar around my neck, isn't it?'

'Once donned, you're stuck with it, I'm afraid.'

'And what about Lobsang?'

'Oh, I've already said goodbye to *him.* Or at least, to his Easter eggs . . .'

Now, below, the glaciations were taking hold, with the landscape alternating as they stepped between tundra and an open polar desert where winds blew ice crystals across frozen ground.

'Like in the song,' Agnes murmured. 'Winters without end.'

'Sister?'

'I think I might go have a nap. Old lady's privilege.'

'Shall I wake you for lunch?'

She smiled as she stood. 'Certainly. I couldn't miss the lions and hippos you promised me ... Oh, one more thing. *Troy.* Troy is his name, your grandson. Remember me to him.'

'I will, Agnes. Thank you.'

15

LEE MALONE AND Dev Bilaniuk waited with Stella Welch and Roberta Golding outside the fence of the GapSpace facility, under the thinly clouded sky of a June day, in this remote copy of north-west England. Their luggage was heaped up in the dirt.

A twain was approaching, a dot on the horizon, quickly growing in Dev's vision. It looked small, its grey envelope unmarked save for splashes of solar-cell panelling, its gondola plain and cramped-looking. Such craft had been plying the Long Earth for forty years; it was a mundane sight. And yet this ordinary craft represented something extraordinary. For the twain was going to take Dev and Lee to the Grange, the home of the Next, where they were to consult on a project inspired by a message from the sky.

'You know,' Dev murmured to Lee, 'before I ever crossed to the Gap I was able to *imagine* how it would be there. A hole in the Long Earth – a step into space. Exotic but comprehensible. Whereas now, with this "Grange", I've literally no idea what we're walking into. But I suppose if we could imagine what the Next get up to, there'd be no *point* to them.'

'I wonder why the twain's flying in,' Lee murmured, sounding practical.

'Huh?'

'I mean, why not step into the air right above us?'

'No doubt there's a good reason,' Dev said. 'Which we're too dumb to understand.' He glanced over at Stella and Roberta, who stood waiting patiently in their modest coveralls. 'It is frustrating being members of a sub-race, isn't it?'

Lee grinned. 'I don't know. It's fun trying to second-guess them.'

The twain descended with a hum of smooth-running turbines, and a stair let itself down from the side of the gondola.

A man clambered down briskly. Tall, thin, aged maybe forty, he wore a peculiar garment that was basically khaki shorts with wide braces; the shorts were quilted with pockets, and tools of various kinds dangled from fabric loops. Otherwise his chest and arms were bare, as were his skinny legs, and Dev was gratified to see him shiver in the coastal breeze, brisk even though this was June.

Lee was still grinning. 'Also, the Next have truly awful dress sense.'

'I heard that,' said Stella, who looked as if she was suppressing a smile herself. 'Unlike you vain creatures, we choose practicality over looks. This man is called Jules van Herp. He lives at the Grange, but we asked for his help today because—'

'I'm one of you,' Jules said immediately, his own grin wide and nervous. He shook hands with each of them. 'Not a Next, I mean. What does that make me? A Before?

Ha ha. Come on, grab your luggage and climb aboard the twain. Let's get out of this wind and be on our way . . .'

Jules led them up the stair and into the gondola, and the twain closed up behind them. The turbines hummed, and Dev felt a surge as the ship immediately began to move through the air.

While Stella and Roberta went on elsewhere, Jules led Lee and Dev along a smooth-walled corridor into a small, windowless cabin. Jules shut the door behind the three of them and fussed around, pressing panels to make seats fold out, and opening a cupboard containing drinks and snack food. 'Take a seat, help yourself . . .'

As they put down their luggage, Dev and Lee exchanged wary glances. Dev ran his hand over the smooth, feature-less grey wall. 'No windows. What's this material? Some kind of ceramic? And if I tried this door—'

'I wouldn't advise it. Look, try to make yourselves comfortable. The trip's going to be short, but—'

There was a sensation like a plummeting fall, almost as if they'd crossed over into the gravity-free realm of the Gap, and a sense of deep, shuddering cold.

Jules grinned. 'There's going to be a lot of *that*.'

Dev grabbed the back of a seat, reflexively. He saw that Lee was shivering.

She said, 'That was like no step I ever took.'

Dev said, 'It might have been a soft place. I've heard of them. Like Long Earth wormholes, fixed tunnels from one world to another. It's like they sap the energy out of you, so I hear. In which case we could already be anywhere, geographically and stepwise.'

Lee glanced around at the blank walls. 'Stella and Roberta are in some kind of observation lounge, I bet. While we can't see a damn thing—'

There was another gulping, swooping fall. Dev felt deeply nauseous, but tried not to show it.

'Shit,' Lee said. 'That *hurts*. Like a punch in the gut.'

And another shuddering transition.

Jules said, 'You'd better sit down.'

Lee and Dev fumbled for seats.

Lee looked at Jules. 'Why do the Next keep the location of this Grange of theirs secret in the first place?'

'Wouldn't you? There has been at least one military project, semi-officially endorsed and almost carried through, to *exterminate* them. You do understand why you're being brought in?'

Lee, white-faced, shrugged. 'They want to discuss how to respond to the Invitation.'

Of which much more detail had already been received via the Clarke telescope, the huge sea-urchin design being rushed through its construction in the Gap, using the Next's almost magical molecular-level replication and assembly technology.

Lee went on, 'And since we two have been involved at the Gap end of the project from the beginning—'

'Your point of view will be useful,' Jules said. 'The Next like to consult well-informed dim-bulbs, on projects that are likely to affect them. Which is clearly the case here.' He eyed them. 'You'd better get used to that phrase, by the way. Dim-bulbs. At the Grange, they use it without thinking. They don't mean any harm.'

Dev and Lee just stared back at him.

110

'They'll listen to you,' Jules went on. 'They won't necessarily do anything you recommend, directly, but they will take what you say into account as they formulate a wider judgement about what's best. If you want my opinion, being there physically is the main thing, actually, even if they don't listen to a word you say. So that you become lodged in their thinking as they consider other factors. Just by standing there, you're a reminder that humans exist.

'Listen. You're going to see a lot, hear a lot, that will probably shock you. Baffle you, even.' He glanced down at himself. 'Believe me, the way they dress isn't the half of it. Just let it wash over you. As for me, think of me as a native guide. Or an interpreter.'

Dev stared at him. 'You're a normal human – right? Living among the Next. You haven't said a word about yourself. Have you a career, a family? . . . Why do you live this way?' With every day a constant humiliation, he thought, but he didn't express that out loud.

Jules's eyes shone. 'You'll see – or you will if you've got the imagination, and can put aside your own petty pride.'

'You're dazzled,' Lee said neutrally. 'I heard that people can get that way around the Next.'

'But they are dazzling.' Jules plucked at his Next-style clothing, and grinned nervously, looking around the room, as if, Dev thought, he suspected he was being watched by masters he was desperate to please.

Dev looked at Lee, and saw something like pity on her face, pity for Jules. Dev felt only revulsion. *He* wasn't going to lose himself in awe of the Next, whatever he saw at this Grange. He was positive about that.

Another sickening, lurching, chilling fall.

Lee asked plaintively, 'Are we there yet?'

16

THE GRANGE TURNED out to be a series of clearings cut into a lush forest, linked by wide, straight paths.

Roberta and Stella led them away from the landed twain along one such path, walled by tall tree trunks, with Jules following behind. Jules said their luggage could be collected later. The day was mild and fresh, the sky blue, the forest scents strong. Dev swung his arms, trying to get over the nauseous after-effects of the journey.

'We could be anywhere,' Lee said. 'Geographically, I mean.'

'This looks like temperate forest,' Dev said. 'Are those trees some relation to oaks? The leaves are full, like it's summer. So we could still be in the northern hemisphere. But, depending on the local climate, on a particular Earth you can get temperate forest bands anywhere from the equator to the poles.'

'And of course,' Jules added, 'this may not be the native flora at all. Perhaps it has all been transplanted; perhaps you are in some vast fool-the-eye arboretum.'

Looking faintly annoyed, Lee said, 'We work in space. We know the stars, the planets. We could figure out the latitude from the length of the day, even make a guess at longitude if we saw something like a lunar eclipse—'

'But what good would it do you? Even if you knew the geographical location you would have no idea where you were stepwise.'

'We're not natural steppers,' Dev said. Neither of them had been allowed to bring a Linsay Stepper box. 'What if we were – or what if we had our boxes, and tried to step away? What then?'

Jules shrugged. 'To either side the stepwise worlds are *much* less hospitable than this. In a thick band. Even a twain couldn't get through. The only way in or out of here is by soft places, believe me.'

Lee said, 'Then you're imprisoned, just as we are.'

'So what? I trust the Next. They know what's best, for mankind, and for me.'

Lee recoiled from him visibly.

They came at last to a larger clearing dominated by a series of big conical buildings, with trampled, dusty ground between. Roberta and Stella, looking out of place in the sober jackets and slacks they'd worn for the journey, wordlessly led them across the open ground towards the largest of the houses.

Each building seemed to be thatch plaited over a frame of long, straight tree trunks, with heaped-up stone as a low perimeter wall, Dev saw as they passed. There was a central hearth, and smoke seeped out of the thatch of some of the houses. Dev was surprised how basic it looked, how primitive. It might have been a scene from Iron Age Europe. Yet here and there were glimpses of higher tech, metal glinting in the fabric of the houses.

A few adults gathered in knots, talking, all dressed much as Jules was – Dev was starting to think of it as 'naked with pockets' – and children ran around, some of them more or less bare, others dressed in cut-down versions of the adult garments. As they passed, Dev caught snatches of speech: not English, though he recognized a few English terms embedded in there. This was quicktalk, a rattling, high-speed gabble quite beyond his comprehension. The most baffling thing for Dev was the way three or four would gather and all talk at once, evidently capable of listening to one stream of words while uttering another. He could almost see the information being poured from one mind to another in parallel high-speed channels.

A few people nodded to Roberta and Stella as they passed, but none even glanced at Dev and Lee – or indeed Jules, Dev observed. He murmured to Lee, 'They aren't noticing us any more than you'd acknowledge a dog on a lead.'

'Down, Fido.'

The house they were led to was empty of people. The space inside was open; there were no interior walls, though what looked like partition panels were stacked up in a heap opposite the door. Shady corners were lit by free-standing cylindrical lamps, apparently electrical. There was some furniture, low bunks, couches, what looked like a galley area equipped with shining boxes of metal and ceramic. A doorway led to a bathroom.

Jules went bustling off to the galley. Roberta and Stella sat on a couch, took a breath, and gabbled quicktalk for half a minute. Then they turned to Dev and Lee, who stood uncomfortably in the doorway.

'I'm sorry,' said Roberta. 'Come in, sit down. We try to avoid quicktalk when we're in the human worlds. It's such a relief to get back and to be able to express oneself properly . . . This building has other purposes, but it's the nearest we have to a guest house.' She pointed. 'You can fix up individual cabins with those partitions. You'll probably need privacy.'

Lee frowned. 'The implication being that you *don't* need privacy.'

Jules called over, 'They're more civilized than we are, Lee, remember. They don't need to avoid each other as much as we do.'

Roberta went on, 'We'll have your luggage brought in . . . What else? Jules can show you how to use the galley. We generally eat fresh produce from the forest, but you may find it easier to use the food printer units.'

Dev frowned. 'Food printer?'

Stella said, 'Like your own matter printers, but rather more sophisticated. And based to some extent on silver-beetle technology – you know something about that. It's voice activated; you can ask for a wide variety of foodstuffs.'

'Replicators,' Dev said. 'They've got replicators.' He stepped forward to inspect the nondescript ceramic boxes. He could see no power connection; maybe there was some kind of energy-beam technology, invisible transmission.

Roberta said, 'With such devices we have made a major step towards a true post-scarcity society. Hunger banished without labour, for ever.'

Dev couldn't resist it. 'Can it give me Earl Grey tea?'

Lee grinned. 'Hot!'

116

*   *   *

The two of them stayed in their guest house that evening.

That was basically on Jules's advice. They should keep themselves to themselves, and keep away from Next children in particular, he said. Even now, a quarter-century after the establishment of the Grange, many of the adults here had grown up in the human worlds and knew how to deal with regular people, respectfully or otherwise. But the kids born in the Grange were different. To them, humans were just exotic animals.

Jules had grinned nervously. 'They aren't always – kind. Actually, some Next believe it's good for their children to be raised among humans. Because you exert a selection pressure. The truly smart, having discovered they are cleverer than the people around them, soon learn that the smartest thing of all for them to do is to prevent said people from ever finding this out. Roberta said she had a teacher who told her that she should have "Nobody Likes a Smart Alec" tattooed to her forehead in reverse, so she could be reminded of it every morning in the bathroom mirror . . .'

They erected a few partitions and assembled their cot beds.

'So,' Dev said tentatively. 'You want we should push these beds together?'

Lee glanced around at the partitions. 'I can't see any lenses poking through the walls. But I doubt if our privacy has any real meaning for them. Any more than we'd think about a right to privacy for a hamster in a cage. If they thought it was useful or instructive, would they have any ethical qualms about observing the mating habits of this particular species of chimp? You can get your thrills some other way, assholes.' She raised her middle finger. 'Quicktalk *that.*'

17

I N THE MORNING, they breakfasted on eggs benedict and coffee from the replicators. Then Roberta Golding came to summon them to the first of the day's meetings.

The session was to be held in one of the bigger round-houses. Maybe twenty people were already there when they arrived, sitting in rows on the floor or on heaps of cushions: mostly adults, one or two earnest-looking youngsters. They all wore idiosyncratic versions of the naked-with-pockets garments, though crotch and breasts were covered up, and they all carried tablets that looked like they had come fresh from some Low Earth industrial factory.

Stella Welch was already on her feet before an impressive-looking conference screen, speaking in rapid-fire quicktalk. Roberta led Dev and Lee to seats at the back of the room. One or two of the Next glanced around at them; the rest were incurious.

Roberta whispered, 'This is just a preliminary present-ation by Stella on what we've found in the Invitation so far. Hopefully this group will reach a consensus before presenting conclusions and recommendations to Ronald and Ruby later today.'

Lee frowned. 'Who are they?'

'You'll see. The whole thing will be in quicktalk, but I'll try to keep you two informed. A literal translation would be impossible, of course; quicktalk contains many concepts which can't be rendered down into human language. It's quite possible that by the end of an intense session like this, the language itself will have evolved, with new vocabulary, even new grammatical structures—'

'We get the idea,' Dev said, feeling weary. 'Just give us the tabloid-headline summary.'

The screen lit up, and as Stella waved her hands a complex engineering diagram began to assemble itself, component after component dancing across the display in eye-baffling three-dimensional motions. Every so often Stella, with a grasping gesture, would pull some component out of the general layout to magnify it, rotate it, point out features, and the images swivelled in response. Every part looked alien to Dev; even what looked like structural components were intricately shaped, curved, knotted.

All this was presented at a bewildering pace.

Roberta said, 'We're already halfway through Stella's presentation. There's so much to summarize.'

Lee asked, 'This is to do with the Invitation? It looks like an engineering design.'

'None of this was in the message itself,' Roberta said. 'The information embedded in it, which we picked up with the Clarke, was indecipherable. Too complex—'

Lee evidently couldn't help herself. She grinned in triumph. 'Even for you? Ha!'

Roberta was unperturbed. 'We think, actually, that the apparent data content was a kind of lure, a distraction. The Invitation seems to work on a more primal level. On the mind itself. As if the signal content works indirectly – *hypnotically* is not the right word . . .'

As we knew, Dev thought. As observers of the trolls reported from across the Long Earth, for instance – if only these Next had listened. The radio transmission from space was only one element of the signal. The message had washed across all the stepwise worlds, in the form of – what? Dreams, visions, longings? And, according to the handlers of the troll workers at GapSpace, those deep-brained denizens of the Long Earth had picked up their own form of the Invitation too. This wasn't just about humans or even the Next; it was about everybody.

'So it's a kind of – cosmic telepathy,' Lee said uncertainly.

Roberta raised neat eyebrows. 'We prefer to avoid such imprecise terms. But there *is* no English word. Think of it as . . . a vision. A vision which can, perhaps, be fulfilled in engineering terms. And that is what our finest minds have attempted to do. The result is what you have seen today. A Next design in response to an alien vision. The surface level of the message was: JOIN US. The level further down is: HERE'S HOW. But it is a target we have to reach ourselves.'

With the help of mankind, Dev thought, and the trolls, and others, who had all been made ready in some sense by versions of the message of their own.

'I guess I see that,' Lee said. 'A vision of a design. Like Leonardo sketching helicopters centuries ahead of their time; he could see them in his mind's eye. But a helicopter was for flying. What is this thing *for*?'

'We may have to complete it to find out,' Roberta said.

Lee asked, 'Do you at least know where this signal is coming from?'

'It's impossible to be sure, but the origin is somewhere in Sagittarius. We still believe it originates deep in the heart of the Galaxy. In fact, for some time – even before the silver beetle incident, long before the Invitation was detected – we've been monitoring anomalous gravitational waves coming from the black hole system at the Galaxy's very centre.'

'Anomalous?' Dev asked.

'Containing structure that we can't analyse.'

Lee grinned. 'Satisfying to hear there's something else you can't do.'

Dev said, 'So anyhow you have super-advanced aliens trying to get in touch. We dim-bulbs thought all this through a century ago. An interstellar message? Upside, *Contact*. A glorious galactic future. Downside, *A for Andromeda*. Enslavement and extermination.'

Roberta seemed to consider. 'These fictions may be useful input.'

Dev couldn't tell if she was sincere. 'Glad to be of service.'

Now the scale changed, and in the virtual graphic on the screen the individual components melded into a kind of structure – sprawling, flat, intricate. It reminded Dev of a massive solar energy array, maybe, or an antenna farm, hundreds of dishes peering collectively at the sky. Or maybe it was more exotic than that, less orderly, like a rendering of some other-worldly city.

Roberta said, 'The components come in two rough classes, though there is a significant overlap. The larger components are simpler, at least in information content, and are mostly structural. But you can see that even they are often complicated. The smaller components are still more intricate – and smarter. More complexity pound for pound than a human brain. Even a Next brain.'

'Gosh,' Lee deadpanned, and Dev suppressed a smile.

'We believe that – if it is decided to construct this device – our replicator technology here at the Grange will be able to print out many of the smaller, intricate components. But we do not yet have the capability to manufacture the larger elements. Especially given the sheer number of them that seems to be specified.'

'Ah,' Lee said. 'So you'd have to contract all that out to us low-brows. The industrial complexes in the Datum and the Low Earths.'

'Yes.' Roberta listened a moment. 'Some of the attendees note the practical difficulty of working with humans at all, in an age of dissolving central governments and a weakening corporate culture. And then there is the group known as the Humble, an ideological Next–human collectivist movement that has gained particular traction in the industrialized Low Earths where much of this work would need to be done. Perhaps you have heard of a spokesperson for that group – Marvin Lovelace – a former colleague of mine who now spends most of his time in the human worlds. Marvin is suspicious of the motives of those who sent the message – suspicious of their manipulation of our consciousness.'

Lee smiled. 'Like Dev said. *A for Andromeda*.'

'Actually it is useful to have an expression of opposing points of view. We Next are far less paranoid than humans.

'But others raise the question of urgency. Time may be short, you see. If large-scale human industrialization collapses altogether, then it may not be possible to progress the Invitation project for some time – not until we Next have developed large-scale manufacturing facilities, presumably robotic, under our own direct control. A window of opportunity is closing. Others in this group are reminding us that because of the urgency, preliminary efforts have already been made to pre-prepare the human populations of the Long Earth for such a project.'

Dev asked, '"Pre-prepare"? What does that mean?'

Roberta said, 'Our main tool to date has been viral narratives—'

'Viral what?' Lee scowled.

'Memes,' Dev said. 'I think she's saying they're introducing ideas into our culture to control us.'

'That's outrageous. What gives you the right to meddle with our minds?'

'Well, that is a moral dilemma. In fact the debate about our relationship with the human world has been intense since the teachings of Stan Berg. As far as dealing with the signal is concerned, *should* we proceed with such a project without a full consultation with you? After all, the consequences are likely to impact humanity as well as the Next.'

'Damn right,' Lee said sternly. 'You mean you've seriously considered *not* consulting us at all?'

Roberta glanced at her. 'In the course of your early mechanized wars, millions of horses were slain in the combat arenas. Before the conflict, did you give such animals a veto on participation?'

'I'm no damn horse.'

Dev was distracted by the latest image in the screen, which expanded as the virtual camera pulled back; now individual components were lost in a sea of complexity. The viewpoint tipped up to a horizon crowded with technology – and Dev saw, to his amazement, that that horizon was *curved*.

'Roberta, how big is this thing going to be?'

She shrugged. 'We don't have all the specifications; we're still not sure. When it's fully assembled we suspect it will be larger in area than most states. Smaller than the continental USA.'

Lee stared at her. 'Larger than a *state*?'

The group was stirring. The conversation was breaking up into small huddles, while Stella closed down her display. A couple of members hurried out, looking earnest.

Roberta said, 'I think we have a consensus.'

'We do?' Dev felt bewildered. 'It would take a bunch of human scientists or engineers days, weeks, to come to a conclusion about this. If they ever did at all.'

Roberta said gently, 'It is easier for us to talk things through. We are able to discard personality – pride, personal clashes, territoriality – more readily than you can. And our logic allows us to resolve many preliminary questions; we can all see the obvious answers immediately. We tend to find it easy to agree on tactics, you see. It is only at the strategic level where we have significant disagreements. In this case, of course, the debate is over whether to accept this Invitation – to fulfil the vision – or not. Which is where Ronald and Ruby come in.'

Lee tapped Dev's shoulder. 'Take a look.'

Dev turned to face the door.

He saw that a kind of wooden litter was being carried into the room, on the shoulders of half a dozen Next. On the litter, sitting side by side on upright chairs with loose harnesses, were two more Next. They wore versions of the usual shorts and vests with pockets, and their bodies looked normal – human adult, maybe rather skinny, Dev saw, if not wasted. An attendant was supervising a drip that fed into the arm of the one on the left. Ronald or Ruby? He couldn't actually tell which was male and which female.

But all this was in the background. For it was the heads of these creatures that he couldn't help but stare at: skulls swollen like balloons, with scattered patches of dark hair on what looked like painfully stretched skin, and more or less normal human faces diminished in proportion.

As this bizarre procession made its way through the hall, Dev noticed a young Next, a normally proportioned woman, staying very close to the litter, though she played no part in carrying it. Her face was closed in, expressionless.

With great care, Ronald and Ruby were set down before the big screen, facing the rest of the group. One, perhaps

Ruby, the woman, took hold of the accompanying girl's hand.

Roberta whispered, sounding almost starstruck, 'The girl with them is Indra Newton. She's a cousin of Stan Berg himself, and comes top of every scale we measure ourselves against. Thought to be the brightest of the new generation, perhaps the brightest since Stan himself, and a crucial interpreter for the lollipops.'

Dev couldn't take his eyes off them. Lollipops?

'My God,' Lee murmured. 'What is this?'

'One of our experiments,' Roberta said. 'One attempt to circumvent the legacy of our human nature and its restrictions. In this case the size of the skull, which restricts the growth and development of the brain. With this new kind, the foetuses are capable of *stepping* out of the womb, bypassing the birth canal altogether.'

Dev said, 'I heard of this. In the wild. It's in Joshua Valienté's account of his first expedition into the High Meggers. A kind of elf developed that trick, somewhere out in the Corn Belt.'

'That was where we got the idea,' Roberta said. 'According to Valienté it was Sally Linsay who called them "lollipops". We found them, extracted the relevant gene complex. *Those* creatures did nothing useful with their larger frontal lobes. Perhaps with time, we, however . . . Ronald and Ruby are already significantly more intelligent by most measures than our finest scholars. They are not yet twenty years old. They have become a kind of arbiter of disputes – as in the present instance. To that extent the experiment worked . . . And now it is Ronald and Ruby who have been central in interpreting the alien

127

vision in design terms. I think they are ready to speak.'

'Already?'

'They were briefed on the issue of the Invitation before this morning. It will not have taken long for Stella to summarize the conclusion of the earlier session for them—'

'Welcome.'

With a start, Dev realized that the two lollipops were watching himself and Lee. The one on the left had spoken. The single word had been uttered by a frail, papery voice, the voice of the very old – not of a teenager. But it had been in English. And was there a smile on that distorted face?

'We welcome our guests,' the lollipop said. 'Dev Bilaniuk, Lee Malone. You should hear what is decided, for it will affect you and your families. My name is Ruby. This is Ronald. As you can probably tell, this isn't our full-time job. Personally I make a living as a professional ballerina, while Ronald here is a football quarterback.'

Dev stared, disbelieving. A *joke*? Lee laughed, nervously.

'Now, as to the issue at hand, you should know that Next science has already diverged sharply from the human—'

'Too true,' said Ronald, his voice just as weak, yet subtly deeper. 'Roughly speaking, we went back to Leibniz, who argued with Newton, and started again from that point. I mean, talk about schoolboy errors!'

Stella Welch coughed.

Ruby smiled. 'I apologize. Our own science is a work in progress, and we would be well advised to be humble – as indeed Stan Berg cautioned us.

'In our science, indeed our philosophy, we Next have learned to take our lead from Berg's Rules of the Three Thumbs. He advised us to *be humble in the face of the universe.* So we will be in this instance. We should accept this vision from the Galaxy with gratitude; while proceeding with caution, we will not be so arrogant as to assume it is necessary for such a superior race to seek our destruction. "Join us," they said. We have no reason to believe this Invitation is a deception.

'*Apprehend*, Berg said. We should embrace the universe in its totality – and if the perception of this Thinker, this machine from the sky, is a better window to the universe than our own senses and devices, then again we must accept the gift.

'And Berg said, *Do good.* We will need your help with this endeavour. But we will ensure that such help is obtained with your full consent, that you will be used ethically, and your safety will be paramount. Indeed, the safety of all of us, of all the worlds. We, personally, will take necessary steps to ensure this is so.'

And Dev wondered what those 'necessary steps' might be.

Ronald stirred, and raised a stick-thin hand. 'I understand the decision is not yours alone; nobody speaks for all mankind. Nevertheless we would appreciate your feedback. Do you concur with our conclusions?'

Lee and Dev exchanged a look. Dev was aware of Indra Newton staring at them, blank-eyed, almost as if puzzled by their presence.

Lee pulled a face. 'This is all just words. In the end, they can do whatever the hell they like.'

Dev forced a grin. 'Maybe. But I always was a contact optimist. That's why I went to work at the Gap in the first place, I guess. Let's build this thing. When do we start?'

'Just tell me this,' Lee said to Roberta and Stella as the meeting started to break up. 'You said that humanity was being pre-prepared. What "viral narratives"?'

Roberta said, 'Stories. Passed on by word of mouth. How else is one supposed to transmit a message to humanity, now that it is scattered across the Long Earth? *Stories*: bits of narrative, like viruses attaching themselves to your childlike imaginations.'

Lee pressed, 'Stories such as?'

Roberta smiled. 'Such as a story of Earth West 314,159 . . .'

18

As it happened, like the encounter with the lollipops, this was another incident from The Journey: Joshua Valienté's first exploration of the deep Long Earth, in the company of Lobsang, all of four decades before. An incident never fully reported, a tall tale now resurrected, spun, and whispered into cars across the Long Earth, all to further the Next's purpose . . .

This was around a couple of weeks into The Journey. Joshua had already made the remarkable if disquieting discovery of the lollipops, an unexpected new breed of humanoid.

Joshua woke one morning to find the *Twain*'s stepping halted. They were in the Western section of what would later be called the Corn Belt: Earth West 314,159.

It said something for Joshua's exhaustion that he hadn't noticed the stop. And when he glanced out of the windows he saw immediately why Lobsang had called a halt at this particular world.

A world like a bowling ball, utterly smooth, under a cloudless deep-blue sky.

'A Joker. Like we saw before,' Joshua said.

'Indeed.' Lobsang glanced at a tablet. 'The last was at West 115,572. I thought this time we both ought to take a look.'

'We, Lobsang?'

'I'm allowed some curiosity.' He smiled. 'Don't worry, Joshua, I am sure I'm safe in your hands . . .'

They stood in nothingness.

No. Not quite.

Joshua let go of the ladder from the hovering airship and took a tentative step forward. He was on a plain, a flat surface, featureless, a soft eggshell blue. Above him the sky was a white abstraction, a dome. He took another step, turned around. As far as he could see, this empty plain stretched away, in every direction, to a misty horizon under that sky. It was like an artefact, not a world. An abstraction, and inverted – white above, sky-blue below.

In the middle of it stood two grimy humans – or one and a simulation. They cast no shadows, Joshua saw now. The light was diffuse, that empty sky illuminating the land, although for all he knew it could be the other way around.

Lobsang looked just as baffled as Joshua felt. He stepped forward, clapped his hands, shouted, 'Hello?' The sounds were swallowed up without echoes.

Joshua looked around uncertainly. 'What is this, Lobsang?'

'There have been accounts of worlds like this,' Lobsang said. 'Including the one we found. Cueballs, travellers are calling them. A kind of Joker – an eerie place you'd hurry through.'

'A flaw in the Long Earth, then?'

'Maybe. Or . . .'

'Yes?'

'This is my wild theorizing, Joshua. Some kind of inter-section – I mean, with another Long world. Like two necklaces, crossing over at this one place.'

Historians would note Lobsang's remarkable prescience in this remark, given that at this point in The Journey the pair had not yet encountered Sally Linsay, queen of the soft places. Then again, the extent of Lobsang's knowledge was always a mystery.

'Two worlds crossing . . .'

'Worlds merging somehow,' Lobsang went on. 'Mingling. Until you're left with this – abstraction. All that's left is what they have in common, the most basic features.' He jumped a couple of inches in the air. 'Gravity. This world has mass, then. Size. We could measure the distance to that horizon, if we bothered. It's like a mathematical model, not a world at all. A set of numbers with no detail.'

'Or like an emulation in a computer game.'

Lobsang sighed. 'Joshua, I am like an emulation in a computer game.'

'Then why the glow, the blue ground? . . .'

Lobsang stared around. 'It's like the stuff everything else is made of. The light that shines behind reality, giving it substance . . . Don't look at me like that, Joshua. You should remember my cognitive capacity is rather larger than yours, my processing speeds orders of magnitude faster. I have a lot of time to *think*. Even while people like you are talking.'

'Fair enough.'

'And I think about the nature of the Long Earth. Even about Platonic realities, and . . .'

'And then you smoke a bit more?'

Lobsang said nothing.

'Come on. We've logged it, let's move on.' Joshua reached out for the ladder to the airship.

But Lobsang was standing a little way away, and staring into the air. 'Joshua. Look at this.'

They were like raindrops, perhaps. Mist particles. All around Lobsang, perfectly spherical droplets of water hung in the air, quite stationary.

In retrospect, 2030, when he had gone exploring with Lobsang, had been a pretty good year for Joshua Valienté. It had even made him famous.

That wasn't how 2070 was turning out.

19

JOSHUA WAS STUCK in a nightmare.

Dumped on the ground.

Blood in mouth, dirt under cheek.

Being rolled on his back, to a flood of pain from his leg. Being handled like a doll in the hands of some coarse idiot child, limbs pulled this way and that. When he struggled, feebly, more hands pressing him down.

Huge figures all around him, black-haired bodies glimpsed through a film of blood. All of it suffused with agony.

Pass out. Wake up. Pass out again.

He lived this over and over. The nightmare lasted for days.

He came back to himself slowly, bit by bit.

He lay there and let it happen. After all, what choice did he have?

He thought of the jigsaw puzzles he used to dig out of the back of cupboards at the Home. Battered old relics in torn boxes, depicting scenes of worlds that had vanished before he had been born: range riders in the Old West, Mercury astronauts in silver spacesuits. Lost dreams.

Working alone, sometimes for hours on end, he'd painstakingly sort the pieces into their categories: corners, edges, bits with sky or sea or silver-spacesuit fabric, *edges* with sky or sea or spacesuit silver . . . You just had to be patient, one piece at a time, and slowly, slowly, the picture would emerge. And the more of the picture you got, the more you were going to get.

Spacesuit silver. He wondered why he was thinking of that.

It was dark, then it was light. Days passing.

It would soon be fall, he thought, on this world as on all the worlds of the Long Earth. Soon the days would be getting shorter, colder. Nothing he could do about that now. He just had to endure.

A dull ache in the leg was his constant companion, and he fretted about the state of the break.

Also his trousers, ripped to pieces. He always had been lousy at sewing. That made him want to laugh, but his chest hurt.

The sky above him was the first part of the puzzle to come clear. A blue sky, with scattered cloud. How long had he been lying here?

He smelled dirt, and the dense animal musk of trolls, and heard running water. No sign of humanity, not even the smell of a campfire. He was still out in the High Meggers. Nobody had come, nobody had found him, then. He had no idea whether he was even still in the world where he'd made his stockade—

The troll face, looming over him, seemed to come out of nowhere. He flinched back.

The troll, startled, ducked back too, only to return more circumspectly, curiously. This was a young animal, he saw now, very young, a cub, its rounded face a mask of thick black fur, its features still babyish – almost human-looking, if you ignored the beard. This certainly wasn't the older troll that had saved him after . . .

After he'd been run down by the baby elephant with a mask like a *Star Wars* stormtrooper. He remembered now. And the mother who'd carelessly stomped on him.

'Hoo!'

The troll moved abruptly, approaching him again. Lying in the dirt, helpless, Joshua cringed back from the fast, determined motions of this powerful young animal – and he *was* an animal, after all. Joshua had to force himself not to step out. He had to believe he was better off here than anywhere else. And besides, the trolls would probably just step after him.

Suddenly there was a hand behind his head, a strong hairy paw, lifting him. Another hand before his face – cupped, with a splash of water in the palm. Joshua reflexively opened his mouth, and the water spilled in, more than he'd expected, gritty and cold. He gagged, but, determined, he swallowed.

Then he was dropped with a thump that sent a fresh wave of pain shooting up from a battered body. 'Hoo!' An adult troll lumbered across his field of view, and away.

As Joshua lay there, gasping, he started to sense more trolls, moving around him. Of course there would be more trolls. A youngster like that wouldn't be alone. Now he heard their massive movements, their leathery feet scuffing in the dirt – a few snatches of song, like samples of an opera in Klingon.

'Well,' he said. His own voice sounded odd, very scratchy; his mouth felt Para-Venusian dry. 'I sure could do with another sip of that water.'

As if in response another troll loomed over him. This was an adult, a big male, not old; it wasn't Sancho. The male peered curiously into Joshua's eyes, and poked his cheek hard enough to hurt.

'Ow!'

'Hoo!'

He raised Joshua up, a little more gently this time, to a half-sitting position. Joshua glimpsed the young troll behind the male, and a female, standing there, looking on with what seemed like curiosity, if not concern. Beside her was another cub, what looked like a female to Joshua, though with all that black fur it was hard to tell the sex even with the adults. She clung to the leg of the adult female, as if she was shy. This could be a family. He knew that trolls in the wild could be monogamous, with little family groups sticking together within the larger bands of dozens or more. As far as he knew, nobody was sure if the adult males in each 'family' actually were the biological fathers of the offspring they cared for.

All this was set against a nondescript background: a dusty plain, a small copse with fruit bushes sprouting at its periphery, what sounded like a stream flowing not far away. Good country, if you were a troll. Joshua could still be in the world where he'd started building his stockade, or he could be far away.

Wham. Without warning, food was rammed into his

138

mouth – a slab of bloody meat, some kind of vegetable. The adult male was feeding him, roughly, but it felt like he'd been punched, and his mouth was suddenly so full he thought he would choke.

He raised his hand and managed to yank out the bulk of the food. He dropped the meat in the dirt; it could be raw elephant for all he knew. But then, more cautiously, he picked up the vegetables, a broken-up root like raw potato, something green and tangled, something else soft and red – a kind of fruit. As he began to chew on the root he felt ravenously hungry. 'My compliments on the side salad.' The big male, still supporting him, tried to stuff more food into his mouth. But Joshua blocked the move, and instead picked out manageable chunks from the male's offering with his own hand.

The female, with the two cubs, crept closer, watching him. He was aware too of a wider band, more trolls at the edge of his vision, staring curiously. It struck him that maybe they weren't used to seeing humans as *old* as he was.

'I'm grateful,' he said around chunks of food, still chewing. 'I don't know how I got here. I guess my buddy Sancho dumped me on you, and I don't see him around anywhere . . .' He sighed. 'But I have a feeling I'm going to be imposing on you a while longer. And I can't call you "adult male" or "non-specific-gender cub". You're Patrick.' He pointed to the adult. 'You, the mother, you're Sally. I knew a Sally once . . . The boy is Matt, the girl is Liz. Where the hell did I get those names?' He shook his head. He pointed to his own chest. 'And I'm Joshua Valienté. Look me up in the long call.'

Then he plucked up his courage, and, moving with caution, looked down at his damaged leg for the first time. To his huge relief it looked straight, more or less. His trousers were, however, shredded even worse than he remembered. The leg wasn't splinted, of course, or bandaged, and from the waves of pain he felt as he moved, he evidently hadn't been treated with anything resembling an anaesthetic.

But if he could get the leg healed enough that he could stand unaided – and if he stayed alive – he had a reasonable prospect of stepping back to some inhabited world. And once back at Valhalla or a Low Earth, he could get some decent corrective surgery.

If.

He looked into the faces of the watching trolls. Patrick's face crumpled quizzically. 'Oh, for a troll-call. Look, I suspect you saved my life. Thank you . . .'

Suddenly a wave of nausea caused his stomach to clench. He rolled away from Patrick, the adult male, despite flares of pain from his leg, and painfully vomited the half-chewed meal he'd consumed.

Then he sat back, cradled in Patrick's arms once again. Waves of heat pulsed through his body, his head. 'Shit. I got infected. No surprise, I guess.'

Beyond Sally, he saw a flash of spacesuit silver in the dirt.

He squinted, cursing elderly eyes, trying to see more clearly, trying to sit up. The silver scrap was an emergency blanket. Heaped in the dirt beside it he made out other gear: his desert-camouflage pack, his outer coat, his aerogel mattress, his sleeping bag, the glint of his knives.

It looked like Sancho had had the wit to empty out his stockade and bring his stuff here. Again his chances of living through this had just got incrementally better.

'Sancho, you're my hero.'

'Ha?'

'And spacesuit silver! I knew there had to be a reason that was bugging me. I guess I saw it out of the corner of my half-asleep eye. Patrick. Help me. Please bring over all that stuff . . .'

It took some anxious sign language to get the message across. It was the male cub, Matt, in fact, who got it first, and soon the family were working together to lug over the gear. The human artefacts looked tiny in their big hands.

By now Joshua was starting to feel dizzy, nauseous and seriously thirsty. He tried to prioritize, to do what he needed to do before the incoming tide of delirium rolled over him. First he gathered all the gear under the survival blanket, for protection from the weather. Then he dug a small radio transmitter out of his pack, set it in the sunlight for power, and started it broadcasting short-wave radio pleas for assistance. If anybody happened to come through this world, they ought to hear it – if they were listening, unlike most combers these days, and if they could be bothered to help. A long shot but better than none.

Then he found some antibiotics and gobbled them down dry.

He was almost finished. He found it hard to concentrate. But there was one more big job he needed to get done before he succumbed to the darkness.

Patrick and Matt were still here, father and son, curiously poking at the heap of gear. He grabbed their arms, and made them look at him. 'I need to fix my leg. If I roll around while I'm ill, I could snap the damn bone again. And with a splint the chances of it healing straight are much better.' He rummaged through his pack. 'I have this elasticized bandage. I'll show you what to do. But I need you to bring me some planks. Timbers. Straight branches . . .'

He was babbling. They were staring at him entirely without comprehension. He went into a sign-language pantomime, grabbing a couple of twigs from the ground nearby and pressing them against his leg, gesturing at the forest clump.

Again it was Matt who got the idea first, and Joshua wondered if he'd had some exposure to humans before.

It seemed to take for ever for them to find and bring over a couple of suitable branches. Joshua chugged a pep pill to stay conscious a little longer. He considered sacrificing one of his precious ampoules of morphine. No, he'd survived without that so far; he had no idea what was yet to come before he got out of here . . .

When Patrick started wrapping the bandages tight around the splinted leg, the pain was astounding, even compared to what had gone before. It wasn't just the superhuman strength but his careless rough handling that made it so bad. Patrick, Joshua knew, was doing his best. Joshua managed to sit up, and pushed and prodded, trying to make sure the bandages weren't too tight; that way lay a dead leg and gangrene.

At last he lay back, and spat out the bit of wood he'd

clamped between his teeth. 'OK, it's my fault, Agnes! You warned me.' His words dissolved into a scream as Patrick put the big muscles of his back into yanking the bandage. 'I asked for it. My bad, OK? Just make it stop! Make it stop! . . .'

20

DURING THAT SUMMER of 2070, as Joshua Valienté endured a sabbatical that had become a stranding, and Dev Bilaniuk and Lee Malone glimpsed the future of mankind at the Grange, Nelson Azikiwe undertook a long journey of his own. A long stepwise journey, despite the discomfort of stepping itself. But it was worth it, for Nelson. For he went in search of a grandson he had only just discovered existed.

Despite his elderly eyes, Nelson was one of the first to spot the storm approaching this living island, this Traverser.

He was sitting on the soft, pale sand of the island's north beach – or rather, on the sand-covered flank that this island-like creature chose to present to the low northern sun that morning. The Traverser, which Lobsang, its discoverer, had chosen to call Second Person Singular during Nelson's first visit all of thirty years ago, was always in motion, always responding to currents and breezes, to the cycle of the seasons – always under way, following its own imperatives.

The sea stretched before Nelson, small waves lapping at

the shore, further out placid and flat and a deep rich blue: placid for now, anyhow. This was the Tasman Sea, and somewhere to the east was New Zealand – or rather an uninhabited footprint of the Datum island group of that name. This balmy world was seven hundred thousand steps West of Datum Earth.

And above the island, patiently station-keeping under the control of its onboard AI, hovered the small two-person twain that had carried Nelson all this way. Sleek, glittering with solar-energy panels, the twain was a reminder that Nelson did not belong here, that his own home was far distant, around the curve of the planet and many steps away along the mysterious chain of the Long Earth. But for now, here he sat, on this beach that wasn't a beach, with his son, Sam. A son he hadn't known existed until a few months ago.

Sam was twenty-nine years old, almost as dark as his father, naked to the waist and looking as fit as a decathlete. Now he squinted up in the air. 'Your ship moving. Knows storm coming.' He pointed north.

'*The* storm *is* coming . . . Never mind.' Since he'd arrived at the island, Nelson had learned that as he'd grown up Sam had always been made aware by his mother, an island-born woman called Cassie, that his father was not one of the other men of the island, but had been the 'han'some clever fella' who had visited all those years ago, and, only once, had walked into the jungle with her . . . Cassie had done her best, with the limited resources available to her, to give Sam enough of an education that he would be able to converse with his father when Nelson returned, as Cassie always had faith that he would. She'd done a good job, and it wasn't

Nelson's place to pick holes in the young man's grammar. And besides, Sam's native language was a perfectly respectable creole, dominated by English but laced with many other tongues. It was Nelson's failing that he couldn't speak the local language, not the other way around.

Now Sam pointed, scanning his finger along the northern horizon. 'See. Black smudge?'

'It seems so far away. Harmless.'

'Far, not harmless, here soon. Sky ship turn to face wind?'

'If it needs to it will fly up above the weather . . . Do we have to shelter?'

'Oh, island look after us, no worries.'

And Sam meant that literally. Sitting here on this authentic-seeming beach, with the island under Nelson feeling every bit as solid as its geological counterparts, it was almost impossible to believe that the island was no island, no inanimate lump of coral or rock, but a living thing, evidently sentient to some degree, and capable of caring for the cargo of living creatures that dwelt on its back – including generations of human beings. Yet you only had to be here for a few days to observe for yourself that that was true.

He was maundering again. Sam was watching him patiently.

'I'm sorry, Sam. Off with the fairies.'

'Show you.'

'Yes?'

Sam reached into the pocket of his trousers, an elderly pair of jeans long faded to blue-white. He produced a small figurine and passed it to Nelson.

Nelson cradled it, turned it over. It was a slim form carved in ivory – well, there were dwarf elephants, even mammoths, on this island, and when they died they would bequeath plenty of ivory for such purposes. The limbs were mere suggestive scratches, but the face was a more detailed cartoon. And there was a splash of some red pigment in the hair.

Nelson felt a warm shock of recognition. 'Cassie. And she's smiling.'

'Yes.'

'She always did wear red flowers in her hair, I remember that.' It was as if Nelson was back in his study when that avatar of Lobsang had first broken the news to him about his distant family. He was a very old man, he thought, suddenly subject to the most intense emotional experience of his life. 'I never meant it to happen, you know.' He glanced at Sam. He felt ridiculously embarrassed to be discussing such matters as his son's conception with the man himself.

'Mother say *she* meant it. As soon as you show up—'

'Yes, yes, all right. And I was being pushed from the other direction too.'

'By friend Lobsang? I know story.'

'That's him. He implied it was almost my *duty* to get someone impregnated, as a donation to the gene pool of the island's human population. Ha! Well, in the end . . . It was love, Sam. Brief as it was, a singular moment as it was. Can you believe that?'

'Mother say so, always.'

'Despite Lobsang banging on about gene pools, somehow I never really imagined that anything would come of it – that she actually would get pregnant. That *you* might exist. Let alone little Troy! Simply beyond my imagination. I suppose you can blame half a lifetime in the Church of England for that. If I'd known, I would have come back.'

'No.' Sam took back the ivory piece and held it tenderly. 'Mother know. Your life far from here. I was gift from you, she said, and later little Troy. Father, when people die here, not bury dead like England.' He got the pronunciation slightly wrong – Ann-GLAND. Nelson did not correct him. 'We come from island. We return to island. Chambers, full of living things – green and pink – there we lay dead.'

Nelson imagined vats of life deep within the island's carcass, dissolving the corpses of its passengers – humans, yes, and presumably the other animals that inhabited its surface. 'It seems appropriate,' he said gently.

'We keep nothing of dead,' Sam said. 'Not like you speak. No ashes. No stones on island – wash away! Instead, markers. In chamber deep in island.' He looked down at the little figurine. 'This hers.'

'I would like to see that.' This travelling island had been sailing its stepwise oceans for centuries, at least. That chamber of the dead must be full of little statuettes like this, rows of sketchy figures and smiling faces, the most antique peering out of deep generations. 'You know, I was older than your mother, by a considerable margin. I did not expect to outlive her.'

'She die forty-seven year old. A good age! Old go away smiling, make room for lots more babies.'

'Like little Troy.'

148

'Like Troy.' Sam took his father's hand, his strong brown fingers wrapped over Nelson's rougher, liver-spotted flesh. 'My mother saw grandson, happy and healthy. What more want?'

And there was a deep booming noise, rich, resonant. Like a thousand bass-voiced monks chanting. It seemed to come from within the island.

'What in Jupiter was *that*?'

Sam stood, and carefully tucked the figurine of Cassie back into his pocket. 'Island call. Come on.'

Nelson stood, stiff after sitting too long on the sand. The booming continued, and he thought he could feel it through his feet, the island's fake ground itself vibrating. And he saw that the storm was a black mass of cloud now, piling up in the sky, the uppermost clouds streaming. Soon the clouds would blot out the sun. He blinked up at the sky, looking for the twain, but it was already out of sight.

Sam took hold of Nelson's hand again as they walked slowly up the beach.

Nelson saw that the great lids were already opening, ridged discs hinging up on tremendous muscles like the opening of giant oysters or clams: slabs of the chitinous carapace that underpinned the surface carpet of rocks and dirt and living things. Within the openings revealed, Nelson could see rough ramps leading down into chambers that glowed softly with a deep-blue underwater light.

And from all over the island, people were coming, men, women and children – some babies in arms, a few very old, and *nobody* as old as Nelson himself – all of them making their peaceful way down the ramps and into the island's interior. There was no sign of fear or panic. The adults chatted as they marched down the ramp and into the gloom. Older children ran around their legs, shouting, their voices echoing as they swarmed down into the cavernous inner chambers. People seemed happy, excited by this break from the routine.

Nelson shook his head. 'They're like a crowd at a Christmas sale. Or the way Christmas sales used to be . . .'

'What, Father?'

'Never mind.'

'Down ramp before animals come. And before storm . . .'

Over Nelson's head, the clouds covered the sun; it grew suddenly dark, distinctly colder. And Nelson heard a shrill trumpeting sound. The mammoths were coming! Nelson felt a deep visceral thrill.

He let his son lead him down the ramp.

21

'SLOW DOWN, TROY! I'm not as young as I was . . .'

But the ten-year-old, slim, lithe, wearing only a kind of loincloth, was an explosion of energy. 'Come *on*, Granddad! Fun come see horses spinies *elephants*!' And, holding Nelson's hand, he tried to haul him deeper into the Traverser's innards.

'Now, Troy, gentle with Granddad.'

Troy's mother was called Lucille. As far as Nelson could tell she was a permanent partner for Sam. It obscurely pleased him that Troy was growing up with at least a semblance of a normal family around him, that he knew who his mother and father were. Not that Nelson was judgemental about such things. After all, it had struck him the first time he visited the island with Lobsang that in such a small community, relationships were necessarily going to be flexible, moral judgements pragmatic.

Now Lucille, short and pretty, was quietly admonishing her son. 'Besides, under-under, quiet! Look at other children. Little Moll, Rosita, Parker, quiet under-under, good as gold . . .'

They were all in a chamber of a very organic kind, with

smooth, curving, enclosing walls, moulded – no, *grown* – into complicated shapes. It was like being inside some vast sea shell. Nelson was a big man. He towered over these compact islanders, and he had to duck to avoid thumping his head. But the chamber was surprisingly roomy.

And the light from overhead, coming through layers of translucent Traverser carapace and filtered through seawater, was a bright, oceanic blue-green. They had indeed submerged.

He briefly wondered about insects: flies, spiders, ants, termites. It was hard to imagine *them* trooping two by two into the Traverser's natural holds, yet such creatures were necessary for any functioning ecology. He imagined they had evolved their own ways to survive these periodic inundations.

Meanwhile those taken into the Traverser's great belly were safe. He looked around the chamber, where the people milled around, set out blankets, talked quietly. Among other vocations Nelson had once been an engineer, of software at least, and he tried to think that way now. How did the Traverser *work*? This dry, air-filled room must serve as a buoyancy chamber, doubling as an airtight shelter for the animal inhabitants – and the people. The air smelled fresh enough, though there was an odd, salty, organic tang to it, like seaweed maybe. He wondered how long the air would last, in fact. Probably a good while; the island, a mile long, must be riddled with air-filled chambers like this to be able to float at all. And maybe, he mused, the Traverser had some ingenious way to replenish the air it stored.

Now, it seemed, his grandson was determined to be

his guide on a tour of some of those chambers.

'Oh, Troy, leave poor Granddad alone!'

'I'll be fine,' Nelson said, lowering his voice to the soft level that seemed to be assumed by everybody else in here, underwater, *under-under*. 'I'm glad of a chance to see all this. Don't worry, I won't let him wear me out.'

'Well, all right. Just this once. No tread on good boys and girls nappin' like supposed to.'

'Won't. Come *on*, Granddad . . .'

They made their cautious way across the chamber's uneven floor, stepping over people with smiles and apologies. As Lucille had said, the drill seemed to be for people to settle down in little family groups, sitting, lying down, talking softly. Some of the children were napping, curled up with each other or against their parents. Others were playing quiet games with shells and beads and boards scratched on to sheets of what looked like eucalyptus bark.

'Makes sense,' Nelson whispered to Troy.

'What, Granddad?'

'For everybody to be sitting still and sleeping. Makes the air last longer.'

Troy looked puzzled, but Nelson was pleased that he seemed to be trying to figure that remark out, rather than dismissing it or arguing about it.

Nelson supposed most of the island's human population must be gathered in this one place. In the gloom it was hard to count heads, but he estimated there must be about a hundred. There couldn't be many less to provide a population genetically diverse enough to stay stable across the generations – a diversity aided by the occasional injection of genes from outside, like his own, he reflected with some embarrassment.

On the other hand there wasn't room for many *more*. As far as Nelson could gather the people practised abstinence, or used non-penetrative sex or withdrawal methods, and it seemed there were various contraceptive treatments available from the island flora. None of these methods was accident-proof, of course, but overall the people seemed to be able to keep their numbers in reasonable balance. Nelson had wondered (but hadn't enquired) if, in the course of surviving booms and crashes and food shortages in the past, they'd learned the hard way how to keep the population size down. Certainly having a short life expectancy helped, as Sam had observed: the old vanished gracefully, leaving room for the young.

Nelson tripped over somebody's leg in the dark. Again he'd become lost in his maundering.

'Grand-*dad*! Careful!'

'I'm sorry, Troy. You lead the way, I'll watch my feet . . .'

Troy led Nelson, always just a little too quickly, up and down ramps and through short corridors, and they pushed on through more chambers, many just as roomy as the big dormitory but mostly empty. It was all very organic, the walls smooth and curving with no edges at floor or ceiling, and short connecting passageways shaped like back-to-back trumpets smoothly leading off from one chamber to the next. Nelson was undoubtedly crawling around within the anatomy of a living creature, and a far greater one than he was. He felt minuscule.

Closest to the upper carapace, the overhead chambers,

translucent and allowing through the greenish light, were all filled with scummy water. Nelson wondered if the plankton and other organisms growing in there were encouraged, in order to replenish the oxygen of the inner air, as he had speculated. And for the plankton, he supposed, protection from the browsing creatures of the sea was the reward for their dribble of oxygen.

In some of the lower levels, Nelson came across a still stranger sight. The underside of the island, when it was visible, was complex, encrusted with huge shapes, some of them big tubes with blobs of green stuff growing at the ends.

This arrangement baffled Nelson, but Troy seemed to know all about it. 'Dolphins. Whales, little ones. Porpoises. Swim in for food. Wiggle and wiggle in tubes!'

And Nelson thought he saw it. Maybe this was a mechanism – one of several, perhaps – that the island used when it needed to move through the water. It lured the big sea mammals into these food-providing tubes, and in return for the snacks that grew there the animals swam their hearts out, gradually pushing the island the way it wanted to go.

Shelter in return for an air supply, food in return for locomotion. The whole arrangement reeked of smartness, Nelson thought, as they wandered on, smart bits of naturally evolved engineering as all parts of this strange symbiotic creature laboured in harmony to support the whole.

And yet he saw no evidence of anything like a central nervous system: no nerve trunks, no spinal cord. Nelson suspected that Lobsang, who knew far more about these matters than Nelson did (of course Lobsang knew more about almost *anything* than almost *anybody*), might have said that Nelson was being parochial. The Traversers appeared to have descended from colony creatures, from communities of living things. A Traverser needed to think, but to do that it didn't need anything like a human, or indeed a mammalian, brain. Perhaps the Traverser's consciousness emerged from a network of interactions of its onboard community of living organisms. Take those plankton communities in the upper chambers. On one level each algal cell was busily looking after its own business of feeding and reproducing, while on another level an algal community was itself a very complex network. Similarly, aboard the Traverser, a dwarf horse uprooting a mouthful of long grass was eating lunch, but at the same time that very action could be a 'thought' of a higher consciousness.

Maybe multi-species cooperation and cohabitation were actually the norm in the Long Earth – indeed, the norm for terrestrial life. Even during his time on the island Nelson had witnessed different species of dolphins swimming together. And during The Journey of '30, Valienté and Lobsang had even reported discovering, some nine hundred steps from home, a group of hominid species of variant forms, the product of diverse stepwise evolutions, happily living side by side. Once, Nelson supposed, you might have witnessed such scenes on the Datum itself – but in the course of its inglorious career, *Homo sapiens* had pretty much seen off any cousin species closer than the chimps. And, isolated, humans had come to believe that ruthless competition, even the extermination of rivals, were inevitable. Nelson was determined to discuss all this with Lobsang when he got the chance – if Nelson himself survived the trip back, if Lobsang ever emerged from his latest electronic womb . . .

He heard the whinny of a horse. The animals were close.

They came to a chamber containing a group of mammoths, apparently dwarfed, but still an astonishing sight to Nelson. From what he remembered of his palaeo-biology, these were more like Columbian mammoths, low-latitude browsers, than the woolly variety adapted to colder climes. They seemed to be a group of females and young; the adults stood together, twining trunks and gently clashing tusks, while the young sheltered under their feet. There was a puddle of water for them to drink, in a hollow in the floor, but no food that Nelson could see. Their rumbling voices were like the rolling of boulders.

This chamber seemed large to Nelson, but was presum-ably claustrophobically small to wild animals – especially plains animals like mammoths – certainly far smaller than many zoo compounds Nelson had seen. Yet the animals waited for their release as calmly as the humans in their dormitory. He wondered now if there was some-thing in the air, a gentle tranquillizer evolved by the Traverser to keep its inhabitants subdued while they were confined. On some Traversers – such as the very first Joshua and Lobsang had discovered, on a world much further out than this – the animal specimens were kept almost anaesthetized, it seemed; within the bulk of the creature they had called First Person Singular the travellers had seen birds, small animals, even elephants like these

157

immersed in some kind of fluid, neither awake nor asleep, neither walking nor swimming. Perhaps there was a whole range of such storage strategies. No one knew.

The Traversers, he reflected, carried some strange beasts, but none so strange as themselves.

With Troy leading him on tiptoe, Nelson wandered on.

They found horses, small and hairy. And what looked like wombats, what looked like armadillos, what looked like sloths – an eclectic mix of creatures, many of them extinct on the Datum Earth, yet presumably prospering still on this world and its stepwise neighbours. It was the nearest he could imagine to a realization of Noah's Ark. Every so often he glimpsed something smaller – a rat, a mouse – but he and Lobsang had long ago concluded that this 'collection', if there was any purpose behind it at all, was the result of a strategy to select animals with a body weight of around an adult human's, give or take an order of magnitude. The mice and rats were just as much visitors here as Nelson was.

But he and Lobsang, he remembered, could only guess as to the meaning of all this. Lobsang had suspected that the Traversers, once natural creatures, the products of Darwinian evolution, had been *modified*. Engineered subtly, for some conscious purpose. 'Perhaps they are indeed collectors,' Lobsang had once mused. 'Latter-day Darwins, or their agents, scooping up interesting creatures for – well, for science? To populate some tremendous zoo? Simply for their aesthetic appeal?' But such conversations had taken place a long, long time ago, and Nelson still had no answers.

The horses whinnied and stirred, and Nelson felt the Traverser itself shudder and rock. It was a queasy, massive sensation, like riding out a mild earthquake.

He felt Troy's hand slip into his own.

'Troy? Are you all right?'

'Yes.' But the boy didn't sound convinced.

'Does it often do this? The Traverser.'

'Not often. Sometimes. Upset.'

'By the storm?'

'Not storm.'

'What then? . . . Oh, look, never mind. Come on, shall we go back and find your mum and dad?'

22

THREE DAYS AFTER the storm had passed, Nelson found himself in a small sailboat, resting on the placid sea – perhaps a half-mile from the island that was not an island, to his west. Sam and his handful of crew busied themselves with their chores – tending lines, checking their nets and lobster pots. A fishing trip was hard work, yet as with everything the islanders did there was always an element of play. All but naked in the rich morning sunlight they laughed, joked and competed over the strength of the knots they could tie, the size of fish they could lure from the depths of this remote sea.

Even Nelson's twain was back. When the storm had cleared, the ship had returned to its station-keeping over the island, and hung like a translucent fish in the bright, warm air. It was a relief to be in the open air again, and all seemed well in the world.

Nelson himself was content to rest. He'd treated every year of reasonable health in his eighth decade of life as a bonus, and all of these islanders were so much younger than him – let them do the work; let the fish come to Nelson's line if they willed it, otherwise not.

Around noon, or so he judged it from the position of the sun in the sky, Sam approached him. Nelson came to himself slowly; he'd evidently been dozing. Sam set up a kind of umbrella of palm fronds for shade, and produced a leaf basket that turned out to contain water, the juice of some exotic fruit and the baked flesh of fish. Nelson ate gratefully, wishing only that his palate, dulled with age, was capable of appreciating the spices better.

Sam, chewing on his own portion, eyed his father. 'Leave tomorrow?'

'Day after at the latest. Doctor's appointment, son. When you're my age – well, that twain up there rattles with the pills I have to take.'

Sam smiled. 'Stay. Sunshine. Fishing. Come live with us.'

Nelson sighed. 'But I don't deserve that. All I ever did was stay a few nights and saddle your poor mother with a bun in the oven. Sorry to be crude about it.'

'Happy alive, Father. Happy for gift of my life. Happy with Lucille, with Troy. Happy, happy. You come back, we take care of you, as long as—'

'As long as I've got left?'

'As long as like.'

Nelson sighed. 'And I'd entertained fantasies of taking you all back to England. We're not going to agree, are we? And so we'll end up apart. I'll go my way and you yours, which is the worst of all solutions—'

And it was then, as he was speaking of departing, sitting in this still boat on a semi-infinite sea, under a perfect sky, that he thought he heard Troy call for him.

* * *

161

Afterwards he was never sure if he had heard that call or not. Later still, Nelson remembered how Troy had thought the Traverser had been in some distress days earlier. Could the island-beast have known what was coming?

Certainly, some of the boat's crew seemed to be aware of *something*. They sat up or stood, frowning, and stared around at the horizon.

Then one young man stood straight and pointed west. 'Look!' he cried, anxious, troubled. 'Island! Island!'

Everyone in the boat, sitting or standing, turned and looked that way. And Nelson could immediately see why the lookout was so concerned.

The Traverser, which had been a low dark mass on the ocean, fringed by the green of its central forest, was gone. Not submerged – that process always took some time. Gone, vanished – *stepped away*, Nelson realized, with a deep jolt of shock.

The crew flashed into action with the vigour and decisiveness of youth. Nelson realized they anticipated an incoming wave – the sudden disappearance of a beast the size and shape of a small island meant that a lot of water was going to be displaced – and they tied down pots and bundles of gear. One kindly young man even slipped a rope around Nelson's waist, for security. Nelson was barely aware of this gesture, or of the surge of the boat under him as the great wave passed. Sam, cut off from his family, tearfully roared out his pain even as he worked.

And Nelson, exhausted, terrified, tearful, looked up at the twain hovering in the turbulent sky. 'Lobsang! If you can hear me – help, Lobsang! Help me get Troy back!'

23

Almost from the beginning of the Next's subtle campaign of pre-preparation of mankind for its participation in their coming project, Jan Roderick had been aware of the game, even if he couldn't have put into words what he was perceiving – even if he wasn't *aware* he was aware, Sister Coleen thought. Now there were even more stories, tall or otherwise, a flood of them – eventually Sister Coleen would learn that they all contributed to the meme-plex clustering around the Invitation – stories passed from mouth to mouth among the fissured human communities of the Long Earth, and eagerly scrutinized by Jan when he found them.

Stories such as – Sister Coleen saw, reading over his shoulder – the tale of the man who became known as 'Johnny Shakespeare', supposedly dating from about twenty years after Step Day:

Mr Clifford Driscoll, born in Datum Massachusetts, was a teacher of English. His particular passion had always been for Shakespeare, and he made no apologies for that. To the benefit of those of his students who were capable of listening and willing to learn, that passion fuelled an anxious, intense but compelling teaching style, and an often very successful one.

In those pre-Yellowstone days his early career had been conducted in small public high schools in his native Datum Massachusetts. Here – and unlike on the new worlds of the Long Earth – Shakespeare, along with all of the Datum civilization's cultural heritage, was at least *available* to Mr Driscoll's students, accessible at the touch of a keypad, a whisper into a phone. But, he came to feel, his students' attention had been constantly diverted from their studies by their technological toys, by the endless roaring background noise of the Datum's high-tech, crowded culture – as well as by the timeless distractions of each others' developing young bodies.

And Mr Driscoll himself grew increasingly restless. In his fifties, a bachelor, celibate for more than twenty years, and approaching the last stretch of his career before retirement, Mr Driscoll formulated a new goal. He must go where he was needed. Where he might be *useful*.

It was with a kind of missionary spirit that he found a teaching post in a school in what he thought of as one of the colony worlds, West 3, in a small stepwise-Massachusetts town with a booming population and an economy dominated by lumbering. For Mr Driscoll, at first, this was a romantic place to work, an island of human endeavour carved into the great silence of a global forest. And the colony's fast growth rate, some years after Step Day, provided him with classrooms pleasingly crowded with students.

But there were problems.

Even as early as the 2030s, the America of West 3 was no primitive culture. The larger towns already had connectivity through fibre-optic cables, TV, phones. It was not yet saturated with technology; here the students found less to distract them. But that did not make room for English literature in their heads; it did not make room for Shakespeare. And *these* young people were destined for lives working in lumberyards. The Datum and its millennia of culture seemed a glittering and remote abstraction. What use literature to them? What use Shakespeare, in such a world?

That question gained still more profound significance in Mr Driscoll's mind as he learned more of the Long Earth into which he had taken a few tentative steps.

He made an ally of Chet Wilson, a hobbyist engineer who ran hugely popular hands-on technology classes in the school's extensive workshops. Wilson, from rural Massachusetts in the Datum, cared only for his gadgetry. He was a man out of his time: he would have looked at home under the bonnet of a Model T Ford, Mr Driscoll thought, and if he could have got away with whittling all day, he might have done just that. A character as unlike Mr Driscoll's earnest culturedness would be hard to find. Yet they found common ground in their passion for their subjects and a desire to teach.

One day Mr Driscoll idly asked Wilson how far out the wave of human colonization had spread across the Long Earth.

Chet Wilson sucked his teeth and said, 'Let me give it some thought.'

After an interval Wilson said, 'Nobody knows, is the

165

truth. I do know there's a big belt of farmed worlds that start out beyond a hundred thousand.'

'Did you say a hundred *thousand*?' Mr Driscoll was already out of his depth.

'Not all the Earths in between are going to be populated. Not yet. But you know how people breed, when they get the chance.'

Mr Driscoll was appalled. 'All those Earths. All those children, those young minds! Who will know only logging, and farming, and digging for iron ore. Or just wandering around picking fruit. And *their* children will grow up knowing less still. What will become of our civilization's heritage after a few generations, Wilson? Tell me that! It will be as if thousands of years of struggle to *learn* and *remember* were just a dream . . . I must think about this.' Muttering to himself, he wandered off.

Wilson, calm, said nothing.

Twenty-four hours later Mr Driscoll returned to the workshop, bubbling with enthusiasm. 'I have it, Wilson. I have it!'

Wilson eyed him and moved a bit further away.

'Shakespeare! That's the answer. What represents the crown of our civilization? Shakespeare and his works! And how can a human world ever be called civilized if it does not know Shakespeare? That is to be my mission now, Wilson. I have already handed in my notice at the high school. I will not linger here, wasting my remaining years before handfuls of indifferent students. Instead I will take Shakespeare to the Long Earth! And thus I will shape rude minds. "The play's the thing, wherein I'll catch the conscience of the king . . ." Conscience, yes, that's it. I will give the Long Earth its conscience.'

'How?'

'How what?'

'*How* are you gonna take Shakespeare stepwise?'

'Well, I haven't worked it all out, not yet,' blustered Mr Driscoll. 'I can go out there and speak of the Bard . . .'

'Won't do much good if they can't read it.'

'That's true, that's true. A travelling show, perhaps, to stage the great works? No, no, too complicated a process, and I am no impresario.' Suddenly he shot to his feet. 'Ah! I have it. I will carry copies of the complete works in some compact edition. Paper, of course; one cannot rely on electronics in the true frontier worlds, I am sure. One edition per town, to be copied and disseminated. But even that, given so many Earths . . . One per world, then! A symbolic act, which may inspire others to emulate my donation, and spread the word of the Bard laterally, so to speak.'

'Gonna need a stage name.'

'A what?'

'So everybody hears about what you're up to. Something memorable.'

'Ah! I see. Like a secret identity. The wandering minstrel, perhaps.'

Chet Wilson sucked his teeth and said, 'Let me give it some thought.'

After an interval Wilson said, 'Johnny Shakespeare.'

'But my name's not John. I'm afraid I don't see—'

'Like Johnny Appleseed. With him, apples. With you—'

'Shakespeare! Yes! Wilson, you're a genius. One world

at a time, like Appleseed wandering across the Old West, I will plant the seed of Shakespeare to flourish on each new Earth. And thus will the great tree of our civilization grow, as far as man has travelled – or at least, as far as I myself can step. I must announce this straight away. And I will order a box of books from a Datum publisher and make a start—'

'Gonna need a big box.'

'What do you mean?'

'Well now, there's said to be people scattered over the worlds out to Earth West 1,000,000 and beyond. If just one tenth of one per cent of those worlds is settled, you're gonna need a thousand books. How far you reckon you could carry a thousand books?'

'Well . . .' Mr Driscoll had never been a particularly practical man. Now he saw his scheme collapsing before it had started. He sat down, helpless. 'What am I to do, Wilson?'

Chet Wilson sucked his teeth and said, 'Let me give it some thought.'

The next day Wilson called Mr Driscoll back to his workshop.

'Now this here is only a prototype. It's gonna need some tinkering. But I reckon it'll do the job . . .'

The thing on Wilson's workbench struck Mr Driscoll at first as a kind of grotesque crab. It was a book, a complete edition of Shakespeare, but it stood on a set of spindly legs, just a few inches off the bench, and Mr Driscoll glimpsed miniature manipulators of some kind dangling from the underside.

'Wilson – what is this?'

'You ever heard of *matter printers*, Driscoll?'

Wilson's solution to Mr Driscoll's dilemma was simple in principle and, given a reasonably mature matter-printer industry, straightforward in practice. *This* was a complete edition of Shakespeare that was capable of reproducing itself.

'So you come to some new world. You set this little guy down on the floor of the forest, and let him go to work, while you light up your pipe and sit back.'

'Well, I don't smoke, Wilson.'

'Smoking's optional. Here's the thing.' Wilson mimed scuttling legs with his fingers. 'He rushes over to some tree – a fallen trunk will do, even a sapling. And he starts to chew up the wood into pulp to make paper, and then he finds gall and such to make ink. And then, page by page—'

Mr Driscoll saw it. 'Out pops Shakespeare.'

'The same. It'll take him a day or so to spit out his copy.'

Wilson struck Mr Driscoll as the kind of man who, working in a high school, had probably had to train himself to use phrases like 'spit out', as opposed to less salubrious alternatives.

'All nicely bound and everything. There's a master copy on his back here, he has a crawling laser reader to scan the text, to check there's no error creeping in.'

'And there I am, a day later, with a brand-new Shakespeare to hand over to a hungry young civilization. Marvellous, Wilson. Marvellous!'

Wilson droned on some more, about how the printer

was capable of limited self-repair and maintenance, again using components derived from wood. 'With a little nanotech you can make almost anything from carbon. Even diamond to fix the laser scanner, or build itself a new one.' And he went on about how as long as the printer didn't drift from its programming, there would be no problem . . .

Mr Driscoll was no longer listening. He was already dreaming of the speech he would make to announce his new venture to the world.

As soon as he had assembled his travelling kit, Mr Driscoll went back to the Datum and made his way to Brokenstraw Creek, south of Warren, Pennsylvania, where the original Johnny Appleseed – whose real name had been John Chapman, born the best part of three centuries earlier – had planted his first nursery. There Mr Driscoll set up a tablet on a wall to record the moment for posterity, as, alone, with his matter-printer Shakespeare at his side, he declaimed his intention to carry the Bard to the new worlds:

'To older generations this technology would have seemed strange indeed. But today, in a marriage of the supreme achievement of the arts and sciences of the Datum Earth, it will inspire young minds and nurture civilization across the new Earths. It is just as in Shakespeare's time. The Bard's London was a world city, at the heart of an emerging global culture, and through his plays Shakespeare brought that new world to his audiences. And now in this newly emerging panorama of many Earths, I – oh, excuse me . . .'

The recording had to be abandoned because the matter

printer was nibbling at his chair leg, seeking wood to pulp.

And then, with a twist of the control of his Stepper box, Mr Driscoll set off.

At first all went well.

Mr Driscoll soon shook off his inexperience and became a seasoned Long Earth traveller, his breath deepening, his legs strengthening, his feet hardening, even his stomach becoming used to the stepping nausea. He didn't stop at every world. He decided to go as far into the Long Earth as he could manage, scattering his literary seed here and there, and relying on time and Shakespeare himself to take care of a wider diffusion.

When he did stop, it would be for a few days. He would send his matter-printer master edition off to the forest to spawn, and wait for the new copy of the works to be produced. Sometimes he would camp out. Other times he would introduce himself locally, and perhaps stop to deliver a talk, a reading of the Bard, teach a class or two. Then, with the gleaming new complete Shakespeare delivered, he'd be sent on his way, generally with gratitude and a pack full of food and a bottle of fresh-squeezed lemonade.

Word began to spread ahead of his arrival. In some worlds he would be greeted by farmers or their children, and offered a ride to the nearest township.

In three years he covered hundreds of worlds in this way. He felt a vast and deepening satisfaction at the success of his project.

Then he came to Earth West 31,415, in the far Ice Belt.

171

He released his master printer, and after his usual refreshing night's sleep in a forest glade, went to retrieve this world's brand-new copy of the Bard. He soon found the master copy, dormant as usual, in a pose that Mr Driscoll, no engineer, always interpreted as resting after a hard night's work. And beside it was – not another reading copy, with pages still moist, the gall-based ink printing bright – *another master copy*, another crab-like gadget, a copy of the book on a series of spindly legs. Puzzled, he reached for the new copy – but it scuttled off out of his reach and out of sight.

Mr Driscoll was more irritated than alarmed. He was not a practical man, and was used to machinery of all kinds letting him down. He set the true master copy off on its way to another part of the forest – perhaps there was something peculiar about the trees just here, he wondered, not very scientifically – and waited another night. The next morning there was a fresh reading copy of Shakespeare, sitting there on a pile of leaves, just as specified.

Mr Driscoll picked it up, took it into the nearest town, and spent a pleasant day talking to some vaguely interested farmers' children in their quaint little school. To Mr Driscoll's taste this was a particularly pleasing community who, Amish-like, had decided to eschew modern technology as much as possible when shaping their new world.

And the next morning Mr Driscoll stepped on, thinking no more of Earth West 31,415.

Until, ten days later, an agitated farmer pursued him stepwise and demanded that he come back.

* * *

When he returned to 31,415, he was taken to the forest glade where he had released the master Shakespeare – only to find the glade had vanished. It was as if a whole bunch of trees had uprooted themselves. 'Hmm,' said Mr Driscoll, baffled. '"Fear not, till Birnam wood do come to Dunsinane . . ."'

'What? What? Look at this, man. Look what you've done!'

The farmer dragged Mr Driscoll deeper into the forest and now Mr Driscoll saw that the patch of cleared ground was not empty, but filled with crablike creations that crawled and rustled and clambered up the trunks of the surrounding trees, pages on their backs stirring like ladybird wings. They were Shakespeares: not readers' copies like the ones he was leaving behind on the worlds he passed through, but more masters, matter printers making replicas of themselves. And those copies were making copies in turn, spreading out through the forest . . .

'What are you going to do about this?' cried the farmer.

'Me? What can I do?'

'We've already lost about a ton of lumber, we reckon. In ten days! And it's spreading faster all the time.' He grabbed Mr Driscoll by the lapels. 'You know what you've done, don't you? We came all this way to escape this modern technology bullshit. Now you come here with your stupid books, and you've unleashed a nanotech disaster on us. A grey goo! Well, it's all your fault, peckerwood. What are you going to do about it, eh?'

There was only one thing he could do. 'I will get back to the Low Earths as fast as a twain will take me.'

'And then?'

'And then I'll ask Wilson.'

'A ton of lumber in ten days, eh?' Chet Wilson sucked his teeth and said, 'Let me give it some thought.'

After an interval Wilson said, 'What you got, you see, is a mutation.'

'A mutation?'

'The master Shakespeare was always capable of doing more than just churn out the pages of the book. Well, I told you as much. It could create spare parts for itself, even for the replicating mechanism. Designed to recover from drastic damage. That backup process has just gone a little too far, that's all.'

'A little too far? Are you mad, Wilson?'

'Now it's not just fixing itself, it's making a whole new copy. Don't blame me. Probably the way you operated it.'

'Me?!'

'You should have just turned it off and on again. That usually works. The original master evidently reset itself and recovered. But the little rogue baby it produced—' He chuckled indulgently. 'What a rascal!'

'But – but – I refuse to accept any responsibility for this mess. And even so, I don't see how a two-pound book could have churned up a ton of lumber in just ten days.'

'Ah, well, that's exponential growth for you. Breeding like rabbits once they get started, see? In the first day one becomes two. In the second, two become four. In the third, four become eight . . .'

'Yes, yes.'

'After ten days, you've got a thousand copies, plus

change. And a thousand copies of a two-pound book is a ton, my friend. *That's* where your lumber went.'

'Well, it isn't my lumber.' Mr Driscoll's non-mathematical mind tried to grasp these concepts. 'But if I understand you right – on the *eleventh* day, one ton will become two. And then two will become four. And then—'

'That's the idea.'

'Where will it end, Wilson? Where will it end? And what should I do?'

'"Exit, pursued by a bear,"' said Wilson.

The following few weeks were a sensation, at least for the inhabitants of Earth West 31,415, and for the Datum federal government agencies called in to help.

The colonists were hastily, resentfully evacuated, as after twenty days a thousand-ton lumber forest had been demolished.

After thirty days, a million tons of trees had been chewed up, leaving a scar visible from space.

And after forty days a billion tons had gone, and the continents' surviving animals were fleeing the rising Shakespearean sea.

Just fifty days after Mr Driscoll had released his original master copy, almost every tree on Earth West 31,415, indeed the bulk of the planet's continental biomass, had been converted. The books of the Bard roamed the devastated plains, hungry for more.

Mr Driscoll called Wilson from the penitentiary where he was awaiting trial.

'It's terrible, Wilson! They say the books are mutating

again. Eating other kinds of vegetable matter: grasses, shrubs. At the ocean shore some are venturing into the water, devouring the seaweed. In the interior some of them are turning on each other. Bard eat Bard! And they blame me! "Blow, blow, thou winter wind, thou art not so unkind as man's ingratitude." Well, the government has declared a quarantine, and is thinking of sending in some kind of clean-up operation . . .'

'Good idea. Gonna need a code word for that.' Chet Wilson sucked his teeth and said, 'Let me give it some thought.'

After an interval Wilson said, 'How about "The Taming of the Goo"? Whaddya think of that, Driscoll? Driscoll? . . .'

Discovering such stories only made Jan Roderick determined to root out more. And Sister Coleen grew increasingly anxious about him.

24

Joshua's time with the fever was like being underwater, he thought later. Like he wasn't truly asleep but immersed in a shallow lake, and looking up through a rippling meniscus at the world of air above, a surface over which he saw day and night flap by, and the big faces of trolls peering down at him, like moons.

Sometimes they moved him. He would be picked up by Patrick, the big younger male, a hairy arm around his back, a hand under his armpit. His bad leg would send fresh pain shooting through his system, and he would struggle and protest feebly. Later, to his shame, he remembered some of the language; it would have made Bill Chambers blush.

Other times, as he rose out of his reddish murk of sleep towards the daylight, they tried to feed him. He wasn't hungry but he was always hellish thirsty; he would spit out the food and demand water. Sometimes they let him get away without eating, but other times they forced him. The male would prop him up and let his head dangle back, mouth open, and the female, Sally, would drop in stuff, roots and leaves and the sour juice of some fruit or other, and he would choke and shake his head and try to spit it out. But Patrick clamped his mouth closed, and Sally would stroke his throat, and he would swallow; he had no choice.

Afterwards he figured they had been trying to feed him some kind of herbal medicine, no doubt evolved through chance discoveries over millennia: wisdom stored in the trolls' strange collective consciousness – their long call. Given that he eventually recovered, he guessed it had worked. Though the modern antibiotics from his pack that he gulped every time he was awake enough to remember no doubt helped too.

He knew that the trolls were saving his life. It was just that trolls were always so damn *rough*. They were big muscular humanoids, and their method of hunting was to gather in a group and *wrestle* a beast the size of a young elephant to the ground. Mothers even dragged their infants around dangling by one hand or by a scruff.

'As nurses go, these trolls need to up their bedside manner . . .'

He discovered he'd said that out loud. He was in one of his more lucid intervals, then.

He was lying on his back, peering up at a cloudless sky. And the air was cool, cooler than he remembered before the fever heat cut in. The fall must be coming on this Para-Venus. He wondered how long he'd been lying there. And he still didn't know how bad the winter would get. You could tell the rough character of a world from the band it was in, but you had to live through a cycle of seasons, or more, before you truly understood it. And before you knew if you could live through it . . .

A troll's face swam into his blurred vision, peering down at him. He saw a grizzled, crumpled face surrounded by greying black hair. For a moment he was befuddled.

'Sancho!'

'Hoo.'

'Hi, buddy. You saved me. You and your relatives—'

Something soft and pink and bright came sailing in from left field, hit Sancho on the side of the head, and rolled away.

'What the hell?'

'Ha!' Sancho turned that way, glared, and disappeared from his field of view.

Joshua managed to turn his head to the left. He saw Sancho hobbling in pursuit of one of the kids – Liz, maybe. Evidently it was she who had thrown the cheerleader's pom-pom at him. She ran off, laughing as only a troll could laugh.

A *cheerleader's pom-pom*. Where the hell had a troll acquired a cheerleader's pom-pom? Not only that but Joshua thought he recognized the pinkish colour scheme.

'Sancho!' Joshua tried to prop himself up on his elbows, to see more. But the very effort exhausted him, and when he moved it felt like the contents of his head had been liquefied, and he fell back in a faint.

25

CAME THE DAY he was cured.

Well, it felt like it. He woke from what seemed to have been a normal sleep. His vision was clear, there was only a dull ache in his head, but he was still thirsty.

Experimentally, he sat up. He felt shivery-weak in his upper body, and briefly dizzy as he moved his head, but that passed. His right leg, stretched straight out before him, was a sight, the bare flesh filthy and strapped by bloody bandages between two massive branches; the trolls did nothing delicately. But it ached only dully now, a bone-deep throbbing that, he feared, he might have to put up with for the rest of his life.

Glancing around he saw that his kit was close by, in the lee of a nearby rock bluff, still protected by the emergency blanket. Save for his own rummaging for drugs, it seemed undisturbed. He dug into his pack until he found one of his knives, and slipped it into his belt, at the back. Trolls or not, he felt a lot safer with some kind of weapon to hand.

There was no water here, however, and his raging thirst was his first priority. That and maybe the relief of a painfully full bladder. He wasn't far from the bank of a shallow, sluggish river – a dozen paces, no more. No distance, if he'd had the use of both legs; a heck of a challenge given the state he was in. He looked around again. There was nothing nearby he could use for a crutch. He tried pushing himself up with his arms, and folding his good leg underneath, but his bad leg was an impossible obstacle. Soon his weakened muscles were trembling, and he slumped back to the ground.

A troll face swam before him, a vision from his illness. It was the female cub, Liz. Looking around, he saw a few more trolls grooming in a huddle in the middle distance, a handful by the river. Most of the band seemed to be away.

Liz was a bright youngster, and she could immediately see what he wanted. Without hesitation she got her hands under his armpits and, with effortless strength and the usual troll roughness, boosted him to his feet. He yelled as his gatepost of a leg swung in the air, but Liz was still there, and he stayed upright. He threw his arm over her shoulder, and he was stable, balanced on his left leg.

He managed a grin. 'Thank you. You're just the right height for this, you know that? Now – water?' He pointed at the river, and at his mouth.

She set off that way, but too quickly, and he found himself dragged along, hopping crazily, his bad leg scraping in the dirt behind him. 'Hey! Slow down, speedy.' Hop, hop. 'One step at a time . . .'

As they moved away from where he had been lying, he saw the ground was scuffed and stained for some distance around his gear. He remembered, dimly, how they had been moving him around. They must have cleaned him up after he soiled himself, or at least moved him out of the mess, over and over. Trolls had been observed to care for their sick and elderly; maybe they knew to move the immobile, to avoid such problems. Even so he badly needed to clean up properly, and he ought to strip off and inspect himself for bed sores and such – not to mention a good look at that leg.

He felt a sudden surge of shame that he had been so helpless before these trolls, and was flooded with gratitude for what they had done. He hugged Liz's massive football-player shoulders. 'Kid, you're the best nurse I could have found.'

'Hoo?'

He got to a rock where he pissed like Austin Powers.

Then Liz helped him to the river. The big old troll he called Sancho was sitting by the bank, picking fleas from the long, muddy hairs on his legs. He looked up incuriously as Joshua approached. At his side was a fuzzy pink ball, splashed with mud: the cheerleader's pom-pom.

Joshua nodded to Sancho as, with Liz's help, he struggled to sit on the muddy earth by the water. 'Like I said before, I reckon I owe you a big thank-you too, old buddy. My first responder.'

Sancho shrugged – a very human gesture. Then he went back to his assiduous hunt for fleas.

Joshua was distracted by that brilliant pink pom-pom. Since when did a troll carry any possessions around at all? Let alone a cheerleader's pom-pom. 'But it's none of my

182

business, buddy. You carry that pom-pom, you do what you like.'

Sancho didn't even glance around.

Joshua turned back to his own concerns. Gingerly, sitting on his backside, he pushed himself closer to the river, dipped in his hand, and splashed water into his mouth, over his face. Then he poured it over the encrusted filth on his bad leg. He longed to immerse himself completely, but he was wary of whatever must inevitably be lurking in the water. He made a mental note to start using purifying pills for drinking water – but then he'd survived up to now, for the unspecified period while he was ill, with his only serving vessel being the cupped palm of a troll. Maybe he'd developed some kind of immunity over his years in the Long Earth.

Clouds crossed the sun, and that deep ache in the leg intensified. Great, he thought; he was going to become one of those old farts who felt the weather in his bones.

He peeled back bandages and the remnants of his trouser leg. On the exposed skin of his leg there was mud and blood and what looked like dried pus, and as the layers of filth washed away there was a stink of rot. But he also found some kind of vegetable matter tucked away in there: leaves, roots, a kind of greenish scrape on his skin. More troll medication? If so, it seemed to have worked. The place where the skin had broken had never been stitched up, but it had healed reasonably well. He'd have one hell of a scar to scare his grand-nieces with, back in Reboot. But, he saw with relief, there was no sign of infection, no evidence of gangrene – and if that had developed, for all the trolls could have done, he'd have lost his leg, and probably his life, in short order.

He felt his way along his shin, cautiously, slowly, to the break itself. He found a hard knob of bone in there. It ached when he prodded at it. So he stopped prodding. Not a perfect match-up, then. But he had been able to walk, supported by Liz. If he could make himself crutches of some kind, he'd be mobile. It could have been a hell of a lot worse.

And, as he gingerly peeled back more of his elasticized bandages, he found something else unexpected. The rough-and-ready splints had been tied in place, not just by his bandages, but by lengths of cord, evidently taken from his pack, that had been neatly knotted.

'Will you look at that?' he said aloud. 'Trolls with pom-poms. Now trolls tying knots. I bet you never observed that, Lobsang, did you?'

'Trolls tie knots.'

The words sounded like they came from a small bull-horn. Joshua, startled, sprawled comically in the river-bank mud. Words in English! It was totally unexpected.

The laughter of a troll billowed over him. It was Sancho, of course, watching his antics. Sancho, holding a troll-call.

Joshua faced him. 'That was you!'

Sancho lifted the troll-call again. It was the size and shape of a clarinet, a tube encrusted with a kind of circuitry, and worked when held close to the mouth. 'Trolls tie knots! Good knots big knots tight knots.'

'You've got cheerleader pom-poms and now a troll-call. What the hell?' But of course, if he didn't speak through the troll-call, Sancho couldn't understand a word. 'Give me that thing.'

Sancho handed over the troll-call.

Individual trolls were smarter than chimps, but not so smart as humans; some experts thought they might be about equivalent in intellect to the long-extinct *Homo erectus*. It was in their collective behaviour that the trolls were so intensely intelligent: in their cooperative hunting, and in the long call, the unending chorus that seemed to encode their race's deepest memories as well as being a rolling account of the present – what food the scouts had found just over the horizon, which infant was showing signs of tiring on the march.

But still, individual trolls did have a language, of hoots and pants, of gestures, and, yes, of song – a language more sophisticated than any chimp's, that was for sure. To communicate with them, all you had to do was translate that language.

And that was what Lobsang, decades ago, with his pioneering troll-call, had been able to do.

Joshua turned the instrument over in his hands. That this device looked a lot more sophisticated than Lobsang's old prototypes wasn't much of a surprise. What was a surprise was that this eccentric, elderly troll was carrying it around with him. And when Joshua turned the instrument over, he found an inscription on a small plastic plaque:

PROPERTY OF
UNIVERSITY OF VALHALLA
AT DOWNTOWN TWO
DO NOT REMOVE

Joshua smacked his head. Valhalla! *That* was where he'd seen pom-poms like those before. His son Rod, then known as Dan, had attended a school in Valhalla, the greatest city of the High Meggers. Dan hadn't stuck around long enough to go to college there himself, but he and Joshua had taken in a few football games.

Joshua turned and stared at Sancho. 'You've got something to do with the University of Valhalla?' Then he raised the troll-call and repeated his question.

Sancho frowned, listening. Then he took the troll-call back, his leathery face crumpled with concentration. Every linguistic structure from the basics of grammar on down differed between trolls and humans; all the troll-call could do was offer a kind of best-guess translation.

At last Sancho pointed to his own chest. 'Faculty.'

'What? You're on the *faculty*? Of a *college*? Oh, I get it. They've been studying you, right? Like Lobsang in his troll reserve. Hmm. Or maybe *you're* studying *them . . .*'

'Tenure! Sancho got tenure! Hoo!' And he dropped the troll-call in the mud, hooted, splashed, and folded his big hands over his head, obviously hugely amused.

Joshua wondered if he was still in a fever dream.

As the evening drew in, the rest of the trolls returned. Some brought food – armfuls of root vegetables, small game. The big female Sally carried over her shoulder the carcass of what looked like a young deer, but probably wasn't.

They gathered close to the spot where Joshua had been lying for so long, near the bluff. The vegetables and fruit were roughly shared out.

Now he was more capable, Joshua saw that this was a good site, backed up against a bluff for defence, not far from a watercourse. Not so unlike the site he'd chosen for his own stockade, he remembered. You could hide in the rocks if those armoured elephants charged. There were even overhangs for shelter from those pesky pterodactyls.

Joshua watched as the adults butchered the deer-like creature. They used stone blades, hastily selected from a scatter on the ground, to slit open the skin. Then, with the skin hauled off and discarded, they dismembered the carcass, slicing off the limbs, hauling out the entrails and organs. It was an efficient piece of butchery, even by human standards, although Joshua supposed humans would have taken more care to set aside the skin and sinews for use later. And humans mostly wouldn't have stuffed their mouths with raw meat while the butchery was still going on.

Joshua, meanwhile, sitting quietly with his back against the rocky bluff with Sancho, found himself the centre of attention. Sally and Patrick both came over, and hooted their pleasure at seeing him mobile, awake, smiling. Matt rolled a kind of somersault and would have thrown himself at Joshua to wrestle, if, to Joshua's relief, Sancho hadn't blocked his way with a huge forearm.

Then Patrick offered Joshua a slab of raw meat. Joshua took it, nodding gratefully. 'Thanks, but it's a little rare for me; I think I'll just run it through the microwave . . .'

It was the work of a couple of minutes, even stuck on the ground as he was, to assemble a hearth from some flat stones, a few handfuls of dried wood and windblown brush that had gathered in crevices in the bluff. With his flint fire-starter and a few scraps of paper for kindling, he soon had a blaze going. The trolls were entranced. Soon children and adults started hauling over larger chunks of wood to feed the flames.

Joshua got Patrick's gift of meat on an improvised skewer, and held it out over the flames. Fat sizzled, and soon the smell of barbecued meat caused the trolls to start patting their bellies.

'You . . . popular.' That was Sancho with the troll-call.

Joshua grinned, and took back the call. 'Well, I'd better be, I'm likely to be around here for a while. I ought to start earning my keep. And, look, Sancho—'

'Ha?'

He shook his head. 'I thought I knew trolls. I've been meeting trolls for forty years. My best buddy was the world expert on trolls for a while . . . Evidently not any more. And I never met a troll like you before.'

Sancho considered this – whatever the hell he made of it. Then he took the call back and hooted. 'Smarter than the average troll.'

'Hm. I wonder who taught you *that* line.'

'Librarian.' He poked his chest. 'Sancho Librarian.'

The word was clear and unmistakeable. 'What? . . . I wish Lobsang was here. He'd love this.'

'You stay. Join us.' Something about that remark seemed to amuse the old troll, and he started to laugh. 'Join us. Join us!'

The others gathered closer, and laughed along with Sancho as they ate, mock-wrestled, cuddled. And they started to sing, an exquisitely beautiful multipart song that rose like the smoke into the air.

As Joshua sat by his fire, it took him a while to recognize the tune. '"Surf's Up"! Sancho, remind me to tell you about Sister Barbara some time – she loved this song. She was a Californian, y'know. The Surfin' Sister, we called her . . .'

'Hoo?'

And Joshua wondered what a troll Librarian was for.

26

As far as Sister Coleen was concerned, Jan Roderick should have been grounded for running off to Madison West 3 the way he did. Not *encouraged*, by being taken on some open-ended jaunt into the higher worlds. Not *rewarded*.

And why was Sister Coleen the one who had to take him?

Sister John smiled. 'Coleen, you're only going to West 31. It's hardly the High Meggers.'

'But he's already been over to 3 by himself. He says if he doesn't find – whatever it is he wants to find – on 31, he's got a whole string of more worlds in mind to visit.'

'So he does. Ask him to show you the numbers. 3, 31, 314 ... He's got it all worked out, a regular little strategy.'

'But as far as I can tell he doesn't even know what *it* is!'

'If he did know, there'd be no point looking for it, would there?'

'So am I supposed to just go on and on, as long as he wants?'

'I'm sure you'll use your common sense, Sister.'

'But *why me*? I'm a city girl.'

'Seriously?'

'You know I am. Born and raised in Madison.'

'In Madison West 5, you mean. Believe me, Sister Coleen, I know West 5 is our nation's capital now, but compared to the big Datum towns before Yellowstone, West 5 is Dodge City.'

'Where?'

'Never mind.'

'What about his numbers? I don't do math, Sister. I can't even read a recipe.'

'Well, *that's* true.'

'Why not send Assumpta or Joan—'

'Because he likes you, Sister Coleen.'

'Really?'

'Compared to most of us around here, yes.'

'How can you tell?'

'A lifetime's experience. Look, Sister, no more arguments. It will be a growth opportunity for you, and a chance for him to prove himself. Pack your luggage – backpacks only, Coleen!'

'Impossible,' breathed Sister Coleen, who *never* travelled light.

Sister John smiled, and handed her a battered paperback book: the *Stepper's Guide to the Long Earth*. 'Go on, off you pop. Existential mysteries don't solve themselves, you know.'

'Is that what Jan calls this?'

'If he had the vocabulary, he would . . .'

* * *

So, after a day's preparation, with Sister Coleen in practical jumpsuit and wimple, with each of them carrying a lightweight backpack and Stepper boxes on their belts, off the two of them went.

They left the Home at West 5 in the morning. A steam-powered tram took them into a downtown district dominated by the big wooden barn of a Capitol building that now housed the US Congress, itself a copy of the destroyed original on the Datum.

There they got out and stepped, heading for Madison West 31. Neither of them were great steppers, however, and Sister Coleen insisted they take it slowly, leaving ten or fifteen minutes between each step, even though the nausea pills they'd taken were pretty effective. So it took several hours to step across a patchwork of Madison footprints, each more or less built up, though none so much as West 5.

They broke for lunch at a snack bar in West 20.

It was about four in the afternoon by the time they reached West 31. This was September, but the day in this world was warm and bright. The geography of this footprint of Madison was virtually the same as West 5, of course. Here was the Capitol mound, and a short walk away, no doubt, they would find the lake. But there was no sophisticated development here, just tracks cutting through the prairie towards the lake shore. It seemed odd that such a nearby world should be so empty. But even after the great exodus of people that had followed the Yellowstone eruption and the evacuation of the Datum, just the first dozen or so worlds to East or West had soaked up almost all the fleeing population. Each world, after all, was a whole Earth the size of the original, each stepwise America a continental wilderness to match the homeland.

There was, however, a travellers' rest on top of the Capitol mound here in West 31, under a flag that fluttered bravely on a pole, a holographic US-Aegis Stars and Stripes. Sister Coleen had looked this place up, and had arranged a reservation. Now she plodded up the mound, with Jan trailing. They both had muddy boots by the time they reached the porch.

You *might* call this huddle of single-storey apartments a motel, Sister Coleen thought dismally, if motor cars ever came this way – and if you didn't know it had been converted from a temporary barracks hastily thrown up by the US Army in the days of chaos and flight after Yellowstone, when the stepwise Madisons had become refugee camps. Still, the check-in was friendly, and their adjoining rooms were clean.

Once in his room, Jan barely bothered to unpack before he spread out his tablet and his hard-copy notes across his bed, and set up his little home-built radio kit on the room's small table. He snapped a switch, and immediately screens started to glow. With a sigh, Sister Coleen left him to it. She'd seen him like this before.

In her own room she boiled a kettle of water on the small gas stove. It was self-catering here, evidently, and without electricity; heating and lighting came from bottled biofuel gas. When she wanted to wash, she'd have to boil another kettle. And she hoped Jan's batteries wouldn't run down too quickly.

She took mugs of coffee through the connecting door

into Jan's room. Intent on his radio, he still had his outdoor coat on. She set a mug down hard on the table beside him.

He winced. 'Don't spill it on my stuff.'

'I won't. Now, you listen to me, Jan. You're going to drink this coffee, and you'll take off that coat, and then I'll prepare you something good to eat, and you're going to eat it.'

He looked at her and smiled. He was a thin-faced, under-nourished-looking boy, but, she always thought, when he smiled he lit up the room. '"Good to eat"?'

'Cheeky. Just remember I'm in charge.'

'Course you are, Coleen.'

She pursed her lips. 'Sister Coleen to you.' She was not much more than twice his age, and she'd learned she had to be authoritative around the Home's older children. Friendliness backed up by a steel core was the way. She glanced around at the cabin: bare walls, scuffed floor. 'What a place. It looks like the soldiers who built it only just moved out . . . I wish you'd dragged me to West 3, where you went first. They have real motels on West 3. With electricity. And showers.' She sighed. 'And if we don't find whatever it is you're looking for on this world, we're going to have to move on, aren't we? Where next?'

'West 314, maybe.'

'314? That seems a long way.' She glanced around at his tablet, his papers; he had a ring binder full of computer downloads and clippings from grainy Low Earth newspapers. 'Well, here we are, following this trail of yours. Maybe you'd better help me understand. Where are these numbers coming from, Jan?'

He stared at her. 'Isn't it *obvious*?'

'I always hated math, and I hate puzzles even more. Just pretend I haven't the faintest idea what you're talking about.'

He took his ring binder and flipped through it until he found a page covered with rows of numbers. 'Look at this.'

She leaned down to read. The digits began:

3.14159 26535 89793 23846 . . .

She shrugged. 'So? Lottery numbers? Astrology?'

'Sister, these are the first three thousand digits of pi.'

'What pie? Oh, *pi*. Something to do with circles?'

'That's it. What you get if you divide the circumference by the diameter. The digits go on for ever.'

'Unlike my attention span. Let me look at that again. Three point one four one five . . . Oh. I get it. So we're searching for worlds that follow the digits of pi.'

He looked pained. *Well, duh.*

'You started at Madison West 3. Now you've come to West 31. And next, 314.' She felt pleased with herself for puzzling out the pattern, even if he'd had to hold it in front of her face. But there was a further consequence. 'But that means, if we don't find what you want here or 314, it will be *3,141* . . .' The number sounded huge to her. 'Where's that? Is it even still in the Ice Belt?'

'Of course it is, Sister.' He dug out a chart of what looked like a rock column, colour-coded. He'd marked some of the layers with big red asterisks. 'Look, I have this Mellanier chart of the Long Earth. You can see the Belts – here's the

Ice Belt and the Mine Belt and the Corn Belt – and I marked the worlds in the coded messages.'

'I see . . .' She was thinking ahead to practicalities. Even a few hundred worlds would be a long way to step on foot. Sister John had told her to take as much time as she needed, and assured her that her credit, backed up by the Home's accounts, was good. Probably local twains went that far, crossing the stepwise Madisons. But to go *thousands* of worlds – would they have to go cross-country to one of the big Long Mississippi hubs? Just how far would Sister John want her to take this? . . .

Jan was watching her steadily.

'So these – pi worlds – have got something to do with the stories you've been collecting, have they?'

'Yes,' he said with a kind of stretched patience. 'The stories show up in the news, or the online feeds. People gossip about them, and they kind of go viral. And then you start getting stories about the stories. And *then* you start to see the patterns.'

He showed her clippings in his ring binder, and archived pages downloaded on to his tablet. Here was a strange story of a woman who couldn't step, but she could *see* into the stepwise worlds. She had been called Bettany Diamond, mother of two. Sister Coleen remembered seeing some version of this story on a trashy strange-but-true documentary; Diamond had died in the year 2030, in the middle of a post-nuke riot in Madison. And, it turned out, the woman had spent much of her later life here, in a small community in West 31.

And then there was the legend of 'Johnny Shakespeare'. That particular story, a strange-but-maybe-true fable of the Long Earth, had been written up in a book for children. And he, supposedly, had let his self-replicating Shakespeare volumes loose on Earth West 31,415.

'You see?' Jan stabbed the page with a grubby finger. '*That* was the one that gave me the real clue. The first five digits! It was staring me in the face . . .'

Coleen thought she heard a woman's voice, very faint, as if far off. This was a very quiet world.

Distracted, she turned back to Jan. 'So you believe that all these stories—'

'I think they're a *message*. I think they've been *planted*, in the news, on the internet, the outernet. All you've got to do is put together the clues, see the pattern. And then it's obvious.'

'What's obvious?'

He shook his head, impatient at her slowness. 'That something important is happening on one of these worlds.'

'The pi worlds?'

'Yes! People are *doing* something. And they want help.'

'How can you tell?'

'Because they're asking for it. What else can all this mean?'

Again she heard that faint voice. 'And now you're here, and you've got your radio transmitter, and you're broadcasting – what?'

'My name, where we are, and the pi digits. I'm telling them I know they're calling, that I understand.' He tapped his set. 'This is a short-wave radio. It will be picked up anywhere on this Earth.'

'But what kind of help can they possibly want, from . . .'

'From a kid like me?' He glared at her, defiant. 'Maybe if I'm smart enough to figure out the code, I'm smart enough to help. Even if I am just a *kid*.'

'I'm sorry,' she said quickly. 'It's just that it's all so strange for me.'

'But you can't deny it's real.'

'I guess not . . .' Again, that voice. She glanced to the grimy window. 'Can you hear somebody? The lady on reception said we were the only guests here.'

He stared at her. Then he lunged at his radio and turned up the volume.

Suddenly the voice was crystal clear. '. . . Stay where you are, and keep broadcasting. We've located you from your signal, but it will take us a few hours to reach you. Thank you for responding to our message, and for taking the trouble to come. My name is Roberta Golding, and I look forward to meeting you. Don't try to reply; this message is on a loop. Be assured we're on our way. Stay where you are, and keep broadcasting . . .'

Sister Coleen and Jan just stared at each other.

Then Jan jumped to his feet and ran around the room, punching the air. 'Yes! I was right!'

Sister Coleen longed to join in. But she said, 'Well, now, just be sensible, Jan. We don't know what this is about, yet.'

'It's going to be *fun*—'

She grabbed his shoulders to make him stand still; he was panting hard. 'But I'm still in charge,' she said. 'Deal?'

'Deal.'

Of course he would have promised anything to get to

meet this Golding woman. Sister Coleen sighed. 'I suppose I'm glad I'm not going to have to trek off to the High Meggers, or wherever . . . Now, before this lady shows up, will you calm down, and take your coat off, and get washed, and have something to *eat*?'

27

I N THE EVENT it was not until the next morning that Roberta Golding arrived.

And when she did it was in a small helicopter that descended from the empty blue sky of a Wisconsin fall day, landing before the Capitol mound. Jan, of course, was thrilled.

'I'm sorry it took so long. There are only a handful of us responders on each of the target worlds; I've had to travel from the Manhattan footprint.'

Sister Coleen frowned. 'Target worlds?'

Jan whispered, 'She means the pi worlds.'

'Oh . . .'

Jan was all for going for a joyride on the chopper, but Roberta insisted on coming up to their rooms in the motel. 'You asked *me* to come see *you*, after all,' she said to Jan. 'And if we're to work together, it's important that I get to know you.'

Jan was round-eyed. 'We're going to work together?'

'If,' said Sister Coleen firmly as they walked back to the motel. 'She said *if*. And I'm still saying *if* too, young man. Let's just see how this pans out.'

Roberta stood in Jan's room, gravely surveying his materials, glancing at his tablet, his home-assembled radio kit, his cuttings file, showing every evidence of approval. Although it was hard to tell what she was thinking, Sister Coleen admitted to herself. Roberta, in her forties perhaps, was slim, serious and bespectacled; she wore a sober, anonymous trouser suit. And she was rather inexpressive.

Eventually she nodded to Sister Coleen. 'He's done well. And I do understand how difficult life can be for such a child. And for you, of course. I was once like him. Many of us were.'

'"Us?" "Such a child"? Ms Golding, you haven't said a word about what's going on here, who you are—'

'We are the Next,' said Roberta simply.

Sister Coleen stared.

Jan said, '*Cool.*'

Sister Coleen pulled herself together. 'The Next. OK. And is Jan right? I mean, that you've been sending out messages of some kind?'

'He is. We are engaged in a project. A big one, a construction project which – well, it's far too large for us to handle alone.'

'What kind of project?' Jan snapped. 'What construction? What's it for?'

'We don't know yet. We'll have to build most of it to find out, I suspect – if we build it at all, and that's being debated. But, you see, we received a message too, from – somewhere else. You'll learn all about this if you join us.'

'But I know what it is. A SETI signal. Like in *Contact.* It was in the news, for a while.'

Roberta smiled. 'It started that way, certainly. But it soon vanished from your news bulletins, didn't it? Strange news from the High Meggers – not as immediate as the latest sabre-rattling between the US and China, say. Jan, evidently you have a longer attention span than most of your kind.'

'"Your kind."' Sister Coleen frowned. 'I don't like that. What is it you call us? *Dim-bulbs?* So you need help from us dim-bulbs for this great project, do you?'

Roberta said mildly, 'We are still few, and with limited resources. You are many, and have the resources of worlds.'

'So why aren't you approaching the big engineering companies? Even the government?'

'Oh, we are. You may hear of this. We call ourselves the Messengers – well, we have incorporated under the name.' She smiled. 'The Messengers, Inc. Yes, we have taken out contracts with many of the world's largest engineering concerns – that is on the Datum Earth and the Low Earths, even at Valhalla. But the project is bigger even than *that*, it seems.'

Jan asked, 'How big?'

She smiled. 'Not as big as a planet.'

Jan goggled.

Sister Coleen couldn't take that in. 'OK,' she said. 'So you sent out these stories—'

'We needed a way to ask for help from *everybody*, from all the worlds, from ordinary people, the public. But it is only human contact that unites the Long Earth. And what better medium to send a message than coded into stories, passed by word of mouth from one human being to another? Of course it needed to be a message heard only by those capable and willing to help.'

'Such as a ten-year-old boy?'

Jan said quickly, 'But I *did* understand, Sister. It's not just the numbers. It's what the stories are about. That tells you something about the project. The story of Bettany Diamond is saying that it's something to do with how we see the worlds of the Long Earth. The Cueball story says it's about how the different Earths are connected up. And Johnny Shakespeare – well, he rebuilt a whole world, by accident. Just like your big project, maybe.'

Roberta eyed Sister Coleen. 'You see, Sister, it does depend on which ten-year-old boy you ask.'

Jan said, 'But what can I actually do?'

Roberta touched his radio. 'You built this from a kit, did you?'

'With some upgrades,' he said matter-of-factly.

'Jan, if you can make something like this, you can make stuff for us. We'll give you the specs of a replicator – like a matter printer. And with that, you can make parts.'

'Parts? To do what?'

'Well, we don't necessarily know. Not yet. None of us knows for certain. I guess when it's all put together, then we'll know. This is crowd-sourcing, as they used to call it, working across the whole Long Earth. The final assembly will be on Earth West three million—'

'Let me guess.' Sister Coleen flicked through Jan's notes to the pi digits. 'Earth West 3,141,592. Right?'

'You're getting the idea, Sister. We chose that world especially. Although the idea for the pi numbering came from events on West 3,141.' Her smile was thin. 'Even the Next had no influence over *that*.'

Sister Coleen wasn't sure what she meant. 'And, 3,141,592. That's a long way away. Is it past the Gap?'

'Indeed. We don't know what this machine is going to do. To build it a long way away seems a good idea. If we build it at all.'

Coleen said, 'I remember when it was in the news, a lot of people didn't like this thing. Maybe it's some kind of trap, like a big bomb they're getting us to build to blow ourselves up.'

Roberta laughed. 'It might comfort you to know that we too are exploring such dangers, at greater depth.'

Coleen scowled. 'If I wasn't used to being patronized by the senior Sisters I might take offence at your tone.'

Jan said, 'Will I be able to come see it?'

'I don't see why not. But you'll have to talk about that with Sister.' Roberta stood up. 'I think we're done for today. We'll be in touch.'

Sister Coleen said, 'We live at—'

'The Home in Madison West 5. I know.'

On impulse, Jan tugged Roberta's hand. 'Pi is in *Contact*. That's what gave me the idea about the code numbers in the first place.'

Roberta smiled, and winked at Sister Coleen.

Who was already trying to figure out how she was going to explain all this to Sister John.

28

Nelson's first impulse, when he had seen his grandson vanish in the belly of the disappeared Traverser on that warm world seven hundred thousand steps West, had been to call on Lobsang's help.

His son Sam and the other fishermen had immediately struck out for the nearest land – a verdant but uninhabited island. Here there was food and water and fuel for fires; here, Sam said, after conferring with his fellows, they would wait for the return of the Traverser with their families. What else could they do?

But Nelson knew there was little hope of the situation simply resolving itself. Whatever new phenomenon the Long Earth was now displaying was far greater in scale than the human. And to deal with it he needed the help of an entity greater than the human.

So he had recalled his twain, and headed straight back to the Low Earths.

Once back home, Nelson had learned that his own experience in that remote footprint of the Tasman Sea was part of a wider phenomenon. With the help of online resources, and buddies including his old friends the Quizmasters, he'd discovered that his own Traverser, seven hundred thousand steps out, had not been unique in its disappearance. Traversers had always been able to step, of course, from one world to the next. *But now they were disappearing altogether,* along with whatever freight of life they carried, as authenticated by various bewildered observers on several far-separated worlds.

Where were they going? How did they travel? And *why now*? Nobody had any answers.

But of course it wasn't the issue of the Traversers itself that Nelson cared about. It was Troy, lost in the belly of the vanished beast. Troy, his grandson, found and lost in a matter of weeks . . . And Sam, Nelson's son, abandoned too, left adrift on that island close to the footprint of New Zealand with the rest of the tiny fishing fleet.

Only Lobsang could help. But Lobsang had disappeared.

Eventually he learned that Lobsang was in a virtual reality, a refuge, itself locked inside a kind of corporate firewall. As Nelson battered feebly against this barrier, a butterfly against a window, he got to know Selena Jones at transEarth, Lobsang's gatekeeper, rather too well.

In the end, it was not until December of 2070 that he got the break he needed, when he attended the funeral of Sister Agnes, at the Home at Madison West 5. This was a strange, eerie affair. Nelson gave a eulogy, and helped carry a coffin that felt peculiarly heavy. The hymn being sung had been 'Morning Has Broken', with a discarded ambulant unit of Lobsang's playing the Rick Wakeman piano accompaniment, and pretty soulfully too.

And it was at the funeral that he met Ben Abrahams, né Ogilvy: Ben, the adopted son of Agnes, and of Lobsang. Ben had helped Lobsang hide away, and now agreed to help Nelson find him.

But, he warned Nelson, it would mean undertaking a journey even stranger yet . . .

29

As the travellers came down from the final mountain pass, they descended at last below the snow line. Nelson found himself walking on solid rock, the footing cold but firm under his thick boots in this Himalayan spring. He paused for a moment, beside Ben Abrahams. Side by side, the two of them must look as fat as trolls, Nelson suspected, swathed as they were in layers of clothing, in their thick trousers and padded jackets and mittens and Tibetan-style woollen hats, and with their breath steaming from their mouths.

Nelson raised his face to the mountain before him. It seemed to rise almost vertically to the crystal-blue sky – a wall of granite laced with brilliant-white ice.

Ben Abrahams pointed. 'The village is in the valley just down below.'

Glancing down, Nelson saw threads of smoke rising, and in the huge silence he thought he heard the clank of cow bells, all of it dwarfed by the tremendous presence of the mountain. 'Imagine living under *that* all your life. Humanity is irrelevant here.'

'Yes. Hell of a view, isn't it? Oh, sorry, Nelson—'

'For using the H word? Don't worry about it. My dog collar is long ago and far away. It's a relief to be able to stand on firm ground, though, isn't it?'

'That it is, Nelson.'

'Although,' Nelson said, thinking about it, 'I'm not as winded as I ought to be, given what we just came through. And given how high up we are.'

'More than two miles above sea level.'

'And given my age.' He looked at his mittened hand, turned it over. 'But then this isn't me, is it? Not my body.' Which wizened husk was lying in a kind of sensory deprivation tank in a Low Earth transEarth facility right now, surrounded by scanners, and with internal monitors that had wriggled up his nose and into his ears, while his consciousness was projected into this unreal place.

He shuddered.

Ben asked, 'Are you cold?'

'No. Call it existential angst.'

Ben grinned. 'Just forget about it. The outside. Accept what you see, what you feel. We crossed by the pass above—'

'Yes. I can remember. Kind of. I remember what went *before*.' The weeks of effort it had taken to get permission to access this simulation. 'And I remember the hike – but the way I remember reading an entry in somebody else's diary. I don't recall making any particular individual step. Even the last step I took, before standing right here . . .'

'Don't push it, Nelson,' Ben said. 'Your memories of the trek are mostly mock-ups. No deeper than they need to be.'

Nineteen years old, Ben was calm, strong, assured. His

accent was a kind of backwoods twang, incongruous for a young man so obviously well educated, Nelson thought. But then, with his adopted parents, Lobsang and Agnes, he had spent his early years in a backwoods community.

'So this place is—'

'Not far from Ladakh. West Tibet. Now within the boundaries of India, and preserved from the worst of the Chinese occupation of the country as a result. And then, when Step Day came, this was the focus of the main migrations out of the Datum, as Buddhist communities gathered here and spread out into empty footprints of the Himalayas – empty of the Chinese, that is. What you see is a recreation of the Datum community as it was pre-Yellowstone, pre-Step Day. Lobsang asked for that specifically.'

'Yes. Lobsang. Who we came to see.'

Ben, his face round-cheeked inside his fleecy hood, glanced at him with faint concern. 'It was your idea, Nelson. You wanted to come here—'

'I remember now. I'm sorry.'

'Don't be. Nelson, this kind of memory muddle isn't particularly uncommon. It's just that there have to be horizons within a sim like this. Cut-offs to the memory, as well as physical boundaries. A sim can't be infinite, or infinitely detailed; you have to start a sim *somewhere*, from some base in space and time. And at least if we come walking down from the hills like this, we will be fully consistent with the sim itself. We shouldn't give Lobsang himself any cognitive problems.'

'Then let's get on with it.'

But Ben hesitated. 'You're sure it's necessary to do this?

Lobsang has been living a normal life, growing up in here for years.'

Nelson smiled. '"Normal" for a Tibetan-Buddhist novice monk?'

Ben sighed. 'I don't exactly monitor him daily. My studies at Valhalla keep me far away. I have kept a closer eye on him recently, since my mother's health began to fail . . . He's going to have to come to terms with her death; that's one issue. Also, with Lobsang, there have already been signs of some cognitive disturbance. As if he is distracted by something. Maybe that comes from within himself, or maybe from outside this artificial environment.' He glanced at Nelson. 'Maybe he knew you were coming.'

'Or maybe whatever caused – the reason I'm here – has disturbed Lobsang too.'

'Come, it's not far now. I'm sure the villagers will make us welcome, and we can warm up. They're always kind to strangers – well, you have to be, in a place like this . . .'

They wandered down into the village, side by side. The only vehicles on the track they followed were bicycles and a couple of hand-drawn carts.

The place seemed small and cramped to Nelson, a huddle of single-storey houses. There were some modern buildings, constructed of breeze blocks and corrugated-iron panels, but most of the houses and communal places were built of old, worn stone. Nelson imagined the labour as each block had been cut and hauled down from the mountain; once brought here the stone would be used and reused, over and over. He saw cattle penned behind a wall on the outskirts of the village, big beasts with thick black hair and curling horns and bells around their necks. And as they entered the village itself there were more animals, dogs, goats with thick coats of hair, seeming to wander at will.

The people peered at them curiously, their expressions not unfriendly.

They were shorter than Nelson, though he was tall anyhow. Men and women alike, they looked rounded in their heavy coats. But many of them wore modern western gear – quilted jackets and lace-up boots and Day Glo mittens. There were few children around, but then this was a working day, a school day; the adults would be at work in the fields or the nearby towns, the children in their classes. The younger women and men struck him as very handsome, and the older people seemed to have faces as hard and leathery as old saddlebags.

Nelson paused at a prayer wheel, an upright cylinder half as tall as he was, and elaborately decorated. 'Almost pointlessly beautiful,' he murmured to Ben.

As they stood there, a very old man came up and grasped Nelson's hand and shook it vigorously, gabbling something Nelson couldn't understand. Nelson just smiled back.

Now a man who looked about sixty approached the visitors. He wore what looked like an elaborately coloured robe under his top coat. 'Mr Azikiwe, Mr Abrahams? My name is Padmasambhava. Please call me Padma – Lobsang always did. We corresponded, Mr Abrahams—'

'Call me Ben.'

'And of course, Mr Azikiwe, we met at Lobsang's funeral

– oh, twenty-five years ago? Strange to think of that, in the circumstances.'

Nelson said, 'That's what being a friend of Lobsang does to you. I remember it well. And I'd shake your hand if this old fellow ever lets go of me!'

'He's one of the oldest residents of the village. He's guessing you are either African or American. Either way he says you're welcome here, as a friend and supporter of the Dalai Lama. He is ninety-two years old. And, in case you're wondering, his avatar is an authentic replica of the real thing, his physical body.' He said more quietly, 'About five per cent of the people you see are avatars of living people. The rest are computer-generated simulated personalities. Granted it's often hard to tell who's who. And I, in fact, am rather more elderly in reality than the figure you see before you.'

'In that case I'm impressed. This fellow's pretty limber.'

'He prostrates himself before the Buddha in his family shrine one hundred times a day, every day. Excellent way to keep the back supple. Please, come into my home, get out of the cold for a moment . . .'

Padma's home was a small house at the edge of the village. The walls were decorated with colourful hangings, the floor with a thick carpet. There was an elaborate shrine against one wall, neat, symmetrical, brightly coloured with gilt frames around red panels; the shelves were crowded with tokens and small Buddha statues.

'Please, sit. I would offer you tea, but Lobsang is not far away. I'm sure you would prefer to meet him soon.'

'It's why we came,' Nelson said.

'I should say that this is actually a home of my cousin's, not my own. I am abbot of a monastery in Ladakh – that is, in the real world, the Datum. But, as you know, I have long been a close friend of Lobsang. I have worked with him regarding spiritual matters for many years. When he decided to, ah, immerse himself in this environment, in the latest iteration of his existence, I was happy to devote a proportion of my time to accompany him, to be his spiritual guide as he grows up in this place.'

Nelson imagined he had as close a relationship with Lobsang as anybody in his 'family' – by which he meant Agnes, Ben, Selena, and of course Joshua Valienté. For all Lobsang's claims about his origin – that he was the soul of a Tibetan motorcycle repairman reincarnated into a gel-substrate supercomputer – none of them, not even Nelson, had ever explored the full implications of that idea. Yet something in that exotic background clawed him back, over and over. And here he was again.

Ben said, 'That's very kind of you, sir.'

Padma regarded him. 'And it is forgiving of you, his adopted son, not to feel resentment at this absenting of himself from your own life. Lobsang has chosen to start again, in a sense, to grow up immersed in the traditions of his ancestral faith. You are so young yourself. Physically and spiritually Lobsang has made himself younger than you. How strange!'

Ben shrugged. 'I always knew my parents were – different. Even before they told me the truth about their own nature. Even before they told me I was adopted, in fact.'

And even before alien planet-eating monsters showed

up in his home town of New Springfield, Nelson thought.

'Ah,' said Padma. 'One can never fool a child.'

'But I was an orphan – who knows what would have become of me if not for Agnes and Lobsang? I guess I can forgive them for being *odd*. They were what they were.'

'You are wise for such a young man. And as for the money that is being expended on this place . . .'

Nelson grinned. 'I asked around at transEarth. This simulation is consuming the GDP of a small nation.'

'But Lobsang can afford it. And you are certain that you must disturb him now?'

Nelson glanced at Ben. 'Ben asked me the same question. I'm afraid so. He's the only one I can turn to . . . Put it this way, *he* would never forgive me if I didn't call on him. But I have a feeling that what's going on out there is serious enough that he's going to have to know anyhow, sooner or later. He is, after all, Lobsang.'

There was a shrill whistle, the sound of boys cheering.

'Ah.' Padma smiled. 'Sounds as if somebody has scored a goal.'

'A goal?'

'It may be an opportune time to intervene. If you'll follow me . . .'

In a rough field behind the village, under the looming mountain, teams of novice monks were playing soccer, a half-dozen per side. All the boys, aged somewhere between twelve and fifteen, were wearing purple robes and had shaven heads. One side was celebrating a goal, while the other was riven by arguments.

'Now I've seen everything,' Ben said. 'Novice monks playing football.'

Padma smiled indulgently. 'Young men cannot study thousand-year-old manuscripts about the nature of consciousness all the time.'

'What baffles me,' Nelson said, 'is how they can tell who's on which team.'

Padma laughed, a big booming laugh that seemed to echo from the mountain.

Now Nelson heard what looked like the captain of the losing side berating his midfielders. 'Look – I know it's not your position, but when the defender goes forward you drop back to cover him. You back him up. You always need back-up!'

Ben and Nelson exchanged a glance. Nelson said dryly, 'I think we found him.'

Padma beckoned the losing captain over. He came at a jog, young, healthy, breath wreathing pink cheeks. But he stared at Nelson and Ben, and slowed, and his face fell. Nelson felt his heart break, just a little. Already the Himalayan dream was over for this boy.

'I know these people, master,' the boy said to Padma.

'You do. This man is your friend – your good friend of many years. And this fellow – well, *he's your son.* Your adopted son.'

The boy's face worked. 'Why have they come?'

Nelson stepped forward. 'It's my fault. Blame me. I persuaded Ben to bring me here. I felt it was important.'

'They need you out there,' Padma said gently.

'I remember.' The boy pressed his fists to his eyes. 'I remember! Why did you come?' He was weeping, Nelson

216

saw with a shock. The boy crumpled, squatting, the tears leaking from behind his clenched fists.

Padma knelt down with him, stiffly. 'Remember, Lobsang. Remember your teaching, the texts. *To realize one's true nature is a liberation.*'

'We're only one goal down! Oh, why did you come? Why?'

30

As the winter turned to spring, the troll band seemed content to hang around the rock bluff where they'd brought Joshua.

As he got on with his convalescence, and waited for a pickup that might or might not come, Joshua had re-established his own camp at the bluff. He'd set up his small tent, with his aerogel roll-out mattress and his sleeping bag. His radio still worked, pumping out its general-purpose beacon signal: *Here I am.* And, as a second thought, he spread out the remnants of the space-suit-silver survival blanket across the top of the bluff so it could be seen from the air, just as Bill Chambers had suggested – at least, when Sancho wasn't borrowing it. Of course you had to be wary of what kind of attention you attracted to yourself; he hadn't forgotten those big pterosaurs. But he figured that at this point the advantage he could gain from being picked up by some Good Samaritan and returned to the human worlds far outweighed the risk of danger. And besides, the trolls were here with him. They'd provide some warning of, if not protection from, aerial threats.

In the meantime, he lived among trolls.

Their hunting was a beautiful process to watch. Scouts panned out across the landscape, and indeed across the worlds, returning with information about threats, storms, or sources of food and water and shelter, and they would sing out that information to the group. More scouts would go out to check up on these reports, and then return to sing out their findings. Very quickly the band would converge on a solution – to Joshua's ears it was like a scratch choir suddenly and triumphantly bursting into a perfect rendition of the 'Ode to Joy' – and off they would go, in search of goodies. This was the essence of troll collective intelligence, Lobsang had come to believe, adapted for an existence spread across a sheaf of stepwise worlds. A troll band was like a bee swarm, with scouts returning from stepwise worlds to dance out news of food or threats to the main group.

Now he had time to watch them more closely – and maybe for longer, in one continuous period, than anybody out in the wild before, he mused – Joshua thought he spotted more novel aspects of their behaviour. Such as when scouts he didn't recognize showed up – granted it was hard to be sure with all that hair who was who anyhow – and they would join with scouts from 'his' band, and maybe others, and go into a different kind of gathering, hooting, jumping and floor-slapping, even mock-wrestling at times, dozens of trolls from several different bands all over each other.

'It's like a Boston New Year's,' Joshua said to himself, watching, bemused.

But though there was obviously a strong element of

play here – and flirting, as a few male–female pairings would periodically spin off from the whole – Joshua was sure all this had something to do with the collective, that every gesture, every hoot and cry, was a thought being expressed or received.

In a way there was no such thing as a troll; there were only *the trolls*, the collective – the way no bee was a true individual, separate from the hive. And Joshua knew about bees, having spent many scary hours as a small boy helping Sister Regina maintain the Home's single hive. A troll band saw and sensed as a whole, and remembered through the dances and the long call. And this new behaviour he witnessed seemed to fit in with that. Beekeepers knew that drones from hives miles around would sometimes gather in a kind of congress, and urgently share information in their buzzing aerial dance. In the same way, maybe that was what was happening here – troll bands spread across miles, and across many Earths stepwise, sharing their intelligence of opportunity and threat.

'Must tell Lobsang,' he said. 'Always something new in the Long Earth.'

And, when a very young cub died of some condition Joshua could neither identify nor treat, he witnessed behaviours he had heard of before, when the cub was buried in a crude, scraped-out grave, and the band gathered round and scattered flower petals.

It was either his good fortune that the trolls happened to be sticking around during his recuperation, or else his even greater good fortune that they were choosing do so, that they were being kind to this raggedy old human with his busted leg.

More good fortune than he deserved, he thought in his blacker moments.

The trolls hadn't asked for him to show up, after all. And it was his own stupid fault he'd gotten himself injured. Out in the High Meggers there were plenty of humans who would have left him lying in the dirt, after having robbed him of anything worth carrying away. Even Sally Linsay might have abandoned him, he reflected with sour humour, seeing his death by starvation or between the jaws of some predator as a fitting reward for his carelessness. The Long Earth was a tough place, a raw place, a place that didn't owe you a living. In the end the dumb got winnowed out – and even the great Joshua Valienté, the best-known pioneer of them all, wasn't immune to that.

Except it wasn't happening that way. Thanks to the trolls.

He did want to think that he was giving something back to the trolls.

After all, they had a lot in common. Trolls and humans were believed to share a deep common ancestry that dated back to the African savannah on Datum Earth. The ancestors of the trolls had gone off into the Long Earth to become super-stepper hunters, while the ancestors of humans had hung around on the Datum and moved out across the continents, becoming clever survivors, banging rocks and splitting atoms. But, Joshua thought, they must share deep primal memories of those common early days – memories of the teeth of leopards. Here there were no leopards that Joshua had seen, but there were carnivores so ferocious that elephants had needed to evolve armour. Trolls were big, heavy, clever animals, but for all the complexity of their song, for all the power of their muscles, trolls were as naked in the wilderness as *Homo habilis* two million years earlier. He'd seen them in the dark, how they huddled together backed up against the rock face of the bluff. How they woke when noises came out of the night, and the parents snuggled their young closer. How a cloud of fear hung over the group.

So Joshua played his part to assuage that fear. He showed the trolls his tools, his knives, his small handguns, and what he could do with them. And he made sure there was a fire blazing at every sunset, a fire he and the trolls kept fed through the night.

'Call me man-cub, Sancho.'

'Hoo?'

So they stayed with him while he recovered, and conversely he stayed with them.

But he was not a troll.

The weeks and months wore on, and he was stuck out here on a voluntary sabbatical that had become an enforced exile.

In the end it was Helen he missed the most.

Looking back he felt bemused at the time he'd wasted, the time he'd been away from her. Their years seemed so brief, in the end. He would hold her diary, which had survived the months of his illness. 'Helen,' he said, 'if I get out of this fix I will come see you on Datum Madison, where you lie, if I have to hop there on a pogo stick to do it. I swear it.'

It was when he was in this mood that the old troll Sancho would come join him.

* * *

It was the middle of the day, and the sun was high. Joshua was sitting on top of the bluff, wearing a battered broad-brimmed hat, his shirt open.

It was the warmest it had been since before the winter, and the air was a flat, oppressive blanket. He could see a good bit of the landscape from up here, and nothing much was moving. Some of the trolls sat lolling in what shade the bluff offered, but most were out of sight, probably off food-gathering on some neighbouring world. Elephants were hanging around the river, further upstream, trumpeting thinly as they splashed water over their armoured faces.

And here came Sancho, carrying his translator troll-call, courtesy of Valhalla U. His ageing body heavy, he climbed the bluff stiffly – though not so stiffly as Joshua with his rigid right leg and home-made crutch. Sancho sat down by Joshua, wrapped the spacesuit-silver blanket around his shoulders, and surveyed the landscape with a faint air of old-man disdain.

Then he reached out a hand like a boxing glove, in a silent request. Joshua sighed and handed over his sunglasses. 'Just don't bend the damn frame again.'

'Hoo,' said the troll, jamming the glasses on his wide face. Somehow, Joshua had to admit, the glasses suited him.

Sometimes they would sit side by side like this for hours, in silence, each chewing blades of grass. Like two old-fart boatmen by the Mississippi, Joshua mused, silently letting the hours wash by like the waters of the river itself.

And sometimes they spoke.

Sancho spat out a volume of greenish phlegm. 'Alone.' He handed over the troll-call for Joshua's reply.

'Who, me? Or you?'

'Why alone why?'

Joshua shrugged. 'I like to be alone. Or used to like it.'

The old troll pursed his lips and squinted, listening. Joshua always wondered how much of his meaning was getting through. You had to shout and hope with the troll-call.

'Kid alone?'

'Yeah. I was alone as a kid too. I had friends who cared for me. I think I'd bust the troll-call if I tried to explain Sister Agnes.'

'Hoo.'

'*You're* alone. I can see that. Where's your family?'

The troll spat again, wrapped his arm over his head like an orang-utan, and scratched a filthy armpit. 'Family happy healthy hungry, far away. Babies with mom-and-pop. Mom-and-pop with babies. Old trolls, me, wander off. No babies, no mom-and-pop, wander off. This band, this band, this band.'

Joshua imagined a sub-clan of elderly, solitary trolls, their own cubs grown and independent, the females no longer fertile perhaps, wandering the stepwise landscape, not exactly alone – he guessed a true loner wouldn't survive long – but drifting from one band to another. Had humans ever observed this behaviour? They had probably just assumed the old members they saw in any given troll band were grandparents, even great-grandparents, hanging around to help out the younger generations. Even Lobsang might have fallen into that trap, watching the trolls in the restricted environment of his Low Earths reserve, where old folk such as Sancho wouldn't have had their usual freedom of movement.

Now Sancho tapped his skull. 'Librarian.'

'Yeah. You said that before. You're a Librarian. Is that what they called you at the college? What does it mean, Sancho?'

'Big head. Lots of remember.'

'Memory?'

'Lots of remember. Remember for trolls. Old time, long time past. Weather. Before people.'

'Hm. Before Step Day. When the golden age for trolls ended . . .'

'Head full.'

'Full of what? Memories, I guess. Stories? So is that how you earn your corn? You take your stories around the population?'

'Librarian.'

Joshua smiled. 'Yes, buddy. And I guess all you know is fed into the long call . . .'

He could see how useful such information could be to the trolls, as it would be for any human group. It was always worth cherishing a handful of old folk who could remember what they did the last time the once-a-decade flood came, or the big storm, or the famine, or the bad winter when there was a particular kind of mushroom you could find in the snow to keep you alive . . . Maybe in the case of the trolls there would be information from the deeper past, from generations ago. Memories of volcanic eruptions and quakes and even asteroid strikes, lessons about how trolls had lived through such disasters before.

Joshua started to picture Sancho's mind as a cavern, deep and dark and mysterious, crammed with treasure, with information – with *remember*.

Lobsang had been a student of the trolls since the days of The Journey back in '30. Once Lobsang had told Joshua how culture, unlike an instinctive behaviour, was stored outside the genome, outside the body, beyond any one individual's memory. So human culture was stored in artefacts, books, tools, buildings, a whole heap of inventions and discoveries passed down from the past, there for each new generation to access. It was the same for trolls, except that everything *they* knew about the world was in the long call, the song that was outside the head of any one animal. Lobsang had spoken of the long call as analogous to a computing system, a vast, adaptable network of information encoded in the music.

Well, maybe the Librarians, tough old survivors and full of experience, were like high-density memory stores embedded in that evanescent network, deep caches of the wisdom of a species.

As Joshua reflected on this, Sancho patted his arm with odd tenderness. 'Mom, pop, little kid alone, boo hoo. Old fart alone, who cares?'

The troll felt sorry for him, Joshua realized suddenly. This *animal* felt sorry for him. Resentment sparked briefly. Joshua had never been comfortable under the scrutiny of others, and certainly didn't welcome pity. But that feeling faded quickly. 'You saved my life, old buddy. I guess you earned the right to feel that way.'

'Boo hoo,' the old troll said gently. Then he wrapped

his other arm over his head, and got to work cleaning out the opposite armpit.

That was when Joshua heard a dull droning noise, drifting down from the sky. It didn't sound like any kind of insect swarm, or pterosaur.

Sancho didn't seem perturbed.

'That sounds to me like an aeroplane, old buddy.'

'Hoo?'

'Give me those things . . .' Joshua snatched the sunglasses back from the troll, and jammed them on his own face. He struggled to his feet and peered around, leaning on his crutch, hand over his eyes against the sun. The sound seemed to echo around the arid landscape. It took him a few seconds to spot the plane, a gleaming speck in the bone-dry sky. But it was heading his way now, maybe drawn by the silver gleam of the survival blanket.

When it flew over the bluff with a waggle of wings, Joshua could see the aircraft's smooth white hull, unmarked save for a registration number, and the stylized Black Corporation Buddhist-monk logo that marked a capability to fly stepwise. The wings were stubby, the tail-plane fat, the main body a squat cylinder.

The trolls were profoundly uninterested.

But Joshua grinned. 'Only rode in a plane like that once in my life. And I know who that must be.' Leaning precariously on the crutch, he took off his hat and waved it in the air. 'Rod! Rod Valienté! Down here!'

31

T HE PLANE LANDED without fuss maybe a half-mile
from the bluff. Joshua set off in that direction,
hobbling on his home-made crutch.

Sancho and the other adult trolls displayed a supreme
indifference to the miracle of technology that had suddenly
appeared out of an empty sky. Matt, though, bounded
ahead of Joshua towards the plane, a bundle of curiosity
and energy on the dusty ground.

Matt had reached the plane by the time a hatch opened
and Rod clambered out. He'd already changed out of his
flight suit into a practical if faded shirt, traveller's jacket,
jeans and a broad-brimmed hat, and he carried a heavy-
looking white pack on his back. Matt jumped up and down
before him, slapping himself on the head and rolling in the
dust. Joshua could see his son kneel down, grinning, to
speak to Matt, and then he took something from his pocket
and threw it in the air. Matt caught it one-handed, hooted
and rolled, and then scampered back towards the bluff.

Rod walked in and met his hobbling father not a
hundred yards from the bluff. He slowed, somewhat
warily, as if assessing Joshua's mood. 'Hi, Dad.'

'Rod.'

'Look, Dad, I know I'm breaking your sabbatical. I can also see you're in trouble.' He patted the pack, which Joshua guessed contained medical supplies. 'Well, I came prepared. You're either going to tell me I took my time getting here, or to piss off. Right?'

'Rod—'

'But I didn't come out looking for you on a whim, or just because you're overdue. I have some news for you—'

'Shut your yap.' Joshua stumbled forward and embraced his son. Rod smelled of the plane, of engine oil and electricity and a new-carpet cabin smell. Joshua dreaded to think what *he* smelled like. 'I am in trouble. I busted my damn leg. Thanks for coming, son.'

They broke, awkwardly, and began to plod, at Joshua's snail pace, back to the bluff.

If they were shy of each other, Matt was shy of neither of them. He came back, trailed by his sister Liz, and they both rolled and hooted alongside Rod as he walked. Rod dug into his pockets again. 'Here, you guys, plenty of sugar for both of you.' They snatched the white lumps out of the air and crammed them into their broad mouths.

'You're good with trolls,' Joshua observed.

'What, is that a surprise? Dad, we, my family, we live among trolls. Or they live among us. You ought to know that. You would, if you ever spent any time with us.'

'OK, OK. But you won't stay popular with their mothers and fathers if you keep feeding them sugar.'

Rod raised his eyebrows. 'It's gen-enged, Dad. No dental caries, and slips through the digestive system harmlessly. You're behind the times.'

They reached the rock bluff, and Joshua's rough camp. Sancho still sat on top of the bluff, wrapped once again in the survival blanket. He observed Rod's approach with a grave but remote interest. Rod bowed to him and said, 'Hoo?'

'Hoo.' Sancho turned away, evidently accepting Rod as simply as that.

Joshua said, 'This band of trolls saved my life. Especially Sancho here, after the break. I wouldn't have made it otherwise.'

Rod looked back at Sancho, and nodded. 'I'm impressed. Not surprised, but impressed. Let me get that leg seen to.'

They settled in the shade of the bluff. Rod dropped his pack and unzipped it. In with the med gear he had a small cooler bag, from which he extracted bottles of cold beer. He handed one to his father, with an opener. 'Anaesthetize yourself. Valhalla's finest.'

Sitting in the dirt, Joshua popped off the cap and took a long, luxurious draught. 'That is unreasonably good.'

Rod took a beer for himself, and eyed Sancho. Then he passed a bottle up to the troll.

Sancho took it – the bottle was almost lost in his huge black-haired hand – and eyed it suspiciously. He reached for his troll-call and asked, 'Lite?'

'No way,' Rod said.

The troll grunted, flipped off the cap with a tooth like a tombstone, and took a long pull on the bottle.

Rod washed his hands with a sterilizing fluid, pulled on surgical gloves, and got to work on Joshua's leg. He cut away the rough bandaging, and levered away splints that were stuck to the flesh by chewed-up vegetable matter, a mass of dark green. Rod poked at this. 'A troll poultice?'

Joshua shrugged. 'I guess. I was out when they did this for me. I reapplied some of it myself.'

'I've seen them do this. They gather the stuff, grind it up between their back teeth, and plaster it on. There's a lot of folk medicine stored in those big heads of theirs, and specific to the worlds, or the bands of worlds, they visit . . . There's no sign of infection. Hell, I'd be able to smell it by now. I'll clean all this away, give you a shot of antibiotics.' He looked at his father. 'Look, all I know is field medicine. I'll be clumsier than the trolls probably. You want a painkiller?'

'I'll let you know.' As Rod got to work, Joshua leaned back, cradling the beer. 'So how did you find me?'

'Not hard. Your old buddy Bill Chambers helped a lot. When you were overdue, he called me.'

'Overdue? How the hell could I be overdue? I'm on a sabbatical. By definition, you're not "overdue" on a sabbatical.'

Rod just laughed. 'Bill showed me a spreadsheet he keeps on you.'

'A *spreadsheet*?'

'How long your average stay is, with ninety per cent confidence limits, before you check in with him. Bill knows you as well as anybody, I guess, ever since you were both raising hell in that Home in Madison of yours.'

'I don't check in with anybody.'

'Of course you don't, Dad. So he knows how long you'll be out. And he also has a way of predicting where in the High Meggers you'll go next, based on all the places you visited before. You could call it an algorithm.'

'An *algorithm*?'

'He keeps all this stuff in a box file.'

'A *box file*?'

'Anyhow, once you were overdue, Bill put the word out, and I came looking in the likely spots. And once I'd found the right world I was led here by your radio signal, and the survival blanket draped over your buddy there—'

'*Ouch*.'

'Sorry. You sure you won't have a painkiller?'

'I could take another beer.'

Rod passed him the bottle, and continued working. 'I'll be honest, Dad. When I set off, I did wonder what I'd find. Or if there'd be anything *to* find.'

Joshua frowned. 'Is that what you think? That I was on some kind of death march?' But was it really a shock that Rod should think that way of him? He imagined Bill Chambers's face, as lined and leathery as his own, peering at him sceptically. *I warned ye, if ye kept on goin' out there alone, ye'd get yerself killed, ye fecking eejit. You don't know half the truth about yourself, do ye? . . .*

Rod flinched at the bluntness of Joshua's words. But he said, 'It is difficult for the rest of us to figure out why you need to take these sabbaticals, Dad. Over and over.'

'It's what I've done all my life. Ever since I was trusted by Agnes and the Sisters to be away from the Home for a night on my own.' He struggled to explain. 'Ever since Step Day, when the Long Earth opened up – for me, personally, anyhow – to go back to the Datum, to billions of people packed together on a sliver of a world, a world no thicker than the edge of a knife – it grips your mind like a fist.'

'Hmm. But you're closer to seventy than seventeen now, Dad.' He gestured at the damaged leg with a gloved hand stained vegetable green. 'And it could have been even worse. Bill told me you usually avoid worlds where the troll population is large.'

'They're supposed to be solitary trips. Trolls, bless them, can be kind of noisy neighbours if you're in search of silence. Or, the Silence.'

'So you were lucky. Dad, you have people who need you. Family.'

Joshua glared at him. 'Family who walked away from me.'

Rod looked away, concentrating on his medicine. 'Yeah, well, maybe things are different now.'

'Different how?' Joshua thought back. 'You said you had news for me. What news?'

Rod shrugged. 'Good news, bad news. And some news that won't surprise you.'

'Tell me what won't surprise me.'

'Lobsang's asking for you.'

Joshua sipped his beer, leaned back and laughed. 'No, that doesn't surprise me, damn it. I thought he disappeared again, that he had another of his periodic breakdowns.'

'As I understand it, he did. But your old buddy Nelson Azikiwe went to bring him back.'

'Went where? Never mind. So there's some new crisis blowing up in the Long Earth, is there?'

'Isn't there always? And they want you back, Dad, Nelson and Lobsang—'

'Same old same old. Tell me the bad news,' Joshua said bluntly.

233

Rod looked at him. 'Sister Agnes died.'

'Ah. OK.'

'There was a kind of service, at the Home. I'm sorry, Dad. I know how close you were.'

'Sure. Even after she was brought back by Lobsang, she was still Agnes. Adds up to a lot of decades, I guess. But we said our goodbyes. So what's the good news?'

And now, Joshua could swear, Rod blushed under his tan. 'Sofia is pregnant. Now, Dad, if you don't remember who she is—'

'Sofia Piper. Give me some credit. Your . . .' He hesitated, not wanting to use the wrong word. 'Partner?'

'Close enough.'

'So you're going to be a father.' Again, was that the right word, when it applied to Rod's extended family? 'A biological father, I mean.'

'Sure. And you're going to be a biological grandfather,' Rod said dryly.

Well, that was good news. And unexpected. In fact, a shock. It felt as if the world was reconfiguring around Joshua, as if everything around him, his relationship with his son, even the rocks and the trees and the trolls, had a new significance.

And so much for any auto-destruct loops inside his head, if they existed in the first place.

'Wow,' he said at length.

'So what are you thinking?' Rod asked.

'I don't suppose you have any cigars in there.'

'Have another beer.'

'You always said you weren't going to do this. Have a kid of your own.'

Rod shrugged again. 'We're human beings. A complex mystery. Guess what? We changed our minds.'

'You fell in love with this Sofia, is what you did.'

'I guess. Having her nephews around us the whole time kind of influenced us as well, I think. We always hated saying goodbye to them. The rest of the family threw a party when they found out. That's our way.'

'OK. But, Rod . . .'

'Yes?'

'Thanks for coming out. Thanks for telling me.'

Rod looked embarrassed. 'Well, I had to come save your ass anyway. I couldn't *not* tell you—'

'Thanks anyway.'

'Whatever.'

And, Joshua decided, now *wasn't* the time to remind Rod about Oswald Hackett, and the Fund, and the gruesome genetic legacy of the Valientés. Joshua had chosen to live with it and move on; maybe Rod had made the same decision.

Rod sat back at last and started peeling off his surgical gloves. 'Done. That will hold until we get you back to Valhalla or the Lows. So.' He glanced at the sky. 'Time for lunch?'

'Why not? I've been sharing with the trolls. My camp-fires, my spices, their meat. Rod, I've got to tell you that troll cuisine is most suitable for somebody who's really, really hungry . . .'

Rod grinned. 'I know that, Dad. I'll go get some more beers from the plane.'

32

THE KILLER STAR glared out of the early evening sky of Earth West 3,141.

It was bright enough to cast a shadow, Sister Coleen saw, even in competition with the setting sun. Brighter than any star of the usual constellations – brighter than Venus, brighter than the moon. But the sky in which it shone was obscured by drifting smoke. On the horizon a bank of forest burned fitfully, a line of fire spilling down a hillside like a special effect from *The Lord of the Rings* – another of Jan's favourite movies. And a river beneath the airship's prow seemed to be choked with the bodies of some big herbivore species, whole herds dead and washed away.

'A supernova,' Roberta said grimly.

'Good grief,' said Sister Coleen.

Jan arrived, wide-eyed, still holding the hand of the young sailor who'd brought him to this observation deck.

When the time had come for Jan to be taken to the Next's project on West 3,141,592, for the leg to Valhalla Roberta had booked passage for the two of them on a commercial twain, an ordinary ship. The crew were used to handling kids and had been good with Jan. Now the boy stood between Roberta and Sister Coleen and stared out, uncomprehending. Coleen rested her hand on his shoulder.

Roberta said, 'Now, Jan, here's what's special about *this* pi world. Incredible to think that all this came from a star maybe a thousand light years away, a collapse that took just a second . . .'

'A supernova,' Jan said. 'I read about that.'

'A distant supernova, yes – not distant enough. There'd have been no warning for the creatures of this world. The first wave of destruction would have arrived at the speed of light, with the image of the detonation itself: high-energy gamma rays, X-rays, battering down as soon as the explosion was visible. The ozone layer would have been stripped away, the surface pounded by solar ultraviolet. It was probably so sudden it would have overwhelmed even most stepping creatures. And the supernova isn't done yet. There's a wave of cosmic rays on the way, travelling slower than light, that will arrive here in a few years.'

'Ma'am, we still don't have a full count of human casualties,' the sailor said. 'The first reports came from travellers trying to pass through a few days later. Of course the Long Earth is a kind of disorganized place. They'll probably have to wait for missing-person reports to come filtering in.'

'Gee,' Jan said simply, in a small voice. 'Do they know which star it was?'

'Not yet,' Roberta said. 'The astronomers at Valhalla U or the Gap will probably be able to figure it out. There are plenty of candidates. Big bloated stars, any one of which, through some chance event in this particular universe, might have gone up. Sirius, Canopus, Rigel, Altair, Deneb, Spica, Vega—'

Jan looked at her. 'Vega?'

Sister Coleen hadn't known about this event either. 'And it's scary this is so close to home. You think supernovas are things that happen out in the High Meggers. Not here—'

'Not here in the Ice Belt,' Roberta said. 'Not in the Datum's home belt, no. We estimate that a nearby supernova should affect only one in ten million stepwise worlds. So it's unlucky to find one so close.

'Now, Jan, this is about the worst damage this universe can inflict: an extinction event that can span thousands of light years. But you mustn't be scared of it. If the supernova hammers you, there's nothing to be done about that. We must be humble in the face of the universe, as we Next say. But with time, and granted a *lot* of time, life rises, intelligence recovers, the building starts again. And if the world is Long, the recovery's even quicker. In a few years, when it's safe, people will be coming back, right here. Trolls too. Bringing animals, seeds. Restoring this Earth to life.' She bent over, slightly, to face Jan, stiff, a little awkward. 'And, Jan, now we've received the Invitation. A message from some kind of people far away. So you see, for all the horrors of things like supernovas, the universe is filled with life.' She studied the boy with a rather forced smile. 'It must be.'

Jan seemed to think this over. 'Vega, though,' he said at length. 'That's where Ellie Arroway went. I know it's just a story. But I wonder what happened to the folks up there.'

33

ROD HAD DECIDED to stay on a few days. There was no rush to get back, he told his father, although Joshua wondered how true that was, given Rod had a pregnant partner out in the green – and given what Rod had told him about Lobsang asking for him. But Rod said he wanted to make sure Joshua's leg was stable before committing him to what was going to be a long journey home, if an easy one inside the step-capable plane.

So they settled in.

The trolls took to Rod at once, Joshua observed. Of course his gambit of handing out sugar lumps hadn't hurt. But Rod was young and healthy and evidently used to trolls, and he was also a hell of a lot more active than Joshua had ever been, even before he busted his leg and became a dependant. He played games with the youngsters, with Matt and Liz – throwing, chasing, racing, mounting mock-hunts. He was savvy enough not to try to join in the trolls' favourite play activity of wrestling, as even a cub, as Joshua knew from experience, had a grip strong enough to crack a rib. He checked out Joshua's traps and set a few of his own. And of course there was the fire that he and

Joshua banked up every night, to deter the teeth and claws of the dark – and to produce the vast quantities of cooked meat that the trolls consumed with relish.

In the evenings they had long, slow, rambling conversations – as slow as Joshua's healing process had been, it felt like sometimes, and maybe that wasn't a bad analogy. A lot of healing to be done, between father and son. But Joshua was intrigued at Rod's news of what was becoming a sensation across the Long Earth: the Invitation, some kind of SETI message from the sky, and rumours of a tremendous industrial project being managed by the Next, so the gossip went, out in the High Meggers – indeed, beyond the Gap. Always something new in the Long Earth, Joshua reflected.

On the third day of his stay, Rod won even more fans among the trolls by helping out with a hunt.

It started with excitement as troll scouts, flicking back and forth between stepwise worlds, reported back in snatches of song that they'd come across a big old male elephant, wounded somehow, who had got left behind by his bachelor herd. Joshua sat with Rod and Sancho and listened as the trolls' unending song absorbed their reports, and more scouts flickered across to investigate the find. Sancho kept up rough commentaries for Rod and Joshua through the troll-call.

And when the younger adult males and females got together to prepare for the hunt – arming themselves with stone knives, the song becoming sharper and ever more exciting – Rod picked up a couple of his own knives, and a spear Joshua had been idly whittling from a straight and smooth sapling trunk, and jogged over to join the band.

240

Joshua couldn't resist going too. This would be by far the most spectacular kill the band had attempted in the time he'd been with them. So he had Sancho help him up, and they hopped between the worlds until they found the site of the kill, so they could watch.

The trolls had already surrounded the bull elephant. The beast had a huge tear at the top of one thigh, presumably inflicted by some big predator, and, distressed, was unable to move far. The ground under his feet was already stained with his own blood.

And now the trolls closed in.

The bull fought back. He trumpeted and tossed his head, using the big mask of armour plating over his face to keep out the hammer blows of troll fists, and swiping at his circling assailants with leading edges of sharp bone. Rod, Joshua was relieved to see, stayed well out of this close-range battle, as the trolls strove to beat and stab and club the bull into submission.

But when the bull scattered his troll tormentors with a particularly vigorous effort and stood briefly alone, trumpeting and raising his trunk, Rod hurled Joshua's spear. The point slammed into the bull's cheek, at a vulnerable spot just behind the facial armour. The elephant shrieked, and blood gushed from his mouth and trunk. As Rod stood back and watched, the trolls closed in once more, clubbing the dying animal to the ground.

Sancho, watching impassively, used the troll-call. 'Good throw.'

'That's my son.'

Sancho looked Joshua up and down. He asked, witheringly, 'True? Yours? Ha!'

241

* * *

By the end of the day the trolls were replete with elephant steak, and were relaxing. Mothers suckled their infants, the males inspected their armpits and other orifices for fleas and parasites, the cubs rolled around languidly mock-wrestling, and some of the younger adults patiently knapped tools, practising the skill and adding to the litter on the floor that was their endlessly replenished store-house. One or two couples had the usual noisy, explosive, blink-and-you-miss-it sex. And the unending song hung like a cloud over the group, a comforting murmur.

Joshua sat with Sancho as usual, with the big troll wrapped in the silver blanket he had made his own. And Rod was with them tonight, still splashed with some of the blood of the elephant he'd helped kill and butcher.

Joshua ventured, 'I know I said it before, but I wish I'd known how well you got on with trolls.'

'That's because you've never seen me out in the green, Dad. Me and my family. This is how we *live*. We encourage our kids to do this. Be with the trolls. I mean, you have to make sure the children stay safe – trolls are big heavy animals and can be clumsy . . . But the benefits outweigh that. Trolls are pretty different from people, and to get along you have to discover what you have in common and build on that. It clarifies the mind.'

'Hmm. You're learning what it is to be a sapient, in this complicated universe. While all the time you *think* you're knapping a blade or building a fire.'

'That's it. And our kids just soak up the lessons. Such as, clear up your mess.'

Joshua smiled. 'I can play that game. How about – learn from your mistakes?'

'Don't steal.'

'Don't take – in fact it helps if you can give.'

'Know yourself.'

That one surprised Joshua. 'As deep as that?'

'Why not? The treatment of trolls in the Long Earth has got a lot better since your day, Dad.'

'My day? I'm not out to pasture yet, son.'

'Didn't you once petition President Starling about cruelty to trolls?'

'Yes, but he was plain Senator Jim back then. Still, perhaps it made a difference in the end.'

'We ought to turn in. I'm thinking of preparing the plane tomorrow, for a launch possibly the day after.'

'What's the urgency?'

Rod grinned. 'Only that we're running out of beer now that your pal Sancho has the taste for it . . .'

As it happened, that plan never worked out.

34

Long before Rod had shown up in the plane, Joshua had been walking, every day a little further.

For most of the winter he'd used crutches – branches brought in from the forest clumps by Sally or Patrick and then shaped with his own knives. It had taken some work to get them to the right length, and to make them reasonably comfortable to use he'd sacrificed one of his shirts to make cushions stuffed with moss to ride under his armpits. He'd also fire-hardened the flat tips of the crutches where they hit the ground, but even so they wore rapidly.

Still, every day, further.

He would walk around the bluff, and to the forest clumps, and along the bank of the river, trying to restore the strength in his good leg, his arms, his back. His best recourse in the case of most threats remained just stepping away, which would put him out of range of all predators save humanoids, such as elves. But, he'd figured, if he was ever going to attempt to step his way back to the more inhabited Earths he was always going to need some mobility, just to escape from threats like floods, and avoid geographical shifts like the rise of the Valhallan worlds' inland seas. Hence the crutches and the determined hiking.

Then of course Rod had shown up. Now Joshua had decent crutches of Valhallan manufacture, fold-out light-weight affairs from the plane's medical stores, and he had a much easier way to get back home, in the plane, than by stepping out of here. But still he walked, every day, building up his strength. After all, you never knew; he and Rod were a long way from home, and if the plane failed them they might still need to rely on their own strength to survive.

This particular day Joshua was stumping along the bank of the river, idly listening to the wash of the trolls' song, its casual beauty all around him as usual. This remained a dangerous world, and wherever he walked he always carried a selection of weapons: his knives, his bronze handgun. And he tried to make sure he was in sight of plenty of trolls. Glancing around now he saw Sally playing with Liz by the bluff, and some of the males further away, flickering as they stepped in and out of the world, maybe scouting out a hunt. There was old Sancho sitting cross-legged on top of the bluff, wearing Joshua's silver survival blanket like a cape. Joshua had to smile at the sight: a hairy Superman. Rod was visible in the middle distance, working on the plane.

And then, as he worked his way down the river bank, trying to stay clear of the clinging river-bank mud which could swallow a foot or so of his crutches, Joshua saw young Matt, alone, crouched by the water, singing and idly drawing shapes in the mud with one forefinger.

Nobody else was close to him. Nobody to come running if the worst happened, with a choice of options for 'worst'.

Which was odd.

How had Matt got himself so isolated? Troll cubs had good instincts for that kind of thing – and, as Sally Linsay had always said, if you didn't develop good instincts you didn't last long out in the High Meggers. Something must have made Matt *think* he was still close enough to the others that the usual alarm bells hadn't sounded.

Joshua reached Matt and stood there, breathing hard, his bad leg a dead weight. Swivelling on his crutches, Joshua searched the empty landscape nearby, the river bank, the water. Save for the troll cub at his feet he was alone – no other trolls in sight from here. Matt didn't even look up. He was just a troll by the river, playing in the mud, singing softly, joining in with the group's ongoing song, drawn into the music . . .

The song. That was it, that was what didn't fit. The song was too damn loud. That was why Matt hadn't been alarmed; he'd been listening to the song and, consciously or not, he'd read its volume as signifying plenty of trolls close by. But they weren't. And if the trolls *weren't* singing the song he heard, who was? Or *what*—

As if on cue, at that moment the animal burst from the water. And all Joshua could see was teeth.

The river beast was nothing like the gator-like river hunters Joshua had seen, and studiously avoided, before in this world. This was some kind of humanoid in fact, a kind unfamiliar to Joshua, with a massive body, over-muscled and sleek with streamlined fur, and a mouth, yes, a mouth that looked like it was full of alligator teeth. Joshua would never have believed that a thing like an otter on steroids could ever have evolved a way to sing so beautifully.

But in retrospect, when Joshua had a chance to think it over, the development of this kind of predator was obvious.

Predators evolved to exploit the weaknesses of their prey, and one stratagem was to lie, to deceive the credulous. Thus carnivorous flowers lured insects into their lethal maws with colourful but mendacious promises of nectar.

What characterized the trolls above all was their song. An individual troll was drawn into the song, was immersed in it, was distracted by it. The song was an expression of the identity of the group, within which an individual, especially a cub like Matt, felt as safe as he ever could be. So, if you as a hopeful predator could *mimic* the song . . . You didn't need to capture the full richness of it; you didn't need to relate the history of every troll back to the primeval Datum Earth savannah. You just needed to capture whatever essence of it entranced a young troll and caused him to lose that natural caution, to make him feel safe when in fact he was in lethal danger.

Just a few heartbeats of distraction: that would be enough.

For Joshua, time slowed to a crawl.

Matt hadn't moved, even now, even as the singing killer raced up the beach at him, its mouth gaping blood-red. An adult troll would just step away from such a danger, but juvenile trolls tended not to step if they were separated

247

from their parents, for fear of getting lost. So Matt would keep on sitting there, just long enough . . .

'Not on my watch, damn it!'

Joshua threw aside his crutches and, even as he toppled, reached for his weapons with two free hands, and hurled a hunting knife. He managed to lodge the blade in one big cold eye. 'Yes!' Then he fired his electric handgun right into that gaping mouth, aiming for a dangling organ at the back of the throat that burst like a balloon, splashing blood.

The beast turned its wounded head, roaring. And, driven on by its own inertia, it came crashing to the ground, just missing Matt, who scrambled out of the way, and Joshua too, who fell and rolled aside.

Thwarted, the beast wriggled on its belly and slid smoothly back into the water, trailing a stream of blood.

Joshua struggled to sit up, and looked for Matt. The cub was staring around, bewildered. They needed to get out of here. The beast had been injured but hardly disabled, and Joshua had to expect its return any instant, with a grudge – but his crutches were out of his reach—

Strong troll hands grabbed him under the armpits, and he was hauled away from the water. His bad leg clattered over the ground, and he howled in agony. But he saw that Patrick had picked up Matt and was hurrying away with him. The cub was safe.

More of the adult trolls came running now, hurling boulders the size of Joshua's head into the river, yelling and beating their chests. The singing beast surfaced again, blood trailing from its mouth and a clear liquid dripping from its broken eye. It faced a bunch of angry, wary trolls.

Even so, Joshua could see it tensing for another spring. The trolls gathered closer, their shouts ever more defiant.

Then Rod came running through the group. Wearing his orange flight suit – evidently he'd come straight from the plane – he was yelling, and he brandished a kind of fat, bright red pistol.

'Rod! No! Get back!'

But Rod surely never heard his father over the shouting of the trolls and the roar of the singer beast, and he wouldn't have obeyed him in any case. He ran past the trolls and right up to the singer, dwarfed by its bulk. He held up that pistol – now Joshua recognized it as a flare gun – and fired it at point-blank range into the singer's jaw.

The result was spectacular. The flare burst inside the beast's huge mouth; the animal vomited smoke that was illuminated from behind by glaring orange light. The trolls scrambled back, as scared by the flare as by the singer.

But the singer, though howling with pain, wasn't finished. Smoke still pouring from between its jaws, it bent down, effortlessly scooped up Rod like a doll in its small forelimbs – and vanished.

Joshua, still calling for Rod, struggling to stand without his crutches, saw it all. It had stepped! Of course it had; it was a humanoid; Long Earth humanoids stepped. Now Joshua himself frantically stepped into the worlds to East and West, one step, two; he couldn't stand, he was sprawled on the ground, but he could *step* – Joshua Valienté had always been able to step. But there was no sign of them in the worlds next door, though a few trolls huddled there, having instinctively stepped away from trouble. No sign of the singer beast, or of Rod. And though he called until he was hoarse, and stepped over and over again, somehow Joshua knew that wherever Rod was, it was further, much further away than this.

At last he returned to the trolls' base world. As soon as he arrived back, Sally came running over, Matt's mother. Weeping, she wrapped her arms around Joshua's chest and held him close.

His mouth full of black hair, he struggled against her, struggled to speak. 'You've got to help me. I lost Rod, I lost my son. You must help. Sancho! Get me Sancho . . .'

35

As the Navy twain USS *Charles M. Duke* made its final stepwise approach to Earth West 3,141,592, Admiral Maggie Kauffman, standing in the observation lounge at the prow of the ship, was aware of the craft's deliberate reduction of its stepping rate. And she could see why the *Duke* was slowing, for though the mid-American landscapes of these last few worlds seemed uninhabited, the skies were full of traffic: big cargo-carrying twains that flickered in her view as they made their own steps towards the destination. Some of them hauled engineering components so big they had to be carried outside the holds of the craft themselves, slung in cradles beneath the gondolas. Hence the caution. You couldn't step into a place already occupied by another solid object, such as a twain, and it played hell with your steering if you tried, and you didn't want problems with that given the size and complexity of some of the loads being shipped in here. Maggie refused to be impressed by the scale of the operation, however, as ships and cargoes flickered in and out of existence above the barren ground.

'It's as if the whole damn sky is a badly edited 3-D movie,' she groused.

Standing with her was Captain Jane Sheridan, extracted from other duties to deliver Maggie for this bizarre tour of inspection of the Messengers, Inc. installation. 'There *is* a massive flow of materials and labour in and out of Apple Pi,' Sheridan said. 'There's no industrial concentration like it outside the Low Earths. Even Valhalla doesn't compare, and that's the largest city in the High Meggers.'

The result, in these neighbouring worlds, was a sky full of ships and cargo.

'And none of this existed a few months back, right? Which is no doubt why Ed Cutler was beat up to get some kind of control over the situation, and why he in turn beat up on *me* . . . You know, I'm old enough to remember that first jaunt of Joshua Valienté's, when he *discovered* the Gap. Now here we are a million worlds further on, and there's all *this*.'

Jane Sheridan was a very able young officer who had probably been born a decade or more after Valienté's Journey, and she politely declined to respond to Maggie's old-lady mumblings. 'It's all been a fantastic rush since the Messengers, the Next, began their programme of contracting out the design, manufacture and assembly. Traffic control has been an issue. As you can see. The Navy has already designated clear loading zones in Apple Pi itself. The one we're heading to is reserved for Navy and other government traffic. The base is called Little Cincinnati, by the way; that's the footprint we'll be in. All these control procedures are initiatives of officers in situ. Of course, ma'am, you may want to review all that when you've got your feet under the table.'

Maggie grunted. 'Unless I can persuade Ed Cutler to pass this dream job to some other sap. Just tell me this – *Apple Pi*?'

Sheridan shrugged. 'I'm not sure where the name came from, ma'am. But you know that the Next who initiated this project selected the target world partly because of its stepwise designation—'

'The digits of pi, OK. And some bozo thought that was funny?'

'Well, we are the Navy, ma'am. And it is a footprint of North America that's being rebuilt here.'

Maggie stared at her. '"North America, being rebuilt"? That seems an odd way to put it.'

'Best if you see for yourself, ma'am,' Sheridan said diplomatically. She pointed down. 'There's our own ground spotter.'

A guy in a yellow high-vis jacket waved paddles, and Maggie heard a crackle of radio communication. For the last few worlds the visual spotters stepped ahead of incoming twains at walking pace, one world at a time, to ensure there were no collisions.

'Almost there, Admiral . . .'

Even given the crowded skies of the neighbouring worlds, it was a shock to make the last step into Apple Pi.

After the usual vegetation-green landscape in the world next door, suddenly the twain hovered over a carpet of technology. There were heaps of components everywhere, some evidently metallic and painted with a dull-red corrosion-proof paint, some of more enigmatic materials

– ceramics, perhaps. Many of the components, especially the big ones, had an oddly organic look, not like regular engineering at all, with sweeps and curves and blisters, like spray-painted seaweed, Maggie thought, on a huge scale.

From the air it looked to Maggie like she was flying over some vast engineering storage yard, a yard that filled the landscape from the middle distance all the way to the horizon, into which twains descended industriously, like bees dropping into a field of flowers.

The Navy drop area below, kept clear of Messenger engineering as Sheridan had said, was a broad slab of concrete marked with roughly painted landing zones. Ground vehicles skimmed between a scatter of temporary buildings, prefabricated units or just canvas. Maggie saw there were a number of ships already down, tethered to mooring pylons. For all the scale of it there was a sense of haste, of improvisation. A Stars and Stripes, holographically enhanced, hung limply on a flagpole.

And all of this under a mundane American springtime sky, blue with scattered clouds, a faint threat of rain in the afternoon . . .

She grunted. 'I wish I knew what in hell this is all about.'

Sheridan said carefully, 'I rather think the senior commanders hope—'

'That I'm going to figure it all out for them? In their dreams.'

As soon as the twain was anchored, Sheridan led Maggie, escorted by a couple of junior officers, down a staircase to the ground. The air, after the processed atmosphere of the twain, was oppressive and smelled of engine oil, hot metal and wet concrete, and, stepping down the stairs in her heavy uniform, Maggie felt every one of her sixty-nine years.

There was a reception committee waiting for her at the bottom of the stair, beside a small electric ground vehicle.

'Oh, Christ,' she said. 'There's Ed Cutler himself. I'm being thrown in the deep end.'

'I'll be right beside you, ma'am.'

Cutler came forward to greet her. Aside from a couple of junior officers – both armed, Maggie noticed – his only companion was a middle-aged woman in a sober business suit, who hung back, formal, reserved. Maggie thought she looked familiar.

'Admiral Kauffman,' Cutler said, saluting. 'Welcome to the nut house.'

She saluted back. 'Glad to be here, Admiral Cutler.'

'Call me Ed. When we're in private, anyhow. I think we've known each other far too long for formalities, you and I . . .'

Maggie inspected him sceptically. Ed Cutler was just as she'd known him all the years, in fact the decades, they'd worked together. Thin, intense, fragile, devoted to order and control, he was a man a lot better suited to a desk job than to the complex realities of the field. More than once Maggie and her officers had had to save the day for him, for instance the time he'd lost his head while the Navy and other agencies were trying to contain a more or less peaceful rebellion in Valhalla. Yet he was a survivor. And he was a man who followed orders no matter how inimical

255

they might be to him personally. That was why his superiors valued him, why promotion had followed promotion.

And now, beyond his own retirement age, he had the rank of admiral, and was commander of USLONGCOM, the vast military command zone that comprised all of the Long Earths – and in practice, out here in the High Meggers, only President Damasio herself wielded more power. But nothing Ed Cutler ever attained or did was going to impress Maggie.

'Well, here I am, Ed. Shall we get on with it?'

Ed grinned at Sheridan. 'There you are, you see, Captain. That's what I value most in the Admiral here. Decisiveness. Urgency. Yes indeed, Maggie, we've a lot to see. I've done my best to sort this mess out, but you're better suited to a job like this, and I need to get back to my other responsibilities. Look, I know you've had no proper briefing notes. That's the damn Long Earth for you – every communication has to be carried by the Pony Express. I've arranged an introductory tour for you, to get you started right away.'

'Thanks.'

He turned and gestured to his companion, the woman. 'First I need to introduce you—'

'We've met before.' The woman, hair tied tightly back, bespectacled, smiled thinly and extended her hand.

'Roberta Golding,' Maggie said, remembering, and she took the woman's hand. The shake was firm, determined. 'Yes, we have met. After the Happy Landings incident . . .' Where Ed Cutler had had an extraordinary part to play, Maggie reflected, when he had smuggled aboard her ship a nuclear weapon intended to eliminate the Next altogether. That was a quarter of a century back. And now here he was standing beside this representative of the Next as if she was a business partner. 'Strange times, Doctor Golding.'

'Strange indeed, Admiral. Though it's "Professor" now. Not that such titles matter in the face of all this.' She gestured around.

'Your project, you mean.'

'Well, it isn't *ours*. We Next, and our human allies, are just – facilitators, I suppose. The project belongs to the Sagittarians – which is one name we have for the agency at the heart of the Galaxy who sent the Invitation in the first place.'

Maggie sighed. 'Straight off the twain, and I'm already discussing galactic alien intelligences with an authenticated superhuman megabrain.'

Sheridan caught her eye. 'That's why they called in the Navy, Admiral.'

Roberta said, 'I for one am glad to see you, Admiral. I do remember your decisiveness over the Happy Landings affair – and your good judgement. I hope that your presence here will progress the project.'

Maggie frowned. 'What I'm here to progress is national security.'

'Of course. But the two objectives need not be in conflict.'

'We'll be the judge of that,' Ed Cutler said briskly. 'Very little of this project is under the control of the federal government, let alone USLONGCOM – even though it is all entirely within the US Aegis. And it's all been so darn *fast.* Come and hop aboard this electric runabout.' He turned and led the way; the party filed aboard the little vehicle, selected seats, fixed seat belts. 'I want to show you some of the work being done here, Maggie. Stuff on the ground. Who we've got working here. And our, umm, guests.'

'Guests?'

'You'll see,' he growled. The vehicle pulled away, driven by one of Cutler's armed junior officers. 'As I recall, you were the first to appoint non-humans to your twain crew. First trolls, then those damn dogs.'

'Beagles. They're called beagles.'

'That's one reason I pushed for your selection for this job. You're probably going to feel right at home in this zoo. Look, Maggie, we've had direct pressure from the administration to deal with this. I spoke to President Damasio herself. Hell of a thing to have dumped in your lap in the middle of your first term. And from the administration's point of view this came out of nowhere. All we were aware of initially was a huge diversion of manufacturing capability from the Low Earths, even from the Datum. And the creation of more capacity, in fact.' He glanced at Roberta. 'None of us knew the Next were so damn wealthy, in human terms.'

'We do command significant resources,' Roberta said. 'Amassed through selling appropriate ideas and innovations to human entrepreneurs, and investing the proceeds. This is carefully done, to avoid destabilization.'

'Carefully done, my ass,' Cutler growled. 'Maggie, the first we heard was squawks from some of the post-Yellowstone reclamation and conservation agencies about the industrial resource that was suddenly being diverted away from their projects. And then we had a flood of patents from get-rich-quick types who got their mitts on bits of ET tech. Then came campaigns from the paranoid types who think it's all some kind of alien trap, a Trojan Horse.'

'You forgot the Chinese,' Jane Sheridan said with a flash of humour.

'Cripes, yes. Who want a piece of the alien pie for their own economic purposes. And because of *that* you have Long Unity desk jockeys here too . . .'

Actually Maggie quietly approved of the Long Unity, a kind of low-key offshoot of the old UN that was extending carefully into the Long Earth, offering help, support, connectivity across an increasingly scattered mankind. The Long Unity, at least, was harmless.

'To get all this built the Next've been using sly ways of influencing folk, recruiting them to the cause. It's all over the Aegis. Not just the big industrial combines: cottage industry stuff. Hobbyists. Kids in home workshops, building pieces of it. We only discovered all this after the fact. Well, the President set up an advisory committee. You've got the National Science Foundation, NASA, the DoD, the National Security Council, the security agencies, and every goddamn futurologist and think tank we can find. But the whole operation was up and running before we were properly aware of it; we've been playing catch-up from the start.'

'And so they called in the Navy.'

Cutler grinned. 'Well, hell, we were here already. Because we're everywhere. Maggie, you know as well as I do that things have kind of dissolved in the years since Yellowstone. It's only the Navy that has kept its shape, especially in the form of the twain fleets. Yes, they sent for the Navy, because across the Aegis there's nobody else to send for . . .'

The President sent for the Navy, Maggie thought sourly, and the Navy sent for me. Well, it was obvious the science was going to be a big element here. She made a mental note to send for Margarita Jha, who had served as her science officer on expeditions that had taken them to even stranger places than this . . .

Cutler was still doing his best to alarm her. 'We don't know what kind of threat we're facing here. What does this—' he waved a hand at the industrialized landscape '—this almighty boondoggle mean for our economic capacity? And although it's contained within the US Aegis – within this copy of the North American landmass – that seems to be chance, it's where the Next happened to choose to build the thing; *they* don't recognize our international boundaries, as you know, Maggie, any more than we care about chimp territories in the jungle. So how are we going to square all this with the Chinese and the rest? What's it going to do to our relationship with the Next? *That* is a strategic question, believe me. And, above all – what *is* this thing? What's it for? What will it be capable of doing when it's complete?'

Maggie glanced at Roberta. 'Reasonable questions, I would think. Given that all this is being built in the US Aegis.'

Roberta said smoothly, 'Well, the location was specified in the Invitation – as we discovered once we

260

had begun to decode it. As to what the Thinker is for—'

That was the first time Maggie had heard the name. 'The Thinker? What the hell is it thinking about?'

Roberta smiled. 'We believe it will tell us itself, when it's ready.'

Cutler snarled, 'And in the meantime we have to trust it, and you. And all we get out of you Next is the same platitudinous bull crap.'

Maggie said, 'The President's experts must have some ideas.'

Cutler shrugged. 'Only guesses. You know me, Maggie. I tend to side with more conservative opinions. The woolly space dreamer types tell me I'm paranoid. Why would anybody bother to reach out from the centre of the Galaxy to harm *us*? Well, I say, they've reached out all that way for *something*.'

Roberta said, 'We too are divided. But most of us believe implicitly in the benevolent nature of this project. This gesture from the stars.'

Cutler glanced at Maggie meaningfully. 'And *we* remember New Springfield.'

Maggie understood Cutler's unspoken meaning. If Roberta Golding was wrong, if this machine did turn out to be harmful after all – well, then, it would be Maggie's duty to stop it.

If she could figure out how.

36

ONCE OUT OF the relatively clear spaces of the Navy camp, they drove along narrow dirt tracks through a landscape crowded with incomprehensible machinery.

Cutler pointed to a wooden post with a red-painted top and a number etched into its side. 'You can see we're trying to impose some organization on this place.'

Roberta said, 'To a large extent the whole facility is self-organizing. The Thinker itself has, or at least is incrementally developing, a knowledge of its own necessary layout—'

'All of which wordy bullshit is no use to your average truck driver from Detroit trying to find his drop point. So we've sent up a couple of Navy twains to map and number the emerging zones, according to a system of our own.'

Roberta said dryly, 'Painting all those little signposts does keep a lot of people in uniform gainfully occupied.'

'Yeah,' Cutler said entirely without irony, 'that's another advantage.'

They entered what Roberta called a manufacturing zone. The cart rolled to a halt outside a kind of factory, a long, low building of aluminium walls and big glass ceiling panels. As she walked in, crossing a floor of hastily laid concrete, Maggie saw what looked like assembly lines, and some equipment she recognized: angular construction robots that she'd expect to see in a twain shipyard, automated forklift trucks shifting loads to and fro, and a big overhead frame from which heavy chains dangled. More robots than people, she figured, but the people she could see were hard at work. What they were working *on* was the mystery.

Cutler said, 'I picked this site to show you because it has a cast of characters of a representative type, as you'll see . . .'

'Including my young friends from the Gap.' Roberta abruptly took the lead, striding across the floor to a small workshop area, curtained off floor to ceiling by dust-excluding translucent sheets. At their approach a couple of workers emerged: a man and a woman, both looking no older than thirty to Maggie, and wearing blue coveralls with GapSpace logos at the breast. The woman was holding a slab of some glass-like substance.

The man spoke. 'Good to see you, Professor Golding.' He indicated himself and his co-worker. 'Dev Bilaniuk. Lee Malone. Both GapSpace employees and shareholders . . .'

When Maggie and Cutler were introduced, the workers didn't seem fazed by their high ranks or military uniforms. Or, indeed, particularly interested, Maggie thought.

Lee said, 'We were told you would want to see what we're working on. This is a sample.' She held up the slab of material. 'Actually this item failed its integration tests, so it's safe to remove it from the sterile area. We'll break it up for components and reuse them later . . .'

Maggie was allowed to hold the assembly. It was indeed glass-like, with a complex internal structure dimly glimpsed, like some fantastically complicated quartz crystal. And yet it was evidently artificial, for she saw subcomponents within: what looked to her like silicon chips, threads of wire or cable, and tiny light sources that glowed in constellations, green and gold. 'It's like a whole world in there,' she said.

Lee smiled. 'Beautiful, isn't it? It wouldn't be meaningful to say that we *made* this. It's more a question of self-assembly – well, it's that way for all the Thinker's components, save the simplest structural pieces.'

Dev said, 'We were assigned to this work because of our technical experience with GapSpace. Even using the Gap, the space programme depends a lot on miniaturization. Actually, we two got involved in the first place because we were working on the in-Gap RT that detected the Invitation.'

Maggie asked warily, 'RT?'

'Radio telescope,' Roberta murmured.

'Tell her what she's looking at,' Cutler snapped.

'It's one of the smarter submodules,' Dev said. 'I mean, most of the components seem to be smart to some extent, and the whole assembly, when completed . . . Well, we haven't got a handle on how smart *that* will be yet. What you have there is an approximation to a kind of computronium.'

That left Maggie flailing again. 'A what-now?'

Roberta smiled. 'A human name for an alien technology.'

264

Lee said, 'A substance where every grain – even every molecule, every atom – is devoted to information processing. This is probably some way short of the ultimate realization. But we can recognize computing systems on a variety of scales, all the way from the mechanical – see those little levers? – down through the electronic, transistors and such, through chemical and nano and, we think, quantum.'

Dev said, 'But we think the real beef is in the material structure itself. It's a kind of diamond, engineered carbon, just as it looks. More advanced as a material even than space elevator thread.'

Roberta said, 'And an innovation which alone is revolutionizing human industries.'

Cutler rubbed his chin. 'Makes you think about the scale of what's going on here, doesn't it? You have rivers of twains in the sky, a steady flow of raw materials across the Long Earth. And you have *this*, in the palm of your hand, with a computer in every damn molecule.'

Maggie said, 'How smart, exactly?'

Dev said, 'Well, we estimate the data store at ten to twenty-two power bits per gram.' At Maggie's blank expression, he said, 'That's, um, ten billion trillion bits—'

Roberta said, 'By comparison, a human brain, and a Next one come to that, stores around one hundred trillion bits. Smaller by a factor of a hundred million. In fact the number he quoted is ten times more than mankind's estimated current global data store.'

Cutler snorted. 'That doesn't sound so much.'

Maggie said, 'But he said, *per gram*.' She hefted the

block. 'What does this mass, about a kilogram? And it can store ten times as much as all humanity's knowledge, the whole of the Library of Congress, *per gram*.' She glanced around at the facility. 'This is overwhelming. Damn it, Ed, you should have sent me some kind of brief.'

'Would you have believed it? Come meet a few more of our citizen volunteers . . .'

'Carly Maric.'

'Jo Margolis.'

'We're from the beanstalk facility at Miami West 17 . . .'

These were two bright, nervous twenty-year-olds who were applying experience of massive engineering gained from a space elevator construction project to one of the larger components. What they were building was a glistening, seamless structure of some pale, smooth substance, with a flaring base leading up to a complicated peak where something like a ball joint connected the lower entity to a flaring shield. Maggie thought it looked like the knee joint of some Dali-esque surreal monster.

'We've *no* idea what it's for. Or even if it's finished yet,' Carly said.

'But we just loved working on it,' said Jo. 'Some of the pieces are made by conventional manufacture. We do some iron smelting here, there's steelwork, but most of the metal components are built of aluminium that's flown in by twain from stepwise extraction operations. There's some stuff built of fancier materials like carbon composites. And then there's *this*. If I'm honest, we don't quite know what it's made of. The chemists could

266

tell you. It kind of grew in a big vat, layer by layer.'

Carly said nervously, 'We have to look it over, check tolerances, keep an eye on the flow of materials into the vat, the temperature—'

'We just love being here, General,' Jo blurted out.

'Admiral,' Maggie corrected her automatically.

'I mean there was just no work at home, not since they mothballed the beanstalk.'

And Maggie, who had commanded some peacekeeping missions at troubled, half-derelict industrial sites in the overdeveloped, underused communities of the Low Earths, sympathized completely.

But as they moved on, Cutler grumbled, 'So much for a message from the stars. Sometimes it's like a damn welfare scheme. We've even got the Humble here, just like those Low Earth industrial wastelands.'

'The Humble?'

'Think of a labour union run by sanctimonious Next. You'll see soon enough. And you'll have to find a way to deal with them, and good luck with *that*,' Cutler said blackly.

The factory tour continued. Maggie's last encounter was, surprisingly, with a little kid with a matter printer. He was no older than ten, eleven. He just sat there feeding scrap into the machine's hopper, and out the other side came objects rather like heavy bolts, a couple of inches long, with broad heads but lacking any thread that Maggie could see. He'd been doing this for a while, evidently: there was a box of the bolts beside him, half-filled.

A nun sat with him, reading a novel on a tablet. She smiled and introduced herself as Sister Coleen; the boy

267

was called Jan Roderick. They were from a children's home in Madison West 5.

'Not just any home,' Cutler murmured to Maggie. 'The same home that produced the great Joshua Valienté. You'd think one would be enough . . .'

Maggie knew all about Joshua Valienté, and the Home. She bent down. 'You made all these?'

'The matter printer did,' Jan said simply.

'Well, yes—'

'But I programmed it. I go around collecting waste material at the end of the shifts, and I recycle it into things like this.'

'All very efficient,' Roberta said approvingly.

Maggie asked, 'Do you know what these things are for?'

'No. But nobody knows what any of this is for, not yet. They must be good for something or they wouldn't want them, would they?'

'I guess not.' Maggie studied Jan. And she thought of the couple from the Gap, the girls from the space elevator. Their shining enthusiasm. This project was certainly capturing imaginations, it seemed, from kids' homes in the Low Earths all the way to space workers. 'Why are you doing this, Jan? What's the appeal?'

Jan looked at her as if he didn't understand the question. 'There was an Invitation from the sky. It said, JOIN US. And then there were the messages from the Next people, and I figured *them* out for myself. The viral stories. The number clues that led to this world, Apple Pi.'

'That's true,' said Sister Coleen ruefully.

'And that's why I'm making these.' Another bolt was

268

finished; he bent over, picked it out of the printer's hopper, stowed it in the box with the rest, and pressed the printer's restart button. He grinned a gappy grin up at Maggie. 'JOIN US. That's what it said. I'm helping.'

Cutler tapped Maggie on the shoulder. 'First, join *me*. I got a couple more items to show you before your coffee break . . .'

37

S HE WAS DRIVEN at some pace past a fenced-off compound:

COMMUNICATIONS AND COMMUNITY CENTER
ACCESS THROUGH SECURITY GATE ONLY

Within, Maggie glimpsed huddles of tents, a few permanent buildings, and disparate-looking groups, some gathered around campfires, some singing songs, one lot mounting some kind of demonstration up against the wire. All on the inside of the fence. Marine grunts, blank-faced, wearing heavy body armour and carrying blunt-looking weapons, stood outside the fence and stared back in.

'Heavy containment for a "communications and community" operation,' Maggie murmured to Cutler.

'Yeah. I'll loan you my Lieutenant Keith; she turns out to be good at dealing with the wackos . . .'

' "Wackos", Ed?'

'Protesters against the project. We've had to do some security screening; we stopped a couple of bombs. Oh, and some who love it all a little *too* much, on the other hand. They turn up here at random – that's stepping for you – and we just have to round them up from all over the Thinker site, and that's a big area, believe me. They're in a cage in there, whether they know it or not. We "officially" interview them, and we have a closed-circuit comms system so they can make their little video programmes and jabber and scribble away to each other. But they are in a cage, and that's where they'll stay. As long as they stay calm, and keep back from the fences, everybody's happy.'

She thought she heard distant music, a gentle, lulling singing, as if by some vast but distant choir . . . She tried to focus. 'What kind of protesters?'

'You name it, we got 'em. UFO nuts. Conspiracy theorists who think it's all the Communists making a comeback from the stars.'

'Or Hitler,' said Sheridan with a grin. 'Old Adolf's a candidate too.'

'I'd be disappointed if he wasn't.'

Cutler said, 'Then you have Christians wondering about the state of grace of these people in the Galaxy who sent the message, whatever they are, and some Islamists who fear the Thinker is blasphemous – maybe we're building some kind of image of God. On the other hand there are some Christian cultists who believe we should build it precisely because it will destroy the world and bring on the Coming of Christ. Take your pick.'

'To be fair,' Roberta said, 'many of the Next express similar views, at least concerning the unquantifiable threat the project poses.'

Cutler said, 'It's more serious than that, Maggie. These

egghead Next are no more united than we are. There's a faction of them here – I told you – call themselves the Humble. They can call strikes, walk-outs, go-slows. But they're not just agitators. They're a kind of . . .' He waved a hand, searching for the word. 'A *cult*.'

Roberta smiled. '*Cult*. Actually I think that's quite an appropriate word, Admiral. They claim to be following Stan Berg's teachings – are you familiar with Berg, Admiral Kauffman? I myself attended the Sermon Under the Beanstalk . . .'

Maggie raised her eyebrows at Cutler, who shrugged.

'But they are perverting Berg's words. *Be humble in the face of the universe*. That's translated by the Humble as – be humble before me! *Do good*. Sure. As long as the good is what I say it is, as long as it's good for *me*. *Apprehend*—'

Cutler snorted. '*Philosophers*. We got a zoo of 'em here. You know how you can tell a philosopher? By how many words he uses when he beefs about the john being blocked. Ah, it's all hot air. But you need to keep a watch on them, Maggie.'

'I can see you have it all under control, Ed.'

He eyed her, evidently unsure if she was mocking him. Indeed, she was unsure herself.

They drove on from the compound, and Maggie saw they were heading for another fenced-off area, this one much more extensive. The fence itself was enormously long, running from horizon to horizon; she was reminded of the supposedly rabbit-proof fences that they used to build across Australia. Everything about this project seemed to be on a monumental scale, even the fences. Looking through this latest barrier, she saw more activity.

Wide, sprawling buildings. Watchtowers where supervisors, or maybe guards, peered down at the action. Big components being manhandled by teams of hefty workers – hell, no, they were too massive for humans . . . And she heard that singing – rich, detailed, an unending round.

'Trolls,' she breathed. 'You've got trolls.'

'No,' Ed said gleefully. '*You've* got trolls. You always did like the damn hairies, didn't you? Well, be careful what you wish for. It's like the UFO types in their tinfoil helmets. These beasts just turn up, and you got to put them somewhere. So we built this fence to keep them out of the more fiddly stuff. Not just trolls, actually. Some of those other humanoids have come wandering in. The kobolds, the ones that can speak a little English. Hell, they speak it better than the average marine.'

Jane Sheridan put in, 'Hey, don't knock the kobolds. If not for Fingers's swap meets I'd have run out of underwear long ago.'

'*Join us*,' said Roberta Golding, with a smile. 'The Invitation wasn't just for us, you know. Not just for humans or Next. And it was broadcast on more channels than just the radio spectrum. Which is why the humanoids are showing up here.'

Maggie goggled at all that. 'Run that by me again? . . . No. Later. We need to talk, Professor Golding.'

'Of course—'

'Down!'

Suddenly Ed Cutler had his hand on Maggie's neck, and was forcing her over, sideways and down into her seat in the vehicle. Around her she heard weapons being drawn, triggers cocked.

And then she heard a gruff bark, like a big dog, or a wolf.

Maggie grinned. 'I know that bark.'

'Stay down!'

'Let me up, damn it, Ed! Nobody shoot, and that's an order.'

A certain natural authority worked in her favour, as usual. Ed, nominally her superior, backed off and let her straighten up. The rest, Jane Sheridan and Ed's officers and guards, lowered their weapons warily.

Something was running at the fence, from the far side. A huge, vigorous body, on four legs: a wolf, unmistakeably, a huge one. Even Maggie flinched when it reached the fence.

But it pulled up and stopped, panting. Then it raised itself up on its hind legs – not like a dog standing for a trick, more like a human straightening up, a male, low of chest, short in the legs, but standing comfortably. Now it could be seen that the beast wore a kind of jacket, replete with leather rings and deep pockets. And it carried a wrench in one paw-like hand.

Maggie got out of the vehicle, went to the fence and pressed her hand against the wire. 'You too?'

'We hear-hhrd. *Join us-ss* . . . We r-rrhode the twains-ss . . . I saw you-hrr ship.'

'Good to see you, Ensign Snowy.'

'And you, Add-hrr-mirrh-al.' And the wolf snapped a brisk salute.

'Give me strength,' murmured Ed Cutler.

38

HER FIRST FEW hours' dash around the Thinker facilities in this remote footprint of Ohio left Maggie overwhelmed, exhausted. All she wanted was to retire to her cabin on the *Duke*, and drink some single malt, and chew over her impressions so far with Joe Mackenzie – or, failing that, since good old Mac was long dead, with a compatible soul like Jane Sheridan.

But that wasn't an option, it seemed.

As the light of day began to fade, the electric cart returned them to the central landing area where the *Duke* was still tethered. And alongside it now hovered another ship she didn't recognize, sleek, jet-black, very expensive-looking, obviously private. Lights gleamed from an extensive observation deck built into its lower hull.

'That's where we'll be guests for dinner,' Cutler said smoothly.

'Guests? Of whom?'

'An old friend.' He glanced at her. 'Don't worry, you'll get a chance to freshen up. We had spare uniforms shipped aboard earlier. You do smell a little of dog. And we're going to take a ride. A proper view of your new domain, from the air.' He grinned at her, almost evilly. 'You ain't seen nothing yet, Kauffman.'

Maggie had pulled long watches before. She rolled with the punches.

And maybe it helped that her capacity for surprise had already been so dulled when, a couple of hours later, in a glittering observation lounge crowded with guests, she met her host, in his wheelchair. A servant, a young man who looked as massive as a troll, stood stolidly behind him.

'Douglas Black,' she said, staring.

He grinned, almost elfin, his face a crumpled but suntanned mask. He was totally bald, his scalp covered by huge liver spots, and his eyes were large behind thick glasses. 'The same.' He held up a spindly arm, a bony hand.

She tucked her peaked cap under one arm, and had to suppress a childish shudder of revulsion at the prospect of taking that claw-like hand, but when she did so the flesh was leathery but warm. 'I haven't seen you since—'

'2045,' he said without hesitation. 'When you deposited me on Karakal.'

'Earth West 239,741,211.'

'Well remembered. My Shangri-La. My refuge against illness and ageing. And it worked, as you can see.' He lifted up his arms, looking oddly like a clumsily worked string puppet. 'I'm a hundred and six years old. Yet, I think you'll agree, I don't look a day over ninety-eight. And *that* joke is even older than me. Welcome to my humble vessel.'

With a soft shudder, the airship began to rise.

Looking around, Maggie saw that immense windows and transparent panels in the floor offered a wide view of the receding ground. The setting sun cast long shadows across a carpet of Thinker components. Her view expanded further as the twain rose. There was the 'rabbit fence', the compound of the trolls and beagles, itself a vast expanse, but, she could see now, even that was an island surrounded in the further distance by more of the Thinker construction . . .

'Here.' Ed Cutler stood by her; he handed her a glass of champagne. 'I suspect you need this.'

Black raised a glass of fruit juice. 'To health, long life and a fruitful cooperation.'

Maggie smiled. 'I can hardly not drink to that.' The champagne was exquisite, delicate – but too refined for her tastes, she knew. She'd swap a bucket full of it for a measure of a decent single malt . . . 'Look, Mr Black, I'm new to all this.'

'I know.'

'You said *cooperation*. Cooperation over what?'

Cutler growled, 'You can blame Professor Golding and her collaborators in Messengers, Inc. for that. The Next were worried that the project wasn't progressing as well as it could – the development's been patchy. The industrial concerns they're consulting with on the Low Earths either don't have the capacity or can't deliver the quality. Shambolic organizations like the Long Earth Trading Company, for instance.'

'And so they came to me. Naturally,' Black said. 'The Black Corporation has set the standard for high quality, high capacity, rapid delivery and innovation for eighty years already. I could hardly refuse such a challenge as this, Captain Kauffman!'

'Admiral.'

'Although I admit to some concerns. Principally that we don't actually know quite what it is we're building, do we?' He smiled coldly at Cutler. 'You see, I'm a sceptic too, Admiral Cutler. If I left my ship, you would no doubt lock me up in your compound with the millennial catastrophists. As for myself, I believe one should hope for the best but prepare for the worst, always. Admiral Kauffman, I'm sure we'll have many fruitful conversations on the subject in the days to come . . .'

But Maggie was increasingly distracted by what she was seeing, as the transformed landscape opened up beneath the rising twain. In amongst the vast carpet of machinery there were still patches of bare earth, even stands of forest, and the lapping technology stayed away from river courses and standing water. But otherwise it covered the land. And Maggie started to see patterns emerging that were nothing to do with the local geography: round structures, larger circles enclosing nests of smaller ones.

Cutler stood at her side. 'As we get further up, it's easier to see the whole thing. Even though it's obviously incomplete.'

'What's with the circles?'

'That's the dominant design element, that we can detect anyhow. The smallest are around ten paces across – the size of a small apartment, maybe. Then they scale up, clusters in rough powers of ten. A hundred yards, the size of a city block – a thousand yards. The poindexters think this is something to do with distributed processing. The whole thing's a kind of computer, remember. You get some problem broken down into pieces that are worked out in these circles and subcircles, and then it's all gathered together at the top level.'

'It's a privilege to see this emerge, isn't it?' Black said, rolling up in his chair. 'A vision from an alien mind, I'm told, and designed and built by the superhuman Next. Remarkable.'

Maggie said, 'I admit I'm surprised to see you here in person, to tell the truth, sir. You did seem comfortable at Karakal.' She looked at Cutler. 'This was a Joker, in the far reaches of the Long Earth. Low gravity and high oxygen, and Mr Black had a theory that those environmental conditions would extend human life.'

Black said, 'Well, I appear to have been correct. I'm the living proof!'

'You hoped to attract others like yourself. The elderly rich, seeking a retirement community.'

'It was to be a kind of brains trust for mankind,' he said ruefully. 'An arena for medical innovation, funded by myself and the other struldbrugs. But it was not to be, alas. I was doomed by geology.'

'Geology?'

'Admiral, I was foolish enough to fund an investigation into *why* that particular Earth should have such low gravity – why it should be so less massive than the average. Unfortunately for me, my hired rock hounds returned with an answer. All Earths, it seems, contain radioactive materials, and on all Earths these can gather to form tremendous natural nuclear reactors – or naturally occurring fission bombs. On a huge scale.'

He spoke of the early Datum Earth, of concentrations of isotopes of thorium, uranium, plutonium, gathering in great lodes at the boundary of the outer core and the mantle. Gathering, and ultimately going critical . . .

'Some theorists believe that such detonations split the moon from the Datum Earth, or at least expelled the mantle material that went on to form the moon. The largest nuclear explosion managed by mankind was the Tsar Bomb; that created a fireball six miles across. The Datum's moon-creating detonation would have been equivalent to ten *trillion* Tsars. And on Karakal, it seems, there were even larger explosions.'

Cutler whistled. 'Yeah. If it stripped away so much mass that it actually reduced the planet's gravity, it must have been a hell of a bang.'

'And some of my investors, hearing that my precious refuge was actually a relic of nuclear detonations, were deterred. By the fear of residual radioactivity, you see.'

'That's absurd,' Maggie said. 'The fallout, even the isotopes that created the detonation, must have decayed away aeons ago.'

'I know! But these are precious souls who are highly motivated to preserve their own skins – and are wilful in terms of placing large investments. The slightest hint of a sniff of a problem with a place like Karakal and it was doomed. I still have a residence there, I and a few others. But my dream of a Shangri-La of the Long Earth is finished.'

Cutler said, 'Well, I guess we're glad to have you with us despite that, sir. Aren't we, Admiral Kauffman? . . . Admiral?'

Still the twain rose; still the tremendous sprawl of the engineered landscape extended beneath Maggie. She was

280

losing her perspective. Her eye sought patterns; maybe there was still a hint of that circular motif in there, circles upon circles, overlapping, like craters on the moon.

'No more bullshit, Ed. How big is this thing going to get?'

'You ain't seen nothing yet.'

'You spoke of these circles. A hundred yards, then a thousand, then ten thousand – what's that, six miles?'

He nodded. 'We threw up a couple of satellites. You can pick out the circular groupings, or at least the pattern-seeking software can. Six miles, yeah, then sixty, then six *hundred*. And it's still growing, even without our help. As to how they're building it so fast, three words, Admiral: *alien replicator tech*. Deployed here, on Aegis soil. You and I need to have a conversation about that. On the outer edge there are some kind of self-replicating components that are starting to spread out of their own accord—'

'*Six hundred miles?*'

'Just here, we're hovering over the Cincinnati footprint. You understand that this version of North America isn't quite identical to our own, on the Datum ... East–west the Thinker already stretches from Washington DC to St Louis, north–south from Detroit to Atlanta, Georgia. It avoids the major water courses, so it's lapping around the Great Lakes, for instance. But to the east it's already spilling over the Appalachians.'

'My God. It must cover half the continental US.' *Per gram*, those bright kids had said. This stuff was smarter than all humanity put together, *per gram*. And here was a concatenation of it half the size of the nation itself. 'What the hell are we building here, Ed?'

'You're in charge now, Maggie. You tell me.'

Behind her, Maggie was peripherally aware of a figure in a plain black robe approaching Black.

'Mr Black? I'm sorry to bother you. We've never met, but your people were kind enough to invite me aboard. I couldn't help but overhear your conversation about the risks involved with this project: the Invitation, the Thinker. I represent a dissident group of Next, a conservative group, who, like you, are concerned that we should – how did you put it? – prepare for the worst. I wonder if we could talk about cooperation? We call ourselves the Humble. My name is Marvin Lovelace . . .'

39

I N THE END the trolls had to drag Joshua away from the river and back to his camp by the rock bluff. Sancho was at his side, grave, solid, that silver blanket as ever around his neck, and he offered Joshua a shoulder to lean on as he hobbled back to the bluff, defeated. Even as night fell, with Joshua far beyond being able to move any more, he raged at Sancho for not saving Rod, and he shouted for help into his radio, to Lobsang, to Sally Linsay – even to Sister Agnes, and he was ashamed of himself about that. But there was no one to hear.

He slept at last.

He woke up with a face crusted with tears. In the night, Sancho had carefully draped the survival blanket over him.

At least he felt calmer. Or maybe it was just another stage of his exhaustion.

And when he looked around, in the morning light, he saw that the area around his campsite was laden with gifts, of roots, butchered meat – even lengths of tree branch, perhaps a wistful attempt to provide him with better crutches.

Seeing Joshua was awake, with Sancho sitting beside him, the trolls came cautiously to see him. He was subject to playful backslaps and shoulder punches that more than once knocked him over, despite Sancho's admonitory growls. Evidently he was a hero for saving Matt. And, most embarrassing of all, Sally offered him sex. (Well, he *thought* that was what she was doing when she faced away from him, bent over, and backed up like a small truck reversing . . .) The offer, once refused, thankfully wasn't repeated. But he did get the sense that he had been accepted into the group more deeply than ever.

But Rod was not here. And nobody seemed to be trying to find him.

Two days after he had lost Rod, he was sitting with Sancho on top of the rock bluff, on their customary old-fart perch, as he thought of it. 'I can't stay here, Sancho.'

'Ha,' said Sancho thoughtfully, pulling at his spacesuit-silver blanket.

'What I need to do is *find Rod*. And if I can't find him, I'll find a way home. Maybe in that plane. Get help. And then come back for him. After all, he came all this way for me.'

'Hoo.'

'And what about you, buddy? Sooner or later, I guess you'll find some other troll band and start all over again. Don't forget to tell them about the singing river ape. That was a new one on me.'

Sancho reached for the troll-call. 'Danger.'

'Yes, big, big danger. A predator that's evolved to take out trolls. Curse you, natural selection! You're always one step ahead of the game.'

Sancho seemed to be thinking hard. Coming to a decision. Then he said, 'Find.'

'What?'

Groaning slightly, Sancho lumbered to his feet, adjusted the blanket over his shoulder, and held a hand out to Joshua. 'Find.'

'What? Find who? *Rod?* Will you help me find Rod?' Suddenly excited, suddenly energized, Joshua clumsily propped himself up on one crutch. 'Find him how? Where? Do you *know* where the singer took him?'

The troll wouldn't answer that. Instead he gestured at the camp, Joshua's scattered heaps of stuff, augmented now by Rod's gear from the plane.

'Yes, yes. I get it. I need to figure out what to bring.'

Joshua scrambled down from the bluff. Rod's white medical pack was still there. Joshua sat in the dirt, opened up the pack and piled in whatever necessities he could see to hand – knives, matches, his handgun, a length of rope. He kept the medical stuff, but it broke his heart to dump the last couple of beers, unopened, in the dirt. One last item – he grabbed Sancho's battered pink pom-pom and stuck it in the bag. All this at top speed, before the troll could change his mind.

Then he zipped up, pulled out rucksack straps, and, still sitting awkwardly, hauled the case on to his back. 'OK, buddy, I'm packed.' And he tucked the troll-call into a jacket pocket, to forestall further conversation.

Sancho grinned, a wide toothy orang-utan's grin. Then with one huge hand he grabbed the scruff of Joshua's neck, lifted him to a standing position, and *shook* him, as if straightening out the legs of a string puppet. Joshua gagged, half-choked by his own shirt; his dangling leg ached, and he fought to keep hold of his crutches. Even the straps of his pack dug into his back.

'Hoo!'

And he fell into a hole between the worlds.

40

I T WASN'T LIKE stepping.

With a step you transitioned from one world into the next, a world more or less identical save for such details as civilizations and extinction events, like stepping between successive frames of a movie. And then you stepped again, into another frame, and then another . . .

This wasn't like that. This was a plummet.

It was more like travelling through soft places, through which Joshua Valienté had passed too many times with Sally Linsay. It had been a Long Earth theorist called Mellanier, an academic rival of Sally's father Willis Linsay, who had first posited the idea of soft places purely on theoretical grounds. Linsay pictured the Long Earth as a necklace strung with the blue pearls that were whole alternate worlds. Simple stepping allowed you to move along the chain, from one pearl to the next. But Claude Mellanier hypothesized that the necklace might get tangled up, in some higher-dimensional jewellery box, with strands overlaying strands. And he argued that it might be possible to break through into an adjoining strand, and thereby travel, in one jump, *much* further through the Long Earth than any simple step would take you. You could even move geographically across the Long Earths using soft places, unlike regular stepping. It was said that the most gifted steppers among the Next could *manufacture* their own soft-place routes . . .

Joshua Valienté thought of soft places as being the Long Earth's equivalent of wormholes, like in *Contact*, and they were about as pleasant to fall through. This was something like a soft place – but a soft place with greased walls.

It made a kind of sense. Trolls were stronger physically than humans, and they'd spent a couple of million years out here busily adapting to the strange conditions of the Long Earth. Of course their most advanced stepping, their soft-place tunnelling, was going to be a tougher ordeal than anything a mere human would choose to face.

But it was galling for Joshua, who had been the poster boy of stepping since he was thirteen years old. Now, maybe, he knew how it felt to be a phobic, like his brother-in-law, poor Rod Green, who had been made physically ill by stepping even if he was sedated and carried over on a stretcher. Always something new to learn about the Long Earth, it seemed – even about the trolls.

And, in a blur, with the troll's strong hand at his neck the only firm reality, he thought he could see Sally Linsay's face, hear her mocking voice. *Not so tough now, are you, Valienté?* This *is the reality of stepping. Like what it really feels to be a fish out of water . . .*

'Leave me alone, Sally.'

'Hoo?'

Suddenly he became aware that he was no longer being

held up by Sancho. He was standing, supported by his crutches.

But he was surrounded by milky, glaring emptiness.

It might have been one of the white-out blizzards he'd been caught in during the Datum's long volcanic winter, or even another Cueball Joker. But the temperature was neutral, and he felt soft moisture gathering on his face. Under his feet too was the most featureless of surfaces, like a pale-white sand. But then he saw what looked like a worm cast, just to one side of the dangling boot of his damaged leg. Not a Cueball, then.

He looked up at the troll, who loomed black against the white mist. 'Where the hell are we, Sancho?'

'Hoo?'

'Damn it . . .' He fished the troll-call out of his jacket pocket and tried again. 'Are we there yet?'

'Beach,' the troll said simply.

'Huh?'

Almost comically Sancho cupped his hand to one hairy ear.

And now, straining, Joshua could just make out the rush of a breaking wave. He turned to look that way.

He was in a mist, a sea fog maybe, close, moist. But the mist was lifting now, and he could see a littoral strewn with what looked convincingly like seaweed, and a greyish ocean on which languid waves rolled, breaking almost elegantly at the shore with a rush of broken shells. The horizon was still entirely hidden.

Joshua, his head spinning from his cosmic ride, was struck by the mundanity of it. 'So where, Sancho? What beach?'

Sancho shrugged. 'Beach.'

Joshua laughed softly. He was already tiring of standing, so he let himself slide down his crutches to the sand, splaying his bad leg before him, and gazed out as more of that calm sea was revealed to him. 'Who cares what beach, right? Joshua, you need to think like a troll. A beach is a beach is all one beach, spanning the Long Earth – and a good place to feed . . .'

Sancho tapped him on the shoulder. 'Climb.'

'Climb? Climb what, where?'

'Tree.' The troll pointed inland, and started to march that way.

'Tree?' Joshua stood again, with difficulty, and turned away from the sea. The fog was lifting rapidly – well, it must be morning here, as it was on the world they'd come from, as it was presumably on all the worlds of the Long Earth. And in the morning light the sea mist burned off to reveal, as he looked inland, above the beach—

Structures. Like towers.

Big ones, each one a central pillar with what looked like buttresses splayed on the ground at its base, and draped in mist above. A whole array of them, still no more than silhouettes against the pearly fog. Buildings? No, they looked too organic for that. In fact even those splayed buttresses looked like tremendous crabs.

He saw the hunched shoulders of the troll disappearing into the mist as he tramped steadily up the beach, towards one of the 'pillars'. Joshua hastened to follow, fumbling with his crutches. The mist lifted further. And Joshua had a sudden shift of perspective.

He was looking at a *tree*, a big one, with a fat solid trunk and a heavy, massive root system that had fooled him into thinking of a crouching beast, a crab, and branches and a canopy still out of sight in the rising mist above his head. A big tree, but just a tree – with more of the same beyond, he saw, as slim silhouettes congealed out of the mist. Some kind of sparse forest, then, towards which Sancho was leading him at a ground-consuming marching pace.

'A forest is a forest,' Joshua muttered as he pivoted himself forward on his crutches, over and over. 'Like a beach is a beach. Except – here we are. Why this forest, why these trees? . . .' Perhaps there would be answers when they reached the forest itself.

But they were still on the damn beach. Joshua's crutches were still sinking annoyingly in the soft sand, his bad leg aching with every move, his armpits sore and chafed already from the crutches. And those trees looked just as far away as ever, despite the troll's steady march towards them.

'What the hell is this, am I on a treadmill? . . . Ah, quit complaining.' Joshua got his head down, gritted his teeth, and endured. 'I'm coming, Rod.'

The going got a little easier higher up the beach, where there were scraps of dune grass to bind the surface. That gave way to a grassy, sandy sward, and then rows of dunes that rippled gently across the landscape. 'Gently', that is, unless, like Joshua, you were trying to walk through them on one leg up a sandy hill and down into a grassy hollow, over and over. But Joshua moved as fast as he dared, not risking a fall, trying to keep Sancho in sight in the still misty air.

The dunes gave way to a plain, a grassy scrub dotted

with low bushes. The fog was still thick enough to obscure the horizon – and, Joshua realized with a renewed shock, those big trees themselves were *still* far enough away for their trunks and roots to be greyed by the lingering ground mist, the fog above still cloaking the branches and canopy.

He stopped thinking, and just concentrated on one step after the next, one crutch-pivot after another, following the back of the receding troll. But unease prickled. If he'd been able to make out those root masses from the beach, beyond the bank of dunes, how the hell big must those trees be?

He didn't realize how big they were, in fact, until at last he reached the base of the trunk of the nearest tree, and he found himself walking into the root system. Not around it, or over it – *into* it, like an ant approaching an oak tree. Sculptures of wood lifted out of a mulch-strewn ground around him, soon rising up over his head. And these were just the roots. If he hadn't seen it from further away, from this close Joshua would never have recognized this enormous structure as a tree at all. And yet there was Sancho still fearlessly leading the way into the root mass, even though the troll's own mighty bulk was dwarfed by the giant formations all around him. Joshua felt diminished, as he struggled to keep up.

And he was struck by how quiet it was, not a bird's call to be heard.

At last the troll stopped before a wall of wood that rose up sheer from the ground. Fallen branches littered the earth at its foot – branches that looked hefty enough to serve as tree trunks in most forests Joshua had visited.

Even Sancho was panting now, but he thumped at the wall with one big fist. 'Tree,' he said.

'Well, I can see that.' Joshua let himself slump to the ground, and looked up. The trunk was so vast it showed no obvious curvature, not from this close to. It was a wall that stretched to left and right as far as he could see, and up into the steadily rising bank of mist. At first glance the surface, a blackish bark, had seemed smooth, but now he saw crevices and flaws. Joshua gulped water from a flask, and grabbed the troll-call. 'Three questions, Sancho.'

'Hoo?'

'Why the hell did we have to *walk* all this way from the beach? Couldn't your damn seven-league-boots stepping bring us closer?'

Sancho just shrugged.

'OK. Second. Why are we here?'

In answer, Sancho started digging in the mulch at the foot of the trunk-wall. He threw aside what looked like huge dead leaves to Joshua – until he perceived that these were only fragments of leaves, shreds of much bigger structures. Now one of those immense fallen branches was exposed in the mulch. Without hesitating, with one hand, Sancho got hold of a thick splinter at the branch's broken end – and with a dismissive gesture flicked the branch into the air, a hefty timber the size of a reasonable tree trunk cartwheeling away, falling slowly, languidly, before coming to rest with a slow-motion clatter some yards away.

Joshua just stared. 'Wow. I know trolls are strong, but this is ridiculous.' Curious, he got to his feet and hobbled over to the fallen branch. Here was the splinter that Sancho had grabbed hold of, a jagged dagger of torn wood. Experimentally, leaning on his crutches, Joshua got hold of the splinter, and pulled.

And the whole branch lifted up off the ground, a pillar of wood twenty feet long at least. It wasn't quite without weight, but it felt like a papier-mâché mock-up of a tree trunk rather than the real thing. 'Wow,' Joshua said again. 'If I had two working legs, *I* could send this thing spinning. Hey, Sancho. What is this stuff?'

'Reaching-wood,' was all Sancho would say, as he rummaged through the leaf litter, working his way towards the big trunk-wall.

'Reaching-wood? But—'

'Hoo!' With that triumphant call Sancho at last produced something from the dirt. A cylinder, Day-Glo scarlet.

Joshua's heart skipped a beat. It was Rod's flare gun. And, Joshua saw, it was sticky with blood.

He wondered how Sancho had known to look just here. Maybe he was guided by scent, or something in the long call. It didn't matter.

'OK. I get it. This is where the singer beast brought him. What do we do now?'

The troll looked up at the trunk-wall, and grinned. 'Climb.'

41

THERE WAS ONLY one way Joshua Valienté, sixty-eight years old and with a busted leg, was going to climb this mountainous tree. And that was on the back of a troll.

Joshua found it more than a little embarrassing to be so helpless, but Sancho was brisk and sensible. He let Joshua sort out his pack, folding up his lightweight crutches and stowing them away, hanging the troll-call on a cord around his neck. Then he helped Joshua clamber up on his back, arms around the troll's huge neck, with a couple of loops of rope around their waists for safety. Sancho seemed so practised at this that Joshua wondered if he'd been used as some kind of bearer in the past, maybe for one of the big logging concerns like the Long Earth Trading Company. A humanoid with a big roomy mind and a generous heart, used as a mule by some bunch of money-grubbing lumberjacks? Well, that was people for you.

And then, with his human cargo safely attached, the troll looked up at the immense trunk-wall, spat on his hands, and began to climb.

The bark was marked by knots and pits, and Sancho had no trouble finding handholds. Even the troll's feet were mobile and clever, seeking out holds with almost as much articulation as the big hands. As Sancho climbed, Joshua could feel the immense muscles in the troll's shoulders and back working under his hairy skin, and despite the dead-weight burden of an old man, Sancho seemed not so much to climb as to swarm up the trunk face in a continuous liquid movement. Trolls had often made Joshua think more of orang-utans than of gorillas, and the likeness to the orangs had never seemed more striking, the troll's arms and legs matched in their length and strength and suppleness.

And while Joshua was marvelling at the skill of the troll, they rose steadily into the air.

Soon the ground was far below, littered with fallen leaves and branches that looked, from a height, almost normal scale. But when Joshua looked up, this wall of bark receded up into the still rising mist, and if there were any branches they weren't visible yet.

And, looking around, leaning back as he clung to Sancho's muscular neck, Joshua could see those other trees now, their trunks tremendous vertical shadows off in the mist. Some of the trees seemed to be wrapped in cables – huge vines or lianas perhaps, dimly visible in the mist, maybe some kind of parasite. This was a true forest, of many trees, but the individual specimens were so vast, and, presumably, necessarily spaced so far apart, that it didn't *feel* like a forest. The trees were more like immense buildings, like skyscrapers. This was Datum Manhattan rendered in wood.

The troll moved steadily, but not quite tirelessly. Every so often he stopped, and Joshua could hear the rumbling of his huge lungs as he took deep breaths.

And as he climbed Sancho picked at the surface of the bark before him. He was careful not to damage the bark itself, but plants grew here, things like ferns and orchids and bromeliads, taking their sustenance directly from the air. Some of these epiphytes bore fruit that Sancho stuffed into his mouth. And he dug bugs and beetles from crevices in the bark – more crunchy snacks. Joshua himself stuck to his bottled water and energy bars from Rod's pack, but he was impressed. Life everywhere, living on or in this great tree. Once Sancho disturbed a bird like a huge wood-pecker, the size of an eagle but gaudily coloured, which flapped away, cawing in disapproval, while Joshua ducked for cover. Maybe this was why he'd heard no bird call on the ground. The birds lived just too damn high.

And still they climbed. Warm, comfortable, lulled by the steady rhythm of the climb – and feeling as safe as he ever had, in the care of this remarkable troll – Joshua slept.

He was woken when Sancho stopped once more and, gently, began to disengage Joshua's ropes.

Joshua saw that they had reached branches, at last.

The sun was going down on this world, the world of these immense trees, and the low light cast milky shadows through the still lingering mist. They must have climbed nearly all day. And Sancho and Joshua were dwarfed by a three-dimensional tangle all around them: the trunk, the vast branches, leaves like green flags. The branches were themselves huge structures, the size of mature Datum oak trees – branches that seemed too massive to support themselves, but if they were made of that anomalously light 'reaching-wood' then Joshua supposed it was feasible. Now, Joshua realized, there was noise, the calls of birds – or something like birds – and the squeaks and cries of animals of some kind, echoing in this vast roomy structure in the sky. This was wherethe life was, then, on this world: high above the ground. And presumably this was only the lower level of the canopy of this giant forest.

Sancho looked up suddenly, nostrils flaring, intent. Joshua thought he could hear a snatch of long call, drifting from the mist above.

Looking around, Joshua saw that Sancho had evidently stopped here because he had found a kind of pond, water collected in a junction of branch and trunk. A little way from the pond, Sancho gently let Joshua down and wrapped the safety rope around a side-branch, massive in itself. Then he worked his way back to the pond for a drink.

Guessing they were here for the night, Joshua reinforced the rope attachment with a couple of knots of his own. Then he dumped his pack, carefully tying that to the branch also. He dug out Sancho's survival blanket, and a lightweight sleeping bag for himself. The branch surface was tricky to work on, every square inch infested with mosses and lichen and fungi, and slippery, treacherous under hand and foot. He felt oddly breathless as he moved around, as if it was he who had been exercising hard, not the troll – and by comparison the troll barely seemed fatigued at all, though his big chest heaved at the air.

He joined Sancho by the tree pond. Sancho was using his hands to guzzle down the water. Joshua filled an empty flask, but he strained the water first and dropped in a purification tablet.

After that, Sancho sat over the pond, in the patient posture he'd had when hunting those rabbits in their underground lairs. Joshua sat beside him, still and soundless. But he could see nothing in the pond, nothing but some kind of lily-like plant spread on the surface, and the gentlest of ripples—

Sancho plunged in one huge hand, creating a vigorous splash, and in a single motion drew out a fist containing a kind of alligator, struggling and snapping. The gator was dwarfed and pale, but Joshua thought it was nevertheless more than capable of taking off a finger. But Sancho slammed its head against the trunk surface, and the gator's struggles ceased immediately.

Sancho stroked its crushed skull, as if comforting it. Then he ripped a sliver of bark from the trunk and used it to slit open the creature's belly. When he offered Joshua a handful of raw meat, still warm and dripping, Joshua demurred. He had salted meat in his pack along with some of the survival rations from the plane. 'I mean, if we could build a fire up here—'

Even without the troll-call, Sancho seemed to pick up on that word: *fire*. He made urgent sign-language gestures, *no, no*, and grabbed the call. 'No fire! No fire!'

Joshua held his hands up. 'It's OK, buddy, just a suggestion. No fire. I get it.'

Sancho seemed pacified, but he kept his eye on Joshua

as he chewed on his gator meat, as if Joshua might suddenly whip out a blowtorch.

Once they'd eaten, with the light diminishing, they huddled up together, side by side, troll and human under survival blanket and sleeping bag respectively. Despite the persistent urgency to keep looking for Rod, Joshua felt somewhat relieved to have stopped moving; even as a passenger he felt exhausted.

And he still had that nagging breathlessness. How *high* were they? He thought back to Denver and its footprints: the mile-high city. Whenever he'd flown in there it had always taken him a couple of hours to adjust to the thinner air. Was it possible they were *that* high? Sancho had been climbing steadily and swiftly for hours. And even if they were a mile high, it was clear they were nowhere near the top of this tremendous tree . . .

A *tree*, miles high? And not just one mighty Yggdrasil, there was evidently a forest of them. How was that even physically possible?

But, mile high or not, he was surrounded by life, all around him and high in the unseen canopy that still lay above him. Lying there in the gathering dark he thought he saw some animal moving through the branches, a shadow against shadows – not a squirrel, or squirrel analogue, not a climbing primate type as you might expect – this looked like a *deer* to Joshua, a big quadruped animal skipping lightly along the thick branches. And he heard turbulent ripples in that pond nestling in the crook of the branch, something as big as that alligator Sancho had taken or even larger, hunting in its mile-high domain. This was a vertical landscape.

Trees!

Trees had been Joshua Valienté's companions since Step Day itself, when, as a thirteen-year-old boy, he had found himself stepping across from a suburb of Madison, Wisconsin, into forest. It was the same everywhere, in fact. Most Earths were great tumbled forests. Mankind had only arisen on Datum Earth – and only on the Datum was the world forest gone, the legacy of millennia of patient clearances by smart axe-wielding apes.

But Joshua had learned, with the help of Sister Georgina in the beginning, that trees were more than just background scenery. Their trunks stored much of the world's biological matter, they fed whole ecologies thanks to roots that penetrated water sources hidden deep underground, and just as he'd seen here their crevices and cracks provided homes for animals and insects and even other plants. All this was fed ultimately by the energy of the sunlight falling on the leaves of the canopy. On this world the logic of the tree seemed to have progressed as far as it could, with the ground more or less abandoned save for the world-trees' mighty roots.

But if he was already something like a mile above the ground, how high could the ultimate canopy be? He knew there were limits to the size of trees, on the Datum anyhow. Sequoias, say, could grow no higher than the structure of their wood could sustain the load of the trunk above it, and no higher than it was possible for the tree's internal structures to lift water from the ground up to the leaves. So you were looking at two, three hundred feet. Not a *mile*.

Maybe these trees worked by some other logic. They had to.

And *where* was he?

He remembered one Joker he and Lobsang and Sally had found during The Journey, their first pioneering expedition into the High Meggers forty years ago. That had been somewhere between the Rectangles and the Gap, as he recalled the milestones from that tremendous trip: a world where, with the *Mark Twain* high in the clouds, leaf-laden branches had scraped the keel . . . And he had a vague memory of an account of one of Maggie Kauffman's Navy-twain expeditions into the unknown reaches of the extreme Long Earth. Somewhere the best part of a quarter of a billion steps out, they'd made a sighting of a world, or a band of worlds, studded by immense trees. Had they been as big as these specimens, though? Of course the wisdom was that trolls and other stepping hominids had not spread further than Gap worlds in either direction, contained by those natural vacuum traps to West and East. So much for that; give trolls a soft-place capability and they could be anywhere. Joshua imagined little clusters of trolls dotted throughout the greater Long Earth, spreading out stepwise from wherever their favoured soft places delivered them . . .

Could Joshua *really* have come that far out with Sancho and his super-stepping? Maybe so. He seemed to have left his usual feeling of location in the Long Earth back on the river bank with Patrick and Matt and the rest, but he *sensed* he was well beyond the High Meggers, wherever he was.

Don't question it, he told himself. Let someone smarter than you figure it out, one day. He wasn't Lobsang; Joshua's way was to experience, to cherish, not to analyse. And besides, nothing mattered save for his search for Rod.

'It's like Step Day,' he said aloud. 'Looking for the lost child in the stepwise forest. We're coming, son. You just hang on. We're coming.'

Sancho grumbled and snorted in his sleep.

42

T HE NEXT DAY was more of the same. More of the troll's
steady climbing.

The *whole* day.

Joshua, clinging to Sancho's back like a child to its
father, grew numbed. Out of condition, maybe still suffering the after-effects of the infection, he was barely aware
of the world around him. And the troll climbed on and
on, with a kind of liquid grace that belied his bulk. The air
seemed to grow thinner with every breath, but Sancho
was climbing just as vigorously as he had from the start.

The light grew brighter. Looking around, Joshua saw
they were out of that bank of mist now – no, he saw, peering down over Sancho's shoulder, they had actually
climbed above a *cloud layer*, out of which the mighty trunk
of the tree rose up defiantly, reaching for the sky like a
space elevator. They had evidently left behind that first
layer of canopy too, for the trunks of this tree's companions
stood all around, bare and clean, rising from the clouds.
He vaguely remembered reading, probably with some
Sister or other, that the carbon that went into making all
that wood in a tree's trunk came from the air. If so these

trees represented one hell of a carbon store. Perhaps, in fact, this was naturally a world high in carbon dioxide, and the trees had evolved in response.

And here he was speculating on evolution while gasping like a beached fish and clinging to a troll's hairy back. 'Stick to the point, Joshua.'

They seemed also to have clambered above most of the vertical wildlife that the tree nurtured. The few branches they passed were sparse and stubby, and in the crisp light the puddle-lakes like the one where they had spent the night were now scarce. Joshua supposed that they were above much of the weather here too; rainfall would be rare.

But Sancho, without food and water almost since they had woken, seemed indifferent. He just climbed on and on.

Joshua could only endure. He clung to Sancho's back, his face buried in thick black troll hair.

When Sancho next stopped, Joshua groggily saw that the sun was setting again. Below him were more layers of clouds – cirrus clouds this time, Joshua thought, a fine layer through which could be glimpsed deeper cloudscapes below, all of them threaded by the trunks of the trees – and above him, beyond the branches, only an astronaut's sky, deep blue, specked by a handful of brilliant stars, empty of cloud save for only the palest icy streak.

He was dimly aware that Sancho was untying the ropes. He gently unloaded Joshua and settled him in a crook of a branch. Beyond him the curious faces of other trolls hung like moons (*what* other trolls?). Joshua was confused, nauseous, breathless – and cold, and Sancho seemed to

305

realize that, for with rough kindness he tucked the sleeping bag around Joshua's inert body.

Joshua lay back. Above him those branches combined in a canopy draped with huge leaves, like blankets spread out to dry in the sun. A second canopy, then. Why not? Up here in the clear cloudless air the conditions for photosynthesis must be ideal, he thought dimly, ideal for gathering the unending sunlight from a cloud-free sky – a harvest that nourished the growth of all he had seen below him, in the miles of their ascent.

Miles?

Could that really be true? How high were the highest cirrus clouds? Twenty, thirty thousand feet? Rod the pilot would know. He was maybe three, four miles high, then. At least. And he could see, leaning back, that the trunk of this vast tree went on even beyond this canopy layer, on up towards the blue-sky heaven. How tall could this tree grow? *Five* miles?

Joshua laughed. 'Sally, you should be here to see this.'

And there were trolls up here.

In the declining light he saw now the shadows of adults and cubs, big heavy trolls with big deep chests, moving cautiously. Maybe they lived up here permanently and their bodies had adapted to the thin air. There were whole families up here. They were eating fruit and grubs and what looked like haunches of meat, and they drank water from cupped leaves. As he watched them feed, he thought they were careful not to consume anything of the tree itself. He'd read somewhere that some trees, oaks for instance, evolved poisons against persistent herbivores.

Silhouetted against the deepening purple of the sky,

they looked like heavy fruit, hanging from these impossible branches, miles high. And he could clearly hear, floating on the still air, the trolls' eternal song.

'Yes, you should be here, Sally. You'd love it.'

He pulled the blanket closer over him, tugged his hat down over his ears, and tried to sleep.

He woke once in the night, growlingly thirsty. He tried to call for Sancho, but his voice was a scrape.

He raised his head. All around him the trolls were visible in the light of the brilliant stars, huge mounds huddled together as they slept. When he called again for Sancho, a heavy hand touched his shoulder. He turned to see Sancho's heavy, rather mournful face.

'Water . . .'

Joshua expected Sancho to go to the medical pack for one of Joshua's flasks. Instead he held up a kind of greenish sac, an organic object, oddly streamlined – it was like a teardrop, Joshua thought, heavy with liquid within. Sancho expertly ripped a hole in this with thumb and forefinger, held it up over Joshua's mouth, and clear, cold water trickled on to his tongue. When the sac was empty, Sancho just held it up and let it go.

And the empty sac sailed up into the air, up over Sancho's head, until it was lost against the details of the branches above.

Somehow this didn't seem at all surprising to Joshua, in this fantastical place. What else were things supposed to do but float off into the sky? He patted Sancho's shoulder in thanks, and settled down to sleep again.

43

WHEN HE WOKE, in deep-blue daylight, his head felt much clearer, his thoughts sharper, the vague nausea that had plagued him receded. Evidently he was adapting to the altitude – adapting suspiciously well, in fact. Maybe this world was more oxygen-rich than the Datum. After all, a planet full of giant trees could well have a messed-up atmosphere. He hoped Maggie Kauffman would get somebody sent back here to study the place properly some day.

In the meantime he badly needed a piss, more water, and food, in that order. He sat up – but too sharply, and his head swam briefly. A strong troll arm wrapped around his shoulders, to save him from falling back: Sancho, of course. And, looking beyond Sancho, Joshua saw that the rest of the trolls seemed to be congregated on one long, fat branch.

Joshua grinned, and gently pushed Sancho's arm away. 'Thanks, buddy. Let me see if I can water this mule by myself.' He made sure the rope around his waist was tied tight to the branch, then cautiously stood, bracing himself against the rough surface of the trunk wall. Then, facing away from Sancho, he unbuttoned and released the flow. His urine splashed against huge branches and fell in yellow droplets down into the deep air, and Joshua wondered vaguely how deep they would reach before evaporating, or maybe freezing out. Yellow hail!

And how would it be if he did stumble, if his rope failed, if *he* fell from here? He would soon reach terminal velocity even in this thin air. It would surely take many minutes to reach the ground, sailing down past the trunk of this sky tree, crashing through layers of branches and startling the aerial fauna of this strange forest. Or maybe he wouldn't fall at all. Perhaps he would just float up into the sky, like—

The memory came back to him, clear and sharp. And as he stood here on one leg, before the wall of the trunk, he could swear he heard a kind of gurgle, as if from buried pipework, water rising through some kind of plumbing.

He turned, almost falling in the process, grabbed Sancho's shoulders, and reached for the troll-call in his pack. 'Sancho. Water.'

'Fire,' said the troll gravely.

'What? No, Sancho, water. Like the pod you fed me with last night.'

Sancho pursed huge lips, then reached into the crook of a branchlet and produced a green sac, one of a stash, of the kind he'd given Joshua before.

Joshua grabbed it. It was just as he remembered, and, given it was a sac of water the size of a grapefruit, it felt remarkably light. He ripped it open eagerly, dumped out the water – 'Hoo!' said a surprised Sancho – and then released the empty bag.

Just as before, the sac sailed upwards, rising like a party balloon lost in the sky.

Excited now, Joshua said to Sancho, 'Show me.'

'Hoo? Water?'

'No, I don't want the water. I want the bags. Show me where you get the water bags.'

And Sancho, understanding what he wanted, but evidently puzzled by Joshua's behaviour – he kept saying 'Fire', which puzzled Joshua in turn – led him to the tree's trunk-face. Here a gash had been crudely cut, presumably by stone tools laboriously carried up from the ground. A gash wide enough for a troll hand to reach inside. Joshua could see nothing, but he could easily reach inside the cut and feel around.

And he found more of the sacs, full of water, rising up through a smooth-walled channel deep within the tree.

He sat with Sancho, Joshua chewing on compressed rations, the troll under his survival blanket, just as if they were back in their old codgers' places at the bluff.

With a little more thought – 'By God I wish Lobsang was here! *Or* Sister Georgina!' – Joshua believed he began to see the secret of the sky trees.

'Here's my theory, old buddy. Here's how these impossible trees of yours aren't impossible after all.'

'Hoo?'

'Those water sacs are like little balloons. Once they've lost their water ballast, they just float up into the air. So, just like a toy balloon, they have to be filled with something, some gas that's lighter than air. *Hot* air? No, they weren't even warm to the touch. What then? Helium or hydrogen, I figure – just like a twain. But where would a tree get helium from? That stuff's pretty rare, as far as I know, on most worlds anyhow. Hydrogen, on the other hand, is everywhere.' He remembered table-top chemistry experiments Sister Georgina had run with him in the Home. 'You can get hydrogen from water. H-two-O. You pass an electrical current through water, and the water molecules are split into hydrogen and oxygen, and you just collect the hydrogen . . .'

'Ha!'

'Exactly.' He looked up at the higher canopy, where vast leaves, suspended from vaster branches, bathed in the sunlight. '*There's* all the energy you need to drive an electrical current, pouring down from the sky. Somehow, maybe through some kind of natural conductor, a fraction of that energy is passed all the way down to the trees' roots. And I bet you'll find a kind of natural electrolysis lab down there, where groundwater is split to give off hydrogen. The hydrogen is collected in vessels like your water pouches – the sacs. The mechanics of it must be fun.

'And *that's* how water is brought up from the ground, through a height of miles. Carried in natural hydrogen balloons, passing up through internal channels inside the tree itself. And *that's* how come these beasts can grow seventy, eighty times taller than the tallest sequoia.'

'Ha?'

Joshua slapped his forehead. 'And the reaching-wood! I saw it for myself. The whole substance of the wood is full of hydrogen. That's what makes it so light, that's what makes this damn tree able to stand up. Why, maybe it doesn't support its own weight at all; maybe its upper layers are so light they are actually tethered to the ground by the trunk and the roots, like a twain on its cable. I love it!'

'Fire!'

'Yes, buddy! What about fire? Hydrogen is pretty inflammable. Sure, that's why you didn't want me building a campfire in the tree canopy the other night, right? And lightning strikes here must cause a hell of a mess. Although I imagine the trees must have evolved some way to resist fire. After all, they are full of bags of water . . . Loggers, though. Maybe *that's* why something as obviously useful as reaching-wood, ultra-light, has never been brought back to the Low Earths. Because anybody who happened on this band of worlds – if anybody has made it out this far – has, on their first night, casually built a campfire . . . *Ka-boom*. Goodbye, loggers.'

'Fire?'

'I know, I know. What would Lobsang make of this? He'd try to figure out how it evolved, that's what. I guess as soon as the hydrogen buoyancy trick emerges at all, there'd be a race to be tallest, strongest, the one to trap the light. No wonder the trees grow as high as they do, until the cold or the lack of oxygen limits them . . .'

'Fire! Fire!'

For the first time in long minutes Joshua paid attention to what the troll was actually trying to say to him. It wasn't just the word; Sancho was pointing out to where the rest of the trolls were gathered, out at the end of that long limb, suspended in the sky. Joshua peered out that way, cursing aged eyes. And he thought he saw something at the very end of that branch, a stranger fruit yet – some kind of big heavy animal, bigger than a troll. Cornered, out on that branch, trapped by the trolls.

And a splash of bright orange. Flight-suit orange.

Joshua's heart seemed to stop. He grabbed the troll-call again. 'That's my boy.'

'Cub,' Sancho agreed.

'You found him. Shit. Sancho, I could kiss you. But now we have to go get him, right?'

'Fire!'

Joshua thought it over for one second. Then he dug in his pack and pulled out a box of matches. 'This is what you want me to bring to the party?'

'Fire, cub, fire!'

'Somehow we're going to use fire to get Rod back? OK, buddy, I'll follow your lead . . . I have a feeling we won't be coming back this way.' Excited, bewildered, determined, Joshua tucked the matches into his jacket pocket, and hastily bundled up the rest of his gear into the med pack. Then, as he clambered on to the troll's back, wrapping rope firmly around both their waists, Joshua muttered, 'So, a tree-climbing croc has my son, and I'm crawling across a five-mile pillar of hydrogen, on the back of a troll, with a box of matches in my pocket. What can possibly go wrong?'

44

JOSHUA WAS SURPRISED to see how graceful the singer was, with that flexible, well-proportioned humanoid body, as it clambered around its branch. He'd first encountered the singer in a river, after all; but if it was a natural swimmer, it looked like it was just as good a tree-climber as any troll.

Joshua didn't know how Sancho had known the singer beast would come to this world, to this particular tree. He didn't know how he and the local band of trolls had cornered this animal, out at the end of its branch. But if it was adapted to hunt trolls in the first place, maybe it used the same super-stepping passageways Sancho had used to bring him here. Once again it struck him that there was evidently a hell of a lot he'd yet to learn, along with the rest of humanity – even Lobsang – about trolls, and their lifestyles, and their capabilities, and their predators.

Anyhow, right now that singer animal was backed up, close to the end of this branch that hung impossibly high and long in the sky – trapped by the massed trolls that had evidently driven it up there. And Joshua could see his son now, apparently unconscious, draped over the branch at the feet of the singer. Joshua couldn't tell from this distance if Rod was dead or alive, or, if he was injured, how badly.

All that for later. Now he just had to get his son back.

Sancho stood beside him, holding a chunk of reaching-wood, a section of branch – a rough tube. 'Fire.'

Joshua studied the log. 'What are you thinking? Smoke him out somehow?'

Sancho shoved the reaching-wood cylinder into Joshua's arms, losing his usual phlegmatic patience. 'Fire!' With one finger he tapped Joshua's pocket, where the matches were.

Joshua studied the cylinder more closely. It was deceptively light, like all reaching-wood, and obviously organic, but peculiarly shaped. 'This is a chunk of the tree, right? Hollow inside – the wood stuffed full of hydrogen – short and straight, almost streamlined. And these grooves on the outside surface are almost perfect spirals.' Then he thought he had it. 'Wow. Are you serious? I bet the troll-call has no translation of *missile*... But why would a tree *grow* natural hydrogen-fuelled missiles? ...'

'Fire!'

'Right, right, I get it, I know. Don't think, just do the job. You're the boss, Sancho.' He eyed the singer beast standing over his son, snarling with that big ape head at the trolls goading him. 'OK, but let's have a practice run first...'

Joshua pointed the 'missile' out into the open air, away from the trolls and the singer. Then, improvising as he went along, he packed the base of the tube with dry leaf matter, and cut a stub off a candle to serve as a fuse. 'Not having any ambition to blow myself up now I'm so close to Rod . . .' Then he struck a match, lit the candle stub, and backed hastily away.

The organic matter smouldered, sparked and flared, hydrogen vessels popping. It went briefly quiet, and Joshua thought maybe he'd created a dud. But then a bright white flame erupted from the base of the 'missile', and the tube soared away into the air, trailing a thread of billowing smoke. Joshua saw how it spun on its axis, those spiral flanges catching the air, and as a result it flew straight and true just where Joshua had aimed it – until, quite quickly, it ran out of gas, and, flaming, fell away into the open air.

'Well, I'll be,' Joshua said, astonished. 'I think this might actually work.'

'Hoo!'

'Let's do this.'

In the end it was a question of timing.

The trolls were hunters, used to cooperative operations. So the troll band kept up their barrage of cries and fist-waving at the singer, which snapped and snarled back, posturing over Rod's prone body. All this was to distract the singer from Sancho, who silently, calmly, almost without a sense of threat, crept forward from the pack and edged a little closer to the animal, and to Rod.

And Joshua forced himself to concentrate on setting up his second branch-missile: the first and last he'd ever fire in anger, he supposed, and he had to get it right. He tinkered with the aim, improvising a kind of launch rail with twigs and sticks, and sighted along the slim body of the branch, cursing his failing eyes.

When he thought he had the alignment as right as it would ever be, he didn't hesitate. Again the lit match applied to a candle stub, again the smoulder and pop of hydrogen-soaked leaf matter. He limped back out of the way, and got into cover.

The fuse burned down.

Again that flare of rocket power, again the flame and the smoke as the missile surged away – and it slammed straight into the belly of the singer beast. The animal fell away from its branch and went tumbling into the air. Joshua howled his triumph.

But so massive was the singer's body that the missile, still burning and spinning, was deflected, and began to soar back towards the tree, spiralling in the air, leaving behind a complex smoke trail.

Even as the troll band yelled and whooped in exultation, Sancho dashed on all fours along the branch, and picked up the limp form of Rod as if he was no more than a bundle of rags. But Joshua was distracted by that flare of light far below. His missile, still burning, had shot back into the body of the tree – and, as Joshua watched, it slammed into the trunk at a junction with a thick branch. There was a deep, heavy explosion, and the whole tree shuddered.

'Oops.'

But here was Sancho, with Rod.

Joshua helped the troll lay his son out on the surface of the branch. He checked Rod's pulse at his neck, leaned over to hear his breath, felt its warmth on his cheek. Then he ran his hands quickly over Rod's limbs. Joshua, eyes brimming with tears, working fast, forced himself to be

317

methodical. 'He seems intact,' he told Sancho. 'Pulse steady, breathing, no broken limbs. Any internal injuries – well, that'll have to wait until he wakes up. Dehydrated, probably starving hungry. We're lucky the singer didn't just kill him – or maybe that's an animal that likes to consume its prey warm.'

'Fire,' said Sancho.

'Sancho, buddy – thank you.'

'Fire! Oops! Fire!'

And now there was a tremendous blast, coming from deep within the body of the tree. The branch they clung to creaked and swayed.

Glancing around, Joshua saw that the troll band had scattered, the individuals clinging wherever they could get a hold. Further away, branches were cracking and breaking, huge chunks, themselves the size of mature trees, falling away into the air. A brilliant glow shone from further down the trunk; there was a rising plume of smoke – and now more explosions, as, Joshua guessed, more natural concentrations of hydrogen were breached.

He stared at Sancho, aghast. 'What have I done?'

'Oops!' Sancho yelled. And he picked up the limp Rod, threw Joshua bodily over his other shoulder, and ran back along the branch of the exploding tree.

As he was jolted along, head hanging upside down, fresh detonations battering his hearing, Joshua muttered, 'Eat your heart out, Colonel Quaritch.'

As Joshua and Rod figured it out when they talked it over later, you didn't evolve to be a sky tree, a five-mile-tall reservoir of intensely flammable hydrogen gas – a five-mile-tall *Hindenburg* – without developing strategies to survive fire. Even to exploit it. For, thanks to lightning strikes and meteor falls and volcanic events and other natural calamities, there would always be fire on any world, even those worlds not yet visited by Joshua Valienté with a box of matches.

For the rogue missile had sparked a cascade of explosions that, with surprising speed, blew the mighty trunk of the tree apart. The tree itself could not survive, and much of its substance was lost to the flames. The colossal pyre created a plume of smoke and ash and water vapour – the product of burning hydrogen in oxygen, Joshua realized, the opposite of electrolysis – that reached for the stratosphere.

But out of that plume sailed significant bodies of reaching-wood, naturally separating from the disintegrating tree: branches, chunks of trunk. Many of these were rather like trees themselves, with slim trunks, branches with clusters of leaves, roots dangling in the air like the tentacles of an octopus. These sailed out of the carnage, slowly settling to the ground. They were seedlings, Joshua guessed, saplings, the descendants of the tree and the repository of its genes, the seeds of the next generation. There even seemed to be two kinds, like pollen, like flowers – male and female, maybe.

And meanwhile, to ensure those seedlings had room to flourish, from out of the dying tree's central blaze flew sparks of liquid light, trailing smoke plumes that were soon miles long. These were branch-missiles like the ones Joshua had ignited with his matches, but here serving their true purpose. Fired blindly and at random, but in all

319

directions, these splinters of fire sailed into the foliage of the dying tree's equally mighty neighbours. Not all the missiles reached a target; not all the targets succumbed to the flames. But enough missiles got through, enough neighbours were destroyed, to ensure that the originating tree's seedlings had at least a fighting chance of finding open ground to root in and sunlight to drink in, away from the shade of more mature competitors.

Of course as each secondary tree was detonated in turn, more missile-branches arced out across the stupendous forest, until a good fraction of it was ablaze. Joshua wondered briefly if the whole damn continent was going to go up in a tremendous firestorm. But he soon saw that the fire was stopping at wide avenues that cut through the forest, natural firebreaks. And, above his head, heavy grey clouds seemed to be gathering: laden with the water vapour rising from the burning trees, maybe they would be a source of rain that would limit the fire further.

Lobsang, on some tree-choked world, had once told Joshua that he believed forests could be seen as living things in themselves: a collective almost like troll bands, sleeping in the cold, drowsy in summer, with the sap rising daily like a single tremendous heartbeat. So it was here – just a different lifecycle, on a different scale. The hydrogen forest was using the fire to spread its seeds, but the blaze itself was self-limiting, it seemed. In a century or two the young trees would grow and the forest would heal, stronger than ever, and it would be as if this inferno had never happened, its only trace a layer of enriching ash in the topsoil.

As the forest turned into a natural if spectacular

battlefield, as a flood of animals fled from the bases of the burning trees – things like deer, things like rabbits, even a few troll bands – one seedling gently sailed towards the ground with an elderly troll clinging to the slim trunk, a human being draped over each of his powerful shoulders.

45

A T LAST ROD opened his eyes.

Joshua, sitting by him, tried to hide his relief. He pushed a lock of hair back from his son's forehead. Rod's face was ghastly pale, but, Joshua told himself, that could be an effect of the eerie light in this cavern to which Sancho had brought them.

Rod tried to speak, licked his lips, tried again with a voice that was a dry rasp. 'Dad?'

Joshua could barely hear him over the soft echoes of the unending long call. 'I'm here. Don't talk too much.'

Rod was lying on a bed of moss, with survival blankets above and below, his own orange flight suit bundled up under his head for a pillow, the white med pack open on the ground nearby. Now Joshua lifted Rod's head slightly and held a cup of water for him. Rod drank greedily, to Joshua's relief.

'That's good,' Rod said, his voice stronger now. 'Tastes kind of . . . organic. But good.'

'Are you hungry?'

Rod thought about it. 'No. I don't think so.'

'Good. I've been trying to feed you while you slept. Or

when you were half-awake, anyhow. A broth your mother would have approved of, with some of the trolls' patent herbal medicines sprinkled on top.'

'Yum.' He glanced around. 'Where are we?'

'Somewhere around West 230,000,000. Probably. If the records of the *Armstrong II* are accurate—'

'Dad. I don't care. I mean, this place we're in. What is it, some kind of cave?'

'Something like that.' Joshua looked around, at the complex roof over his head, the mushrooms and ferns the size of small trees themselves, the soft greenish glow that shone from the roof and walls and permeated everything – and the underground lake, its shore a few paces away, tranquil, glimmering, itself so vast it was almost as if it had a horizon at the place where the earthen 'sky' of this chamber descended to touch the ground. He tried to remember how he had first struggled to take it all in, when the trolls had brought them both down here two days ago – or was it three? Time was fluid in this unchanging light.

'Take it easy,' he advised his son now. 'Let it all sink in. We're in no rush. And we're safe here. As safe as we would be anywhere in the Long Earth, I think. Thanks to the trolls.'

'I can hear the trolls,' Rod said now. 'That song they're singing.'

The mostly elderly trolls who inhabited this place – evidently 'Librarians', like Sancho himself – liked to spend their days sitting in small groups, four or five or six of them singing softly together, and the voices of those groups themselves combined, as if the whole was an ensemble of individual small choirs. The result was music that washed around the cavern in an unending wave, breaking, intensifying, complexifying, every so often coming to a peak as all the 'choirs' joined in together.

'I never heard a song like it,' Rod said.

'Get used to it. Down here they sing all the time.'

'It's beautiful, though.'

'It's part of the long call, I think. And yet there's something familiar about it. I'm trying to remember . . .'

'This is a troll place, isn't it? A refuge. They saved us.'

'Oh, yes. After you saved one of *them*. I have never put my hope in any other but in you, O Sancho.'

Rod, settling back on his pillow, pulled a face. 'What, old movie lines even now, Dad?'

Joshua frowned. 'Not a movie line. On the other hand I can't remember where it does come from.' He massaged his temples. 'Something older than any movie. Sister Georgina would have known.'

Rod was looking around. 'Dad . . . I don't remember how I got here.'

'What do you remember?'

He shook his head. 'That animal in the river, that seemed to be hypnotizing little Matt.'

'And you charged in. If you pull a stunt like that again—'

'Oh, can it, Dad, you'd have done the same. So after that?'

'You were taken away, by the singing beast from the river. Rod, as best I can figure it, that animal is a humanoid predator that specializes in taking trolls. And it seems to be based here, on this world, which is a kind of locus for

324

the trolls, if not a home world exactly. Good hunting for a troll-killer. Anyhow, the beast brought you here. To its world.'

'How? By stepping?'

'Kind of. Long story. And we – Sancho and I – had to come get you back. You don't remember any of that? The big trees?'

'What big trees? Dad, I must have been out for hours—'

'Days, actually. The singer had you for days.'

Rod touched the back of his head, wincing. 'Feels like I'm one big bruise back here.'

'The singer must have kept tapping you to keep you out.'

'"Tapping"? Easy for you to say.'

'Didn't feed you though, and you're badly dehydrated. I've been pouring water into you. From the lake, which is why it tastes funny, probably.'

'What lake? . . . Never mind. Why didn't it just kill me? I was prey.'

Joshua shrugged. 'Maybe it was planning some game with you. Have its young hunt you, or practise their fake long calls on you. To it, you must have been just a funny-looking troll.'

'Lucky for me, I guess,' Rod said doubtfully.

'And lucky for both of us that Sancho saved us.'

'Hoo.'

The big troll lumbered up to join them. He squatted down by Rod's prone body, and fingered the survival blanket regretfully.

Rod, feeble but determined, peeled the blanket off his

325

legs and handed it to Sancho. 'Have it back, big guy. I'm done borrowing it.'

'Ha!' With an expression of satisfaction Sancho pulled the blanket over his shoulders, where it looked like it belonged, Joshua thought.

And when Joshua looked back to Rod, he had slumped back to sleep.

46

AFTER ANOTHER TWENTY-FOUR hours, Rod looked a lot stronger, and was getting restless.

'Dad, can you help me up?'

Joshua couldn't, but Sancho could. He wrapped one huge arm around Rod's shoulders and gently lifted him up to a stand, as easily as a child holding a doll. Rod was a little woozy upright, but he drank more water, and waited until the world stopped spinning, he said. Then he had Joshua help him to a corner where he emptied his bladder.

Rod looked around, in a mildly confused way, at the cave, the high roof, the glimmering underground lake – and the trolls, a band of them. Joshua imagined Rod could see at a glance this was an unusual group, with a kind of inverted age profile: full of oldsters, many of them apparently older than Sancho, with just a handful of young adults and cubs.

'I have this memory of you going on about big trees, Dad. But here we are in this cave. So, big trees? Like sequoias?'

'Bigger than that. Trees so high you can't breathe the

air at the top. Trees as tall as mountains, Rod. Trees miles high. All over this planet, as far as I can tell.'

Rod stared at him. 'You sure that singer beast didn't tap your noggin a couple of times too?'

'I'd take you up to see for yourself if it was safe. But I don't need to do that. Look around. Look at the roof of this place, this cavern. You're underground, you understand that, yes? What do you see? What's holding up the roof?'

Rod looked at arching black pillars that came to a dense junction overhead – high enough that there was a faint mist up there, Joshua saw – with rock and earth caked between. 'Ribs. Like the skeleton of a twain. Are they rock? But I've never seen a rock formation like that. It looks artificial – no, organic. Like it grew there.' He looked around, squinting, trying to follow the detail of the cavern roof where it soared to even greater heights over the water. 'My God. Are they *tree roots*?'

Joshua had had time to figure all this out; he felt unfairly smug. 'You know, some trees have root systems that can extend as far beneath the ground as the tree stretches up above it.'

'I'm getting it, Dad. Slowly. All this vast space is just a hollow under the root system of one of your Yggdrasils.'

'Or more than one, yeah.'

Rod held up his hand to create a shadow. 'And the whole thing is *glowing*, isn't it? Glowing with light. But there's no source. No sun down here.'

'Some kind of bioluminescence, I think,' Joshua said. 'The roof, some of the plants. Like in the sea . . .'

'It's kind of gloomy. A lot of green and brown.'

328

'You get to miss the blue sky after a day or two.'

'But there are trees too,' Rod said. 'Trees, growing in a cave.' He pointed to a couple of specimens. 'Big enough for trolls to sit under.'

'Some of them are more like fungi, I think. Big mushrooms or toadstools, suited to the light. Not my speciality, unless they're edible. But there are ferns and shrubs, and some fruiting plants. A thing like a big banana plant. There's plenty more life down here if you look closer. Big beetles burrowing in the bark, ants building nests in the mulch. Most of them sightless, though.'

'All feeding off – what, the light from the roof?'

'I guess. A whole ecosystem fed by a trickle of energy from the sunlight gathered in the big leaves of the canopy, miles above us. And there has to be some kind of flow of air and water through, to keep that lake from stagnating, the air fresh. Well, if you can call a troll's fart fresh.'

'There must be some payback,' Rod said. 'There always is. Some *reason* the big tree spends its energy like this. Maybe having all this stuff going on is good for its roots, or something.'

Joshua said, looking out at the lake, 'You're right. I bet this is where the tree makes the hydrogen it needs. A natural electrolysis tank. And it's all maintained by the life forms down here. Lobsang would know.'

'Hydrogen?'

'I'll explain later—'

'Good to eat,' Sancho said through the troll-call.

'He's right about that,' Joshua said. 'No predators, fruit growing out of the walls: it's paradise for this bunch of old trolls.'

'More like Fiddler's Green,' Rod said.

'Like in *Pirates of the Caribbean*?'

'You and your movies, Dad . . . It's an old sailors' legend, and there were enough old sailors serving on the Valhalla-run twains in my day. Fiddler's Green, where the rum and tobacco never run out, and the fiddlers never stop playing.'

'Just like this. Where old trolls come when they're done wandering the Long Earth.'

'I guess. I can think of worse places to finish up.'

Sancho rumbled through the horn, 'Not finish up.'

Rod twisted to look up at him. 'Not the elephants' graveyard, then. So what do you old fogies do all day down here?'

'Not all old.'

'Mostly,' said Joshua.

The troll tapped his own heavy skull with a forefinger. 'Librarians. Big roomy heads.'

'Ah. With the memories of the race stored away in there.'

Rod frowned. 'I thought the race memory was locked up in the trolls' singing, the long call.'

'It is,' Joshua said. 'But there's more to it than that, Rod . . .'

Rod looked dubious as Joshua tried to explain. 'So all these Librarians from across the Long Earth, all with their heads full of memories, they come here and . . . what?'

Joshua smiled. 'I think Lobsang would say they *synch*. They put together their memories, they correct them, they lock them together – they share.'

As if on cue, the troll song started to rise to one of its rhythmic peaks all around them.

330

'I can even guess how it evolved,' Joshua said. 'The scouts from different troll bands get together in congresses, where they share information about the hunt, about predators, about drought. This is a scout congress but on a much grander scale, much more depth.'

Sancho waved a hand. 'Librarians from all over. Songs from far away. All brought here.'

'Songs of distant Earths,' Joshua murmured.

'Hmm,' Rod said. 'Memories going back – how long?'

'Nobody knows. We do know the trolls have a history that makes ours look like an anecdote.'

'Just as well your generation didn't wipe them all out then, Dad . . .'

'New,' said Sancho unexpectedly.

Joshua and Rod exchanged a look, and then Joshua faced the troll. 'New? What's new?'

'In song.' Sancho cocked his head, as if listening, and then made a kind of beckoning gesture. '*Come, come. Join us.*'

Rod looked startled. '"Join us." Dad, that's—'

'The Invitation. I know. The radio astronomers, the Carl Sagan SETI thing. It was in the news before I left.' He smiled. 'So the trolls are hearing the Invitation too. Well, of course they are. The Invitation is a Long Earth phenomenon. And the trolls are just as important in the Long Earth as we are. More so. *Join us* . . . It all fits. In a way I think I heard it myself.'

'Dad?'

Joshua closed his eyes. 'You know, son, you can criticize me for my sabbaticals, for running away from my family – as your mother came to see it. I was born in the Long

Earth, you know. In an empty world. Except it wasn't empty, not for me. I grew up hearing it, when I started to step for myself. *The Silence*, I called it. The song of the Long Earth itself – the song behind all the songs, the song behind the call of the birds and the rush of the wind. And in a way, when I was out on sabbatical, *that* was what I was looking for the whole time.'

'You know, Dad, I don't think I ever heard you say so many words all together before.' Tentatively Rod rested his hand on Joshua's shoulder. 'I do try to understand, you know. We all did. Including Mom.'

Joshua smiled. 'I guess that's all any of us can hope for.'

'But we can't stay here.' Rod looked up at Sancho. 'We have to go home.'

Sancho growled, 'Take you.'

'Thank you—'

'Thomas Tallis,' Joshua said suddenly.

'What movie was he in?'

Joshua grinned at his son. 'Old English composer – sixteenth century, I think. Georgina played me some of his stuff. I guess it stuck. *That's* what I keep thinking I'm hearing, in the trolls' song. *Spem in alium*, maybe. And that's why I've been thinking of that line: "I have never put my hope in any other but in You, O God . . ."'

'Why should the trolls be singing some old English tune?'

'Motet, I think it was called. I guess our music has been leaking out since long before Step Day. I wonder if Thomas Tallis was a natural stepper . . .'

'Home,' the troll said firmly.

47

O N THE DAY they were to leave the cavern of the Librarians, Joshua caught Rod carving something into the face of one of the big root stems that supported the earth walls. Rod looked faintly guilty when he was spotted, but then he shrugged and stepped back.

Joshua leaned down to see. 'Difficult to read in this light. And the craftsmanship's kind of dodgy.'

'Evidently I don't have the Valienté omnicompetence genes,' Rod said sourly.

'A, R, N—' Suddenly he saw it.

ARNE SAKNUSSEMM

'I hope I got the spelling right,' Rod said.

'I think it varies with the translation.'

'Couldn't resist it, Dad. Read that book when it was on your shelf at home in Hell-Knows-Where.'

'I thought you didn't like all that old skiffy stuff of mine?'

'I dipped into it. There are no rules, you know.'

Sancho ambled over to them now, his survival blanket

as ever around his shoulders. He peered at Rod's carving. He showed no offence at this vandalizing of the sacred tree, but no particular interest either. Then he straightened and held up the troll-call. 'Ready?'

Joshua said, 'To get out of here?' He'd always be grateful for this place of safety, but he'd come to find the subdued and unchanging light depressing, and difficult for sleep. He was looking forward to seeing the sky again – any sky. 'Ready if you are, old friend.'

Sancho held out his huge hands. Joshua and Rod, standing there with nothing more than the grimy clothes they'd been brought here in and the white med pack on Joshua's back, tentatively took hold.

Joshua eyed Rod. 'I guess you don't remember how it was when we came here. Kind of a helter-skelter ride.'

'Dad, I never saw a helter-skelter.'

'A skydive off a space elevator, then. We didn't so much step as plummet. And without your drugs—'

Sancho said sternly, 'One step two step home.'

Rod smiled. 'Dad, let's do it.'

They took hold of Sancho's hands.

48

WHEN THEY GOT back to the bluff with Joshua's meagre camp, and Rod's plane looking safely intact a short walk away, the place seemed deserted. Sancho's troll band were evidently long gone. But Sancho seemed content to stick around for a while.

Joshua insisted on checking out Rod with the medical gear from the plane that he hadn't been able to cram into the white backpack. As they'd both suspected, Rod was fine save for some bruising, a banged skull, and his slow recovery from deep dehydration. Having suffered this attention, Rod was keen to apply a little TLC in turn to his long-neglected aircraft.

When he'd gone, Joshua clambered stiffly up on to the bluff, and with a sigh of relief settled down alongside Sancho.

'Here we are again, old buddy.'

Sancho sat there, his silver blanket over his shoulders. 'Hoo.'

'Like none of it ever happened.'

'Ha!'

'Do trolls get philosophical? I guess you must, given all

you've shown me. You ever think about what it's all for, Sancho?'

'Hoo?'

'What's the point of life? What would a troll say?'

Sancho scratched a hairy chin. Then he raised the troll-call. 'Troll cub. Grow, mom-and-pop. Cubs, mom-and-pops, troll band. The song, sing the song.'

'Yes, yes—'

'Hunt, eat, sleep, screw—'

'Thanks for that.'

'Sing, more cubs. Troll band, long call – get food. Smarter band gets more food. Makes more troll cubs.'

'A troll band is a machine for food-gathering. The better the band works the more food you collect. Is that what you're saying? That's what it's *for*? I guess you'd be hard put to give a better definition of a human society. Yeah, but what about the Long Earth, Sancho? You trolls were out here for millions of years before we stumbled out on Step Day. In fact you evolved out here – the Long Earth shaped you. But why?' He gestured. 'What's the point of it all? These uncounted empty worlds . . .'

Sancho grinned and tapped his forehead. 'Room to run away, from river-singer-beast. Room for long call. Room for *think* . . . And more cubs.'

Joshua thought that over, and smiled back. 'I guess . . .'

Rod was walking back from the plane. 'Hey, Dad? I'm done. We can leave when you're ready.'

'Shit,' Joshua said. Belatedly, he got to his feet. 'Well, let me say goodbye to my buddy.'

Rod frowned, and glanced around. 'Sancho? Where is he?'

And when Joshua looked around, he saw, with a pang of regret, Sancho was gone. He'd even taken the silver survival blanket.

'See you around, you old fart.'

'Dad?'

'Never mind. Listen, could you give me a hand packing up my gear? . . .'

49

B Y THE TIME they got back to Hell-Knows-Where, Joshua had been away from the worlds of humanity for more than a full year. And he found a heap of messages – mostly from Nelson, who, astonishingly, wanted Joshua to come help him find a lost grandson.

He spent some time with Bill Chambers and other friends. He spent more time in hospital getting his leg, and the rest of him, checked over. Well, it worked; he walked in on crutches and out on a walking stick.

It was June of 2071 by the time Joshua Valienté made it back to Madison, Wisconsin, on Datum Earth: his home town.

But here he was, keeping a promise to his wife.

He stepped back into a small community called Pine Bluff, outside the West Beltline Highway, around ten miles due west of downtown on Mineral Point Road. Leaning on his stick, he had his battered pack on his back, his broad-brimmed hat on his head.

He found himself standing on a cracked asphalt strip, lined by the shells of derelict ash-stained buildings, a handful of newer structures sprouting in cleared plots. Constructed of aluminium and ceramic and treated timber – materials imported from the Low Earths – the new builds looked like colourful mushrooms. Neat-looking electric vehicles were parked here and there.

As usual he felt a kind of cultural, even physical shock at returning to the original Earth, the home of mankind. The sheer extent to which the landscape had been shaped, carved up and built over was startling, even compared to the increasingly settled Low Earths, even here in this outer suburb of what had always been a small city. This was the legacy of thousands of years of humans working the planet, ripping up the land and building, building, and then demolishing or bombing and building again. It wasn't until you had walked into versions of the world where only a handful of natural-stepper humans had set foot before Step Day that you truly realized how much difference all that activity had made. And that was even before Yellowstone had turned much of this particular Earth, and in particular North America, into an ash-coated charnel house.

And yet, thirty years after Yellowstone, the Datum was recovering. Standing here in the middle of the road, you had to admit it. This afternoon the sky was a normal-looking midsummer blue, with a litter of cloud. The aerosols and gases pumped into the air from the immense volcanic caldera had more or less washed out now. And the ash had washed away too, although out of town you could still see big reefs of it heaped up by the highways, and if you dug down into the farmers' fields you would usually find a fine layer of the stuff, only a little way under the surface. But even now, even after so many years, he still thought he could smell soot and gasoline fumes in the air, the ghosts of billions of rusted cars. And it was cold, much colder. Thanks to the volcano winter, Wisconsin, they said, was now more like Manitoba . . .

Flowers were growing through cracks in the asphalt at his feet, despite the cold.

'Are you OK, mister?'

'Huh?'

A young woman stood before him, wearing a practical-looking coverall. She had pale red hair; she might have been thirty. 'I own the motel over there. Well, with my partner, Joe. I was just putting out the evening sign, and there you were in the middle of the road.'

He glanced over at the motel. A chalkboard outside the door advertised drinks, food and a selection of delicacies based on Wisconsin cheeses. 'Some things don't change,' he said.

'You got that right. You just stepped in?'

'Is it that obvious?'

'You looked a little lost. Strange coming back, huh? Lots of ghosts.'

'I guess.'

'You aren't Mr Valiant, are you?'

'Valienté. Joshua Valienté.'

'*Valienté*. Sorry. Kind of an unusual name.'

And a name she'd never heard before, it seemed. So much for fame. 'I guess it is.'

'We're expecting you. You're the only guest we have arriving this evening. Umm, would you like to come in to the warm? We'll get you checked in, and you can make yourself comfortable. None of the rooms are air-conditioned, you understand. You have a private room, just as you booked, or what we call private anyhow. There's TV and web connections, on a good day. Oh, and the power goes off at ten p.m. Still, we're better off than we were. We got a Repatriation grant for redevelopment. Have you heard of that? Money to get people to come back to the Datum and rebuild, now that the weather's easing at last, or so they say. I like President Damasio, I think. Didn't vote for her, of course . . . Oh, here I am yapping on while you're standing there. Can I take your pack?'

'No. Thank you.' He began to hobble beside her towards the hotel.

'That leg looks painful. Arthritis?'

'A bad break.'

'You sure I can't help?'

'No, thank you.'

They paused in the shade of an awning, by the chalk sign.

'I had a note you want to visit a cemetery.'

'Yes. Forest Hill. My wife's there.'

'That's on this side of downtown. It's an easy drive in. We have carts you can hire . . . Oh, do you have a current driver's licence?'

He goggled. 'You need a *licence*?'

'I'd be happy to drive you.'

'I don't want to trouble you—'

'I need to go pick up some stores tomorrow anyhow.' She smiled. 'I mean, it's not like there's a bus service. Not out this far.'

Joshua suppressed a sigh. The great Valienté, the Long

341

Earth wanderer, leaning on a stick, forgotten even in Datum Madison, and reduced to getting a ride from some fresh-faced kid. 'Well, that's kind of you.'

'In the morning, then.'

'Thank you, Ms – umm—'

'Green. Phyllida Green.' She stuck out her hand.

He shook her hand, startled. Helen's family had been Greens. It was a common enough name. But Madison was a small city, and the hair colour looked about right. Was it possible? . . . Well, if this was some distant cousin of his wife, it felt OK to let her take care of him, just a little bit. Even if she had never heard of him.

'Are you sure you're feeling all right?'

'I'm fine, Ms Green. Just more old memories.'

'This way, then. Watch the step now.'

50

THE ROOM WAS a hutch, but the walls seemed to be well enough insulated, and Joshua wasn't cold. Phyllida Green made him a meal, omelette and French fries and beans, and she had a refrigerator stocked with some kind of local homebrew beer in recycled Coke bottles.

The web connection was a bust, but the TV worked well enough; Joshua guessed it was feeding off a signal from some satellite. He channel-surfed, the way he always did when he came back to the Datum, if only because it was still pretty much the only place you *could* do that. 'That's one thing you don't get in the High Meggers,' he said to himself. 'A sprained thumb from a TV remote.'

Most of the output, though, was ageing comedy or drama, some of it even dating from before Step Day. There were a few news channels, just the day's headlines delivered by talking heads, with little in the way of field reports. The most interesting stuff was documentaries, even if most of it was pretty crudely made, just a small team and a camera or two burrowing away in the corners of the Long Earth. Here was a piece on hucksters in Miami West 4, under the eggshell-blue thread of a space elevator, selling Stan Berg T-shirts, emblazoned with the eleven words of his Sermon Under the Beanstalk. 'The only Bible you'll ever need,' said one gum-chewing salesman.

Here was some kind of self-styled adventurer in a broad-brimmed hat that looked like it had come straight out of some fancy city store, clutching a copy of the *Stepper's Guide*, and bragging about the places he could take you, if you only signed up to his twain-based Long Earth tour business. 'In a world on the edge of the Corn Belt, I've explored the bed of a bone-dry Mediterranean. On a world far beyond the Gap, I've climbed the flank of the greatest volcano anybody ever found, a thousand times more powerful even than Yellowstone. Thirty-five million steps from the Datum, I've walked the only continent in an entire world, drained by a single river that makes the Mississippi look like a rivulet—'

'Been there, done that. Actually I don't have the T-shirt. Next.'

A documentary on Valhalla:

'With its grid-layout of streets, its industrial zones and parks, the schools and hospitals and shops, and its show-piece central square that has been named Independence Place ever since a bold declaration of autonomy was made here back in 2040, Valhalla has its own history. But as cities go, it is unique. Valhalla is the greatest city of mankind beyond the Datum and the Low Earths, indeed the only substantial city in the High Meggers. And what makes Valhalla unlike any other city in the Long Earth is that *nobody farms* anywhere near Valhalla. The citizens of this place inhabit a thick band of worlds to either stepwise side, worlds which have been kept largely undeveloped, and where people gather fruit from the trees and hunt the big animals. So a population of hunter-gatherers is able to sustain a modern city. This is a way of living that was not possible before stepping. The Valhallans got the best of both worlds!

'But now there is a kind of wistfulness about the place. Some buildings, even whole districts, are dark, boarded up. Even the bars seem half-empty. As if the people are trickling away.

'On Datum Earth, before Step Day, cities used to be magnets of population. People would drift in from the countryside in search of an easier life. But out in the Long Earth it's the opposite. If you can avoid the dirty water and the mosquitoes, living off the land is easy, cheap . . . In the Long Earth people drift *away* from cities, not into them. Even from the steppers' dream that was Valhalla—'

Depressed – remembering his father-in-law Jack, firebrand of Valhalla's Gentle Revolution – Joshua flipped channels.

A documentary about the Long Mars, a quarter of a century on from the pioneering expedition by Sally Linsay and her father:

'In Australia we had forty thousand years of civilization before the savages landed. It's not our fault that Captain Cook couldn't see what was in front of his nose. My daughter, you know, her art is to make shields of eucalyptus bark, and she signs them with handprints on the back – you blow the pigment through a straw and leave a shadow. And in European Ice Age caves you can find stuff that they signed just the same way . . .'

In the background, behind the face of the polite middle-aged woman, some kind of kangaroo went past, across a crimson plain. It looked tall – taller than the spacesuited humans around it – and, maybe in some adaptation to the lower gravity, it seemed to *walk*, one step after another, rather than hop.

'Of course I wouldn't say we were more advanced than you. Not much. But we were settled, we were sophisticated, we were embedded in our landscape, our ecology. We had mapped the continent, not with pictures but with words and songs. And not only that, we *stepped*. Right from the gitgo. There are rock paintings in the Low Earths that prove it. Stepping for thousands of years, because the outback is sure a useful place to have such a skill – *tens* of thousands of years, like it was normal, it was what we did. And then when the rest of you "discovered" the Long Earth, the way you "discovered" Australia, we were there already. No wonder more of us as a percentage went walk-about in the Long Earth after Step Day than any other group on the planet . . .'

And behind the roo, standing up from the smooth flatness of the seabed, were a series of dark bands, slender, vertical, black against the purplish sky of this world. Monoliths. Five of them. The image was sharp, the inscriptions on their surfaces clear, if utterly strange.

'Well, now we have Mars, the Long Mars, another raw, arid, beautiful landscape, and an unending one. We'll probably spend another four hundred centuries singing our way across all of that. Then we'll figure out what to do next . . .'

'Sleep well, Sally, wherever you are.'

346

At last Joshua found an old movie, a favourite of Lobsang's: *The Ballad of Cable Hogue*. He was falling asleep before the final reel, and dreamed of airship travel.

He woke before light.

This place no longer felt like Madison. It was too cold. It didn't *smell* the same – it didn't even smell like the Low Earth footprints of the town, so drastic had the climate shifts been. There was no traffic noise, but, lying there in the dark, without electric light, he heard the unmistakeable howl of wolves, and a gruff grunting closer by, the clatter of a garbage pail. A bear, maybe? Or just a raccoon? Some said that the wildlife of Canada was migrating south, fleeing advancing glaciers: lynx and moose and caribou. Some claimed you could even see polar bears not far north of Madison, in the worst of the winters.

He rolled over and tried to get some more sleep.

51

A LITTLE AFTER nine the next morning Joshua, with Phyllida Green, set off towards central Madison.

The electric cart followed Mineral Point Road, a straight-line drag that led dead east towards downtown, a route that would bring them almost to the gates of Forest Hill. The road surface was reasonably well maintained, the frost cracks and potholes roughly filled, though the edge of the asphalt was colonized by sturdy-looking saplings – pine and spruce trees. There were no markings on the road, no working lights or other traffic systems. Joshua guessed there wasn't the volume of road traffic to justify the upkeep.

It was a different way of life now, here on the Datum, Joshua was learning. The population densities had dropped so much, and the old globalized civilization had pretty much broken down. The days when you would use a cell phone made in Finland, to order a pizza made with ingredients from east Asia, and delivered by some guy who was an immigrant from Chile, were long gone. On the Datum, and indeed the stepwise worlds, people travelled a lot less geographically, and sourced their stuff much more locally, than they used to. Nobody used the roads any more, or the rail, or the planes.

And the countryside through which this road threaded was transformed too. In places the ground was flooded, and culverts and banks had been hastily dug to preserve the road itself. Joshua imagined drains clogging after a few years without maintenance, and the land reverting to the marsh from which much of the city's real estate had long ago been reclaimed. On higher ground, meanwhile, the old prairie had mostly died back, the lovely waist-high flowers that had once characterized this time of year gone, leaving sparse plains colonized by short grasses – it almost looked like Arctic tundra to Joshua. The forest clumps looked ravaged, with the green of pine trees sprouting from clusters of dead oaks and spruce. Even the state tree, the sugar maple, was supposedly extinct here, he'd learned.

The world was silent too, the birds stilled. Joshua vaguely wondered what was going on in the lakes, which ought to be clear of ash and human pollutants by now. He guessed the birds would be back, northern-latitude species anyhow. But what about the fish?

The trouble was that after Yellowstone it was as if the climate zones had suddenly all shifted hundreds of miles south, maybe as much as a thousand, so that the latitude of Madison was now like the southern coast of Alaska had been. And life couldn't react that quickly. Only a handful of the native species were able to prosper in the new landscape. One day, he supposed, the north Canadian flora would transplant itself down here wholesale, the pines and the birch and the tall grass prairie. But for a long while this landscape was going to look desolate.

They did pass a field crowded with strange, swollen shapes, each taller than an adult human being, and with a strange scent of cheese on the air. Joshua remembered how he and Lobsang had found such fungi on a world far beyond the Datum, in the course of their pioneering Journey all those years ago: a fungus that had proven easy to grow and yet highly nutritious, which Lobsang had threatened to bring home and sell to the fast-food industry. Now, in this long post-Yellowstone winter, that discovery seemed to have at last come into its own.

After a couple of miles they crossed the West Beltline Highway. Here there was still a working lights-controlled crossing system, and they had to wait. Though some of its lanes had been closed, and the bridge by which the highway had once crossed over Mineral Point Road was evidently disused, the highway itself was still open, and it supported a trickle of traffic. Most of the vehicles Joshua saw were electric, like Phyllida's, but there was some older pre-Yellowstone stock refitted with big fat gasifier cylinders, fuel derived from the burning of wood: it was a sight like a news clip from World War Two, to Joshua's eyes.

The highway junction was blazoned with bright orange warning signs, and that gave Phyllida the chance to chatter about the radiation-danger Zone system that had been established around Madison. Joshua remembered some of this, but he had never stayed in Datum Madison long enough for it to matter. The Red Zone extended a couple of miles around the Capitol building, or its ruin, where the anti-steppers' nuke had been detonated, back in '30. These days you were allowed in there at your own risk, but there were nightly sweeps by automated units and foot-patrol cops to stop anybody staying over. An Amber Zone stretched the best part of ten miles out from downtown, and so spanned the whole of Madison to the west to beyond the Beltline, to the south beyond Lake Monona and to Fitchburg, to the east well beyond the interstate to communities like Cottage Grove, and off to the north up beyond Dane County airport to De Forest and Sun Prairie. Phyllida said a kind of lobe of amber extended further to the east, because that was where the prevailing wind had happened to blow much of the fallout on the day of the nuke. Here you were allowed to reside, but you were subject to mandatory annual health checks, especially the children. And then there was a Yellow Zone that spread in a rough circle of radius fifty miles around downtown, just to keep you aware of the blight that lay at the heart of the area.

They drove on in, through more built-up neighbour-hoods, mostly abandoned.

'Some people think the Zoning should be dropped,' Phyllida said brightly. 'The residual radiation's supposed to be back to not much above the old background level by now. Except for caesium-137 of course,' she said with an air of familiarity. '*That* is still a menace in the food chain, such as in game and freshwater fish and mushrooms, which was *just* what people were living off after we ran out of food after Yellowstone, wouldn't you know it? But everybody says the ash and stuff from the volcano will probably do you a lot more harm than the radiation ever would. The authorities just want to monitor things, I suppose, and there's no harm in that.'

Joshua shrugged. 'I suppose nobody knows for sure.'

'That's true,' she said. 'People ask about it when they come to stay. We keep pamphlets. Sometimes we get medical teams and so on, come to study the ongoing effects. And sometimes people just come to see, to be tourists. Some of them brag that they've been to all three pre-Yellowstone civilian nuclear strike zones, in Japan and here. Like they're collecting the experience.'

'Odd.'

'They pay their way, and we make a living.' She glanced at him. 'But most of our visitors are like you, with family here – or at least they had family here . . .'

'My wife and I both grew up here in Madison. In the pre-nuke days. We never knew each other back then. After Step Day she made a trek with her family, and they built a town in the Corn Belt.'

'Where's that? I've never been much further than West 5, for the government offices there and the hospitals.'

'Oh, about a hundred thousand steps out. This was before the twains, and they walked out there. And then when we married we lived a lot further out, more than a million steps.'

'Gosh.'

'But when she died, she wanted to be brought back here. She was cremated.'

'You brought her ashes back, then.'

Not me, he thought. *He* had gone the other way, off into the High Meggers yet again, escaping from it all. And Rod, their son, had escaped too, disappearing into the Long Earth green with his elusive companions. It was Katie and Harry, Helen's sister and her husband, who had had to bring her home to Forest Hill. They'd hardly spoken to Joshua since.

He said only, 'Something like that.'

Much of the housing stock here was long abandoned, and thirty years after Yellowstone there were some pretty mature shrubs and trees colonizing front lawns and parks. They passed one big old shopping mall that had been converted into a 'reclamation centre', according to a big federal government sign. You could bring any of the enduring waste you could still find from the pre-Yellowstone years, near-indestructible foam coffee cups and aluminium cans and bottles of plastic and glass, decades old but some as pristine as when they were manufactured. Here, Repatriation money was being used to process such garbage of the past into useful goods to support the future.

By the time they reached Forest Hill they were just a few miles from downtown. There were posts on the sidewalk giving distances to the perimeter of the inner Red Zone. Joshua began to see damage he thought must be associated with the nuke: roofless wooden-framed buildings just rotting away, concrete structures that were windowless shells. But life sprouted wherever it could, the green of weeds breaking through abandoned driveways, flowers swaying on dirt-covered windowsills in the June light.

After she'd parked up, Phyllida offered to walk him to the grave marker, but he refused. She did check he had a working cell phone, and made him promise to call her if he needed a ride home. He chafed a little at this fussing, but a good heart had always been a characteristic of the

Greens. And besides, his pride wasn't what it had been. Not since he'd needed a troll to wipe his backside.

Once he was inside the cemetery, however, and began his hobbling exploration, he regretted turning down her offer of help. He'd logged on ahead and had downloaded a plot number and a rough map, but it hadn't occurred to him that since Yellowstone the cemeteries in Madison, indeed all over the Datum no doubt, had been forced to become a lot bigger than they'd once been. Forest Hill had colonized what had once been a golf course, and also, he figured out, a residential area between its old southern boundary and Monroe Street, an area probably burned out after the nuke. But even in these extensions the plots were squeezed in tight.

It was a gruesome odyssey.

The sun was high in a cloud-speckled sky by the time he found Helen's plot; he was sweating, wheezing a little – maybe there was still some ash in this foul Datum air – and he leaned heavily on his stick as he peered down at the little marker. It was a modest marble slab set in a square of gravel, with the inscription in a neat, apparently machine-worked font. He read the words aloud. 'To the memory of Helen Green Valienté Doak, wife of Joshua Valienté, wife of Benjamin Doak, mother of Daniel Rodney, 2013–2067. And to the memory of Rodney Green, 2012–2051 . . .'

I kept my promise, he told Helen silently.

There was a hand on his shoulder. 'You found her.'

Joshua turned. 'Nelson. Didn't hear you coming. I'm losing my survival skills.'

'You are if a clumsy ox like me managed to sneak up on

you.' Nelson Azikiwe, wearing a sober black overcoat, bent a little stiffly to see the stone.

'She wanted to come back home in the end.'

'I can understand that. Personally, I have a plot marked out in my old parish of St John on the Water. Well, as a former incumbent my name is already on a plaque in the church, in gold leaf.'

'Very tasteful. Helen's family is all over the place. Her father's buried at Valhalla. Katie, her sister, and her family will be staying at Reboot.'

'What about you, Joshua? Where will your final resting place be?'

Joshua shrugged. 'Wherever I fall over, I guess. I'd rather not provide a snack for some ugly High Meggers predator, however. And *especially* not a croc.'

Nelson squinted at the marker. 'So brother Rodney is here with her.'

'That was one reason she wanted to come home, I think. For Rod's sake. He didn't see any of the family before he died, in prison. She had his ashes brought here. I think she always felt guilty about Rod.'

'I remember the story.'

'Here in Madison the perps of the nuke attack remain notorious, as you can imagine. So we tried to keep the existence of this plot a secret. I said we shouldn't even have Rod's name on the stone, but Helen always insisted on that. If the stone was ever desecrated—'

'She will lie safe,' came a new voice. 'You can rely on me for that, Joshua.'

Startled, they both turned.

* * *

The newcomer appeared to be another elderly man, dressed in jeans and a loose jacket, almost as sober as Nelson in his overcoat. He was entirely bald, clean-shaven, his features rather nondescript. The lines around his eyes and mouth and on his forehead gave an impression of age, certainly, but that was indeterminate too.

'You've got a new face,' Joshua said by way of greeting.

Nelson looked the newcomer up and down. 'A whole new ambulant unit, in fact. Impressive-looking. But rather heavy-set?'

Joshua said, 'And you got your arm back.'

'The damaged copy of myself that you brought back from the world of the Traversers, Joshua, had served its purpose. It is now in a transEarth vault, where the various improvisations that were forced on me to survive years of isolation are being studied for potential future value.'

Nelson smiled. 'No sandals and robe?'

'These days I prefer to remain anonymous.'

'Except when you choose not to be,' Joshua said wryly. 'You say you're protecting Helen's grave . . .'

'You know me, Joshua. I see the world turn – all the worlds – I see thistledown fall on a gravestone.' He sighed. 'But I can make other eyes turn away – electronic eyes, at least. The stone isn't even marked on most plots of the cemetery. I made sure you downloaded a version which had the correct entry.'

Joshua frowned. 'So you saw me coming.'

Nelson touched his arm. 'He watches over us with the best of intentions.'

'So he always says, Nelson.' He faced the ambulant unit. 'So what do we call you this time? George Abrahams?'

356

The ambulant unit smiled at last, and its rather stiff face was transformed. '"Lobsang" will do.'

'It's good to see you again,' Joshua said grudgingly.

The unit considered this. 'In spite of everything?'

'Consider that a standard caveat.'

'Indeed. I have missed you too. Well, here we are reunited. Look at the three of us, relics of an age gone by. Do you recall the movie *Space Cowboys*? In which Clint Eastwood and other veterans—'

Joshua held his hands up. 'Know it by heart.'

'Well, rather like the Cowboys, we have one last mission, gentlemen.'

Joshua said, 'So I hear. We're going to find Nelson's grandson, and bring him home. One last hurrah. Though I've no idea how to go about it. Whereas you, Lobsang—'

'I have a plan, of course.'

Nelson seemed eager, energized. 'You do?'

'And I know precisely where we will begin. We will follow a trail of breadcrumbs laid by a much abler agency than even I ever was.'

'You mean the Next,' Joshua guessed.

'And we'll begin just where it all started for you, Joshua. With a boy, in a children's home that once stood on Allied Drive, since relocated to Madison West 5. Back to the beginning, you see.

'Well, that's the plan. We can go back to West 5 whenever we are ready. But I wondered if you might wish to see central Madison first.'

Joshua grunted. 'I haven't been back there since Yellowstone.'

'It's only a few miles from here, and an easy walk. But I

357

have a cart.' He glanced at the two of them, Nelson corset-stiff and Joshua leaning heavily on his cane. 'I thought that might be wise.'

'Perceptive as ever, Lobsang,' Joshua said. He took a breath, stood straight, and turned away from Helen's marker.

52

To Joshua's untutored eye, the open-top electric cart looked identical to Phyllida Green's – a wheeled box of some smooth white plastic. He did wonder how it kept its energy topped up. From supply points in the street?

For the first few minutes Lobsang drove respectfully slowly, and the cart moved almost silently along the roughly restored asphalt of Monroe Street. By now they were well within Phyllida's Red Zone, as Joshua could tell from a plethora of signposts with glaring scarlet warning discs, radiation-hazard symbols, and free-call emergency telephones. Yellowstone ash was heaped up by the side of the road, and filled up the interiors of the roofless houses, as if it had been poured in.

The cart jolted over a bump in the road, making the two old men in the back groan. Looking over his shoulder, Joshua saw that the asphalt had been melted here, and had then solidified in a frozen wave.

They were reaching downtown now, the central zone of the nuclear devastation, and Lobsang slowed further. Here, many buildings had been flattened to their foundations, though others, some of the more solidly built office

359

blocks and public buildings, had withstood the blast to varying extents. Of course nothing had been rebuilt; only gaudily coloured monitoring stations and emergency medical centres had been erected amid the ruins. But the green was sprouting everywhere it could, pushing through layers of cracked concrete and asphalt, despite the radiation, despite the climate collapse. Life going on.

The mound on which the Capitol building had once stood had been blown apart. They slowed to a halt in the rubble. Flowers swayed between concrete blocks.

'I suppose I owe you both an apology,' Nelson said. 'It's my fault you are both here. Drawn away from places you'd much sooner be, I'm sure.'

'Not in my case,' Joshua said promptly. 'I'd got myself thoroughly lost, for once, out in the High Meggers.'

'I'm glad you've been preserved, of course, Joshua,' Lobsang said now. 'If only to hear of your encounter with a new form of troll – new to me, anyhow.'

'Ha! Even you don't know it all, do you, Lobsang?'

'Not yet.'

'And I'm sorry too that I had to bring you back from Tibet, Lobsang,' Nelson said.

The ambulant unit shrugged, a rather mechanical gesture. 'I had to return eventually. To disappear into such virtual environments, into one's own head, is an endless temptation for one such as me. And yet I seem to need such refuges from time to time.' He glanced over the shattered Capitol. 'I remember how you shunned my company for years, Joshua, after the nuclear detonation here. You wondered how I, a being like a god, could have failed to stop such an obvious wrong as the attack on the city. Yet there are times when I cannot even save myself. Here we are in this museum of destruction, where, you know, the young, the Long Earth generations, come to try to understand. And in fact it's the enthusiasm and the curiosity of the young that I hope will lead us to your lost grandson, Nelson. I'm speaking of the Invitation from the sky, and the Thinker engineering project that the Next have developed in response.'

Nelson frowned. 'What has that got to do with Troy and the vanishing Traversers?'

'*Join us*,' Joshua said, understanding now. 'That's the link. The Invitation from the sky. The Next heard it through their radio telescopes. And it seeped into the consciousness of the trolls. Even I heard it, I guess,' he added ruefully. '*Join us*. Like a nagging at the back of my head . . . I suppose the Traversers must have heard it too – somehow.'

'The Long Earth has always been a matter of the mind as well as the body,' Lobsang said. 'You see, Nelson? I have no idea where the Traversers took your grandson, or how to follow them. But the Next are building a giant engine in response to the same Invitation that seems to have lured the Traversers. I believe our best bet of finding Troy and the Traversers—'

'Is to work with the Next, and follow them,' Nelson breathed. 'I see. And how do we do that?'

So Lobsang told them about Jan Roderick, a boy under the care of the Sisters at the Home, and his matter-printing.

'Enthusiasm and curiosity – that's what the Next have exploited to get their engine built. A million kids like Jan,

361

turning out their baffling components, adding to the vast flow of material and labour into their construction site of a world. And now Jan is out there himself. What I intend us to do is to follow the trail leading from the Home on Allied Drive to that construction site. Its location itself is no secret, but through Jan I hope to find a way to contact the project's superiors. And through them, perhaps . . .

'Well. That's the plan. And the very first step is to speak to Sister John. Shall we return to West 5? If we simply step over we'll be at the centre of town, of course, where a more comfortable transport cart is available. This cart will find its own way home.'

'And then we must plan our next steps,' Nelson said firmly.

When they'd gone, the electric cart, its gleaming white flanks stained by soot and ash, sat silently for five full minutes. Some of the insects attending the flowers that flourished in the wreck of the Capitol mound inspected it curiously; finding no nectar, they turned away.

Then the cart swivelled neatly and started to roll back the way it had come, towards the west. Moving almost silently, in all the Red Zone it was the only object in motion larger than a cat.

53

I N THE END it took a month for the Space Cowboys to follow the breadcrumb trail from their first meeting with the Sisters at the Home in Madison, to the moment when Lobsang's twain popped into the air over the world called Apple Pi.

And Joshua, sitting alongside Lobsang on the bridge of this small airship, found himself looking down at a landscape of glistening technology that stretched as far as the eye could see. It was a July morning on all the worlds of the Long Earth, and the low sun threw back highlights from distant surfaces, like reflections from the windows of tower blocks. The carpet of engineering was broken here and there by huge cylindrical shafts, over which heated air shimmered. Everywhere twains hovered like low clouds, vast components dangling in cradles beneath their bellies. It was an entirely inhuman spectacle, save for scraps of natural green where tents and shacks huddled, and corporate and national flags fluttered from poles.

Aside from Lobsang and Joshua, the twain's only other passenger was Sancho the Librarian troll, sought out and brought here at Joshua's specific request. After all the wonders Sancho had shared with Joshua and Rod, it seemed only right that the troll should be here to add this new miracle to his voluminous memory store on behalf of the troll nation. Now Sancho hooted in wonder, his flat nose pressed against a window. Well, that was Joshua's own reaction, pretty much.

The twain was buffeted as Lobsang brought it down. 'There's a lot of turbulence,' he muttered, concentrating. 'All that machinery gives off a lot of heat. In fact those big shafts are cooling vents. They can pump out so much heat they create permanent low-pressure systems – unending rain storms.'

Joshua said, 'A computer that makes its own weather? But it looks like a blight to me. Some kind of vast infestation. From space it must be an ugly scar.'

'Indeed. And that's not a bad analogy. The structure was begun with imports of materials and labour from the other human worlds of the Long Earth. But now, it seems, a kind of self-assembly process has kicked in. Self-replication. It has begun to spread out from its edge, converting the stuff of this Earth into its own substance. Exactly like a parasite, in as much as it will be mostly composed of materials transformed from the raw matter of this world.'

'Like the silver beetles.'

'That is an unfortunate parallel, yes.'

Joshua asked, wondering, 'But what's it all for, Lobsang?'

'If we're ever to find the Traversers, that's what we'll have to discover, Joshua.'

* * *

364

'*I* can't tell you what it's all for,' said Maggie Kauffman. 'Not yet, not definitively. Not even our Next colleagues know that . . . At least I don't think so.'

The Admiral herself met them at the foot of the debarkation ramp, when the twain had touched down in an island in the Thinker that Joshua learned was called 'Little Cincinnati'. Upright in her uniform, Kauffman looked strong, brisk, and a hell of a lot fitter than Joshua was, even though she must be roughly the same age. A young officer stood at her side, a woman, conspicuously armed. Joshua was impressed that Lobsang had managed to get the commander of this operation herself to greet them – evidently, in fact, to welcome them as some kind of consultants. But then, he told himself, he should have learned by now never to underestimate Lobsang.

Kauffman went on, 'Well, the big mysteries will keep. For now it's good to meet you again, Mr Valienté.' Briskly she shook Joshua's hand; he offered his right hand, not the prosthetic left. Her grip was as impressive as the woman herself. 'I've never forgotten how you helped me through that dreadful dilemma of Happy Landings and a nuclear weapon.'

He shrugged. 'I was just trying to help a friend.'

'I suppose that's all any of us can do. Listen, how's that leg of yours? Looks like you've been in the wars.'

'I'm surviving.'

'Maybe my ship's medics could check you over. Military medicine, better than the civilian flavour nowadays. Well, you won't have to walk far. I'll escort you to our tour vehicle in a moment. As for my other guests—' She turned to Sancho.

The troll looked back at her, grizzled, fearless, curious. 'Hoo.'

'They call you Sancho.' As she spoke she signed, in the lab-rat pidgin that had evolved wherever trolls lived and worked, or were confined and studied, alongside humans. 'I apologize that I have no troll-call with me; there will be some in the vehicle.'

Sancho signed back. *So there should be.*

'Maybe he'll be able to help,' Joshua said. 'Sometimes I think he knows more about the Invitation, about this whole strange business, than we do.'

'I've had trolls and other non-human sapients on my crew before. I see no reason to believe the Invitation wasn't meant for them as much as for us. Sancho certainly has a right to be here.' Now she turned to Lobsang. 'As have you – shall I call you Mr Abrahams?'

'Lobsang will do.' He smiled, still and calm as ever. 'I think we're all rather too old for false identities and other silly tricks now.'

'Indeed. What a bunch of oddballs we are, and all as old as Methuselah. Well, it's going to get odder. This way, please.' She led them across the asphalt. 'And, by the way, call me Maggie. But not in front of the lower ranks . . .'

Joshua hobbled on his stick through an orderly layout of tents and prefabricated huts. Electric trucks and carts rolled through a grid of dirt tracks, and military personnel, mostly young, crisply uniformed, hurried to and fro with gleaming tablets and bundles of paper. Above his head a forest of antennas probed the sky. This small camp was evidently a node of command and communications, from which Kauffman was controlling the human side of the Thinker operation with the military precision Joshua would have expected. Yet Joshua noted that all this was surrounded by a wire fence, and armed troopers peered down from watchtowers. Little Cincinnati evidently needed big security.

They were led to a small convoy, a couple of heavy-looking armoured vehicles flanking what appeared to be a tourist bus, a big, heavy double-decker covered with blister-like viewing windows.

Kauffman said as they boarded the bus, 'We're going to take a brief tour. I'm behind with my own inspection routine anyhow, and I'm due to witness the installation of a new type of component. Which is in the hands of this young person . . .'

A woman aged around twenty-five stood nervously before them, clutching a kind of crystalline slab, hugely complicated. She was staring at the grizzled troll behind Lobsang.

'Cat got her tongue, evidently,' Maggie said dryly. 'Her name is Lee Malone. She's a volunteer originally from GapSpace, so highly skilled technologically. And I want you to meet our lead driver. Dev Bilaniuk is another volunteer from the Gap.'

A smiling man, aged perhaps thirty. 'Space pilot in training,' Dev said. 'Bus driver pro tem.'

Joshua did the presidential handshake thing. 'I'm sure you'll keep us safe and sound.'

Maggie said, 'I want to impress on you the broad range of communities and interests represented here. The Aegis government has put me in charge of security, policing and overall administration. But this is *not* a military project. In a real sense it is an effort by all mankind, scattered as we are across the Long Earth. So you have volunteers like these two space cadets . . . But it's never been our initiative, I mean humanity's, or under human control.'

With difficulty Joshua climbed into the interior of the bus, following Sancho and Lobsang. The seat belt he would have to wear was more like a harness, but otherwise the bus was pretty luxurious. A half-dozen armed Navy personnel climbed aboard with Maggie.

'Nice ride,' Joshua said, strapping in.

Lobsang smiled. 'I recognize the design of the vehicle. The Black Corporation?'

'You're right, as always, Lobsang,' came a new voice.

A screen mounted on the ceiling lit up to reveal an image of what looked to Joshua like a hospital ward. A very wizened, very old man lay in the bed, propped up by a heap of pillows. A drip snaked into his arm, and a translucent mask was strapped to his face. He said, 'I wouldn't be too impressed by the scale of all this, by the way. Size isn't everything. I'm just about old enough to remember the first cellphones; they were the size of house bricks. I bet on the planet Tatooine or wherever this thing originated, they've got it down to a thing the size of a dime . . .'

'Douglas Black,' murmured Lobsang.

'It's good to see you again! We must discuss the financial performance of the transEarth Institute while you're here.'

'Indeed,' Lobsang said uncomfortably. 'I didn't know you were back.'

'I do rather miss my Shangri-La. But you know me, Lobsang, ever the technology buff. I couldn't stay away from this engineering marvel. I'm afraid I'm not quite strong enough even for a bus ride any more. But I'll be with you in spirit, Lobsang. Looking over your shoulder, as ever!'

'As ever,' Lobsang said neutrally.

Joshua wondered how Lobsang really felt about his lifelong relationship with Black. As Joshua understood it, it had been Black's sponsorship that had restored Lobsang to 'life' in the first place, by providing the innovations, notably information-processing gel, and the funds required to boot up Lobsang's 'reincarnation'. Lobsang had grown far from those origins, in fact into an entity that spanned worlds – but there had always been limits. Just as the Next had only ever used him as a kind of bridge to humanity, so Black had always had a certain hold over him. When Black had disappeared for years to his remote Long Earth retreat, Lobsang hadn't even been consulted, Joshua knew. And now here was Black, back again, in the middle of Lobsang's life.

It was remarkable that Lobsang didn't actually *own* himself, and had never been in a position to buy himself out, despite years of effort by his loyal ally Selena Jones. And that was mostly because of Douglas Black.

Joshua touched Lobsang's arm. 'You OK, buddy?'

'He's up to something,' Lobsang muttered.

'Who, Black? What, exactly?'

'Well, he evidently hasn't confided in me. But he's *not* a man who's content merely to observe. Wait and see.'

Maggie tapped the big screen now, and brought up an

image of three more individuals: an older man and woman, and a young girl, aged maybe eighteen. The woman wore a practical-looking coverall; the man and the girl wore black robes.

'More acquaintances you'll need to make,' Maggie said. 'And these are on the bus with us, though they insisted on a closed compartment of their own.'

Joshua peered. 'They are Next. That woman is Roberta Golding.'

Maggie nodded. 'I've known her a long time. She's evolved into a kind of unofficial ambassador of the Next to humanity. Useful in smoothing out the wrinkles between *us* and *them*.' She grinned. 'So much so that I sometimes wonder if she's actually one of our super-brained overlords at all. Now, the man with her is called Marvin Lovelace. He's a Next also; he's from Miami West 4. Seems he worked undercover there at one time. Now he's out in the open, and is a front man for a group who call themselves the Humble.'

'I know of this,' Lobsang said. 'Next preachers working among humanity, particularly at sites of poverty, unemployment, stress. Based on the teachings of Stan Berg. And they have an agenda that differs from the Next mainstream – if that term has any meaning. Sceptical about the Thinker project, comparatively. In some ways the Next are divided over the wisdom of pursuing this contact just as much as humanity.'

Maggie said, 'Well, I leave the theology to the chaplains. In practical terms, here at Apple Pi Lovelace and the others are like ferocious union bosses. If you want to get anywhere with the labour force, you have to work through them.

But I leave *that* to the corporate management people, the Black Corporation, LETC. That position of power is one reason Lovelace is aboard here today, however. Meanwhile the girl is called Indra Newton. A second cousin to Stan Berg. Super-smart. And, it seems, she's inherited some of his unusually adept stepping ability.'

Joshua remembered. Sally Linsay had got to know Stan Berg. In addition to his precocious moral philosophizing, Stan had been able to step in ways even Sally, the queen of the soft places, couldn't follow – as if he could find, or even *create*, new linkages in the great tangle of connectivity that was the Long Earth. It was a talent that in the end had cost both Stan and Sally their lives, at New Springfield . . .

Lobsang asked, 'So why is Indra here?'

'Well, we don't know that yet,' Maggie said. 'The Next appear to have some kind of strategy in dealing with the Thinker, which evidently involves Indra, but they don't confide in us totally. Even though we are the Navy. OK – introductions done. If you're in your seats and strapped in, this wagon train can roll . . .'

54

A s the bus set off across the compound, Joshua noticed, military vehicles moved quietly into formation ahead and behind, including a couple of motorcycle outriders. Lobsang pointed up, and Joshua saw through skylights a beefy-looking military twain hovering overhead.

'The security seems heavy,' Joshua remarked to Maggie.

'Well, we continue to get plenty of threats here. Though I hope my response is more subtle than my predecessor's. I'm confident we've got security buttoned up tight enough.'

But for all Maggie Kauffman's evident competence, Lobsang and Joshua shared a sceptical glance. And again Lobsang looked meaningfully at the smiling, relaxed face of Douglas Black, huge in the wall screen.

As they passed through the boundary security and rolled out of Little Cincinnati, the landscape outside the window soon became utterly alien.

They were heading east, Joshua saw from the position of the sun – it was about noon, the sun was to the south. The roadway they followed was a straight dirt track, evidently purposely left clear so that traffic like this could pass. But to either side of the track, the substance of the Thinker towered. They drove between diamond cliffs, their very surfaces complex textures of facets and panels. The material was mostly clear, it really was like quartz or diamond, and the captured sunlight, multiply reflected, emerged as a cool blue glow. Joshua had crossed Earths trapped in Ice Ages; very old ice could look like this, he knew, shining like walls of blue light. Yet he glimpsed structure in there producing light of its own, winking stars like trapped constellations. Every so often they drove *over* structures crossing the road, like speed bumps but with more texture – fallen glassy pillars. And more prosaically the bus and its accompanying fleet had to skirt those huge heat-release pits in the ground, circular shafts lined with concrete.

Lee Malone came back to speak to them, though at Maggie's stern glare she sat down and strapped herself in. She held up the component she'd shown them before. 'I'll be installing this later.' A slab of crystal, winking lights. 'You can see why we call this machine the Thinker. Every gram of it is devoted to information processing – to intelligence.'

'And we're driving *through* it,' Joshua said. 'As if we're driving through an immense brain. What the hell is it doing with all that brainpower?'

They came to a place where the engineered landscape seemed to have split along a tremendous fault. The bus slowed, and the passengers peered out at an uplifted cliff that rose a good fifty yards above the level of the road. The edge looked fractured, and sparks, like miniature lightning flashes, crackled across the broken face. But Joshua saw connections, scab-like extrusions, seeping down the uplifted face to the lower levels. A healing process beginning, perhaps. Something about it made Joshua shudder.

'Earthquake,' Maggie said. 'A small one, but it did a lot of damage. Well, I say a lot – minor on the Thinker's overall scale. You'll see it seems to be repairing itself. We did send human crews out here, but they didn't know where to start.'

Joshua, staring at the computronium cliff, thought he saw movement, short noon-time shadows shifting across the broken faces. 'I could swear I see somebody moving.'

'Could be.' Maggie snapped her fingers to attract the attention of a junior officer, who began to make calls. 'This is a machine as big as a continent, Joshua. We've had people trying to *mine* the stuff – there is gold in there, platinum. It's hard to patrol it all, although we do try. Drive on, Dev.'

The scenery soon became numbing. The scale was literally superhuman, after all.

Joshua's head started to nod. The troll *did* fall asleep, and snored enthusiastically.

After around an hour, the bus slowed. Dev Bilaniuk announced they were arriving at Hillsboro – or, rather, a station at the footprint of that Datum community. They drove into another fenced compound, much smaller than Little Cincinnati, just a few acres kept clear of obvious Thinker elements. At the heart of this facility was another wire fence enclosing a much smaller area, with its own watchtowers and marines hefting automatic weapons. Joshua wondercd what secret they were guarding here.

And just beyond, not much further to the east, Joshua saw open countryside. The crystalline layers of computronium that washed around this compound came to a ragged border; this was an edge of the Thinker.

'Everybody out,' Maggie said as the bus rolled to a halt. 'There'll be coffee, food. I'd advise you to use the bath-room on the bus, however; the local facilities as used by marine jarheads and Navy grunts aren't likely to be pristine . . .'

Joshua clambered out of the bus with some difficulty, refusing help. Standing with Lobsang, leaning on his stick, he accepted a coffee.

On the side of the empty bus, a panel was alight with the image of Douglas Black, his head cradled on what looked like fresh pillows. When he saw Lobsang, he made a gesture from Joshua's distant childhood, forked fingers pointing to his own eyes, then outward. *I'm watching you.* Black grinned boyishly.

Maggie was intrigued by Lobsang. 'You're drinking the coffee?'

'For the flavour, and to be sociable. I can ape most human functions.'

'I've ordered food and drink for the troll,' Maggie said. 'A variety. I'm used to provisioning my own troll crew members. I know they're picky.'

'Sancho isn't too choosy,' Joshua said. 'Don't give him caffeine, however. I tried him on an espresso once. Boy, did I regret that!'

An officer came jogging up. 'The lollipops are ready for you, ma'am.'

Joshua and Lobsang exchanged a glance. Lollipops? That word had only one meaning for Joshua, and not a pleasant one.

Maggie led them to the central wired-off compound. 'Just to warn you, what you're going to see is a Next project, not ours. I'm told the individuals involved, or at least their parents, had a free choice about participating. Try not to judge what you see, not to react . . .'

The two Next sat in chairs, facing each other; they had metal frames helping to support their heads, and drip tubes snaked into their bare arms. Their bodies seemed almost normally proportioned, and they were dressed in light robes, like hospital gowns. But their heads were grotesquely swollen, the craniums all but hairless, the big bubble-like skulls overwhelming their small faces. They were evidently a male and female, but it was hard to guess at their ages.

Attendants stood by this tableau, whether Next or human Joshua couldn't have said. But the guards around the wire fence were US marines.

Lollipops. The memory surfaced slowly. It was forty years ago now. Joshua and Lobsang, during The Journey, had paused at a world more than a hundred and thirty thousand steps from the Datum. Here they had found evidence of a slaughter of human colonists . . . And, later, a very strange creature. Trying to help the big-brained elf as she gave birth, in his ignorance Joshua could have killed her.

The creatures in the pen were like Joshua's lollipops, crossed with humans.

Roberta Golding joined them, walking over from the bus. 'They are in no pain.'

Joshua frowned. 'Why do you say that?'

'It's the first question people usually ask.'

'And why the guards?'

Maggie said grimly, 'They're here because people have tried to terminate these two. Even some of our own personnel.'

Roberta said, 'The marines protect Ronald and Ruby from such misguided acts of kindness.'

Joshua stared. 'Ronald and Ruby?'

'They have been genetically engineered, based on a humanoid type you yourself discovered, Joshua Valienté—'

'What the hell are they doing here?'

Roberta sighed. 'We are trying to communicate with the Thinker. It was Ronald and Ruby themselves who led our effort to translate the Invitation's rather abstract and utterly alien vision into practical engineering. So they will always have an intimate connection with it, you see. And this particular location is dense with complex electro-magnetic fields. Now, the human brain, or the processing that goes on in there, is also a matter of complex electro-magnetic fields. And surely those fields could be manipulated by a sufficiently advanced technology: your thoughts could be shaped, your perceptions, your very memories altered, non-invasively but profoundly intimately. So we have brought Ronald and Ruby here in the hope of contact. It is hard to imagine a more complete communication, if it works . . .'

Joshua saw that Sancho had gone to the fence. The

marines looked alarmed, but Maggie waved at them to let the troll pass. Sancho pressed his face to the wire and stared at the lollipops.

Joshua too found himself staring in utter dismay. He murmured, 'Lobsang, tell me. How can people so smart commit something so self-evidently wrong as this?'

'I know what you mean,' Lobsang said grimly. 'Maybe it's because the minds of the Next themselves are so new. A hasty rewiring of a system that is after all millions of years old. Things go wrong when you grow too fast. We believe there are asylums at the Grange and elsewhere for the mentally ill – and of course we know of a few crazies who've made it to the human worlds, such as the Napoleons who escaped from Happy Landings by hijacking a Navy twain.'

'And look at those two,' Joshua said. 'They hardly look healthy, do they?'

Lobsang said darkly, 'But maybe they have their uses. Let's find out.'

They walked back to the group.

Lobsang asked Roberta now, 'So what success have you had with your communication experiment?'

'None,' said Maggie without hesitation.

'Some,' Roberta contradicted her.

Maggie put her hands on her hips and glared at her. 'That's news to me.'

Roberta, slim, quiet, looked at them all through her heavy glasses. 'You must see the difficulty. The Thinker's intellect is almost beyond our ability to comprehend. The totality of all human thought could pass through

378

the mind of the Thinker in a few days. *All* of it, since we left the trees. How can we communicate with such a mind? Ruby has said that the Thinker manipulates whole systems of thought – whole sciences, complete philosophies – as we manipulate words in a sentence.'

Lobsang considered this. 'And yet these two have spoken with the machine, to some extent. Can they say what it wants?'

Roberta looked at the lollipops. '*Join us*. That's still the basic message it's giving us.'

Maggie shook her head. 'Join us? How? Are we supposed to build some kind of wormhole, like in *Contact*?'

'Nothing like that. The lollipops say they dream of opening doors.'

'Opening doors.' Suddenly Joshua saw it. He had, after all, lived through Step Day. 'Stepping. This is all about stepping.'

Lobsang stood back and smiled. 'That's it. We should have seen it from the beginning. And it's just like New Springfield. I was *there*.'

Maggie frowned, as ever wary of rapid developments, of disruption to her carefully controlled order. 'Lobsang, speak to me.'

'Admiral, this Invitation is a Long Earth phenomenon. We know that. What's the most fundamental thing about the Long Earth? *Stepping* – the act of mind and body that enables you to travel from one world to the next. But stepping can be more than that. You remember Sally Linsay and her soft places – her leaps across the Long Earth? Then in New Springfield we found the silver beetles—'

'Who were able to step between different planets,' Joshua said. 'Tangled-up Long worlds.'

Dev said excitedly, 'And perhaps that's why we received the Invitation just now. Because *they* could tell, somehow, that somebody had made that step North, into another world.'

Lobsang and Joshua exchanged a glance. 'The Prime Directive,' said Joshua. 'He's right. *That's* why we received the Invitation just now.'

Lobsang nodded. 'We always wondered where everybody was. They *were* out there, but they were waiting until we were ready – we could only join the party when we discovered how to step in advanced ways. And at New Springfield we achieved the step equivalent of warp drive. Stan Berg was our Zefram Cochrane. And, right on cue, here come the Vulcans.'

Maggie sighed. 'You do realize that nobody here knows what the hell you two are talking about?'

But Roberta said carefully, 'Admiral, based on what I know of our communication with the Thinker – this *feels* right. A partial perception, but a good intuition.' She smiled brilliantly. 'I was always one of those who argued for including humans at the very heart of the project. And this shows I was right!'

'I'm happy for you,' Maggie said flatly. 'So what next, Lobsang?'

'Admiral, we must accept the Invitation. The finer the mind, the more advanced the ability to step. I think this Thinker, this tremendous *mind*, is going to enable us to step out of this world altogether. And we'll go – somewhere else. Just like the beetles.'

Maggie was still frowning. 'I suppose that's why I allowed you two to come here, to make these connections. But I don't like it when things move too quickly. Where, then?'

Lobsang peered up at the sky. 'Who knows? The Thinker may be able to tell us . . .'

'I'd go,' Lee said immediately. They all stared at her. 'I'm just saying.'

Lobsang glanced at Indra Newton, standing some distance away. 'And we may need another crew member. A specialist. In the end, the silver-beetle interface needed Stan Berg, remember, a super-stepper . . . Ah. All of which you Next foresaw, of course. And which is why you brought Indra here.'

Roberta smiled, only a little smugly now, Joshua thought. 'We have tried to anticipate. Yes, we guessed this would involve a new kind of stepping; yes, we did learn from the experience at New Springfield. The stepwise connection with the beetles' world seems to have been made accidentally – serendipitously. But we saw that Stan Berg was able *consciously* to change the connectivity of the Long Earth, even if it drained him to do it. All these suggest capabilities of still higher intelligences, who may *manipulate* their own Long worlds . . . In any event, if Ronald and Ruby are in communication with the Thinker, then we hope that they in turn can coach Indra in any necessary skills.'

Indra said quietly, 'I'm Stan's cousin. The family are intensely proud of his self-sacrifice. If I prove capable of this mission, I would be prepared to join the crew.'

Maggie snapped, 'Who the hell said anything about a

crew? You're speaking of a journey, and, I'm guessing, into the utterly unknown. To hell with self-sacrifice. Will it be safe? Will we be able to breathe? Will we step out into the middle of – I don't know – the heart of a sun?'

Lobsang smiled. 'You're a reader of Mellanier, I can tell.'

'Who?'

'A pod,' said Joshua. 'That's what we need. Like *2001*, Bowman through the Star Gate. We build a pod, and step over in that. Something like a bathyscaphe.'

'Yes,' Lobsang said. 'Good. Something that will last long enough at least for the crew to survive, and *step back* to report on what's on the other side.'

'I'll go too,' Dev said promptly. 'You'll need a pilot.'

Maggie held up her hands. 'Hold your horses. This boat that doesn't yet exist, if it gets built at all, is going to be a Navy boat, and the Navy will get to choose the crew. If any. Which means me.'

Joshua had to grin. 'Of course it does.'

Roberta Golding said, 'This has been a surprisingly constructive encounter. Suddenly we have a plan, a product of us all working together, ourselves and—'

'And us dim-bulbs?' Joshua asked.

The Next woman smiled around at them all, brightly, without, Joshua thought, a grain of irony. And yet he couldn't be sour. A new kind of journey faced him, a new direction. He felt the way he had on the day *after* Step Day, when he couldn't wait to get hold of his Stepper box and stride out into the unknown.

'OK,' Maggie said, glancing at her watch. 'Let's finish

the tour – and we are working to a schedule. Ms Malone, I believe you have a job to complete here.'

'Of course.' Lee dived into the bus, and returned with her slab of computronium. 'We wanted to show you the detail of how we work around here. This component is to be installed at the periphery of the Thinker, not far away. Please, follow me . . .'

Lee led the way to the boundary of the computronium surface.

Joshua, glancing over his shoulder, saw that Douglas Black, as displayed on his screen on the bus, was watching intently. And so too were the Next, Lovelace and Indra Newton; they'd stood back from the lollipop compound, but now, after a significant glance between Lovelace and Black, they followed closely too. Joshua felt a tingle of suspicion. The atmosphere had changed; something was going on here. He recalled Lobsang's suspicions of Black.

Only Sancho did not come. The troll stayed with his face pressed to the wire, his big fingers poking through the gaps, staring mournfully at Ruby and Ronald.

They gathered at the lip of the computronium sheet. Here the smart flooring was only a couple of feet thick, Joshua saw, and not yet anchored in the ground. Beyond, green grass grew, Earth grass innocent of the alien machinery that was about to overwhelm it.

Lee crouched down and held out the component she'd brought. 'See how it will mate into this slot in the edge? Just as the design mandated. The tolerances are at the nano scale, and once it's installed it will be integrated seamlessly . . . Of course tens of thousands of such pieces are installed automatically, every day. But this is actually one of the last wave of components to be assembled and delivered in this way.'

'Self-replication,' Maggie muttered. 'That's what it's beginning to do. Eating its own way deeper into the earth, growing at the periphery . . . Making its own components from rock and air. After that point we won't be able to stop it—'

'Ms Malone, *do not install that component.*'

55

THE VOICE, COMING from a loudspeaker, startled them all.

Lee looked baffled. She stared down at the component in her hands, as if it had turned into a rattlesnake.

Joshua turned. The marines at the heart of the compound were looking puzzled too, and were fingering their weapons.

And Douglas Black, his image bright and colourful in the screen on the side of the bus, grinned. 'Sorry to play the *deus ex machina,* so to speak.'

'You're not sorry about that at all,' muttered Lobsang. 'Joshua, I told you he was up to something.'

Black snapped out orders. 'Marvin Lovelace, you should stand aside. Maggie, you may consider confining him for now.'

Maggie, obviously with no idea what was going on, nevertheless nodded to a couple of marines, who hurried to Lovelace's side. 'Mr Black, if you know something I don't—'

'Oh, many things fall into that category, my dear Admiral. But what's relevant here is that I know what is hidden inside that component of Ms Malone's. You needn't worry, child, it's quite harmless – *now*. But you may wish to take it back to your plant and check it over. Ms Malone is quite innocent in all this, by the way.

'You see, Admiral Kauffman, some time ago I was approached by Marvin Lovelace and others of his associates from the Humble, and was asked to help them perpetrate an undercover scheme . . .'

There had been a kind of weapon built into Lee's component, Joshua learned. A computer virus, or a heavily engineered descendant of those antique threats – a virus manufactured by Next technicians, a weapon designed by super-smart post-humans – in fact, they were told, its design had been *sketched out by Ronald and Ruby themselves*, even as they had designed their impossibly advanced alien machine. Evidently their own conflict about the wisdom of building this thing had run deep. They had wanted to be sure it had an off switch.

'Damn it,' Maggie said. 'All my layers of security around this thing, and here was the true threat – right at the very centre.'

'That *was* the idea,' Marvin said contemptuously.

'It was a schizophrenic stratagem,' Black said. 'And this was our last chance to use it – to act before, as you say, self-replication moved the build process out of human control altogether. Would it have worked? The weapon was designed by Next; I'm not equipped to say. But they needed my help, you see, in ensuring that the virus was loaded into a component assembled in one of my factories, that it was properly delivered . . .

'Admiral Kauffman, I cooperated with these clever but

unwise saboteurs for two reasons. First because I thought these Next contact-pessimists might have a point. Maybe we should retain an ability to stop this thing, in our own interests. And second because *I* wanted to retain control. To have a veto.' He raised a kind of remote control in his bony hand. 'An off switch of my own, in case I decided the virus should *not* be delivered after all. And that has been my verdict. The device really is quite harmless now. And *that* will be the basis of my defence when they bring the prosecutions.'

Maggie turned on Marvin Lovelace. 'Why? Why the hell would you do this? What gives you the right?'

He smiled, his eyes hidden by dark glasses. 'It's not a question of rights. We are Next. We are trying to protect you from yourselves—'

'It was not like that,' Indra Newton blurted. She looked around, uncertain.

Maggie said, 'Go on, Indra.'

'I heard them talk.' Her accent was odd, Joshua thought, as if English was an entirely foreign language to her, studied from machine recordings. 'Not Ruby and Ronald: their dilemma was genuine, deep, philosophical. Marvin and the others were different. They don't care about humans. They don't care much about the Next. They thought the Thinker would be smarter than them, and they didn't want that. *They* want to be the smartest, for ever. And—'

'Yes?'

'They're *bored*. They're surrounded by worlds full of stupid people. They're bored ordering stupid people around, manipulating them. It's too easy. So they want to smash things up, for fun. Why not?'

387

Marvin made to lunge at the girl, but the marines kept him back.

Maggie said, 'I believe you, Indra. I knew a Next once, called David. A super-intelligent monster.'

'Yes,' Lobsang said gravely. 'A bored god. And what is such a god to do? The Olympian gods warred with each other, and consumed human lives in the process . . . It is an intrinsic flaw in Next psychology, it seems. But still, how – disappointing – to witness this.'

'Yeah,' Joshua said. 'You kind of expect more, don't you?'

Maggie said, 'We're not done, Mr Black. You're right: there will have to be an inquiry into this. But why *did* you stop them, in the end?'

'Because – *Join us!* I believe we have to trust these beings who call to us from another star. It's that or turn our backs on the future for good. I want to see your bathyscaphe launched!'

Bizarrely he won a round of applause, from Lee, from Dev, even from some of the marines.

'But,' Lobsang said more cynically, 'you have other agendas in play. You always do, Douglas.'

Black smiled, his face creasing. 'Of course you're right, old friend. It does me no harm at all to cement my reputation with these Next, who seem set to play such a significant role in all our futures. One must ask, you see – who is it who has the most to lose, if some form of *Homo superior* is to walk among us? Oh, it's not the little fellow with his bit of property and his small dreams. *He* will probably be better off, in a better-run world. No, it's the powerful and the rich, it is the politicians, the bankers, the industrialists who will find their position at the very top of our society threatened. People like me. After all, the Emperor of all the Neanderthals will have been just another hairy man-ape to the Cro-Magnons, won't he? But I hope, you see, to leverage what control I do still have over my affairs into some kind of credit with our new lords of the universe. And hence my willingness to pull apart this petty little plot.'

Lobsang was studying him, his artificial face inscrutable. 'A cynic might even suspect you set up the whole thing for precisely that purpose.'

Black raised snow-white eyebrows. 'Lobsang! I'm shocked.'

Joshua patted Lobsang's shoulder. 'To hell with him. One more Journey, Lobsang? Just like old times?'

Lobsang looked around. 'Very well. We've a lot of work to do. And I need to tell Nelson that we're going after his grandson, at last . . .'

Indra touched Joshua's arm. 'And I still want to ride in your pod, Mr Valienté.'

'Bravo,' Black called from his screen. 'Oh, bravo, child!'

56

(Extract from *Make Sure You Get This Down Correctly For Once In Your Life, Jocasta: The Authorized Biography of Professor Wotan Ulm, by Constance Mellanier. Valhalla: Transworld Harper, 2061.* Reproduced with permission.)

TOWARDS THE END of his life Ulm continued to speculate constructively, if controversially, on the nature of the Long Earth, and its access by humans through the process known as stepping. Of course he could be somewhat dismissive of unfounded theorizing, as is demonstrated by this verbatim transcript from a conversation with his personal assistant very late in Ulm's life:

'All this nonsense people spout about the Long Earth, as they've spouted since I was in short pants, and they've got not a jot further. Oh, we hear all about uncurled dimensions in a higher plane. Or, we're told, there are ten to power five hundred and whatnot possible universes out there in the "multiverse", as predicted by string theory. Or there are m-branes and p-branes bouncing off each other like puppies in a sack. What nonsense, all of it.

'Stepping is *human*. And it is in our humanity that we will find its explanation.

'It seems clear to me from a number of my studies, particularly concerning brain-damage cases, that *stepping* – at least, what has become known as the classic "Linsay step" process – has a strong overlap with *seeing*. And by *seeing* I don't mean the simple physical mechanism of the eye, or even the transcription of visual signals into messages in the cortex: I mean the deep inner conscious sensation of seeing, of gathering information from a scene. And from there it is a short conceptual distance between the faculty of *seeing* and the faculty of *imagining*.

'Mixed up in all that is our ability to step.

'The case of Bettany Diamond (reference: Mann, 2029) makes this clear. Here was a woman who could not step, physically, and yet she was capable of *seeing* into the neighbouring worlds. She saw her children playing in a garden, in the stepwise footprint of her living room. Yet she could not touch them.

'Stepping, then, is related to seeing, to imagining. And the greater the faculty of imagination, the greater the ability to step.

'But that can't be all there is, can it? What else, then, Jocasta? If you only had the wit, you would be asking that very question. And the answer may surprise you. The other faculty you need to be able to step, I propose, is that you must be able to convince yourself you are *uncertain*.

'Think of the famous quantum cat in the box, threatened with poison by the disintegration, or not, of an unstable atomic nucleus. Is it alive or dead? Those are two possible quantum states, and quantum uncertainty ensures that we cannot know which is "real" until we open the box to see, and one of those potential states is actualized. Very well.

'Now consider yourself, Jocasta. At any instant your location is described by many quantum states. One has you here, in this room, with me. Another has you on the moon. Another has you down the corridor, making me a better cup of tea than the last dose of tar you inflicted on me. Still another has you on Earth West 2, a step away from the here and now. And so on. Some of these places are far more probable locations for you to be in than others.

'You are certain you are here, are you not? Ah, but just suppose – if only you had the wit – that you could imagine that you are *uncertain* where you are. For if you are uncertain, in a quantum-physical sense, your location becomes uncertain too – *you* are the prime quantum observer of yourself, after all. You become smeared, so to speak, across the adjacent possible, among the infinite number of possible locations where you may possibly be. Then if you subsequently become *certain* that you are actually in West 2, and not here with me in West 1, then *that's where you are* – do you see? You have collapsed the quantum functions once more; you have stepped.

'Imagination, and a kind of wilful uncertainty. That's all there is to stepping, Jocasta. And the finer the mind, the greater the ability to step. We have seen this with natural talents who find "soft places", apparent flaws in the connectivity of the Long Earth, which can carry them thousands of worlds away. Perhaps the even stranger flaw that was discovered at New Springfield was evidence of another kind of mind: a mind capable of stepping into another Long world entirely.

'I say "finer minds", by the way. I think we *Homo sapiens* should always remember that the minds that created the Long Earth were not our own. It was our cousins, the trolls and other humanoids, who went out a million years before us, and dreamed the Long Earth into existence as they went, step by step. Not us.

'And as to *why* such Long worlds should exist at all – consider this. Starting with rocks flying around an infant solar system, it seems to be very hard to make one world capable of producing a mind – in the solar system it took billions of years to produce a fecund Earth. But having made one such world, if you could just run off copies, like pages off a printing press . . . But it is a cooperative process. Sapience conjured the Long Earth into existence. Maybe the Long Earth itself, having nurtured sapience, is now using that sapience to dream its way to infinity.

'What kind of stepping would an arbitrarily powerful intellect be capable of? Even I can scarcely speculate. Certainly I won't live to see it. Perhaps you will, my dear. Perhaps you will. But now I'm tired. So very tired. Turn the lights out when you leave, would you, Jocasta? . . .'

57

O N A BRIGHT October day, more than three million Earths from the Datum, a pod sat at the heart of the Little Cincinnati compound, that island of human enterprise in the great technological ocean that was the Thinker. The squat craft had been set up on a broad concrete square intended for landing heavy cargo twains, but today the only twains visible hovered in the autumn sky above, watchful, camera pods gleaming.

Joshua Valienté hobbled across the asphalt, with Lobsang, Maggie Kauffman and Dev Bilaniuk. They all wore NASA-type blue jumpsuits, and carried breathing masks. They were late, and they were hurrying. A heavily armed and watchful escort of Navy personnel accompanied them, led by Jane Sheridan. There had been specific threats against the project from the more extreme contact-pessimist types, and nobody was taking any chances.

As they neared the pod, camera lights glared in their eyes, and they had to push through a small crowd of applauding workers and other well-wishers. Joshua, pivoting on his walking cane, felt self-conscious, even ridiculous. And yet there was something glorious about it all. As if the ship was to be powered, not by any kind of technology, but by a surge of shared enthusiasm. He wasn't about to express such thoughts out loud, however.

'God damn it,' Maggie snapped. 'I haven't got time for this *Right Stuff* crap. We're overdue as it is.'

Lobsang smiled easily. 'Go with the flow, Maggie. The corporate people and the government have stumped up the funds for all this. We'd never have got our little craft built in three months otherwise. The contact-pessimist lobby in government has had to be bought off too. And the way they're clawing back the money, the way they're generating political credit, is by splashing us across the news as fast as the outernet will carry it. So smile for the cameras.'

'I'm a Navy admiral, damn it. We're selling our souls to this circus.'

'My own life story shows it's always possible to buy your soul back . . .'

At last they got through the crowd, passed inside a cordon of rope, and faced their ship. The craft, a squat cone standing on three legs, was swathed in black and white insulation that was broken by stubby antennas and glistening lenses and attitude-thruster nozzles that gaped like the mouths of baby birds. Any clear area, it seemed to Joshua, was plastered with flags, predominantly the holographic Stars and Stripes of the US Aegis, the Long Unity Earth-in-cradled-hands sigil, and corporate logos: the marching lumberjacks of the LETC, the chesspiece knight of Lobsang's own transEarth Institute, the GapSpace roundel. A couple of trucks were nuzzled up against the ship, pumping fuel, water, air and other necessities into the craft, and white-coated engineers fussed over last-minute adjustments.

This was all very small scale compared to what Joshua remembered from the old Cape Canaveral days of the space shuttle. Even so the pod looked familiar. 'It's like an Apollo command module on steroids,' he said.

Dev Bilaniuk was totally at home with this technology – which, of course, was the reason he was on the crew. 'This is Gap chic, Joshua. Yes, it is kind of like Apollo. The design is based on our own stepper shuttle design, which carries crews across into the Gap itself. And that in turn is based, not on Apollo, but on SpaceX tech – kind of a son of Apollo from the 2010s. Bigger, roomier, modern materials . . .' Dev caressed the side of the ship with one hand. 'We considered a lot of options for the pod. Maybe a literal bathyscaphe, from ocean explorations; those things are pretty rugged. The chassis of a marine corps armoured vehicle was suggested too. But we went for a minimal spacecraft design, in case we found ourselves falling into some kind of Gap; the ship is vacuum-proof, and we might need to regularize our momentum and position to be able to get back, and we'll need attitude thrusters for that.'

Joshua said, 'I thought there was talk of adding a layer of computronium.' He grinned. 'I kind of liked the idea of riding a spaceship made of diamond.'

'And I vetoed it,' Maggie said sternly. 'We don't want to be venturing into the unknown, inside a hull of unknown materials. Let's minimize the variables here.'

Lobsang said, 'I'm reassured to find you riding along with us, Admiral Kauffman.'

'Well, the Navy is sure as hell going to stay in command of this thing.'

'But we don't need an admiral. I'm sure there are many less senior officers who could have fulfilled this mission.' Lobsang sounded as if he was teasing her, Joshua thought. 'Someone younger, with better reflexes, vision, hearing, coordination—'

'All right, Lobsang, thank you. It was my decision. There was room for only one Navy officer after you filled the thing with your damn circus of a crew. And I do have some experience leading expeditions into remote stepwise locations, as you may recall.' She grinned, wolfish. 'And besides, how could I resist a jaunt like this? Also I am *still* one of the few commanders who'll accept a troll on her ship.'

'Sancho's coming,' Joshua said firmly. 'This is as much his mission as mine—'

'Dad! Hey, Dad!'

Joshua spun around so fast he nearly lost his balance on his stick.

There was Rod, inside the roped-off area, but being held back by a white-coated technician. Behind him, beyond the rope, was a young woman, tanned, brunette, dressed in what Joshua thought of as Sally Linsay chic: practical traveller's gear of faded jeans, multi-pocketed jacket, sun-faded hat. And, Joshua could see immediately, she was heavily pregnant – close to term if Joshua was any judge, which he wasn't.

He ignored the techs, the wary soldiers, Maggie Kauffman's exasperated glare, and hobbled over. He and Rod just stood there for a moment, face to face, hands at their sides.

Then the young woman called, 'Oh, for heaven's sake, Rod, we came all this way . . .'

Rod shrugged. Joshua shrugged back. Then they hugged.

'Careful with the astronaut suit,' Joshua said, trying to cover for the choked-up feeling that was threatening to overwhelm him. 'And don't give me a cold, damn it.' He glanced over Rod's shoulder. 'Is that—?'

Rod beckoned. 'Come on over here, Sofia. Oh, ignore those Navy goons. Dad – Joshua Valienté – meet Sofia Piper.'

Joshua shook her hand formally; she had a strong grip. 'Rod mentioned you. And, umm . . .'

She blushed, grinning. 'And the next generation. I know.' She patted her stomach.

Rod said, 'Look, Dad, here you are going off on another jaunt. But I wanted to see you off this time. Even I think this is a pretty cool thing to be doing, as far as I understand it.'

'Praise indeed.'

'And I wanted . . . well . . . ah, shit.'

Sofia just snorted. 'You're as emotionally constipated as each other. Look, Mr Valienté, Rod wanted to make sure this little one met you, so to speak, before you left. Whatever happens we can tell him or her that we were here today.'

'You mean, in case I don't come back?' Joshua grinned. 'You can bet your house I'm coming back.'

'Dad, we don't have a house.'

Maggie Kauffman was at his shoulder. 'You won't be leaving at all, Valienté, unless you get your butt over to that ship right now. There are volatiles boiling off as we speak, and *that's* just what's coming out of my ears.'

'Yes, ma'am.' Hastily Joshua hugged Rod again, and gave Sofia a peck on the cheek – and that was that.

Then he hobbled after Maggie, back to the shuttle.

Dev was standing before the little ship with an expression of pride. 'We need a name. All exploratory spacecraft have names. *Eagle, Intrepid, Aquarius . . .*'

Joshua said, 'How about *Uncle Arthur*?'

Lobsang smiled. 'After Arthur C.?'

'Of course.'

'Seems most appropriate.'

Now Jane Sheridan ran forward with a kind of fat marker pen. 'Allow me.' And in a surprisingly flowing hand, she wrote 'Uncle Arthur' on a white patch of insulation near the ship's snub nose.

Maggie nodded approvingly. 'Shall we board?'

A tech held open a hatch.

There was a low step, which Joshua had to negotiate awkwardly, using his cane. The tech, a bright young woman who looked about twelve years old to Joshua, offered him an arm, which he grumpily refused. Standing in the hatchway he glanced back one last time. From this slight elevation he spotted Rod and Sofia. And, over the heads of the pressing crowd, further away, beyond the engineering facilities and tents and dormitory blocks and chemical toilets of Little Cincinnati, he saw the eerie engineered landscape that enclosed all of this: the mind, artificial and alien, into whose dreams he was stepping today.

None of this seemed real. Or maybe that was just his age. He turned away.

* * *

It was a relief to escape from the October sun, the press of people, the glare of the camera lights, and enter the calm of the clean-smelling, brightly lit interior of the *Uncle Arthur*. Though he hadn't actually seen his ship from the outside before – it had been one hell of a rush to get it built – he'd spent a lot of time in a mocked-up simulator of the interior; suddenly this was just like another training run.

He found his seat, a hefty astronaut couch with heavy harness straps. On this middle deck Joshua was in a central seat, with Maggie settling in to his right and Lobsang to his left. Mercifully Joshua hadn't had to climb the ladder to the upper deck, a few feet above him and separated by a mesh floor partition. Up there sat their 'pilots', if you could call them that: Dev Bilaniuk who ran the ship, Lee Malone, his backup, and Indra Newton, the very frail-looking Next girl whose stepping abilities, it was hoped, would carry them to – well, to whatever destination the Thinker and its makers had planned for them.

Below, visible through another mesh floor, was Sancho. The lower deck was a storage area, and the troll was surrounded by a clutter of stuff – air tanks and recycling units, batteries, medical kit, anonymous white boxes that Joshua assumed were something to do with the mission's science goals. The old troll was lying on his back in a heap of straw, with his big arms folded behind his head, draped in Joshua's old survival blanket.

Joshua rattled his cane on the floor. 'Hey, old buddy. You hanging in down there?'

'Hoo.' Sancho raised a thumb. He looked supremely comfortable. But then, Joshua reflected, he usually did.

There was a clang as the hatch was closed, and the last of the noise from outside was excluded. In the sudden hush, Joshua could hear the whir of fans and pumps. Through the small window before him, a disc of thick glass, he saw the technicians backing off, the well-wishers further out still waving. The armed Navy and marine grunts were still there, facing away from the ship and outwards at the crowds. Joshua knew there were more layers of security, the watchers in the towers and in the airborne twains, even small drone aircraft patrolling overhead.

As he went through his own checks Lobsang murmured, 'So how are you feeling, Joshua?'

He thought about it. 'Kind of like Step Day, I guess. I remember I built my Stepper box as well as I could, and I prepared to close the switch, and I had not the remotest idea what was going to happen . . .'

Maggie said, 'But you closed that damn switch anyhow.'

'Yes, ma'am.'

She grinned fiercely. 'Let's do this thing. Mr Bilaniuk?'

'I'm on it, ma'am,' Dev called. 'We just confirmed the hatch closed and sealed. We also sealed the inlet ports and the air vents. We're now locked in and self-contained, and our environment sensors show that all is nominal—'

Maggie snapped, 'Stop speaking to history and get on with it, man.'

Lee said dryly, 'OK, Indra, are you ready?'

'I think so . . .'

Just like Stan Berg at New Springfield, Indra had the key responsibility, Joshua knew. She needed to be ready to step, not East or West, not across the Long Earth, but *North* or *South*, out of the plane of human imagination altogether. Ready to take the whole of this pod, and its passengers, with her.

Or something like that. In the course of his career in the Long Earth and all its mysteries, Joshua had never tried to follow the more wu-wu theories of stepping. If this worked, then fine. If not, they'd be climbing out of this pod and back on to the concrete with red faces all round.

Lee said, 'Indra, let's go through the procedure one last time. It's just like we rehearsed, remember? I'll set up the systems, and Dev will be in control of the piloting. I need to prime the ship's rocket engines in case we find ourselves in a Gap and I have to kill our rotation velocity. *And* I have to arm the abort system in case something goes wrong with the rockets, in turn. We'd be kind of unlucky if both those things happened, but you have to be prepared. You just concentrate on your stepping. I'll give you a count-down. At five seconds I'm going to set up the abort. Then I'll arm the engine. And then at the count of one I'll say proceed, and you do your stuff at zero.'

'I understand.'

Indra sounded not at all nervous, Joshua thought. But then she was a Next, and one of the brightest. Maybe she'd already thought through the possible consequences of her actions today far more deeply than he ever could, and had accepted the risks. And meanwhile Lee sounded remarkably calm and competent. They were good young people, Joshua thought, obscurely pleased. All three of them.

Lee called down, 'Here we go, folks. Counting down,

twenty, nineteen, eighteen . . . Thank you for observing all safety precautions.'

Joshua looked sharply at Lobsang. 'Have you been showing these kids your old movies?'

'Have *you*?'

Dev murmured, 'Never mind movies. Just remember Shepard's prayer: "Dear Lord, don't let me screw up."'

Maggie snorted. 'That's not the version *I* recall.'

Lee said now, 'Nine, eight, seven, six, five, abort stage, engine arm, ready, proceed—'

And they stepped.

58

Joshua felt heavy, pushed back in his couch. 'Ow! It feels like a troll just jumped on my chest.'

'Hoo.'

'Not you, Sancho. You OK down there, buddy?'

'Ha!'

And the light from outside the window had changed, he saw, to a kind of silvery-blue.

'Everybody stay still,' Maggie said. 'Just lie back in your couches. I don't want any broken bones or heart attacks just from the effort of standing up. Let's take stock. We're on some kind of solid surface; we're not accelerating – we're certainly not falling, we're not in space. But the gravity here, wherever *here* is, is higher than at home. Stop me if I get any of this wrong, Lobsang.'

'Precisely right so far, Admiral.'

'Call me Captain. Aboard my ship, I'm Captain ... How much heavier?'

'About twenty per cent. We're on some kind of super-Earth, maybe.'

'Everybody call in. Lobsang, Joshua—'

'Both fine, Captain.'

'Dev?'

'Everything checks out,' Dev said.

'How are *you*, you lummox?'

'Fine, Captain.'

'Lee?'

'Copacetic.'

'Oh, good grief. Indra?'

'I see stars.'

At that, Joshua couldn't resist it. He loosened his harness and leaned forward to his small window.

He saw a desolate, cratered plain, littered with sharp-edged rocks. Moon-like, perhaps. But there was air here, evidently; the sky was a deep purple-blue. Perhaps there was a sun hidden behind the horizon to his right. He saw a glow spreading there, a hint of pinkness.

But the sky was dominated by stars – and stars impossibly big and bright, compared to the stars of Earth. He counted five, six very bright stars showing discs, maybe a dozen lesser lights, and a more distant panorama of crowded constellations.

Dev asked, 'Can we go out to see?'

'I'd advise against it,' Lobsang said. 'Aside from the higher gravity, the atmosphere is mostly nitrogen and carbon dioxide. Only a trace of oxygen. Rather like a dead Earth. Even in pressure suits the higher gravity makes it perilous. Clearly we were right to prepare the pod, to bring protection—'

'There doesn't seem to be much out there to see anyhow,' Maggie said.

Joshua wasn't sure that was true. He thought he saw

something on the horizon, more complex than the rocky waves of the crater rims. Some kind of structure? . . . His old eyes were too poor to show him more.

Indra asked, 'So where are we?'

Lobsang said, 'The obvious question. Clearly not in the solar system.'

And that simple fact had somehow not congealed in Joshua's mind. 'Wow. Of course not. We just crossed interstellar space. In a *step*.'

'I know where we are,' Dev said.

Lobsang said, 'I'll soon figure out if those stars up there are visible from Earth, and if so I'll be able to tell where we are. You saw that this ship is crusted with telescopes, spectroscopes. As well as atmospheric sensors we can detect temperature, radiation; we have probes for sampling the local rock suite, grabbers to take specimens of any life forms—'

'I don't see any flowers to pick, Lobsang—'

'And the onboard AI is very smart.'

'You know that, do you?'

'Well, yes. As I *am* the onboard AI—'

Dev snapped, 'Will you listen? Sorry. Will you listen, sirs? *I know where we are.* I'm an astronomy buff. I spent a lot of time in the Gap, at the Brick Moon, looking out at the stars.'

'Where, then?' Maggie asked.

'The Pleiades.'

Lobsang waited a few seconds, as his automated sensor suite delivered its results. 'Lucky guess.'

'Was not.'

'We *are* on a planet orbiting one of the principal stars of that cluster. Some of that wispiness up there is probably above the atmosphere.'

'I know it is,' Dev said. 'There's a cloud of interstellar dust crossing the cluster. Easily visible in a telescope.'

'Well, I'm impressed,' Joshua said.

'Well done, Mr Sulu,' Lobsang said dryly. 'But in that case we've only come around four hundred light years from home so far.'

Joshua thought that over. *Only* four hundred light years . . .

'When we get a little further out, it may be more of a challenge to locate our position.'

Maggie held up her hands. 'Enough of the antler-locking. Let's review what happened here. So we – stepped. But instead of passing up or down the chain of the Long Earth, we stepped in another direction—'

'So to speak,' Joshua said.

'And ended up here. On the planet of another star.'

'This is what was expected,' Indra said. 'From the fragmentary clues extracted from the lollipops' partial communication with the Thinker. The Long Earth is a chain of worlds, like a necklace drifting in some higher-dimensional space. It may fold back on itself, or it may cut across *other* necklaces, other Long worlds, drifting in the higher continuum.'

'Like this one,' Maggie said.

'Yes. We think that the Thinker is an engine for *imagining* these more remote worlds, these tremendous jumps. And when that couples with my own will, my ability to decohere—'

'Oops, you lost me,' Maggie said.

'Stepping is a faculty of the mind,' Lobsang said. 'And the Thinker we just built is the most powerful mind our small planet is ever likely to see. Hence this monumental stepping.'

Joshua said, 'So is this how the silver beetles stepped into their own Long world?'

'Yes,' Lobsang said. 'But that was an accident. This time we're in control.'

Joshua said, 'Or the Thinker is.'

Maggie said, 'So what now? You say the theory is we stepped through a linkage between one Long world – the Earth – and another. I thought Long worlds are supposed to be linked to the rise of sapient life. I don't see any signs of sapience here. I don't see life at all.'

Joshua was still peering at those structures on the horizon. 'About that—'

'If it's Long,' Dev said, 'then we ought to be able to step across it. East or West, I mean.'

'Yes,' Lobsang said. 'Just as Sally Linsay and her father stepped across the Long Mars. Allow me.'

'God damn it.' Joshua swallowed his pride and fumbled for his prescription sunglasses, so he could see those distant structures better.

But before he got them over his nose, there was another discontinuity.

The light changed again, and those distant structures vanished – but the heavy weight on Joshua's chest remained.

Maggie turned on Lobsang. 'What the hell did you just do?'

'I stepped,' Lobsang said reasonably. 'The conventional way – West, as it happens. Thereby carrying *Uncle Arthur* with me as a temporary extension of my body.'

'Next time you feel like pulling a stunt like that, consult me first.'

Again Joshua cautiously sat up, and peered out of the window. There were the Pleiades once more – a crowded cluster of stars in the sky – but now their glow was obscured by a pale-blue sky, a scatter of streaky clouds. And, looking down, he saw that the ground was quite different. There were none of those lunar-type craters; now he saw rolling hills, a lake of what looked like blue water in the middle distance.

And life: something like grass, something like trees, with trunks, a crown of branches with leaves.

'It could almost be Earth,' he said. 'If it wasn't for the predominant colour scheme of – *purple.*'

The pod rang like a gong.

Maggie yelled, 'What the hell was *that*?'

'My bad,' called Lobsang. 'I just launched a sounding rocket.'

'I didn't know we *had* any sounding rockets.'

Joshua laughed, though his own heart was thumping. 'Oh, Lobsang loves his sounding rockets.'

'I thought we needed a wider view . . . The results of my sensors are coming in. There's now an oxygen-nitrogen atmosphere out there. Not quite breathable, the oxygen's too high, and so's the carbon dioxide. But it's close. And unstable: I mean, chemically. I deduce the presence of life on this world.'

Joshua said dryly, 'So you just *deduced* the existence

409

of all the trees and grass and flowers we can see out there.'

'Precisely,' Lobsang said without a trace of irony. 'My aerial survey is coming in . . . I can see a good few hundred miles around our position. No sign of sapient life, at least nothing technological.'

'How can you tell so quickly?' Dev called down.

'No regular structures. I have pattern-seeking algorithms to tell me that. Also no sign of forest clear-ances, no fires, no industrial-gas imbalances in the air. I'd detect Neanderthals skulking around their hearths in those forest clumps, believe me. Of course we'd have to do a global survey to be sure. In fact I've yet to see any evidence of large animal life—'

Slam. Again the pod rocked. This time Joshua's port went dark, and he flinched back.

Maggie growled, 'Now what? Lobsang, another rocket?'

'He's innocent this time,' Joshua said, and he pointed to his window. Maggie leaned over to see.

Together they peered into a kind of moist, clammy tunnel, with purple-black walls feebly illuminated by the cabin lights.

'That's somebody's *throat*,' Maggie said, wondering.

Joshua said, 'I think we found evidence of large animal life, Lobsang.'

Dev stood up cautiously and peered down through his own window, from above. 'Oh, wow. I can see it from up here. Think of, think of a turtle. A huge one. With an armoured shell. I mean, those are serious *blades*. And legs like a tyrannosaur. And jaws like a crocodile. I don't *think* he can crush the hull—'

'Step us back out of here, Lobsang,' Maggie called.

'Wait,' Joshua said. 'We don't want to kill that thing. We will if we carry him with us.'

'Leave it to me,' Lobsang said. He pushed a button.

This time there was a sharp knock, as if somebody had punched the outer hull. Joshua heard a kind of bellow, and the beast dropped away.

He turned to Lobsang. 'What was that? A weapon?'

Lobsang said, 'I used one of our impact probes. Non-lethal, but it will have stung. A small shell designed to bury itself in rock to return a mineralogical analysis—'

Maggie said, 'Enough. I don't care. Lobsang, step us back.'

A subtle shift once more, and they were back on the moon-like plain, under the brilliant star cluster.

'I don't get it,' Dev said. 'There should be sapience here. That's why this world is Long in the first place, right? Yet we saw nothing.'

'No,' Joshua said. 'There is something, on this copy of the world at least. Take a look at the horizon, at around ten o'clock. There's a building out there – I think. I saw it before . . .'

Maggie produced a set of big Navy binoculars. 'Some kind of structure. Looks like a bunker. Roofless, abandoned.' She lowered the glasses. 'There *was* sapience here, then.'

'But not any more,' Joshua said.

'And those craters, they weren't in the stepwise world.'

'So they weren't created by impacts, like on Earth's

moon. I guess the folks who lived here, whoever they were, *whatever* they were – they blew themselves up.'

'A race even more stupid than humanity, then,' Lobsang said. 'I'll write that in the log. A notable discovery.'

'There may be survivors elsewhere,' Indra Newton said. 'We know that if a Long world has a purpose it must be to serve as a refuge for sapient life, even against its own follies.'

Maggie said, 'It could take a lifetime to find them. That's for a future expedition. Not for us. Let's go on.'

'But which way?' asked Indra Newton. 'South? I could take us home—'

'North,' said a small voice, from somewhere under Joshua's seat. 'Let's keep going.'

The crew exchanged stares. Then Joshua turned in his seat to look down through the mesh floor; his head briefly swam in the higher gravity. 'Sancho?'

'Hoo?'

'Who the hell's down there with you?'

'Nobody.'

Maggie said sternly, 'Come on out of there, nobody.'

There was a rustle in the heaps of straw that surrounded the big troll, and a couple of supply boxes tumbled out of the way. Then a small human being stood, face tilted up bravely.

It was Jan Roderick.

Joshua laughed. 'Well, that's reduced the average age of the crew.'

'You,' Maggie said. 'The kid from Madison, Wisconsin. Who made all those – bolts.'

Dev called down, 'Hey, little dude. Sit down. OK? Sit on

a bale. Or sit on that troll. We don't want you breaking any bones in this gravity.'

Jan obeyed.

Maggie snapped, 'How did you get aboard?'

Jan pointed at Joshua. 'I said I was with *him*.'

Maggie rubbed her face. 'Oh, for cripe's sake.'

Joshua had to laugh. 'Don't blame me.'

Lobsang said, 'I suppose that once he was aboard, he was unlikely to be detected. We aren't mass-critical, we have no significant internal sensors – not of the kind that would detect intruders. This was not anticipated.'

'It damn well should have been,' Maggie said. 'Suppose he'd been a suicide bomber? When we get back, there'll be heads rolling in my security team. Why the hell did you do this, kid?'

Indra Newton said, 'Is it not obvious? He is here for the same reason we all are. Curiosity.'

'They never would have let me go,' Jan said, gazing up. 'No matter how many bolts I made. I was just a kid.'

'So you stowed away,' Dev said. 'I don't know if I would have had the guts—'

Maggie said, 'Can it, Bilaniuk, don't encourage him. What if we'd had to go back because of you, stowaway? How would that make you feel, if you caused us to terminate the mission?'

Joshua touched her arm. 'Hey, go easy.'

'OK, OK. Lobsang, I take it our life support can sustain the additional burden of a ten-year-old brat.'

'I'm eleven!'

'I stand corrected. An eleven-year-old brat.'

Lobsang said, 'As long as we don't extend the mission

unduly. There's plenty of reserve. It's the lack of an acceleration couch that concerns me more.'

'Ah.'

'All our couches were moulded to fit our bodies.'

'Yeah, I'm not likely to forget the fitting session,' Joshua said wryly.

'We have no spare couch. Even if we did it would not fit the boy.'

'I'm fine in the straw,' said Jan.

'Like hell,' said Maggie.

'Come on,' said Joshua. 'The straw's good enough for old Sancho. And ten-year-old kids are made of rubber anyhow.'

'Eleven!'

'Sorry. Listen, kid. Just cuddle up to Sancho. Can you do that?'

'Sure.'

'Sancho, you make sure he's OK down there, and keep him out of trouble. You got that?'

Sancho waved a troll-call. 'Hoo.'

'OK. Let's go on. But when we get back, kid, and I deliver you back to the Home, you're going to apologize to Sister Coleen, and you'll tell Sister John what you've done, and they're going to ground you for a year.'

'I can live with that.'

'What's that?'

'I mean, sorry, Mr Valienté.'

Maggie glared at Joshua. 'Are we done?'

Joshua shrugged.

'What a circus. OK, people, buckle up. Mr Bilaniuk, Ms Malone, if you please.'

Lee said, 'OK, Indra, same routine as before . . .'
North, again.

59

THE GRAVITY IMMEDIATELY felt gentler. Maybe this time it was actually less than Earth normal. Having got used to the weight of a troll on his chest, now it felt like Joshua was suddenly *falling*, as if the elevator cable had snapped. Joshua felt his gorge rise, and he swallowed hard. He had no prior experience of different gravities, save for falling into the Gap.

The light was different again, a softer greenish-blue.

This time they all quickly unbuckled, and leaned forward. The new sky was a distinct tinge of green. A sun was setting, or rising, greyish-red and smeared by refraction, hovering just above a horizon that looked close by.

On the land there was a blanket, greenish like the sky, lapping against a wall of mountains and spilling into a placid-looking lake. Life, obviously, a tangle, but so unfamiliar that Joshua had trouble making out the detail. Maybe those upright structures, bushy at the top, were trees, or maybe some kind of fungus, like a big mushroom – but no, one of them started to *move*, eerily, with a liquid glide across the ground. And conversely what had looked like a stretch of meadow near that lake started to ripple and pulse, and flowed closer to the water: an expanse maybe an acre in size, moving as one organism.

The *Uncle Arthur* clanged and shuddered.

'Sounding rocket away,' called Lobsang.

'Will you stop *doing* that?'

'Sorry, Captain. Well, I see life out there, Joshua, but not as we know it.'

'To coin a phrase.'

Maggie growled, 'Will you two quit it?'

'He's right, though.'

Jan called up, 'And I can see out the window, a big moon rising. With a *shell*.'

Maggie snapped, 'Hush up, kid. And sit down until I tell you it's safe to move.'

Lobsang said, 'Again the air's an oxygen-nitrogen-water mix, not quite breathable, and somewhat acidic. We seem to be being brought to worlds that are somewhat like our own, with a similar chemistry, but not identical. But the boundaries we use to describe families of life back home – bacterial, animal, plant, fungus and so on – may not apply here. It all looks rather odd. I wouldn't recommend an EVA unless it's strictly required, since we couldn't be sure what we'd be stepping on. Or who.'

'An EVA? You can cut the John Glenn jargon too. You got a fix on where we are yet? Still in the Pleiades?'

'I think we've come a little further than that, Captain. If you look up, you might have a clue.'

Joshua leaned forward stiffly, and peered up at the zenith, where, even as that big sun set, the stars were being revealed. But it was not a starscape he recognized from any world of the Long Earth, and nothing like the Pleiades either. He saw a scatter of star-like objects densely crowding the sky, but some resolved on closer inspection into *clusters* of stars: it was a sky full of a thousand copies of the Pleiades.

And there was a larger structure too. Joshua saw a vast, yellow-orange circle of light, like glowing gas, roughly centred on the zenith, lumpy, ragged, broken. A finer concentric band was contained within the outer one, almost circular too. Offset from the centre of the two bands was a brilliant pinpoint, like a star but somehow more intense, bright enough to sting Joshua's eyes. As his vision adjusted, and he tried not to look directly at that central point, he made out more detail: wide washes of purplish cloud, smaller patches of lurid green, and what appeared to be a mass of stars swarming like fireflies around that achingly bright pinpoint centre. It looked oddly *wrong* to Joshua. As if damaged: a broken sky.

'My God,' Maggie said. 'How many stars are visible to the naked eye in our night sky, Lobsang? A few thousand?' She framed a patch of sky with her fingers. 'There must be tens of thousands up there, hundreds.'

'We're at the centre of the Galaxy,' Indra said simply.

Joshua gasped, and he saw shock on Maggie's face.

'Not quite the centre,' Lobsang said calmly. He pointed up. 'If *that* is the central black hole, then, judging by its brightness, we are something like five thousand light years out.'

Indra said, 'Then we've come around twenty thousand light years from home. At least.'

418

Lee laughed. 'Nobody at GapSpace is ever going to believe *this*.'

Maggie asked softly, 'How safe are we, Lobsang?'

'Good question. The place is a bath of high-energy radiation, X-rays, gamma rays. Nearby supernovas are frequent. The *Uncle*'s hull will shield us to some extent, and maybe the planet's air, but we should not stay long. I've an aerial view of the world from the sounding rocket. You all have tablets in the walls before you. Well, except you, Jan Roderick.'

'Hoo.'

'Sorry. And except *you*, Sancho . . .'

In his tablet, Joshua saw a cratered landscape, as if from overhead. But this was not grey and dead, not like the moon, not even like the Pleiades world. This image was full of colour and detail. Some of the craters were flooded with round lakes that gleamed like coins in the starlight, and the grey-green of the local life swept over circular ranges of rim mountains. 'It's like they terraformed the moon,' he said.

'Speaking of moons,' Jan said, but everybody ignored him.

Lobsang said, 'With the stars crowded so close there are going to be a lot of disturbed comets, a lot of impacts. Frequent mass extinctions. But extinctions can be a spur to evolution—'

'If you survive at all, I guess,' Maggie said.

Jan shouted, 'Will you all please *look out of the window*! Sorry.'

At last they looked. He'd been staring out at a part of the horizon the others had missed.

A moon was rising, Joshua saw. A big fat moon, vaguely elliptical in shape, with coloured bands smeared across its surface. And there was a shell around it: cracked, crumbling at the edges, revealing the gassy world within. But, definitively, a shell.

A shell around a world.

Maggie murmured, 'Well, there's something you don't see every day.'

'It's a moon, all right!' Jan called up. 'I told you so.'

'Actually,' Lobsang said, 'I think you'll find that *this* world is a moon of *that* gas giant.'

Joshua scoffed. 'Don't get pompous, Lobsang. You missed it completely.'

Maggie said briskly, 'Enough of the banter. What I want to know is – *what is that shell?*'

'It's clearly artificial,' Lobsang said, inspecting telescopic images on his tablet. 'There are signs of a kind of ribbing on the underside, where it's exposed. I have a name for it, if you like: a supramundane habitat.'

Maggie chewed that over. '*Supramundane.* Meaning, above the world?'

'These things have been studied, hypothetically. A shell like that around Saturn, for instance, would have a hundred times the surface area of Earth, and about Earth-normal gravity.'

'You say "studied",' Maggie said. 'I don't suppose that includes details on how to build such a thing.'

'But you can see why you would,' Dev said. 'It's a shelter.'

'Ah,' Lobsang said now. 'Of course – I hadn't thought of that. A shelter, from this lethal sky. You'd live on the *inside.* You could plate the outer surface to pick up energy from the local sun. You'd be sheltered from the supernova radiation and the rest. Even a dinosaur-killer asteroid would just pass through, leaving a bullet-hole you'd have time to fix before the air leaked out.'

'But it's all busted up,' Jan said. 'Where did they go? Did they die out?'

Lobsang said, 'Maybe they – moved on. Became something higher, something to which even a shell around a gas giant is just a toy.'

'Cool,' said Jan.

Maggie spluttered laughter. 'Kids today. That's all you've got to say? "Cool"?'

Dev called, 'So what now? I guess we could explore this world stepwise.'

Lobsang shook his head. 'Any stepwise copy will surely still be close to the galactic centre, and unsuitable for us. Let's move on.'

Indra asked, 'North again?'

'North. We have the supplies, air, power, for at least one more jump.'

'OK, people, buckle up,' Maggie said. As they settled down, she said to Lobsang, 'I don't understand why we're jumping around the way we are. I mean, aren't the Pleiades *further out* from the centre of the Galaxy than the sun? I checked it on my tablet here. And then we came all the way in to the very heart.'

Indra replied from above, 'We are moving across a tangle of Long worlds. There is no reason why distances across this tangle, in terms of steps jumped, should correspond to spatial distances, to galactic geography. It is the relations between the elements of the tangle that determine distance. In fact there are some relational theories of physics that describe all our perceptual reality, even such qualities as distance and time, as emergent properties of relations between more fundamental objects—'

'I get it,' Maggie said quickly. 'It's complicated. Let's go see what else is out there. Dev, Indra, Lee, you ready to do your stuff?'

'After the next stop,' Joshua murmured, 'I need to take a bathroom break.'

'You and me too, kiddo,' said Maggie. 'Billion-year-old aliens or not—'

Bright light flooded the cabin,
   There was a sickening sensation of falling,
   And a tremendous splash.

There was darkness outside the windows, and the *Uncle* dipped and spun. Joshua clung to his couch, wishing he'd taken that bathroom break earlier.

Maggie yelled, 'Report, Lobsang!'

'We're underwater!' Lobsang called back. 'Or to be more precise, immersed in liquid of some kind—'

'It *is* water,' Dev called down. 'I'm copying the readings here. Salty, not too acidic. Like ocean water on Earth.'

Maggie ordered, 'Keep us upright, Mr Bilaniuk.'

'In hand, Captain. We have air bags in the nose to stabilize us, and a flotation collar around the base. Also the pressure's not too high. We're built to withstand far worse than this . . . Actually the pressure's already dropping.'

'We're rising,' Lobsang said.

'I know,' Joshua called. 'I can feel it in my bladder.'

Suddenly they broke through into the air. Joshua glimpsed bright-blue sky through the water that streamed off his window.

'On the surface!' Dev called.

Lee said, 'But in that case, why are we still rising?'

Maggie leaned forward and stared out of the window. 'Because we're on some kind of island. And *that's* rising.'

'Cool,' said Jan Roderick.

'Hoo!' said the troll.

Joshua and Lobsang stared at each other wildly.

Lobsang said, 'A rising island?'

And Joshua said, 'Are you thinking what I'm thinking?'

60

THE UNCLE ARTHUR, on its three legs, stood at a slight angle on the sloping beach where it had been deposited by the tide. The sea, receding, lapped gently at the shore. The light outside was eerie, a purplish twilight. The sun of this world wasn't yet up, according to Lobsang. *This* sky was like a bad special effect, cluttered with brilliant stars and lurid clouds through which even more stars shone, gauzy, as if seen through a veil, Joshua thought. Joshua had no idea where he was. This was not the sky of the centre of the Galaxy. But on the other hand it wasn't the mundane sky of home, either. Aside from the light show up there, however, this world was remarkably Earth-like. Even the gravity felt about right . . .

And far out to sea, the back of the Traverser that had raised the pod up from the depths was like a low island, silhouetted, its stately movement only visible to Joshua if he watched it carefully for a few minutes, peering through his small window.

Joshua said, 'So *this* is where the Traversers went. But why?'

'Because they were invited, I suspect,' Lobsang said.

'Even if we were probably no more aware of their form of the Invitation than they were of ours.' He sounded unpleasantly triumphant, to Joshua. 'I always did suspect there had been some kind of intervention in the evolution of these creatures, Joshua. They were turned, by some agency, into collectors. Samplers. Curators, if you like. Waiting for a call from the sky. And when it came, here they travelled, by some super-stepping ability of their own. With their cargo of life, gathered from the Long worlds they came from.'

'Worlds, Lobsang?'

'Sure. Why shouldn't the same strategy have been used on other worlds? Maybe this ocean is shared by Traversers from other temperate, watery planets like ours. And maybe there are stranger oceans out there, where you'll find curators from the ammonia-laced oceans of worlds like Europa, or even the acid clouds of worlds like Venus . . .

'This is the fullest expression of stepping, I think, Joshua. We find ourselves in a cross-connected tangle of Long worlds of different kinds, with many different kinds of sapient inhabitants.'

As with much of what Lobsang said, even from the beginning of their relationship, this went mostly over Joshua's head. He tried to picture it. 'Like a subway map? All those lines, cross-connecting . . .'

'Something like that,' Lobsang said, not unkindly. 'But *this* world is a step beyond, in a sense. A place where many world lines cross, a multiple junction – which is how the Traversers have been able to congregate, coming from so many worlds. This is a Grand Central Station of the Galaxy, Joshua. The air is breathable, by the way.'

* * *

They threw open the hatch of the *Uncle Arthur* and clambered out.

Almost without prior discussion they piled gear out of the pod: a couple of tents, sleeping bags and blankets, bottles of water and packets of food, lanterns, mosquito nets. They needed to stay a few hours anyhow to allow the air supply to replenish itself, and beyond that, by common consent, it seemed to Joshua, they were going to spend some time here, have a meal, maybe stay the night. It wouldn't have felt right to have gone scurrying home without exploring a bit.

'But then we *are* going straight back,' Maggie Kauffman said sternly. 'We made three of those super-steps, and we survived them all. We bought enough risk. We've done our job, we've proved this new way of travelling is feasible, and our responsibility now is to get back to Earth, tell everybody what we found, have our picture taken with President Damasio. We can leave the rest to future expeditions.'

'Actually to future generations,' said Indra Newton gravely. 'This network of Long worlds we have discovered may be infinite. It will not be an exploration but a migration. An endless one.'

'A migration into the Skein,' Lobsang murmured, peering into the strange sky. 'A tangle of Long worlds around the centre of the Galaxy. *The Skein* – is that an appropriate word?'

'It'll do,' Maggie said.

Jan Roderick stared up at Lobsang, who was staring at the sky. It struck Joshua that this was the first time the boy had been close up to Lobsang. 'Mister, you look funny.'

Lobsang looked down. 'Well, so do you.'

'Are you a robot?'

'Long story.'

Jan reached out and poked Lobsang's leg. 'I bet you're not even alive.'

'Am so.'

'Prove it.'

Lobsang leaned down, resting his hands on his knees. 'Well, that's a little tricky. You could break me down molecule by molecule and find not a single particle of life or mind. On the other hand, I could do the same to you.'

Jan thought that over. 'Good comeback.' Then he ran off down the beach.

Lobsang eyed Joshua. 'Some kid.'

'The Sisters have him in hand. I think . . .'

Joshua saw that Sancho was wandering away now, one slow step after another, looking around at the sky, the land, the ocean. The troll stretched his mighty arms, as if glad to be free of the confinement of the pod, and then slumped his shoulders. 'Hoo!'

Joshua grabbed the troll-call and hobbled over. 'So, buddy, how are you feeling?'

Sancho bared his teeth and raised two thumbs.

'Good, huh? But – I'm shy of asking a Librarian this – do you know where you are?'

'Home,' said the troll.

Home. Joshua thought he saw what the troll meant. Home: not the place you were born into, but the place that gathered you in. That was what this 'Skein' of Lobsang's was. Like the Home on Allied Drive. And *that* was a richly satisfying thought.

'Well, they always said it – the Invitation wasn't just for humans . . .'

'Bring Sancho.'

'It was a pleasure, big guy.'

And Sancho went on his way down the beach, singing softly. Joshua was no expert, but he thought the tune was 'Pack Up Your Troubles In Your Old Kit Bag'.

After a brief conversation, the 'adults' – Maggie, Lobsang and Joshua – decided to take a hike into a range of eroded hills, just inland. The 'youngsters' – Lee, Dev and Jan – evidently wanted to blow off some steam, and they kicked off their shoes and began a soccer game on the beach. Only Indra defied the rough age categorization; the serious young Next said her priority was to explore this new environment.

Maggie lectured the soccer players. 'OK. We'll be back in a couple of hours. The slightest thing feels wrong and you get back in that pod and close the hatch and flush the air. And you *will* submit to the tox tests later, in case there's something subtle we missed. Understood?'

'Ma'am.'

'I can't hear you—'

'Captain, yes, Captain!'

'Also, you do *not* drink the water. The ocean's salty anyhow, but you don't touch any fresh water either. You do not *eat* anything local. Life seems sparse here, but the bugs Lobsang tested do not consist of the amino acids you use, they do not use the protein suite you do—'

'Captain, they're just *slime*. We're not about to eat that.'

'No, and it's not about to eat you, and if you did chomp it down chances are it would pass straight through. But we're not going to take that chance, are we?'

'No, ma'am.'

'We're going to stick to the rations we brought. Aren't we?'

'Ma'am.'

'I can't hear you—'

'Captain, yes, Captain!'

As the youngsters ran off after Sancho, Maggie joined Joshua. 'I can't believe they brought a soccer ball into interstellar space.'

Joshua said, '*I* can't believe they're putting a troll in goal.'

'But then I guess we missed a whole ten-year-old boy down in that cargo bay.'

'Eleven—'

'By comparison, smuggling aboard a soccer ball is small beer.'

Lobsang joined them. The crew all carried small back-packs, but Lobsang's was a complex affair, glistening with sensor lenses.

As they fixed their packs, Joshua, leaning on his cane, scuffed the alien sand with the toe of his good leg. 'So, through the Star Gate, huh, Lobsang?'

'Indeed.'

'Where the hell are we? I'm guessing you have a pretty good idea.'

Lobsang glanced up at the lurid sky, the dazzling stars blurred by the colourful clouds, that single brilliant shadow-casting pinpoint. 'I believe we're halfway home.

Back from the Galaxy centre, that is. I'm judging that from the sky above, and from the composition of those stars we see – which, according to our spectroscopes, have a higher content of heavy elements than the stars close to the sun. At a guess I'd say we're around fourteen thousand light years out from the core. About twelve thousand light years in from the solar system.'

Indra pointed out, 'That's always assuming we're moving along the same radius. In and out, to and from the centre.'

'True enough. The Galaxy does have a circular symmetry . . .'

'And yet,' Joshua said, 'here we are standing on a beach, with sand in our toes, the waves lapping.'

'Universal formations, Joshua.'

'I guess.' He looked along the beach, at the soccer game. The shouts of the young folk and the hoots of the troll came drifting in silence broken otherwise only by the lapping of the ocean waves. 'That pod looks remarkably out of place.'

'Whereas those kids,' Maggie said, 'look like they belong here. And the damn troll.'

'Indeed they do. Like the Traversers in their ocean. So. Shall we walk?'

61

I T WAS A very mundane hike, despite that bizarre
psychedelic flag of a sky up above.

They walked up from the beach and through a bank of
dunes. Maggie led the way, striding boldly. Lobsang
followed, the lenses and other sensors on his pack
whirring and swivelling.

Joshua was happy to play rear gunner and stay at the
back of the group, pivoting on the damn cane, not wanting to hold anybody up. Indra Newton, however, walked
beside him, and Joshua was aware that she was keeping an
eye on him. It irritated him that *anybody* should think he
needed watching over. But on the other hand he was kind
of touched; he wouldn't have expected that kind of
thoughtfulness of a super-brain Next like Indra. Well,
people always surprised you.

The hike across the sand was hard work, though. He
kept thinking of that desperate scramble across another
beach, on the world of the Yggdrasil trees.

The going got a little easier for him once they'd climbed
out of the soft dry sand at the top of the beach, and the
ground became firmer. Joshua saw that the sand here was

bound by a kind of moss that looked vaguely green, although Joshua didn't trust his colour sense under this peculiar sky.

And then he nearly stumbled when his cane broke through a kind of crust and sank into the earth. Indra grabbed his arm to steady him.

He found himself looking down into a broken-open nest, littered with clumps of moss, from which an animal and its young all stared back up at him. He was reminded of the rabbit-mole nests he'd learned to crack with Sancho – but this animal was nothing like a rabbit-mole. The beast might have been a couple of feet across, and it had six stubby, almost triangular limbs folding out from a central core; it was something like a big starfish covered in electric-blue fur. But in that central section was a mouth, and three very human-looking eyes peered up at him. Around it were three, four, five smaller copies, wriggling starfish the size of coins. He caught all this in a glance.

Big Mama opened that small mouth and hissed at him, the little ones squealed and clambered over her, and she lifted her limbs and gathered herself into a ball of fur, enclosing the young. Then she rolled out of the broken warren and shot out of sight over the curve of a dune, moving with remarkable speed.

Maggie said dryly, 'I see you're making friends, Joshua.'

'At least nobody's killed anybody else yet.'

Indra said, as they walked on, 'Life, then. But there doesn't seem to be very *much* life here. There's nothing like grass on these dunes.' She glanced inland, to bare, eroded hills. 'I see nothing like trees, though that appears to be a universal biological form. No animal life, save Mr Valienté's – starfish? Even the ocean seemed relatively lifeless, save for the Traversers, of course.'

'You're almost right,' Lobsang said. 'Actually there *is* more animal life. In the far distance – my enhanced vision reveals it, but it may not be apparent to you – there are more starfish, big ones, browsing on the flank of that hill . . .'

Joshua peered where he pointed, but could see only massive shadows moving in the purplish light. 'Starfish world, then,' he murmured.

Lobsang said, 'I think this planet may have been through a mass extinction, relatively recently. A nearby supernova, probably. Hence the sparseness of life, the apparent dominance by one animal group. The starfish may have been chance survivors, perhaps saved by their evident habit of burrowing underground. Something similar happened on Datum Earth after a massive die-back a quarter of a billion years ago. In the strata laid down in the period after, nothing but the bones of animals the biologists called lystrosaurus – like ugly pigs.'

Maggie scoffed. 'As every science officer I ever flew with would have remarked, that's a hell of a lot of supposition on very little fact, mister.'

'True enough. But, lacking any better evidence, one must assume that the place one visits is typical of the world as a whole.'

'But if you're right,' Indra said, 'then we haven't arrived at a typical epoch *in time.* Not if we've arrived just after a mass extinction. Not unless—'

Lobsang smiled. 'Go ahead. Make the deduction.'

'Not unless mass extinctions are commonplace here. So that this *is* a typical time.'

'Good. I believe that's true. Come, let's walk on.' He led the way now, plodding further inland towards the more distant hills. 'We may be near the inner edge of the Sagittarius Arm. Which is one of the Galaxy's major star-making factories, a very active place, quite unlike the placid Local Arm through which our sun drifts – well, as you can see for yourself in the sky.'

'Ah,' Indra said. 'And so lots of nearby supernovas. This is almost as deadly a place as the Galaxy centre. Periodically this world must get a drenching of radiation and high-energy particles.'

Joshua grunted. 'Then we needn't expect to find relics of intelligent life here . . .'

'Not so,' Indra said. 'The world must be Long, or we wouldn't have been led here. And a world cannot be Long without local sapients.'

'Quite right,' Lobsang said. 'Joshua, in the course of the Galaxy's history there has been a great wave of starmaking, washing out from the centre. So the closer you get to the centre, the older the worlds and the suns are. I'd estimate this world is a billion years older than Earth. And on such an ancient world complex life, and mind, may have risen up over and over, despite the drumbeats of mass extinctions. Civilizations here are like children growing up in a minefield – and yet, evidently, some of them do grow, and flourish, and achieve great things. Otherwise we would not be here at all; the Skein could not exist.'

Joshua frowned. 'What "great things" have they

434

achieved, Lobsang? I don't see any sign of intelligence here at all.'

'It may be hard to recognize. Maybe even the starfish creatures were engineered to acquire their subterranean habits, so that if the worst comes to the worst, *they* at least will survive.'

Maggie shook her head. 'More irresponsible theorizing. Fun, though. But my stomach's starting to theorize irresponsibly about lunch. How much further do you want to go, Lobsang?'

Lobsang looked inland, and raised a fancy pair of binoculars to his artificial eyes. In that direction the sky was brightening, the lurid backdrop of stars and inter-stellar clouds becoming washed out. Sunrise approaching, maybe, Joshua thought.

Lobsang said, 'Just a little further. I think I see some-thing at the summit of the next ridge . . .'

'That far, then,' Maggie said. She led the way.

Once again Joshua gritted his teeth and followed. Indra walked at his side.

And they crested a low bluff, and stopped dead.

Standing on the next ridge over, they saw a series of dark bands, slender, vertical, black against the lurid sky of this world.

Monoliths.

62

THE TRAVELLERS HITCHED their packs and hiked hurriedly through the final valley. Joshua struggled to keep up, but he was as eager as the rest.

They didn't speak again until they stood, panting, at the feet of the great structures.

Monoliths. Five of them.

'I don't believe it,' Maggie said.

'Wow,' Joshua said. 'Also there's a guy over there in a monkey suit throwing a bone in the air—'

'Shut up, Valienté.'

'Sorry, Captain.'

Indra said, 'They bear some kind of inscription . . . I recognize the formation.'

'I suspect we all do,' Lobsang said wryly.

'Mars?' Maggie asked.

'Yes,' said Indra. 'This seems to be precisely the same configuration that Willis Linsay and his party encountered on the Long Mars.'

Maggie was tentatively touching a monolith with her bare hand. The face was covered with symbols, like runes, perhaps, each element of which was the size of a human head. The inscribing was clean, sharp, as if made by a laser, and seemed not to have been eroded by time. 'These stones are *big*,' Maggie said. 'And there are a lot of symbols. A lot of information, right?'

'Just as on the Martian versions,' Lobsang said, distracted. 'I'm comparing this with the images Linsay brought back. The symbols look similar – the same alphabet – but the message appears different . . .'

'Nobody knows what the Martian monoliths have to say,' Maggie said. 'In spite of a quarter-century of study. Right?'

Lobsang murmured, 'Willis Linsay believed he made some progress.'

'You don't say,' Maggie said, faintly mocking.

'Perhaps what we are seeing are elements of a key. If we put this together with the Martian inscription, and after much further study—'

'But a key to what, Lobsang?'

Lobsang just smiled. 'We'll know when we have it, I suppose.'

Joshua was trying to get his head around the paradox of the monoliths. 'Willis and Sally travelled stepwise into the Long Mars. And *that* was a Mars not accessed from Datum Earth but from the Gap, far from the Datum across the Long Earth. Meanwhile, here we are having stepped our way into the centre of the Galaxy, and we find a copy of what *they* found . . .'

'My head's exploding too,' Maggie said. 'And if anybody tells me it's because I'm trying to imagine a five-dimensional space with my three-dimensional brain they're on a charge.'

'But I think that about sums it up, Maggie,' Lobsang said, smiling. 'This is life in the Skein. All these Long worlds tangled up together. We're going to have to get used to a universe which isn't simply connected.'

'He means that in a precise mathematical sense,' Indra said quietly.

'Thanks,' said Maggie wryly. 'Well, at least this monument to nothing will give us some shade for lunch.' She opened her pack, sat on the ground at the foot of a monolith, and pulled out plastic boxes. 'We got Navy-issue field rations. Sandwiches. Chicken paste, tuna paste, or . . . paste.'

Lobsang began to open his own pack. 'Maybe we can save such delicacies for later. I also brought along a treat. Joshua, maybe you could lend a hand? We won't need to build a fire; I have a small camping stove.'

Joshua saw that Lobsang had brought frozen oysters, and bacon, and even Worcester sauce. 'Oysters Kilpatrick,' he said with a grin.

'It seemed appropriate,' Lobsang said. 'In honour of an absent friend.'

'All we need is a bunch of sunbathing dinosaurs and it could be forty years ago . . .'

There was a radio crackle. 'Captain Kauffman, Bilaniuk. Come in, Captain, do you copy?'

Maggie puffed out her cheeks. 'Hold that thought, Mr Valienté.' She tapped a button on her pack. 'We're here, Dev. Go ahead.'

'Thanks, Admiral,' Dev said. 'You'd better get back here, ma'am. We don't know how come they showed up like this. Maybe one Traverser calls to another, in this big ocean of theirs. Maybe we were recognized somehow, or at least you were, or Joshua . . . I don't know. Anyhow, it's here. *They're* here . . .'

And Lobsang and Joshua looked at each other.

'I guess the oysters are going to have to wait,' Maggie said with regret.

63

Long before they'd got back to the beach, where the *Uncle Arthur* still stood on a slant, Joshua could see it all.

Out at sea there was not just one Traverser any more, not just the living island that had collected the *Uncle* from the abyss. Now there were many – perhaps a dozen, even more? It was hard to distinguish the low backs of the beasts in the further ocean.

'An archipelago,' Maggie said. 'An archipelago of Traversers. That's not a bad word, is it? And look how they're bumping up against each other.'

'Frolicking,' said Joshua. 'Beasts the size of islands, presumably brought here from many worlds, frolicking together. On any other day that might seem strange.'

Now, Joshua saw, one of the Traversers had come closer to the shore than the rest. Big glistening flaps on its back opened up, and what looked like standard-issue humans emerged, just walking out. Some of them clambered into crude-looking boats they hauled out of the Traverser's interior, and paddled to the shore.

The *Uncle Arthur* crew just watched, open-mouthed.

The woman who walked up the beach was perhaps thirty years old, the boy at her side perhaps ten. All but naked, their feet bare, their legs coated with seawater and sand, they bravely faced the travellers in their high-tech suits. The little boy was clinging to his mother's hand, staring.

Lobsang said, 'You know who this is, don't you?'

Joshua murmured, 'I think you're scaring him, Lobsang. Let me handle this.' Joshua hobbled forward, deliberately smiling. 'Lucille? Troy?'

The woman nodded curtly.

'My name is Joshua Valienté. This is Lobsang. Troy, your grandfather, Nelson Azikiwe, asked us to find you. Well, I'm not quite sure how we did it, but here we are.'

'Huh,' said the woman, unimpressed. 'You took your time.'

64

THE *UNCLE ARTHUR* returned through more star-spanning leaps to Earth West 3,141,592.

For much of the journey Joshua's time was spent trying to explain to his new guests, Lucille and Troy, what the hell was happening to them – and, yes, how he'd find a way to take them back home one day, back to their own ocean seven hundred thousand steps from the Datum, back to Sam and the stranded fisher folk.

And when the *Uncle* arrived back at Little Cincinnati, for once the centre of attention wasn't a continent-sized computer. The sky over the Navy base was dominated by a twain – and not just any twain, Joshua saw, not some Low Earth tub, not some battered old scow from the Long Mississippi run, not even a state-of-the-art US Navy military vessel – this was an island in the sky, huge, with artificial light gleaming from ports in a hardened under-belly. And its envelope hull was made, not of some fabric, but of *wood*, Joshua saw, tremendous panels of it. It was like one vast piece of furniture.

As he stumbled out of the *Uncle*, Jan Roderick's eyes were wide, his mouth a perfect circle. 'Oh. My. Gosh.'

Joshua grinned. 'Not an inappropriate response.'

Lee and Dev, techno-buffs both, gazed up at the ship too. 'Wow,' Dev said simply. 'That thing must be a mile long.'

'Actually a little longer,' Maggie said. 'That, my young explorers, is the USS *Samuel L. Clemens*. More than five times the length of the *Duke*. Douglas Black, the builder of this prototype, owes me a few favours . . .'

'Black,' Lobsang said. 'I knew it.'

And Joshua snapped his fingers. 'Reaching-wood,' he said. 'That's how that damn thing stays up. I knew *that* would leak out.'

Maggie pursed her lips. 'I once glimpsed those forests too, Mr Valienté, aboard the *Armstrong II*. When you came back with your account – well, the opportunity to check it out again seemed too good to miss. Mr Black assures me that all logging will be carried out sustainably. And you've never heard *that* promise before, have you? Anyhow, so I'm informed, it's come to take you all home. Once again I thought we may as well travel in style.'

Jan walked up, looking worried. 'I won't be in trouble, will I?'

Maggie looked at him sternly. 'For stowing away? If you were, was it worth it?'

Jan thought that over. 'Hell, yes.'

Joshua cleared his throat. 'OK, kid, good answer. But just imagine Sister John can hear every word you say. I'm over six times your age, and I still think nuns have super powers.'

'Nobody's in trouble,' Maggie said. 'But you, young man, do need to go back home. Back to school. And I have

443

to get back to Datum Pearl Harbor to report to Ed Cutler, my own Mother Superior—'

'But you mustn't leave quite yet,' came a cultured voice. Roberta Golding and Stella Welch approached them. Roberta smiled at Maggie. 'I hope you will all spare us a few hours to discuss your experiences. We have already downloaded the records from the *Uncle Arthur*, but we believe that your individual responses to the environments you visited will be of value also, however naive.'

'Thanks,' Dev said with a grin.

Indra fired a volley of quicktalk at Roberta.

Maggie grunted, impatient at this exclusion. 'What the hell are you talking about now?'

Roberta said smoothly, 'I apologize, Admiral. We have already come to some conclusions on the basis of Indra's reports. The Long worlds, you see, are evidently not consciously designed, but the result of a kind of cooperation between sentience and the structure of the cosmos itself. As intricate as the co-evolution of the bees and the flowering plants. Now you have glimpsed a – Galactic Club – out there, a community of minds in the sky, in the glorious topology of the Skein. Many of those minds will be higher than ours, of course. I mean, higher than those of the Next.'

'Of course,' Maggie said, straight-faced.

'Indra, young as she is, sees her way to the obvious consequence. We have to rethink our relationship with those other sapients with whom we share the Long Earth. With humans, with the trolls and the other humanoids, even the beagles. Indra suggests that we must draw together some kind of Congress, representing all of us, with parity of expression. A Congress of Sapience.'

'Good,' Lobsang said evenly. 'For you have come to the attention of others. And in the future you will be judged on how you behave towards *Homo sapiens* in the present.'

Joshua grinned. 'Didn't your hero Stan Berg come to much the same conclusion, without having to go to all the trouble of conquering the Galaxy? He left your Grange; he wanted to work with people. And you didn't listen to *him*, as I recall.'

Roberta held up her hand. 'Point taken. We are none of us perfect. We can only strive to do better in the future. In fact we are already planning fresh missions to the Skein.'

'To explore.' Indra smiled. 'And to colonize.'

'Hallelujah,' Maggie said. 'In the meantime I'm going up to the twain for a shower and a change and a decent Navy meal. If any of you want to join me, you're welcome.'

'That is kind,' Indra said solemnly. 'I would indeed like to experience a *decent* Navy meal.'

There was an awkward silence. Indra Newton had made a joke.

Joshua was the first to laugh.

But when the group broke up he pulled Lobsang aside.

'Lobsang – all that stuff about the Long Earth nurturing sapience. Like a Long Gaia.'

'Yes?'

'I remember The Journey. *You* figured all this out forty years ago.'

'Well, that's true, Joshua. But nobody likes a smart ass.' And he winked slowly.

* * *

The next morning there was a surprisingly touching goodbye with Indra. She was after all the first of the crew of the *Uncle Arthur* to be left behind. There were tears, and promises to keep in touch.

Then Joshua and Lobsang boarded the *Clemens* and sat side by side in an observation lounge like a reaching-tree root cavern. Sancho was here too, sitting on a straw bale, wrapped in his tattered spacesuit-silver blanket and with Joshua's bent sunglasses on his face.

The *Clemens* weighed anchor and sailed high in the sky. Little Cincinnati receded beneath them, an island of dirt and canvas in an ocean of computronium that stretched to the horizon, translucent, glistening, flowing over the contours of the landscape.

Maggie Kauffman pushed through the door, a stack of coffees in plastic cartons in her hands. 'So we're under way. Three million worlds to cover back to West 5. Here we go, full fat for Joshua, skinny latte for Lobsang, decaff for the troll.'

'Hoo.'

Joshua grinned. 'If you drop Jan from this behemoth in front of his buddies at the Home, you'll have a friend for life.'

Maggie grunted. 'If I was promised him as a Navy recruit, I'd salute him when he farted. I don't particularly want to reward him for stowing away, but that kid's got brains, initiative and competence. And he's got nerve; I don't think I could have coped with the centre of the Galaxy at ten years old.'

'Eleven.'

She sipped her coffee and pulled a face. 'Which by the way is quite a contrast to the scratch crew of trainees and has-beens we got aboard this ship. This is supposed to be a shakedown cruise for the *Clemens*. The hell with that. We'll cross three million worlds in three days, stepping for twelve hours on, twelve hours off. We're not stepping at night, mind you; I don't think Jane Sheridan trusts her navigators to find their own butts in the dark, let alone the way back to the Low Earths. By the end of this first day we should be at the Gap, where we'll disembark Dev Bilaniuk and Lee Malone. Off to build their own future in space, and good for them.'

'Where are Dev and the rest now?'

'Going crazy on the training deck. Which is a kind of giant playroom a hundred feet long. Let them blow off steam and be young again. Now if you'll excuse me I need to kick more butt . . .' She picked up her own coffee and left.

After a time Joshua said, 'I can feel the first step coming.'

'You would,' said Lobsang.

'Hoo,' said the troll.

Joshua raised his artificial hand. 'Three, two, one—'

The Thinker disappeared, a tablecloth whipped away by some cosmic magician.

Revealed was the landscape of Earth West 3,141,591. Joshua saw a river, hills mantled with forests dominated by some kind of fern, and swathes of green where grew something that wasn't quite grass. Down by the river was a slow-moving herd of some big browsing animal. This was the world next door, a typical member of this nameless sheaf of worlds. But, looking down directly beneath the twain, Joshua saw a few heaps of equipment, a couple of rows of tents. He guessed this stepwise world was used as a store for the Little Cincinnati base, just as the Low Earths around the Datum had first been used after Step Day.

But now there was another step, and the store heap vanished, and the land was draped with a subtly different array of vegetation, of forest and open meadows. Again the ship stepped, and again. The green began to blur, and the river flickered in alternate courses, like a wriggling snake. Faster and faster the steps came. Joshua felt momentarily dizzy as the worlds flashed past, and they snapped from sunlight to cloud to rain and back to sunlight again. But then the stepping rate passed a certain threshold, he lost the sense of individual jumps, and, beyond the reassuring solidity of the twain itself, the world *smeared out*. The basic shape of the landscape endured – the hills, the river valley – but now any life was only a grey-green mist, the river was a blurred band, and around the sun, a constant on all the worlds of the Long Earth, the sky became a washed-out silver-grey dome.

Joshua Valienté, drifting across countless worlds, felt at home.

After the Gap, the twain made one more surprising stop, before reaching the Low Earths: at West 3,141. The super-nova wreck.

Where Sancho, the big troll, wanted off the twain.

He still had his troll-call, and he told Joshua

mournfully, 'Song bad here bad. Trolls dead, cubs dead. Forget forget.'

'Ah. The trolls here are in trouble, and your job is to help them remember who they are . . .'

The troll looked Joshua square in the eye. Peering across an evolutionary gulf a million years deep, Joshua felt he was staring into a distorting mirror.

Sancho said, 'Matt. Rod.' He tapped his head. 'Not forget. Not ever.'

And then he grabbed his troll-call, rolled like an orangutan over to the open door, and he was gone.

Lobsang stood with Joshua at the twain's observation window, drinking more Navy coffee. The troll's silver survival blanket was heaped on a table.

'Won't be the same without him,' Joshua said.

'No.'

'Air's fresher, though.'

'There is that. Quite a vision, that sky,' Lobsang murmured. 'Evil. Thunder . . .'

'Steinman.' Joshua stared at him, rummaging in his memory for the lyric, the name of the track. Once he'd had the whole of the man's oeuvre at his fingertips.

Lobsang just looked at him.

Joshua knew Lobsang of old. Nothing he said was without significance. 'Are you trying to tell me something, you animatronic asshole? Something about Agnes? Rod told me Agnes had died, just as she chose to . . . *What have you done*, Lobsang?'

'I'm sorry, Joshua. I could not let her go. Not all of her.

449

I need her too much. I took it upon myself to recreate in myself her essence and beliefs—'

'You're not talking about another incarnation, another robot body?'

'Not at all. She is most definitely dead. But all of what she was I have built into myself. She's not in any kind of – bottle – somewhere. But she is in the centre of my mind, unchangeable, always cherished.'

Joshua thought that over. 'Well, so she is in me. But I didn't need some kind of artificial download to achieve that.'

Lobsang looked at him poignantly. 'Then I envy you.'

They sat in silence once more, cradling coffee.

'So what's next for you, Lobsang?'

Lobsang shrugged. 'Perhaps I will move out from this string of worlds. I have ambitions to see what becomes of this "Galactic Club". Ambitions or dreams. Maybe the longevity of an artificial being such as myself is better suited to galactic scales of space and time than the human. But I don't intend to abandon my humanity.'

Joshua grinned. 'And you'll take a backup. You always have backup.'

'You're right, of course. And I'll take *her* with me, wherever I go. We'll be together, both of us now, in with the Oort cloud.'

Joshua could almost hear Agnes groan at that old joke.

'I often take Agnes for a ride on her Harley, you know. I care for it as well as I can. It is in a garage – on the Datum, of course, in fact in New Mexico. You can't step over all that iron. Stored properly as you would yourself, Joshua:

450

off the ground, tyres over-inflated, fuel drained from the tank, everything greased up. And out there . . .'

'Yes?'

'Out there, they are doing things properly too. Fixing things together. Empathy and cooperation – good Buddhist principles, by the way. Fixing a flawed creation so that it can nurture life and mind, for ever – even beyond the end of time, perhaps. I can sympathize with that. Once, you know, when I lived in Lhasa, I was a motorcycle repairman. In a sense that's what I always was, what I still am. I fix things.'

'There's no higher vocation, Lobsang.'

'Yes. Though I do have one more pleasant duty to fulfil before I go . . .'

Lobsang smiled – and Joshua had a sudden, sharp, warm sense of Agnes, smiling too behind that artificial face.

65

NELSON AZIKIWE WATCHED as Ken the shepherd grabbed a pregnant ewe and slung it over his shoulder.

To Nelson this was an astounding display of strength; Ken's ewes were no lightweights. But, he remembered, Old Ken had been just as strong. Old Ken, who had first built up this pioneering farm in England West 1, just a step away from Nelson's ancient parish of St John on the Water, on Datum Earth. Old Ken, who had been Ken until he died, had bequeathed it all to Young Ken, who became Ken on his father's death. So it went.

Now Ken – Young Ken – walked forwards towards a hedgerow. And took another step and completely vanished.

Nelson hesitated. For him, every step was a penance, he thought with a sigh. But it had been a long time since breakfast. He fingered the Stepper switch in his pocket, clapped his handkerchief over his mouth . . .

When he'd recovered somewhat, the first thing he noticed, in this England two steps away from home, were the trees of the remnant forest beyond the dry-stone wall around

Ken's newly cleared field. Big trees, old trees, giants.

'I remember,' Nelson said, wheezing a little.

'Umm,' said Ken.

'Your father told me all about it, when they first started coming over after Step Day. The work of clearing the forest. Cutting down the big trees, and setting loose the animals to chomp any optimistic saplings, and so forth.'

'Kind of stuff my dad would know, that, Rev.'

'Yes. Yes, I suppose he would. You know, Ken, I always loved my time here in the parish.'

'Umm,' said Ken.

'But there was always a tension in me, you see. Between the scientist and the cleric. Darwin would have understood, I think.'

'What, Robert and Ann Darwin as runs the *Star*?'

'No, no . . . A distant ancestor of Robert's, perhaps. A tension that drew me away from here. So far away, for such a long time. And yet now—'

'And yet now you've come home,' said a new voice.

Nelson turned stiffly. A man stood by the dry-stone wall, tall, slim, very still, head shaven. He'd evidently stepped in; Nelson hadn't heard his approach. But Nelson recognized him immediately.

'Lobsang!'

It was Ken who responded first. 'I read about you.' He walked briskly over to Lobsang and shook his hand.

'Pleased to meet you,' Lobsang said.

'Good firm handshake,' Ken said approvingly. He turned to Nelson with a grin. 'Is he alive, would you say, Rev?'

453

Nelson considered. '*He* thinks he's alive, and that's good enough for me.'

Lobsang nodded. 'Wait here.'

He vanished.

And returned, holding the hand of a rather bewildered-looking little boy, heavily bundled up for warmth, even though the late autumn day was mild. Then the boy grinned, pulled away from Lobsang and ran forward. 'Granddad!'

Nelson bent stiffly, holding out his arms. 'Troy! Oh, my word . . .'

Lobsang said, 'I told you I'd bring him home.'

'I hope it wasn't too much trouble.'

Lobsang smiled. 'Just a walk in the park.'

66

THE PRAIRIE WAS flat, green, rich, with scattered stands of oaks. The sky above was blue as generally advertised. On the horizon there was movement, like the shadow of a cloud: a vast herd of animals on the move.

And the baby was alone.

Alone, except for the universe. Which poured in, and spoke to her with an infinity of voices. And behind it all, a vast Silence.

Her crying settled to a gurgle. The Silence was comforting.

There was a kind of sigh, a breathing-out. Joshua was back in the green, under the blue sky.

On the move, 'down' was always the direction of Datum Earth. Down to the bustling worlds. Down to the millions of people. 'Up' was the direction of the silent worlds and the clean air of the High Meggers.

But to Joshua Valienté, in the end, down was home.

Leaning on a stick, one prosthetic hand stiff, Joshua scooped up the baby, wrapped her up in a ragged old silver survival blanket that smelled of troll, and cradled her in his arms. Her little face was oddly calm. 'Helen,' he said. 'Your name is Helen Sofia Valienté.'

A soft pop, and they were gone.

On the plain, nothing remained but the grass, and the sky.

Acknowledgements

I'm grateful once again to our good friends Dr Christopher Pagel, owner of the Companion Animal Hospital in Madison, Wisconsin, and his wife Juliet Pagel, for, among other things, a discussion on a happily serendipitous observation that Ellie Arroway of *Contact* appears to have been their neighbour, and an insightful reading of the text. And I'm grateful too to Professor Ian Stewart for his stimulating speculations on the peculiar forests of Earth West 230,000,000, as well as another very helpful reading. All errors and inaccuracies are of course my sole responsibility.

S.B.

December 2015, Datum Earth

BOOKS BY TERRY PRATCHETT

Other books about Discworld

NANNY OGG'S COOKBOOK
(with Stephen Briggs, Tina Hannan and Paul Kidby)

THE PRATCHETT PORTFOLIO
(with Paul Kidby)

THE DISCWORLD ALMANAK
(with Bernard Pearson)

THE UNSEEN UNIVERSITY CUT-OUT BOOK
(with Alan Batley and Bernard Pearson)

WHERE'S MY COW?
(illustrated by Melvyn Grant)

THE ART OF DISCWORLD
(with Paul Kidby)

THE WIT AND WISDOM OF DISCWORLD
(compiled by Stephen Briggs)

THE FOLKLORE OF DISCWORLD
(with Jacqueline Simpson)

THE WORLD OF POO
(with the Discworld Emporium)

MRS BRADSHAW'S HANDBOOK
(with the Discworld Emporium)

THE COMPLEAT ANKH-MORPORK
(with the Discworld Emporium)

THE STREETS OF ANKH-MORPORK
(with Stephen Briggs, painted by Stephen Player)

THE DISCWORLD MAPP
(with Stephen Briggs, painted by Stephen Player)

A TOURIST GUIDE TO LANCRE –
A DISCWORLD MAPP
(with Stephen Briggs, illustrated by Paul Kidby)

DEATH'S DOMAIN
(with Paul Kidby)

THE COMPLEAT DISCWORLD ATLAS
(with the Discworld Emporium)

A complete list of Terry Pratchett ebooks and audio books as well
as other books based on the Discworld series – illustrated screen-
plays, graphic novels, comics and plays – can be found on
www.terrypratchett.co.uk

BOOKS BY STEPHEN BAXTER

Proxima

PROXIMA

ULTIMA

Northland

STONE SPRING

BRONZE SUMMER

IRON WINTER

Flood

FLOOD

ARK

Time's Tapestry

EMPEROR

CONQUEROR

NAVIGATOR

WEAVER

Destiny's Children

COALESCENT

EXULTANT

TRANSCENDENT

RESPLENDENT

A Time Odyssey

TIME'S EYE (with Arthur C. Clarke)

SUNSTORM (with Arthur C. Clarke)

FIRSTBORN (with Arthur C. Clarke)

Manifold

MANIFOLD 1: TIME
MANIFOLD 2: SPACE
MANIFOLD 3: ORIGIN
PHASE SPACE

Mammoth

SILVERHAIR
LONGTUSK
ICEBONES
BEHEMOTH

The NASA Trilogy

VOYAGE
TITAN
MOONSEED

The Xeelee Sequence

RAFT
TIMELIKE INFINITY
FLUX
RING
XEELEE: AN OMNIBUS
VACUUM DIAGRAMS
XEELEE: ENDURANCE

The Web

THE WEB: GULLIVERZONE
THE WEB: WEBCRASH

More details of Stephen Baxter's works can be found
on **www.stephen-baxter.com**

TERRY PRATCHETT

The Long Earth

STEPHEN BAXTER

Earths, untold Earths. More Earths than could be counted, some said. And all you had to do was walk sideways into them, one after the next, an unending chain . . .

1916: the Western Front. Private Percy Blakeney wakes up. He is lying on fresh spring grass. He can hear birdsong, and the wind in the leaves in the trees. Where have the mud, blood and blasted landscape of No Man's Land gone?

2015: Madison, Wisconsin. Cop Monica Jansson is exploring the burned-out home of a reclusive – some said mad, others dangerous – scientist when she finds a curious gadget: a box containing some wiring, a three-way switch and a . . . potato. It is the prototype of an invention that will change the way mankind views its world for ever.

And that's an understatement if ever there was one . . .

'From two SF giants . . . a marriage made in fan heaven – Pratchett's warmth and humanity allied to Baxter's extraordinary fertile science-fictional imagination'
Adam Roberts, *GUARDIAN*

'A triumph . . . accessible, fun and thoughtful'
David Barnett, *INDEPENDENT*

'Literary alchemy . . . in the hands of Pratchett and Baxter, the possibilities are almost infinite . . . **thrillingly expansive, joyously inventive, and utterly engrossing**'
SFX

TERRY PRATCHETT
The Long War
STEPHEN BAXTER

The Long Earth is open.
Humanity has spread across untold worlds linked by fleets
of airships encouraging exploration, trade and culture.

But while mankind may be shaping the Long Earth, the
Long Earth is, in turn, shaping mankind – and a collision
of crises is looming. More than a million steps from the
original Earth a new America is emerging – a young nation
that resents answering to the Datum government.

And the trolls – those graceful, hive-mind humanoids
whose song once suffused the Long Earth – are, in the face
of man's inexorable advance, beginning to fall silent . . .
and to disappear.

It was Joshua Valiente who, with the omniscient being
known as Lobsang, first explored these multiple worlds.
And it is to Joshua that the Long Earth turns for help. There
is the very real threat of war . . .

. . . a war unlike any fought before.

'Two of our greatest imagineers . . . are clearly
enjoying their quantum playground; their playfulness
infuses every passage'
SFX

'A brilliant piece of multiverse-building . . . we can all
eagerly look forward to the next instalment of this
excellent, intelligent series'
TOR.COM

TERRY PRATCHETT
The Long Mars
STEPHEN BAXTER

2040. The Long Earth is in chaos.

The cataclysmic Yellowstone eruption is shutting down civilization. Whole populations flee to the relative safety of myriad stepwise Earths. Sally Linsay, Joshua Valiente and Lobsang have all been involved in the perilous post-eruption clean-up.

But Joshua faces a crisis closer to home. From a long childhood hidden deep in the Long Earth, a new breed of young, super-bright post-humans is emerging – but 'normal' human society is turning against them, driven by ignorance and fear. For Joshua, caught up in the conflict, a dramatic showdown seems inevitable.

Meanwhile US Navy Commander Maggie Kauffman embarks on an incredible journey, leading an expedition to the unexplored limits of the far Long Earth.

And Sally is contacted by her long-vanished father, Willis Linsay – inventor of the original Stepper device. Ever the maverick, he is planning a fantastic voyage of his own – across the Long Mars. But what is his true motivation?

For Joshua, for mankind, for the Long Earth itself – everything is different now.

'Pratchett and Baxter . . . skipping along their quantum string of planets like giddy schoolboys – and what a joy it is to have them back . . . thrilling and ceaselessly entertaining'
SFX

TERRY PRATCHETT

The Long Utopia

STEPHEN BAXTER

It is the middle of the twenty-first century.

The cataclysms of Step Day and the Yellowstone eruption have sent humanity out into the Long Earth. Society, on a battered Datum Earth and beyond, continues to evolve. And new challenges emerge.

In a far-distant world, a cantankerous and elderly Lobsang lives with Agnes in the community of New Springfield and endeavours to lead a normal life. They even adopt a child. But there are rumours of hauntings, strange sightings in the sky. On this world, something isn't right . . .

Millions of steps away, Joshua receives an urgent summons from New Springfield. Lobsang believes that what is blighting *his* Earth now threatens all the worlds of the Long Earth.

To counter this will require the combined efforts of humankind, machine *and* the super-intelligent Next. And some must make the ultimate sacrifice . . .

'A hymn to the joys of unfettered world-building . . . restless inventiveness'
GUARDIAN

'Rich in an awe-inspiring sense of wonder, with mind-boggling concepts thrown out like sparks from a Catherine wheel'
INDEPENDENT

'Beautifully visual and wittily imagined . . . serves to remind us just how bewitching and rich this series is'
FOR WINTER NIGHTS